WHATEVER YOU NEED

BRITTNEY LAUREN

Editing by Ellies Edits

Proofreading by Lily Alcala

Author's Note

Whatever You Need is a romance first and foremost but there are some serious themes some readers may find triggering. Parental illness (non-life threatening), on page gun violence (not between main characters), childhood cancer (dealt with off page), emotionally abusive relationship (not between main characters), explicit language.

For peace of mind, no one dies, they're just all going through it.

This book also contains explicit sexual content and is not intended for readers under the age of 18.

If any of these could be a trigger for you this may not be the book for you and that's okay.

Xo - Brittney

"It's too cliche, I won't say I'm in love"
-Megara, Hercules, 1997

The Playlist

I Can See You -Taylor Swift

Chains – Nick Jonas

Glitch – Taylor Swift

Home Run – The Man The Myth The Meatslab

I won't Say (I'm In Love) – Susan Egan

Alone (stripped) – Kelsy Karter & The Heroines

The Only Exception – Paramore

right were you left me – Taylor Swift

Nothing Really Matters – Jaedynn Latter

Relationships – HAIM

Let It Happen – Gracie Abrams

Hits Different – Taylor Swift

Do I Wanna Know? – Artic Monkeys

Do I Wanna Know? – Hozier

It's All Coming Back to Me Now – Celine Dion

hate to be lame – Lizzy McAlpine, Finneas

Silver Spoon – Erin LeCount

BRITTNEY LAUREN

Surfire - Piano Version – John Legend
Far Away – Nickleback
Want You Back – HAIM
Bitch – Meredith Brooks
The Love You Want – Sleep Token
Give – Sleep Token
Head Over Feet – Alanis Morissette
i wish i knew how to quit you – sombr
Strong Enough – Sheryl Crow
Sweetest Devotion – Adele

ONE

Carina

"WHAT THE HELL IS this?" I asked my empty office. It was the end of the day, and even though the words on my screen blurred together hours ago, I was having a hard time believing he really wrote what was in front of me. And had the audacity to hit the send button.

Maybe if I squinted really hard, the words would change. They would have to because what I was staring at couldn't possibly be right.

A creak echoed out from under my chair as I leaned in closer to my screen.

It didn't help.

How did someone go through life with no pride in their work? While I learned early on most people didn't hold themselves to the same high standard I held myself to, there should at least be a bare minimum.

Decades separated me from the memory of the exact moment I knew I wanted to be a lawyer, but I the fire it sparked still lingered. The desire grabbed hold of me, like wildfire to dry brush, and swept through my chest with unyielding flames that forced me to follow my dreams like a moth to a pyre.

Growing up, I had exactly what I needed to survive, nothing more. Simple four walls with a roof over my head, I never went to bed hungry but I had none of the simple luxuries my other classmates seemed to have. Cable being the biggest difference between me and my friends. Instead of watching cartoons after school, I tuned into the only channel our rabbit-eared TV connected with and filled my nights with cop dramas, and because of this, I knew from an early age what I wanted to do with my life.

My road to a Juris Doctor was long, filled with hazards and pot holes but eventually I made it. Even if it came at a cost, but nothing in life that came easy was as rewarding as something you sacrificed for.

For me, it was people that ended up on the chopping block.

Over the years, I sacrificed relationships, friendships and sometimes even my own parents to get where I wanted to be. Not in a diabolical way, I wasn't stepping all over people or backstabbing anyone in my way on the pathway to success. I would simply forget they existed. I'd blown off dates to study, ditched parties in favor of working to afford college, and if my parents needed me, well, they could leave a voicemail and I would get back to them if I had time.

And I was fine with it. I wasn't winning any congeniality awards; I didn't have a pool of people I could call up anytime it felt like my world was caving in, but I had a steady career I was fantastic at, and it was enough.

It was almost perfect, except for the grating sensation of one person who made it their life's mission to make my workload a living hell, who needed to answer for this asinine email.

I pushed back from my desk. The wheels of the chair rolled me away before I stood, smoothing my hands down the pants of my dark blue suit and which was guaranteed to be full of wrinkles from sitting most of the day, but I needed to catch him before he slipped out.

Noise buzzed outside my cracked office door from the hallway as most of my coworkers began packing up. I looked at the clock in the corner of my computer for the first time in hours and realized it was nearing five o'clock. My eyes started going fuzzy around noon, which was a daily occurrence at this point. Even after all these years, I still wasn't used to the amount of screen time I consumed. I've been trying to convince myself it had nothing to do with my age, I was only nearing my thirty-first birthday after all.

The thick office door bounced off the outside wall as I walked out and beelined it toward his desk. For the entire five seconds it took to get there, I muttered under my breath not to let him get under my skin. I needed to take nothing to heart and everything out of his mouth with a grain of salt. But who was I kidding? He lived there; he thrived in the small part of my brain I'd inadvertently let him into when we first started working together. And he wasted no time making himself comfortable, where he knew all my buttons and how to push them like it was his second job.

Abby's desk was empty as I passed and he was just on the other side. I made a mental note to send her a text to remind her how much I hated it when she gave my cases away.

If he sensed me waiting in the opening, no part of him showed it, even if we both knew I was on my way over. Methodical clicking pierced through the empty air, since most people had filed out, with his back facing me as he continued to type. Either he's oblivious or was keeping me waiting on purpose. My money was on the former.

For a second, exactly one second and not a heartbeat longer, my eyes wandered over his frame, savoring the way his dress shirt stretched across his wide shoulders, which moved slightly with each breath he took. His dark hair, reminiscent of ink pools on paper from my favorite pens, was tied at the nape of his neck as usual. Not my favorite look for him, I much preferred when the strands were free of any constraints, grazing the tops of his shoulders in unruly tangles of waves. Although it was rare for him to wear it down at work, something I'd only caught a few glimpses of in our five years of working together.

I hated having a favorite at all.

Without turning around, he said, "That must be a record for you. I sent that email not even a minute ago, and here you are." He punctuated his sentence with a final hit to his keyboard, and the heavy baritone of his voice filled the air before he swiveled to meet me face to face. I would appreciate the sight a bit more if I wasn't already pissed off. How he leaned into the tilt of his chair, looking up at me with whiskey-colored eyes and a smile I had to will my knees not to go weak over.

"Normally you let me sit in your inbox for a day or so before responding," he taunted, and I had to break eye contact if I was going to make it through the conversation without my anger boiling over. Or any other feeling, for that matter.

"What the hell, Decker," I sneered his name, my hands flinging out from my sides without caution. I couldn't even remember the last time I used his real name, probably not long after he started if I had to guess. It was a rule I imposed on myself and stuck to like a religion. Last name only, it helped me keep everything about our interactions less personal.

Less was always better when it came to Levi Decker, in every aspect.

When his smile widened, my blood pressure skyrocketed.

So much for less is better.

With a deep inhale, I closed my eyes before responding; a meditation trick I may or may not have looked up, for his benefit, not mine. "I asked for that mediation meeting to be scheduled weeks ago because I know her attorney takes the entire month of August off. So why did I get an email from you saying it was scheduled, but not until September?" My voice jumped at least three octaves at the end and then slid into a whine with the next words. "That's too far."

His eyes narrowed as he continued to look up at me. I didn't like it; I didn't like him. And the fact he wouldn't stop staring at me without answering was infuriating.

My hands found their home on my hips as my foot tapped at the plastic covering the floor. "So why wasn't it scheduled? I don't get it, Decker. Did you just not do it when I asked? Too busy looking for ridiculous ties to wear? Or, do you just not like your job?" It wasn't like me to stoop down to a level low enough to pick on someone's clothes, but my filter was non-existent when he's involved.

Pain bloomed in my temples as I clenched my jaw and willed myself to breathe in through my nose and then out slowly. I would give anything to figure out what it was about him that peeled back my skin and set me on edge. If I knew, I could pluck him out of the crevasses of my brain and move on with my life. But until then, I would have to live with the ping-pong game happening. Where I bounce from he was fucking annoying to I want fu—you know what, I wasn't even going to go there.

"Noticed my new tie, did you?" His fingers curled around the fabric, flicking the tail end back and forth. I wasn't quite sure what it was, but at my first glance this morning, all I saw were frogs. "They're frog princes. I got them—"

I cut in, not caring where the dumb ties came from. "Decker, the meeting. What's going on?"

"It's not my favorite one," he said, still looking at his tie. "But not bad."

I was going to lose it. At least most of our coworkers were gone, less witnesses.

My foot popped and kicked the toe of his shoe. Slowly, oh so fucking slowly, his gaze dragged up the length of my body until he settled on my face. A quick shiver rolled down my spine.

He waited a few seconds before speaking again. "I reached out to them the day you asked me to. Their calendar has been booked out that far. Too many people are getting divorced, apparently." He swiveled his chair from side to side as he spoke.

"And you're just now telling me?"

"No, you just now looked at your email."

"What are you talking about?"

"Come on, we both know you put me on the back burner anytime my name comes up. What did you do to filter my name to its own folder and then only look at one email now that you need something?"

My chest heated up as if I had been caught red-handed because I had done exactly that. Decker and I didn't work on cases together unless it was absolutely necessary. Our firm was limited, but we had small miracles, like a paralegal for each attorney. Decker was assigned to Jody. Abby had been mine since I started, and I didn't like to share.

But sometimes with my caseload, Abby needed more hands than she possessed, so if she could tell it'd be a quick mediation or two before the final ruling, she might hand it off. Normally she knew to go to anyone else, but everyone had been a bit overwhelmed. So I reluctantly ended up with Decker every once in a while. I preferred to do all the work myself, but who was I kidding? Paralegals were a godsend; I couldn't do all they did *and* my job. Even I knew that.

"Luckily for you, I went to high school with the woman who does the scheduling at that firm. I'm pretty sure she had a crush on me," he added smugly. "I've been calling over about once a week, today included, and an opening came up, and you're now scheduled for next week. Way ahead of when Alain will be out for the month. Which, fun fact, did you know he goes to Germany to see his family?" He looked so pleased with himself and so annoyingly handsome I had to put some serious effort into not using his stupid tie as a murder weapon.

I may not be a criminal attorney, but no witnesses seemed like a good place got start.

"You're welcome," he said before turning around and continuing his assault on his keyboard. My head fell back, a disapproving noise reverberated in the back of my throat, which he only laughed at. It was a 'you thought I was incompetent, but I'm actually way ahead of you' laugh, and I hated that.

A few strides later, I slipped back into my office chair. Sure enough, as I typed his name in the search bar of my email again, there were more unread emails than not, and a quick chime with a meeting invite popped up for the date he had scheduled. My head snapped up in time to see him roll backward out of his cubicle to throw me a thumbs up. I walked toward my door and closed it, resisting the urge to flip him the bird in the process. I also shut my blinds for good measure.

"Idiot," I said to no one.

I liked a handful of people in this world, loved fewer. It never interested me to tie myself to one person, and working as a family law attorney who mainly handled divorces, I was pretty set on the fact being in love meant nothing.

Love didn't save marriages, love didn't put food on the table or a roof over your head; love was, simply put, a feeling. And I had gotten by just fine doling out love to a select few people, like Abby and Lennon and never a man.

Decker wasn't on either of those lists, I'd like to add. What I felt for him was impossible to describe.

I was fresh off passing the bar when we started at Alcala, Lane and Associates at the same time. After putting myself through university and then law school while my parents worked odd jobs, I had finally reached what they deemed the American dream. Being a first generation Italian American meant a lot of my childhood was a bit more complicated than my peers' but I was damn proud of where my family came from and all my parents did to come here, even if I didn't see eye to eye with them most days.

During orientation, Decker was effortlessly funny and easygoing compared to my fervent note taking and question asking. With his stupid ties and lazy smile that haunted my daydreams, I found myself drawn to him.

Sort of sounded like the start of a great love story, right?

Wrong.

It didn't take me long to realize he took nothing seriously, not just the orientation, and it drove me absolutely insane. He treated everything with no sense of urgency, too careless for his own good, with no fear of consequences in his job. Decker exuded the notion he never had to work for anything in his life and had been walking around doing the bare minimum in life.

As soon as my girl brain, or to be honest, my vagina, caught up with my rational side and stopped ogling over his eyes or hair or smile, the better off I'd be.

My computer pinged again and again with incoming emails, pulling my focus back to my work. Sliding my chair into my desk, I shook my head to get him off my mind. I only needed to clock in a couple more billable hours for the day before I could get out of here to swing by my parents' restaurant to look over some scheduling issues my mom was having.

Everything around me faded to black as the longer I typed. I loved my career, the challenge of the day-to-day tasks and the stimulation of pouring over the facts at hand for a case. I loved the research; the fact-checking. I kind of just liked proving myself right. It was like working a puzzle, finding all the pieces that were needed, laying them out, and figuring how they came together to get the picture. And I was good at it.

My type of law might seem mundane, sad, even. I had a front-row seat to marriages dying, but it worked for me. The paychecks didn't hurt either. It afforded me my shoe indulgence, and I could help my parents open their restaurant. Being a lawyer might be my version of the American dream, but the restaurant was theirs.

Another hour flew by, and I hardly moved from my desk. My back ached, and I couldn't remember when my ass went numb, but it was. I stood to stretch and pulled my hair out of the ponytail that threatened to turn my lingering headache into a migraine. I jabbed the power button on my laptop before snapping it closed and stuffing it into my work bag. I wasn't done working, but I could finish from my couch.

Outside, the setting sun splashed orange-colored light through the office windows, giving everything a soft glow. It wasn't too late, but I knew by this time I was like the last person in the office, which I was used to.

I opened my door and stepped out when a sound from the hall caused my head to snap to the right, and I groaned internally.

Decker moved past the end of the cubicle row toward my office the same time I exited but luckily for me, the doors slid open as we walked up, so we weren't forced to linger in awkward silence and mercifully, it was a brief ride down three floors.

The doors slid open, but before I could move, he spoke up. "Have a good night, Carina." He sauntered out of the elevator, across the lobby, and through the glass doors that led to Main Street while I was rooted to the elevator floor. Standing there like an idiot as the doors shut.

But God, if I didn't love the way he said my name.

TWO

Decker

THERE WASN'T ENOUGH COFFEE to get me ready for the mind numbing day ahead. I had one more week before my second year of law school would be behind me; it was so close I could fucking taste the sweet relief of a break. Between work, classes, and my sister somehow convincing me a late night dinner was a great idea, I was running on fumes. Less than fumes. I was running on a tank that went dry months ago. Each day was a bit of a struggle, but I knew it would be worth it, as long as I could actually make it to the other side. If there was another side at all.

I was tired, simply put, even though I was the one with the bright idea to go back to school at twenty-eight years old—law school at that. Maybe it was seeing all of my sisters live full lives, having kids and getting married, careers they loved, that spurred me on. All I knew was one day I was a paralegal, okay with the fact that it might be all I would ever be, and the next I was taking the LSAT and applying to the University of the Pacific.

Even though I was coming to end of my second year, I was still wondering if it was a mistake. In the beginning I had a handle on it, but the further I got, the more self-doubt crept in, wondering if it was the right move.

But if there was one thing that kept me going on the days where I was running on three hours of sleep, an exam on the horizon and more case law to look up at work than I knew what to do with, it was a five-foot nothing blonde stomping around the office in heels I couldn't get enough of and an attitude that kept me hooked.

Not that she knew any of that.

Carina and I had a relationship cultivated by my own careful design. I clocked her rigid demeanor and her 'I know what's best' attitude the first day we met and made it a silent mission to get under her skin. And the fastest way to do that was to show her that all her rules, lists, and plans meant nothing. Granted, it might have worked too well because I still hadn't made it past the 'she hates me' stage to the 'she hates to love me' stage. But I'd get there, eventually.

A ping pulled my focus to my phone as a message from my sister popped up reminding me of our dinner later on, like I could forget. I shot her a quick reply that I'd be there, as I downed the remains of my coffee and headed back into my room to change.

With a little more care than usual, I dressed with intention. Slipping on dark charcoal slacks and a white button up, deciding to leave the top button undone and forgoing a tie altogether, she never seemed to like them anyway. This may or may not be an outfit Carina's eyes slowly passed over when she thought I wasn't paying attention. As an extra step, I even rolled the sleeves of my shirt up. Only a few inches, any further would show off the ink I tried to keep under wraps. Topping it all off, I gathered my hair at the base of my head and looped it through a tie.

My sister Lola was begging me to cut it before her wedding, saying it would ruin her pictures if I kept it this long. No follow up details, it was cut it or I wouldn't be allowed. She was bluffing of course. No way she was going to leave me, her twin, out of her wedding. Or at least I hoped not. There was fifty percent chance she was meeting me for dinner to plead her case once more, but I only had the capacity to focus on one thing at a time this early and for now that was getting to work on time.

The commute from Cornelia to Fairvale was longer than I wanted, and as I glanced at the clock, I quickened my routine and was on the road in ten minutes. The goal was always to move closer, because even though I was in law school and I could end up anywhere once I graduated, I wanted to stay at ALA Law. Only issue was they didn't even know I was in law school, so when the time came I would be crossing my fingers for an associates position to open.

Rays of morning sunlight hit my eyes, temporarily blinding me as I turned onto Main Street. Even the best of Hallmark's small-town movie sets couldn't compare, where wide glass windows of the jewelry store filled with glittering rainbows when the sun hit it just right, the gallery across from the office that only showcased local artists or the smell of pine drifting out of the wood furniture store whenever I walked by. Fairvale was special; you could feel it anytime you stepped onto Main Street, and I would be lucky to live here.

I made my way to the far end of the street where ALA's office sat, parked in the garage under my office and was at my cubicle in minutes. My laptop bag was barely off my shoulder when Abby rounded the corner, files in hand and a distressed look on her face. "Oh no," I groaned, tossing my bag on the desk.

Abby stopped in front of me. "I haven't even asked you anything yet," she chided, before plastering an innocent look on her face, blinking dark blue doe eyes up at me. I knew what was coming. I liked Abby, I really did, she was the best paralegal in the building, probably anywhere and I would take over anything she asked me to, but I was so tired. I couldn't possibly handle one more thing being added to my already tall as a mountain plate.

"Can't you ask Oliver or Emma?"

"You don't even know what I was going to ask."

I turned to look at her, cocking my head to the side while I waited for the inevitable.

She threw her hands up. "Okay, you're right, I need something. I need you to take one more of Carina's cases." Her big eyes got even bigger, if that was possible, as she stared up at me like I was some average sucker.

The chair rolled back into the desk once I dropped into it. Even though I knew this was where the conversation would end up, I hoped it was something different. Anything really. "Didn't I just take one of hers?" It wasn't so much of a question as it was a reminder.

"That was just for scheduling, not a full case, and you know I wouldn't ask if I wasn't drowning in work, Levi, but I need help."

"Why not Oliver or Emma?"

She stared at me. A serious look overtook her normally bright exterior. "You know why." Her voice dropped to a threatening sort of tone.

Every office had them. You know, the people who seemed to do their job just enough to keep it and not a lick more. "Carina would kill me if I handed it off to Tweedle Dee or Tweedle Dum. You're good, she never complains about you," she said.

I scoffed. If I got one thing from Carina, it was complaints. "I beg to differ, Abby."

"It's true." Her voice slipped an octave higher. "She may complain about you," she said with a smile, "but your work? Never." Her chestnut curls bounced back and forth as she shook her head. Abby's beautiful, for sure, and I was certain men fell at her feet to help her, but the charm she was packing on stirred nothing inside of me. Carina, on the other hand, she could pin me down with the spike of her heel and I would gladly say yes to whatever task she had. And then ask her to do it again.

I held out my hand. "What do I get in return?" I asked as Abby handed over the file with a triumphant look.

"What do you want? I'm close to doing anything to get these cases off my desk."

I raised an eyebrow, and Abby's soft laugh filtered into the air. "You're cute, Levi, but no, thanks. I can stock the office fridge with your favorite drinks for a week?" she offered.

Flipping the file open, I took a quick peek. "Make it two," I said without looking up. A quick scan told me Abby did most of the legwork already, the last thing it needed was to be put in the system and a report for Carina to review. With any luck it would be a quick, sign the papers and be done, type of divorce.

She squealed and danced up onto her tiptoes. "Thank you, thank you, thank you."

Before she disappeared completely, I stepped out of my cube and called after her. "But you have to be the one to tell her." She waved her hand above her head in acknowledgement. "And before I send her the intake email later today." As she vanished around the corner, I was ninety percent sure she would do it. There's no way she'd surprise her like that, she knew better.

We all knew better.

Carina hated her routine being derailed, and for her, that could mean anything. A different paralegal, the opposition not having any availability on the schedule she'd already come up with, or even her favorite pens not being stocked in the supply room. She liked the kind with a really thin tip and runny sort of ink that forced you to wait a minute for it to dry before touching it. Any slight change to what she'd planned would spark a faint blush on the tops of her cheeks, her brows would knit together, forming a small crease in the middle, and her jade green eyes would dart around. You could watch her in real time, form a plan to get back on track.

It was fascinating, and...that was exactly what I needed in order to make this worth it. Carina Pera working through a problem was a glorious sight, and was an elixir I craved.

I tucked the file under my arm and sauntered up to her door. If there's one thing that would get the reaction I was looking for, it was me pretending like I wouldn't take something seriously. My knuckles rapped against her door frame, forcing her head to snap away from her computer screen.

Our eyes connected, and I almost forgot to breathe. It'd been five years of this. At some point, I figured the feeling would fade away into oblivion, but it'd yet to happen. Sure enough though, her face morphed within a second and was already scowling. Air came rushing back into my lungs as a laugh.

Pale yellow sunlight poured in through her office window that overlooked Main Street. If I looked closely, I could even see a sliver of the Orange Grove River. Her office was the second best in our building, and for good reason. It was barely eight in the morning, and I would bet she had been here for a while already. Not that she looked like it because, as usual, she looked as if she could walk into a meeting with the President at any moment. Pale pink manicured fingers hovered over her keyboard, and brilliantly blonde hair flowed down her back in perfect soft waves; I could spend forever looking and there wouldn't be a single flaw.

"Decker," she said, pulling me from a daydream of what she might look like in the early morning darkness before all of this and what I wouldn't give to see it. Her hands curled into slight fists as she stopped typing. "Can I help you?"

I shook my head, attempting to erase the pull she had on me, causing the hair at the nape of my neck to pull in the hair tie. Without a thought, my hand came up and pulled it free from the pinching pain. I would fix it in a minute. When I walked into her office and took a seat in the chair across from her, she didn't protest like I anticipated. Instead, her gaze locked on where I slipped the tie on to my wrist before flicking back to my face.

Interesting.

"I have your new file on," I flipped the manila folder open for the name again, "Kelly Leon, I'll have the initial review over to you by the end of day but it's been a while since I've done one of these from the beginning for you. Do you still prefer paper versions of everything?" I looked back at her. That scowl was gone and replaced with some other look I couldn't quite name.

"What are you talking about?"

"Abby needed help on her desk and asked me to take this one from the top."

She clicked her tongue, irritation morphing her entire body. Her mouth opened to speak, but her cell phone lit up in front of her. She quickly silenced it. "Do you know what level it might fall into yet?" she asked as she rubbed her fingers along her hairline. I forgot she levels her cases. It's funny, no one else did it, or at least Jody, my usual attorney, didn't.

"No, not yet. She just handed it over."

Her phone rang again, which she silenced for a second time but with a little more aggression. "I can leave if you need to take the call." I was halfway up from my seat before she waved me back down.

She turned back to her computer and started moving her mouse around. "You're here now, give me the info and I'll open the file in the system."

ALA was small, so small that an automated system was not something we leaned on, and it's not uncommon for the attorneys to do clerical work as well. Small town work at its finest. I plied her with the basic info from the intake forms that are submitted directly from the client. "She also mentions she's pregnant," I finished with.

Carina sat back in her chair, eyes roaming over the info she had typed out before she hummed in question.

"Is that a problem?" I wanted to ask more questions. My law student brain swirled with them, like if custody agreements could be worked into a divorce before a child was even born and how could you enforce anything legally beforehand. But before I could, her office phone rang.

Her hand shot out to grab the receiver. "ALA Law, this is Carina." Even on a phone call, she commanded attention.

Surprise washed over her face and then did something I had never witnessed before. Something flipped and I no longer understood a single word she was saying.

Rapid fire, Spanish...no, that wasn't right. I leaned in, ears straining to listen.

Italian.

She was speaking lightning fast Italian with whoever was on the other side. It was so quick that when she hung up, I wondered if I dreamt it. Five years we'd worked together and sure maybe not as closely as I liked, but I never knew she spoke another language. What else had I missed?

"I didn't know you spoke Italian," I mused out loud. The scowl appeared on her face again and I took that as my queue to leave, I could finish setting up the file at my own desk.

Carina was a well of surprises, and I wanted to know all of them.

THREE

Carina

Steam hung in the air, thick with the scent of pasta that clung to my skin and dampened my hairline, since we had to keep a pot at a roaring boil throughout the day. The only reason I endured it was because this was my happy place, and I didn't have many of those. It made weeknight dinner shifts at my parents' restaurant at bit more tolerable. And kitchen work was infinitely better than waiting or bussing tables.

Fishing the serving of gnocchi from the pot, I dropped it into the marinara filled pan, causing a flash of flames to erupt. The kitchen door swung open as I gave the pan a few good shakes to coat the pasta evenly. "Two more minutes, Noah," I shouted over my shoulder.

I didn't even want to be here, and the way Noah hovered around me made my already flaming nerves feel like they were being dipped into an active volcano. A million things cluttered my desk at work; new cases, depositions to prep for, billable hours I needed to meet, all of them needing my immediate attention but my all nighter at the office was thrown out of the window with a simple call.

I didn't even get the chance to bitch at Abby for handing over my newest case.

Even so, there was a sense of calm that washed over me when I was here and final touches were one of my favorite parts. Food could be good, great even, but would you really want to eat it if it's just slopped onto a plate and tossed in front of you? I swiped the rim of the plate with my apron and followed it up with a heavy sprinkle of parmesan and parsley on top.

Pain rippled across my lower back as I stood up to admire my work, and nodded to myself once it passed my inspection. Grabbing the plate I had finished first, I slid them both onto the counter and hit the bell, summoning Noah back. He appeared through the heavy plastic swing doors a few seconds later. "This looks great Carina," he praised, or sucked up depending on who asked, as he picked up both plates. Either way it caused a slight swell of pride in my chest, even if it was Noah.

With thirty minutes to close, I clicked off the burners, choosing to believe the last customer had already ordered so I could start my prep work early. Icy air blasted my face as I yanked the heavy door open and stepped into the refrigerator. Tiny white clouds accompanied each breath as I took a minute for myself. Everyone in the service industry knew the fridge was a safe space.

I swiped my phone from my pocket.

Another file, Abby, really?

I didn't need to wait long for a response, I also didn't need to give her any context because she knew exactly what she did.

> **What do you want from me! I'm just one person and you get more inquiries than anyone in the office**

> **but him...**

> **Better than the twins**

My laugh bounced off the plastic containers that surrounded me.

> **I guess... but now you owe me. Drinks on you all night for my birthday**

> **I mean they kinda already were but okay! I'll take it, love you!**

My birthday couldn't come soon enough, I was in need of a drink—or ten.

Was thirty-two too old to be excited for your birthday? Perhaps, but I preferred not to limit myself to the world's simple pleasures. And dancing and drinking were some of my favorites.

I was peeling back the lid on a tub of cutlets that needed to be cooked sooner rather than later when Noah's muffled voice filtered through the refrigerator. Metal groaned as I shouldered the door open and popped my head out, instantly regretting it. A sheepish glint in his eye flickered before it was replaced with one of caution. "Don't hate me," he said quickly.

"Don't tell me something to make me hate you." His face dropped. I walked to meet him in the middle of the kitchen. "It was a joke, what do you need?" My tone was light and reassuring, the exact opposite of what I was really feeling. Which was tired and irritated. I wanted to go home and the only reason you start a sentence with 'don't hate me' means you messed something up which led to probably staying longer than I wanted to in this place.

He fixed his face. "There's a couple still here, and they keep saying how much they loved the dishes, it's the first time they've been here and all that and I may have told them that the restaurants' namesake was the chef for tonight. They want to thank you." He slowly backed away with each word and disappeared out of the kitchen by the end of the sentence, which was a great choice on his part.

I begged my parents not to name the restaurant after me, but they did it anyway. No amount of convincing got them to change their minds.

Checking my reflection in a mirror would've been useless, I already knew what I would see. My apron covered in flour and sauce, my hair in a sloppy knot on top of my head and likely frizzy from standing over the boiling water for the past three hours, but it would have to do. If I had any luck, it would be a younger couple who really did just want to pay a compliment. God love the older generation, but they loved to keep a conversation going long past its prime.

When I stepped into the dining room, Noah waved me over to the booth in the back. Small miracles, the woman looked to be younger than forty at least. Jet-black hair that was pulled back from her brightly animated face while she talked with Noah. I was halfway across the room when my eyes skated over to the man who sat across from her, and my footsteps faltered.

I would know that hair anywhere. That hair haunted my dreams and starred in my nightmares, to the point where sometimes I didn't want to wake up.

Maybe I could sneak back to the kitchen with no one noticing, Noah would come check on me and I'd pretend like I was suddenly too busy. But I thought about it too long, and sure enough, Noah's eyes locked with mine.

With the world's slowest steps, I arrived at his side right as he was saying, "And this is Carina." His hands doing this weird Vanna White thing.

Words escaped me momentarily before I pulled my mask on, envisioning a lock snapping shut on my emotions and squared my shoulders. "Hi, everybody." Way too cheery, even Noah noticed as he flashed me a startled look. What was wrong with me? "How was everyone's meal?" I asked the table and watched as my voice registered with Decker.

Muscles in his shoulders tensed under the plain black T-shirt he had changed into as his hand flexed around the glass in his grasp. But he didn't turn to look at me until I focused on the woman, who was breathtakingly beautiful, might I add. She apparently noticed nothing and launched into a gushing review of the food. She was sweet, so it was easy to keep my focus on her. Anything to avoid looking at him, which was near impossible because I could feel the hole burning into the side of my head from his stare.

After a minute she finally included him in our one-sided conversation. "Wasn't it wonderful, Lee?" the woman asked him. *Lee*, what a dumb nickname, I almost wanted to vomit.

Instead of vomiting, I finally allowed myself to look at him.

It was slow and painful, and I was sorry I did it. His hair free of any constraints, wild black waves grazed his sharp jawline that made me sweat a little. But it was more than that. Until this very moment, I never realized I hadn't seen him in anything other than a button up and slacks. Sometimes a full suit, but nothing like this.

He was in black T-shirt that was maybe a size too small for him but hugged every muscle of his shoulders and biceps in the best way. It wasn't the sight of his skin that emptied my brain, it was the fact he was covered in tattoos from the forearm up until they disappeared under his shirt.

"It was," he agreed with his mystery woman in a rocky tone. His gaze flicked up to meet mine as a small smirk tugged at the corner of his lips. He continued staring at me as the woman promised they would absolutely be coming back. I didn't even remember what my last words to them were before I escaped and hightailed it back to the kitchen.

We saw each other five days a week, for hours a day, and the one time he saw me out of work, he says noting. It was rude. Sure, maybe we weren't friends who chatted about our weekend on Monday morning but I spent more time around him than my best friend, Lennon—not Abby, for obvious reasons—because of work. The least he could do was acknowledge me.

Maybe his girlfriend was a jealous woman and he didn't want to let her know that we worked together. That had to be it, I told myself as I tried to ignore the fact that even thinking the word girlfriend made my gut want to empty itself.

We worked together, I had to remind myself, nothing more.

By the end of the night someone could eat off the floor with how clean it was as I poured what little energy I had left into not thinking about him. Noah could sense enough hate rolling off of me and left me to finish the final walk through the building on my own.

Under the soft bistro lighting bouncing off the exposed brick, I pushed in the wooden chairs and straightened the tablecloths so the red and white checkered patterns aligned with the edge of the table. Once everything was in order, I locked up and began dreading having to see him again in a few short hours. I could ask the universe for some help, bargain with the unknown for him to carry the ignoring-me piece into work and put me out of my misery, but something told me it would be futile.

FOUR

Carina

HOW I MADE IT moonlighting at Carina's without ever running into anyone from work was a miracle. I guess it was only a matter of time, but why, of all people, did it have to be him? Or better yet, why did he have to be with a woman who looked as if she walked off the front cover of Cosmopolitan?

Something about the lack of interaction stuck with me, and not in a good way, more like a bad commercial jingle. Invasive, almost to the point where ripping my head off seemed like a logical solution. I spent the night tossing and turning as his stupid face ear-wormed its way into my dreams until I decided being awake was the only remedy.

Everything in the office was still as I walked through the quiet halls in the early morning darkness, not bothering to flick on any lights as I passed them. Deep flavors of brown sugar and cinnamon burst over my tongue as I took a quick sip from the latte I stopped for as a steady hum filled my office. I set my coffee down and tossed the pastry bag next to it on my desk.

There is exactly one thing on this earth that could effectively bring me to my knees and it was the blueberry scones from Renaissance Cafe. Those damn pastries were so good I had to limit myself to only ordering them before big client meetings, trials, or mornings where the bags under my eyes weren't easily concealed. Today was obviously the latter.

My chair groaned under my sudden weight before I typed in my password to get the day started. The early hour called for simple work, simple, billable work. Billing was the bane of my existence, maybe for most attorneys but a necessary evil if anything, despite the feeling I got each time I was the top biller in the office.

I sifted through emails from clients and shot off answers, researched case law for a client who had a mediation meeting coming up to go over custody and drafted a final divorce decree for signatures. By the time I looked up, sunlight filled my office and I had been at it for hours.

Some of my coworkers were milling in the hallway outside my door, quietly chatting as they started their day. I watched for a moment, their casual conversations and quick embraces, someone shared something on their phone with another that caused them both to laugh. It ebbed and flowed with a familiarity I never quite understood.

Abby was kind of my only friend, I had Lennon too, but honestly it never really bothered me. Lasting connections have always been elusive. For a long time, it was something I struggled with. I mean when you're the only girl in fifth grade not invited to sleepover, it did something to you. It was never a conscious effort to not belong but it always seemed to happen; any time I found someone I had something in common with, I'd find a way to wiggle out of their attempt to get to know me.

And who wanted to pry at someone who was cold and off-putting? The older I got the easier it became to bury myself in school and then work.

I had acquaintances, peers, colleagues, and that was enough. And I never flirted long enough to land myself in a relationship.

No real friends, boyfriends or anything other than surface level connections for me. Until Abby. She blew in unannounced and didn't even bother noticing the icy barriers I had installed. Her warmth melted them enough for her to slip through and then she never left.

The years before Abby, I was content with the way I was living. I worked, and went to school—that was it. It was all I had room for while my goals were in sight. I kept my head down until I made it to the other side, and on the other side was Abby. For the last five years she has gifted me with her loyalty and there was no one I trusted more with the details of my inner thoughts than her. She was my best friend, her and Lennon, because you couldn't have one without the other. They are the two most important people in my life outside of my parents.

But sometimes I wondered if I was missing something.

Or at least I thought I might be, but right as those tell-tale feelings of sentimental bullshit started creeping in, from lack of sleep I assumed, Decker slipped into my view and it all vanished and my icy barrier solidified. This was why connection meant nothing. All it was was a slippery slope into disappointment. And Decker was at the bottom of all my slopes.

"Something I can help you with, Decker?" I slapped on my mask of indifference and let irritation coat my words.

He stepped farther into my space. I tracked his movement, always so fluid and confident, as if he owned every room he walked into and he made himself at home in my visitor chair. "Your file is set up."

"And you came all the way over here to tell me." I deadpanned, sliding my focus back to my computer. "Lucky me," I added under my breath. "Have you—"

He cut me off. "Initial email was sent out last night, along with a meeting request which should also be in your inbox." He looked so pleased with himself and sure enough my computer chimed with an event. "Oh, and Ian Wheeler is representing the husband."

My eyes slid shut at the name as my head hit the back of my chair.

If this was a superhero movie, Ian Wheeler was the Lex Luther to my Batman, or was it Ironman. Honestly, who cared? He was the worst, a villain disguised a do-good lawyer.

"Is that bad?" Decker's words pulled me out of my attempt at quick meditation.

"Wheeler is powerful, the best money can buy. He's the guy you keep on retainer to get you out of any legal bind you can think of."

"Sounds like he's just your type," he quipped.

Every muscle in my back tensed. "You don't know my type, Decker."

There was a slight pause, as if he needed to flesh out his answer before speaking. "True. I have no idea how you spend your free time but I do know that in all the years we've worked together, I've never even seen you with a date to any of our company parties." He leaned back in his chair. "So tell me, what kind of man interests Carina Pera?"

He was toying with me, dangling a ridiculous question in front of me, probably betting I wouldn't bother to answer.

I hate losing, didn't matter if they were one sided bets I made up in my head, so I answered. "Very little actually."

His eyebrows lifted before he replied, "How on brand for you. No one good enough?" It came out as a laugh.

"I don't date," I answered truthfully after an awkward lull.

Why did I say that?

"Never?"

"Not really. Last boyfriend I had was a long time ago. I'm just not into romance and all that, I guess," I admitted, then nipped at my bottom lip out of habit.

Why was I telling him all of this? Talking about why I didn't date was something I pushed to the back of my mind and decided to never talk about, with anyone. So what was it about Levi Decker that made me want to spill my guts to him?

He regarded me with something between curiosity and determination before replying. "Well I'm nothing if not a romantic," he finally said.

I laughed, forgetting all about the file he had come in to talk about. "Is that how you lure the women in on your Tinder profile?"

"As a matter of fact, it is. That, and well a placed shirtless photo."

My only reply was an eye roll but I would be lying if I said I didn't get a sudden vision of a shirtless Decker in my head. I bet he was all lean muscle and strong shoulders and tattoos that traveled the entire length of him.

I expected him to up and leave after our quick revelation of personal facts, but he kept sitting there even though there was no reason for him to come and tell me anything in person at all.

"How long have you worked at Carina's?"

A huffed breath left my chest as I continued to pluck away at my keyboard. "I don't. At least not really. It's my parents' place, I come in when there's no one else to take a shift."

"But you cook? You're not a waitress or something?"

"I prefer the kitchen."

"How often are you there?" he asked, as if he was studying for a pop quiz, and I was back to being irritated. Too many facts of my life were being scooped up by him, and not knowing why he wanted them was making me itchy.

"I don't know, Decker, once or twice a month. Why do you want to know?"

He shrugged.

"I'm glad your girlfriend enjoyed the food last night." It was a low, snide remark, that slipped out without even thinking and I hoped it wasn't mistaken for jealousy. Only he didn't look caught off guard. Instead a jarring laugh burst through stale air as he clutched his stomach.

"I'm sorry, I'm not laughing at you. It's just, that was my sister last night, not my girlfriend."

I was saved by a knock at the door and we both turned to see Abby in the threshold, eyes darting between us, with the echo of his laugh still ringing out.

Decker took that as his queue to leave and stood from the chair and strode toward the door. "Oh and for the record there's no girlfriend, at all, not just last night," he stated and I swear to God he winked at me. Actually fucking winked.

And I didn't hate it?

I must be coming down with something.

He left my office while still laughing, leaving Abby with a bewildered look. Without a second thought she snapped the door closed and turned to me with her jaw hanging open. "Okay what was that?" she asked while dropping a pile of folders before me.

Looked like I wasn't getting any work done this morning.

"*That* was nothing."

"It didn't look or sound like nothing." A smirk took over her face.

"Can't you meddle in someone else's life? What's Lennon doing?" I'd say anything to get the attention off of me. You wouldn't see me squirm under questioning, but I loathed talking about myself.

She scoffed. "Lennon's still pretending to not have feelings for Theo, that's what she's doing. Now back to you."

Abby was like a dog with a bone, fiercely protective over this new piece of information she had on me and wouldn't give up. Didn't matter if I ignored her, she was determined to see it through. "He came into Carina's last night with a woman and because the new waiter can't keep his mouth shut, I was summoned to the table. Didn't even acknowledge that he knew me, might I add." There, that should hold her over.

"And today he's letting you know he doesn't have a girlfriend?" The wheels were turning in her head. It seemed so juvenile, gossiping about a guy. There were bigger things going on in the world than what Levi Decker might mean by telling me he didn't have a girlfriend.

A long pause hung between us.

"Weren't you just bitching about having too much work, why don't you go do some of it?" I finally got around to saying.

She gathered the files with a wicked smile on her face. "I'm sure I do," she said as she followed Decker's suit without questioning me further. My shoulders relaxed a fraction once I was alone but my focus was gone because what *did* he mean? The question would plague me longer than I cared to think about.

My head hit the back of my chair and I contemplated redownloading one of my apps to find someone's bed to occupy for a little while tonight. It had been... I did some quick math and took myself by surprise when I realized it had been months since the last time I had a date or anything that even remotely resembled falling into bed with someone.

I needed to change that, maybe that was causing my lapse in judgement. Any time I found myself being charmed by Decker, it was because I hadn't been properly fucked into a mattress. But before I could grab my phone, he walked by my open door, nothing special, didn't even look into my office, but that was all it took before the thought was replaced with a brief picture of me in a very particular bed. I set my phone down, dating app forgotten.

The day passed in a blur, three meetings that could have been simple messages, two more intake files from Abby and emails that seemed to never stop. I welcomed the interruption when my phone rang and didn't even grimace when my mom's picture filled the screen.

"Vita mia, come stai?" The corners of my mouth ticked up at the sound of her voice. The soft cadence of her Italian has been my favorite sound since I was small, her gentle voice to my Papa's boisterous personality. The line was quiet, and I knew what was coming.

"Tell me, Mamma."

I could hear the soft exhale of the breath she had been holding. "We're short again, piccola. Not for today but do you think you'll be able to come in on Friday?"

My eyes pinched shut and I made a great effort to not bang my head into the desk. "Friday night, are you serious? Why can't any of your real employees work?" She tsked at my harsh words, but mainly at my attitude. I already knew I would say yes, I had no real plans besides taking up my normal spot-on Abby's couch, binge watching movies. "Why can't you or Papa stay?"

"We have a meeting out of town that day and will not be back until late," she answered.

"Of course I'll help. I'll see you Friday, Mamma."

That was all she wanted and quickly ended our call once she got the answer she was looking for.

I needed more of a life, something else to keep me occupied so I could say no to helping because I had actual plans. My fingers tapped in a rhythm against my desk as I stared at my phone.

Fuck it, it had been too long.

The app downloaded quickly, a perk of it being deleted and reinstalled often.

Four left swipes and I was already thinking about deleting it again. And then I saw him.

His first picture was standard, semi close up from his shoulders up. His hair was tied back, and I immediately chastised myself for thinking it would have been better if he lead with a full picture that had his hair down, it was one of his best features. I flipped through the photos and sure enough the second to last one was him sans shirt.

My imagination wasn't even this good, but I was right about the lean muscle, with abs I last saw on a greek statue somewhere, and biceps that looked as if he could rip a tree straight from the ground. Good lord he even had the cut muscle group that made a V shape straight toward his...

"Hey, do you—" a voice interrupted my imagination.

My entire body jarred at the sudden intrusion, sending my phone flipping from my hands and me scrambling to catch it. "Oh, fuck!" I exclaimed, staring in horror down at my phone once I had a grip on it. "Oh no. Oh no, no, no," I whined and glanced up to see Abby staring wide-eyed back at me.

"I wanted to see if you want to pick up stuff for drinks and watch a movie tonight. What happened?"

The words felt foreign as I thought them, and even more ludicrous once I said them out loud. "I swiped right on Levi Decker."

FIVE

Decker

WITH SIX OLDER SISTERS, I was in no short supply of finding ways to occupy my free time, whether I liked it or not. It wasn't easy to field all of their calls while in school but that wasn't an excuse I could use after next week. And Laura knew that, so she was getting in early.

I dodged most of her calls the past month but when she finally got me on the line, she demanded we get dinner since I had already been out with Lola and that we had to do it before the weekend. Probably wasn't the best idea to take her to the same restaurant as Lola, but if Carina was telling the truth she wouldn't be there twice in one week. But if she was, I would blame it on the food. It really was too good to pass up.

The real answer was almost too much to wrap my head around.

Deep in my chest there was a pull to be near her, which was getting stronger by the minute, and nothing seemed to keep it at bay. It didn't matter if I only got her glares and sharp-tongued words, anything was better than nothing. I barely knew Carina despite the years we spent working together but I was beginning to think I'd do unfathomable things to get her to look at me with eyes that held more than her usual discontentment.

Thick, warm air enveloped me as I walked the length of the street toward the restaurant. The kind that stuck in your throat, and made each breath feel like you were choking on nothing. Laura waved me down from the front of Carina's Trattoria with a smile that rivaled the sun, and before I knew it, she pulled me into a hug that threatened to break any one of my ribs. "Laura, get off." The words came out as a strangled breath as I wrestled myself out of her grip.

"I'm so excited my baby brother wanted to spend time with me." She latched herself onto my arm as I opened the front door, finally getting the breeze I needed.

"You told me if we didn't get dinner, you would tell Mom that I was the one who broke the vase last weekend."

She smiled brightly and only nodded as we walked up to the hostess stand displaying a small sign telling us to pick our own seats. We wove around the two occupied tables and slid into an empty booth, near the one I sat in last time.

Laura looked around the dimly lit area before lifting up a menu that had been left on all the tables. They were clearly set up for self sufficiency and I wondered if that had anything to do with why Carina worked here. "Didn't you just come here with Lola?" she questioned and I should have known better. For such a large sibling group, we were unusually close and I could always count on my sisters knowing where I went and with who.

Before I could tell her she was right, the waitress approached our table. "Good Evening, everyone, what can I get started for..." The words trailed off as I looked up and locked eyes with the only person I knew with pieces of jade for irises, which immediately went flat and unreadable.

Fate seemed to favor me lately.

A slow smile pulled at my lips as she glanced at my sister then back to me, mouth slightly parted as she arched an eyebrow in question.

"Don't worry she's my sister too," I remarked, answering the question her eyes were asking me.

She clicked her pen in three quick successions. "And just how many sisters do you have, Decker?" she demanded while pulling out an order pad.

"There's five of us," Laura chimed in, stifling a laugh from her side of the table. The two women smiled politely at each other before my sister continued on "And little Levi here is the baby."

Carina mimicked the 'little Levi' comment and I had a feeling she would stash that into her arsenal for later. We gave our drink order, and as she walked off, I tore my attention from watching her leave, back to my sister.

Under Laura's grin and twinkling eyes, I shifted in my seat, waiting for the inevitable.

"Who is she?"

Being the baby of family meant I knew no peace growing up. Our house was loud at any given time, full of controlled chaos, as my mother lovingly put it. As the only boy, I had my own room for most of my life but that didn't stop any one of them from constantly being in my business. It was a never ending revolving door of girls who always thought they knew what was best for me and if I ever put a toe out of line, they were the first to let me know. Certifiable crazy, every single one, and I loved them.

My hand came up to scratch the back of my neck before I answered, and then tucked a piece of hair behind my ear. "We work together. She's an attorney for ALA."

A surprising look crossed her face. "Why is she working here then?"

It was obvious it was more curiosity than anything but there was an indigent tone behind the words and a flash of protectiveness surged through me. "There's nothing wrong with working in a restaurant. Her parent's own this place, she helps out when they are short staffed, Laura," I shot back, instantly on the defense. She threw her hands up, dismissing me before picking up the menu again as another server dropped off our drinks but my subconscious stayed on alert for my next sighting of her.

Our table was silent until Carina made her re-appearance, and my sister with her new found knowledge that we know each other, made no hesitation to chat her up. "What would you recommend? This seems to be little Levi's new favorite place but he doesn't have a favorite dish."

My eyes practically roll out of my head when Carina snickers softly. "The Penne alla Amatriciana is new and one of my favorites. Really anything though, they are all my mother recipes."

"Well, if it's your favorite, then it's good enough for me," she said and I ordered the same because I had a deep-seated desire to know all of Carina's favorites.

Laura filled me in on her life as a mother of two and the only other topic that occupied our family, Lola's wedding, until the food came and it was every bit of amazing Carina made it out to be. "Mom was not this crazy when I got married so I have no idea what to do with her besides remind her it's not her wedding," she exclaimed before shoveling another bite of pasta into her mouth.

"And Lola really wants you to bring a date, who knows why. I think she's sad that you are now the only one of us not with someone or married. But that's just a guess. Are you going to cut your hair? You know she wants you to," she rambled out in one breath. With two young daughters, I wasn't sure she talked to enough adults and wanted to make sure she got it all out before going back home.

My head dropped into my hands as I listened to her ramble. "You people are too much sometimes, you know that?" My voice was muffled but she heard me. I sat back into my chair and raked my hand through my hair. I grew and cut my hair all the time, it shouldn't have been a big deal but when my sister was asking me to do it, every part of me screamed to do the exact opposite. More importantly, if I cut it, I would be getting rid of the only part of me Carina's didn't seem to hate.

A phone rang and my sister's hand flew to her purse in search of it, lips smashed into a hard line as she read the message.

"Everything okay?"

"It's Brynn, she keeps spiking a fever, and has this nasty cough and we can't figure out why." A worried look passed over her face. "Kevin's out of town and the babysitter said she's warm," she huffed out before her chair scraped backwards. "I'm sorry, Lee, I have to go."

I waved her off. "Go, let me know if you need anything." She rushed past me and was out the door before I finished my sentence. Our plates sat in front of us, half eaten and I contemplated finishing up alone or taking it to go.

"Oof, that's a bad sign. Not even your sister stays through dinner with you, are you that bad of a conversationalist?" Carina's voice floated over me, settling into the parts that were filled with worry moments ago. I grinned up at her and was surprised to see she was smirking back.

"Maybe you'll just have to come on a date with me to find out." A little Hail Mary never hurt anyone and work never seemed like the best place to try it out. Her eyes widened before she scoffed at my blatantly lame attempt to ask her out.

"Nice try, don't ask me that again." The check dropped onto the table but she surprised me by slipping into my sister's vacant seat. "You're the only person here," she stated, as if she needed a reason to relax a bit.

I scanned the room after her statement, and she was right. The room was empty and some of the bigger lights had even been turned off without me realizing. I wouldn't have guessed they closed this early on Fridays since it was barely nine. I tugged my wallet free from my jeans and laid out enough cash on the table between us.

"Thanks Carina, everything was great," I said honestly.

"Don't thank me, you paid to be here." She laughed before leaning her head into one of her hands, the other stretched out onto the table, pink nails tapped out a soothing, rhythmic sound. My eyes flicked between her face and then her hand, as a bubbling sensation flooded my chest, telling me to reach out and touch her. Just once, so I could finally stop imagining what it was like.

When my eyes met her face again, she began absentmindedly tugging on her bottom lip with her teeth, looking around the empty restaurant, and that feeling boiled over, flushing my entire body with want. The want to stay in this chair and watch the way her green eyes sparkled under the warm light of the table lamp. The want to reach out and feel the softness of her hand. The want to pull her onto my lap and see if she molded against me and fit the way I always imagined.

But I didn't do any of that.

"I should go," I said with little meaning because if given the opportunity, I would stay through the night doing nothing but stare at her. Her face dropped a fraction. One blink and I would've missed it. The movement sparked a light and made me think that finally this wasn't all in my head. "I'll see you Monday."

"See you Monday," she replied quietly and I unwillingly walked out of the restaurant.

The night air did little to cool me down. Whatever it was that I felt for Carina only made me feel isolated. It had been years since I first laid eyes on her and yet nothing happened.

Maybe dipping back into dating pool again would put me out of my misery. It wasn't really high on my list of things to do but anything would be better than panting after a woman who was completely unattainable.

Before I could talk myself out of it I pulled out my phone and found the app I needed. If it was fifteen years ago, I'd be in a bar trying to shoot my shot with a woman. Not literally though, because fifteen years ago I was underage but in dating world practices of fifteen years ago, that's what I'd be doing. Instead I was swiping left, and left again. And again. And again.

It wasn't like I lacked matches, but I had to be sure they were in it for more than one night. I needed connection, I needed more than something quick and drifting. I wanted something with room to grow.

Being thirty came with the existential dread of ending up alone. It was a hard feeling to shake, especially when I was constantly surrounded by my sisters, who were all married or almost, and my parents who'd been together for decades. I wanted what they had but getting there felt impossible, like being dropped into a new city without a map.

I almost gave up on the app but then...

My feet faltered and I halted to a stop in the middle of the sidewalk.

There she was, smiling brightly up at me from my phone.

I knew exactly when this photo was taken, and was sure if you could extend it you would see me in the background watching her over an Old Fashioned glass. This was last December at our company's Christmas party. Carina wore a dress made of red silk that hit the floor and pooled around her feet, while dipping low in the front and back. It was hard to forget. For weeks I dreamed of that dress.

I didn't know what to do as my thumb itched to swipe but the words in her bio mocked me. *I can't wait to sneak out of your room in the morning.* A laugh escaped and her words from earlier this week played on a loop in my head, she didn't date. Starting anything with Carina wouldn't help me with finding the one if she's so dead set on not dating.

Even if it was only one night with her, it would be enough to hold me over for a lifetime.

Fuck it.

I held my breath and swiped.

I must be hallucinating, I didn't expect anything to happen but there I was staring at my screen as "It's a match!" popped up.

Like I said, the world had been favoring me lately.

SIX

Carina

ABBY'S JAW INCHED CLOSER to the floor as I filled her in on Decker showing up at the restaurant on Friday...again.

"He. Did. Not."

I hummed before shoveling a handful of chips into my mouth. Abby's couch sported a permanent indent of me which I was adding to while her TV played in the background. Midway through pulling out a chip and shoving it into her mouth, Abby froze, hands flying up in front of her as if stopping some invisible force. "You should invite him to come out for your birthday."

My face pinched at her words. "Or not."

"Okay, so I'll invite him out."

That seemed desperate, we didn't hang out outside of work. We didn't even hang out at work. Suddenly inviting him out to celebrate my birthday would be weird. My mind seemed to make the decision for me before I could really process the repercussions of if I did ask him to come. Then there was the whole matching situation. The notification came across my phone right after he left, throwing me into a state of shock, which would

41

now forever hang in the balance between us. I didn't quite know what to do with that piece of information other than that it was something.

"But why not? You want him—don't give me that look," she said without actually even looking at me. "And there's no way he doesn't want you. Come on, it could be fun. Otherwise neither of you will ever do anything about whatever it is you have going on and you know it." Her voice was on the brink of whining, but I only offered her a blank stare so she wouldn't know how much I liked the idea of him coming.

"Abby," I warned.

"It's not like there's a no-fraternization policy at work. What's stopping either of you?" She had a point even if I didn't verbalize it; her smug face was enough of an answer.

"Why are you so invested in this?" I questioned, and an exasperated sigh exited her as she lounged further into the plush couch.

"I have no one. I'm living vicariously through you and Lennon right now."

I laughed, nudging her with my foot. Lennon was currently in denial about her feelings for her former high school boyfriend, who recently followed her back home from halfway across the globe. But Lennon had an actual reason for denying her feelings.

She was happily married to a man who was kinder than anyone I had ever met, and then he died. Suddenly she was alone, and Abby and I worked our asses off to make sure she didn't let her grief take her. The lingering memory of how distraught she was after his death sent chills throughout my body. I understood why she was so hesitant to put herself out there again, but if she could try, then why couldn't I even wrap my mind around the thought of being close to anyone?

Short answer was I liked my independence. I answered to no one—if I wanted to leave for a weekend, I could pack up and go. Or if I wanted to eat the same girl dinner of cheese and crackers for four nights in a row while staying at the office past nine, there was no one waiting on me who would be disappointed, and that was important to me.

Under no circumstances did I want to change myself to fit someone's idea of who I was or should be. It was asked of me once, and I vowed it would never be the path I found myself on again.

Being in a relationship wasn't for me, no matter how many times my mother reminded me I wasn't getting any younger. But in the back of my head, a thought plastered itself along my brain like graffiti, that maybe my fierce independence streak was a coping mechanism I put in place to avoid the truth that I was too much to handle.

Abby flopped back onto the couch but continued to glare at me, as if I was ruining her favorite activity.

I was skimming through my emails when she finally turned her attention back toward me. "Why are you working on a Sunday?"

I glanced up over my screen to see her face screwed up in disappointment. "I've got a million things going on. Office hours aren't cutting it."

"I don't know how you do it," Abby stated. "But better you than me."

It was a harmless statement but one that turned my stomach; it was like she was saying she couldn't bother working any longer than her posted hours because she had more valuable people or things to focus on. Whether she meant it that way or not, it stung.

I could have a full, vibrant life if I wanted to. Date a different man every night of the week, spend weekends hiking or painting or at the pumpkin patch but I liked to work, and that didn't make me or my life any less important.

There was no void I needed to fill, but I could stand to widen my horizons.

Work had been terrible but at least there were a few highlights.

One, I finally met the man who had been occupying all of Lennon's time. Abby and I ran into Theo Beckett after we ended up leaving the office late. I thought Lennon's husband was perfect for her, but I think Theo was made with her in mind also. Second reason was, in a few short hours, I would be on a dance floor with warm fuzzy bliss flowing through me from one too many shooters, wearing this tiny little gold dress I found online while doom-scrolling as I waited for a client last month.

Abby sat on the other side of my desk, equally as giddy. "And you'll be out of here on time today, right?" She leveled a heavy gaze at me.

"Yes, for the last time. I'm leaving no later than five, you and Lennon will probably already be at my house, followed by dinner and then dancing until I can't feel my feet at Liquid Alchemy." I picked up my cold coffee and drained the last drops. Abby opened her mouth to respond as Decker walked in. My stomach dropped at the sight of him. Monday and Tuesday were crazy, I barely saw anyone at the office, Wednesday I brushed past him in the hallway and by the end of the day, he was long gone.

This is the first time I had even a minute to sit. Which was a good thing because if we didn't interact, that meant there was no chance we would have to talk about, what I was referring to as, the app incident.

"Levi, just the man I wanted to see." Abby glanced over her shoulder, greeting him with a smile. If I could kick her through the desk, I would.

My eyes moved from Decker to Abby who had sat back further in her chair with a smug look on her face. I shot her a warning glance that fell flat.

Decker walked into my office with ease and joined her in the spare chair facing my desk. I flicked my gaze away from my computer screen to meet his. Only for him to hold the look long enough that my insides started twisting.

"Ladies," he said while his legs sprawled out in front of him taking up entirely too much room in my office.

"How's your birthday been so far, Carina?" Abby steered the conversion back to me, knowing full well I'd gone the whole day at work with no one the wiser, which is exactly how I preferred it.

"Oh, is it your birthday today?" Decker asked with a tilt of his head.

I didn't know what to make of his tone, so I ignore it and answered. "Can't complain. The day's almost over, works been easy today. Oh, and Abby left me my favorite latte this morning, thank you by the way. Overall not too bad."

"What?" Abby asked as her face pulled into confusion.

"There was a latte left on my desk this morning. My exact order, a soy brown sugar latte, you didn't..." My voice trailed off as she started shaking her head slowly back and forth. Her lips pulled into a grimace the same time mine did. Decker hid a laugh behind his fist. My stomach soured at the thought that I drank a gift from a stranger.

"Gross," she quipped before shooting up from the desk. "Well I'll see you tonight, don't work late because I will drag you from this office if I have to." Abby waved above her head as she left.

Air hung heavy around us as we stared at each other. Besides the restaurant and a few work parties, I've never seen him outside work. It made me wonder what he would be like without all the constraints of the office walls, or his suit and hair ties. I drank in the way his black button up stretched over his broad chest, the cuffs of his shirt hung open but there was no sign of the tattoos I knew were there. Unfortunately, his hair was tied back, dark strands pulled away from his face, showing off his sharp stubbled jawline, which was pulling all of my focus.

He looked tired.

Decker is usually clean shaven, but it wasn't just the faint five o'clock shadow, lilac lined his eyes and each blink came a bit slower than then last. All tell tale of someone burning the candles at both ends, but I had no idea what he did with his time or what could be draining his energy. The sound of him clearing his throat caused my body jerk from the trail of thoughts I was going down. I tried to focus my eyes back on the computer and not on him while silently cursing myself for the detour. "I came to ask if I could sit in on the initial meeting for the Leon case next week."

That was new, he'd never asked to sit in on any meetings before. "Why?"

"Been wanting to dip my toes in on the other side, thought this might be a good case to do so."

"You thinking of going back to school?"

His gaze flicked away from mine. "Something like that."

"Sure, why not," I answered. It was obvious he was expecting a denial but the look of surprise was worth it.

The silence was back and I needed to fill it, anything would work. "Do you have any plans tonight?"

I needed to fill the silence with anything but that. Wasn't I just threatening Abby over doing the same thing I think I was about to do?

What the fuck was I thinking?

Decker kicked one long leg out and over his opposite knee, leaning back into the seat and stretching his arms up until the came to a rest behind his head. He was the picture of comfort while I was a tangled ball of knots.

Lack of sex did weird things to the brain, and I needed to find a quick way out of the hole I was about to too dig myself into.

"I was only asking to see if you were going to show up at the restaurant again or not," I rushed to say. Only when he smiled it only heightened the feelings that were surfacing. I tried and failed to find something about him that turned me off but either it was something he kept buried, or it didn't exist.

"Oh, I'm definitely coming back. There's about a dozen dishes I still need to try."

Decker

I WASN'T EAVESDROPPING. THAT was my story and if anyone asked, I would cling to it like a raft in messy waters. At some point a line was drawn between Carina and I, one she placed not long after we started at ALA together. It had been five years and she was still as serious as when we started. All no nonsense, focused and shooting down any distractions, but at least in the beginning she was lighter around me.

She would laugh at my poorly cracked jokes, and when I remembered her coffee order and brought her a cup in the morning, she'd thank me politely with a coy smile that made me want to keep it on her face. Then one day it all changed, she turned cool. Conversations cut short and were only work related. No more smiles, no more coffee, no more open door that I was trying to work up the courage to step through to her office. She shut it, bolted the door and left me on the other side without so much as a second thought.

It was the one thing in life that haunted me. I never figured out what it was, and it wasn't like I could simply walk up and ask her, as much as

I wanted to, because it was the one thing we never actually talked about. We had moments, that apparently I read into further than she did.

At some point, I begrudgingly moved on. The amount of silent pining was doing no one any good. If she wanted to stay behind a closed door, I could learn to live with it, but it suddenly felt like the bolt was coming undone. It was progress and that was all the encouragement I needed.

The drink I left her for her birthday was a nice touch, if I said so myself, even if she didn't know it was from me. I wasn't an expert in Carina, but I wanted to be. Instead I'd been gathering little pieces of her, squirreling them away for the right moment.

A moment I thought would never come but that was okay because even a sliver of hope was enough for me to survive on.

When I overheard Abby talking to Carina about going out to Liquid Alchemy for her birthday, it was the day after my soon-to-be brother-in-law arrived in town to see my sister. Lola cornered Kevin and me, demanding we take him out for a bachelor party celebration. What better place than a bar? Seemed like fate to me.

Carina's door may have been unlocked but I wasn't going to test it by barreling through, and knocking it off its hinges, risking what might be my only chance. That would have her shutting me out before I even got in. Instead I was going to slowly creep over the line.

Chase was set to marry my sister in about a month, after doing the long distance thing for the past nine months while he was deployed. Lola was set on being with him by the next time he had to leave which led to a wedding being planned quickly. Chase was only here for a few days and then wouldn't be back until the wedding. I was surprised when Lola even offered to give up a night to have us take him out.

His only request was something low key, and there was nothing more low key than simple beers at a local dive bar.

Kevin was already complaining about a headache from the music after an hour, and I had no clue when Carina and Abby had planned on showing up. For all I knew they didn't go out until midnight and if that was the case, we were never going to make it. Hell, she could've been lost in the sea of people pressing against each other and I would never know.

The three of us leaned on a tall table near the dance floor. Music blared from the far corner of the bar but vibrated under our feet as we silently watched those around us. Kevin wore a bemused look on his face, eyes darting from one person to the other and I wondered how long it'd been since he'd been out at a bar. With a wife, two kids and being a physician, I would guess time for himself was scarce and not spent in a bar. Chase, on the other hand, I didn't know much about and I should change that but maybe on a different day because I came here for a reason.

Kevin tapped the bottom of his bottle on the table, right as my eye snagged on a blonde. I perked up but it wasn't Carina. "So is this the whole night?" he said over the music, taking another swig from his drink.

"What, not lively enough for you, old man?" Chase asked with a grin.

Kevin shrugged a shoulder. "It's a bachelor party and all we're doing is standing around looking at each other. Levi keeps fidgeting like he's waiting for something to happen... just thought I'd ask."

My pulse thumped in my chest along with the beat as his words registered. "I'm not fidgeting," I argued weakly as I willed every muscle in my body to stop moving immediately.

Two sets of eyes tangled with mine. Chase spoke first. "You kind of are. You've peeled the label off your beer, and you keep looking over your shoulder at the door," Chase pointed out. "You waiting on someone?"

Balled up paper littered the table, and there was a slight pinch in the side of my neck.

Was I that obvious?

"You're the one that said no strippers, so yeah this is all we're doing." I brought the bottle to my lips. "Fuckers," I mumbled before letting the lukewarm liquid flow into my mouth. I needed something harder, something that loosened me up and would keep me occupied until we either called it a night or I saw her.

Both men glanced at each other. "Well if this is all we're doing, then we might as well get drunk," Kevin proclaimed as if he took the thought from my head before he turned and stalked toward the bar.

Music continued to shake the walls, but the silence between us was almost as loud. I didn't know much about the guy, and Carina was probably never going to show. Right as I was about to ask him where he and my sister would end up living, the dance floor in front of us seemed to part like the Red Sea and Carina slid into my view like the heavens pointing me home.

I think my chest seized at the sight of her. The beer bottle in my hand definitely slid out of my grasp and clattered against the table causing Chase to side-eye me. In an instant everything became too real and alarm bells began chiming, signaling maybe this was a terrible, terrible mistake.

None of that stopped me from watching her.

Carina stood to Abby's right, with another redheaded woman who resembled her to her left, near the bar on the opposite side of the room. Both women were coaxing the one I didn't recognize into a shot of clear liquid that stood in the shot glasses lined up in front of them. Her smile took up half her face and lasted longer than any other time I'd seen her exude happiness. Even from a distance, it was intoxicating, and each time she leaned into the women and moved her mouth in words I couldn't decipher, it was like another thread was being woven into my chest, tying me to her.

She was all I could focus on.

With the neon lights around the bar, everything was cast in a reddish hue but there was no mistaking that Carina was draped in gold that glittered with every move she made. And with so much smooth skin showing, I couldn't decide where to look first.

Every agonizing moment led to this, and it was worth it.

Carina was beaming ear to ear, throwing her hand above her head and bouncing in her impossibly high heels as the women finally downed a shot that clearly didn't agree with her.

Two minutes ago my ears were ringing with the sounds of people yelling against the music, but the longer I watched them, or lets be realistic, her, the quieter everything got. That was until a man approached, and every decibel came flooding back as jealously prickled at my skin while he talked to them with ease. Even Carina flashed him a warm smile I had been dying to be on the receiving end of.

The sound of glass hitting the table broke me from my trance, Kevin was back. "Okay, boys, this round's on me and then we can go."

"Oh, we're not going anywhere," Chase chuckled. "Someone caught Levi's eye."

I tore my eyes away and looked back to see Kevin scanning the large crowd. "Who? Someone you know?" His tone was light and amused, like we were playing a game of I Spy.

Three small glasses of caramel colored liquor sat in front of him as he continued to crane his neck like an owl. I swiped one of the glasses and threw it back, allowing the burn to coat my throat. Anything to keep me from talking, because there was no use in arguing.

Chase nodded in Carina's direction and a low whistle came from Kevin. Jealousy knocked at my chest for the simple sound. "The one in the gold?" he questioned. "She is...wow."

The back of my hand connected with Kevin's chest with a dull thud. He clutched the spot weakly. "Ow, what was that for?"

"For my sister, dick, you're married."

Kevin held his hands up, a feeble attempt to thwart any further attacks. "Married, not blind. Laura and I like to appreciate the opposite genders together, I'll probably even tell her about this once I'm home, no harm."

"Please don't." The last thing I needed was Laura back in my business. One word from Kevin and she would know exactly who he was talking about.

Carina dragged Abby out to the dance floor, closer to where the three of us stood but had yet to notice me. I had no plan for tonight and that feeling of this being a mistake began to take on a more clear form. I was in way over my head and it was too clouded with the thought of her to figure out what to do.

"Quit staring, you'll scare her," Chase chimed in.

"I'm not staring."

"Why don't you go talk to her?" He asked as I grabbed another shot and downed it.

"Why don't you two go get another round," I suggested without taking my eyes off her. Her arms were tossed above her head with abandon, as her hips swayed side to side to the music, the gold of her dress glinting in every direction. Abby stood in front of her, laughing and moving with the music right along with her. It was mesmerizing, watching her walls come down on the dance floor. Her head fell back in an open mouthed laugh as she rolled her hips back and forth. It wasn't until she spun around, balancing on impossibly high heels that she finally spotted me.

Shock overtook her features. Her pink painted lips parted, forming a small circle as our eyes finally locked. I waited for them to narrow, they always narrowed when looking at me. It was a stalemate that dragged on, neither one of us willing to give up and then fate again smiled on me, a slow smirk spread across her face.

She never stopped dancing though. I followed her hands as she crept them up the shimmery dress pushing me further into a haze. Her body turned and I noticed for the first time her dress was so tight and so impossibly short that one wrong move or one slight bend at the waist and it would show everything. And my cock was the first to react, straining against the fabric of my jeans. I reached down for a quick adjustment and I swore as I tugged her smile went predatory.

My mind flashed with images of her pressed up against a wall, dress hiked up and my mouth trailing farther and farther down—*focus Levi*. I was toeing the line she drew, not jumping, I had to remind myself.

Abby only noticed me after tracking Carina's line of sight, waving before whispering into her ear and then nudging another red haired girl's gaze toward my direction. I was a bug under a microscope with three sets of eyes on me.

Carina's eyes found mine again as she broke away from her group and sauntered toward me. Gold heels to match her dress donned her feet and the haze was back with each step she took. Darkness creeped in from the side until she was the only thing I saw, like a light at the end of a tunnel until the tips of her shoes were inches from mine.

Impossibly light green eyes stared up at me, like a hundred pieces of sea glass that came together to form the kaleidoscope in her eyes. The type of treasure you spend hours on a beach looking for — always worth the wait once you found them.

Being so close I noticed the shimmer in her pink glossy lips as she pulled them into another smile. "Hi, Decker," she breathed and I was washed in the scent of cinnamon that always seemed to follow her.

My chest thrummed. From the music, from the closeness of her, everything. It all shot straight through to that underused organ that sat in the middle of my chest. It had been so long since someone had stirred up any type feeling in me, but she was something else entirely. She stirred, shook, grasped my heart between her fingers and squeezed and I didn't think she even knew she was doing it. And that needed to change.

Something had to change otherwise I was going to lose my mind.

"Carina." My voice deepened without warning but she was so close. Every inch of me filled with the need to reach out and touch her, the same feeling I got when she sat across from me at the restaurant.

Nothing held me back this time.

The golden sequins of her dress were rough under my finger tips as they coasted over a few where her waist dipped inward. "You look," Carina's chest moved with a sharp inhale, pressing into my touch, "beautiful," I finally said.

Pink bloomed in her cheeks at my words before laughing. It was different from anything I'd ever seen. Unfiltered, nothing holding her back, unlike at work where everything always felt, not forced, but as if she'd never let anyone around see her fully.

She was pulling the door open and with how she was looking at me, it had me knocking down barriers she put up. I made my decision, I wanted her, I needed her. Maybe her hating me was an act she put on because we worked together or some other surface level reason. Who knew, but there was something between us.

Lust, attraction, something deeper than co-workers.

EIGHT

Carina

HE WAS HERE. AND not simply here in the building but standing right in front of me. Staring at me, tracking me, warm eyes raking over every inch of my body with deliberate precision. The moment I locked eyes with him, I thought I was dreaming or maybe even fell into a nightmare, either one could have been right and I wouldn't have been able to tell the difference.

My first thought was, it had to have been Abby, going behind my back and telling him to come but then she noticed him and her face mirrored mine. She had no idea he'd be there either.

I didn't believe in fate. I believed in hard work and dedication, going after what you wanted in life and ensuring it came to fruition, but this, this was something else. I wished I had it in me to walk away, or turn around and go back to dancing with Abby and Lennon, to leave him alone and go about my life. But as tequila steadily made its way through my bloodstream, replacing all my usual forward thinking, all I could do was go to him. As if a string I never knew existed tethered me to him.

Why did he have to look so good? No dumbass tie in sight and his hair exactly the way I liked it, down and free.

I let the feeling flood my system and pull me to him, planting the tips of my heels inches away from where he stood.

"Decker," I greeted.

His eyes scanned me, from the tips of my toes, slowly up my body before landing on my face, where he took a few beats before saying my name.

Even with the blaring music and the throng of people crowding around, a quiet moment passed between us. I didn't know what to fill it with; it almost didn't need to be. For a moment it was just us, in a tiny little bubble, where we weren't co-workers, where I didn't have to stuff down all my unwanted and conflicting feelings about him. We were two people trying not to be overwhelmed by whatever was passing between us, but then he reached out. It was a simple touch, not even to skin, but the effect was like water boiling over, and a flash flame roared to life.

"You look," he paused for a second, toying with the sequins on my dress, "beautiful."

It was like waking up after years of fitful sleep. Three simple words doused me in a feeling I couldn't remember ever having before. And over a man at that.

"You're here?" I questioned, leaning slightly into his touch.

"Lucky coincidence."

Didn't sound too convincing but I'd let it slide, it was my birthday after all and I was beginning to think a Decker sized gift was exactly what I wanted. Before I could get another word out, something or someone hit my back, throwing me forward into Decker.

My hands hit his chest, curling into the soft fabric to keep myself from falling over completely as his arms snaked around my waist. It was quick, he spun me to his side as I steadied myself, tucking me under his arm as he lasered in on the guy who ran into me. His fingers curled into the collar of the man's shirt with a force that threatened to lift him off the floor. "Watch where you're fucking going," he growled.

The guy drunkenly lifted his hands in defense, a sleepy smile on his face. "Sorry, man, didn't mean to run into your girlfriend."

Decker's fist tightened in the fabric. "Apologize," he demanded.

I should have told him to calm down, it was obviously a mistake. A hazard of being in local small town bar full of college kids home for the summer and freshly twenty-one. Maybe even correct him that I wasn't his girlfriend. But the alpha-male display of protection was making my alcohol riddled brain want to watch what would happen next.

Why was it so hot?

Why did it feel so good to be in his arms?

I knew this was going against every rule I set for myself, but as the guy slurred a quick apology and Decker let him go with a quick shove, I couldn't quite remember any rules or why I had them. As he faced me, drawing me in closer and his arm tightening around my waist, my head tilted to look up at him.

I liked his eyes, they were warm and kind, the type someone looked at and instantly felt at ease. The exact opposite of what my own convey, or so I'd been told.

"You are feeling awfully bold," I stated, unable to come up with anything clever. He smiled, and I unconsciously pressed into him more. With my chest flush against his, my tits were one wrong move away from spilling out of the top of my tight dress. Or one right move, if I was listening to the alcohol in my system.

Decker's gaze traced downward, away from my face as if he read my mind. "Eyes up here, cucciolo." I stopped myself from snorting out a laugh at the stupid nickname as soon as I said it but he really did remind me of a puppy. Always happy and eager, always underfoot when you didn't want him to be.

"Carina." A voice came from my side, I peeled myself away to see Theo looking around wildly. Levi straightened up next to me, his hand long gone from my body, but not far from me. "Have you seen Lennon? I can't find her." Panic leeched into his voice, kinda cute that he'd be worried about her. I knew Abby and I did the right thing by inviting him out.

"What's up, man, I'm Levi." Levi reached his hand out to Theo to shake.

I scoffed. "A nuisance is what you are, Decker," I intercepted, swatting his hand away. "She was still dancing a minute ago, she's around here somewhere." Theo offered me a small smile and then went in search of her, leaving Decker and I back to whatever was flowing between us.

Something was between us. Something old, dating back to when we first started working together, and I allowed myself to be charmed by him. Before I put a barrier between us, and closed myself off.

Lust, definitely, but underneath there was more to it. I couldn't quite put my finger on it but a few things came to me in the moment. One, Decker being here might be some higher intervention, the world kept pulling us closer over the past couple weeks despite us working together for years. Two, the way his arms evoked a feeling in my chest was something I couldn't even dream up. Three, it had been too long, way, way too long, since someone besides myself made me come and something told me he'd know exactly how to get me there.

Suddenly his fingers slid around my wrist, pulling me back so I was flush with his chest again. Even in my heels the top of my head barely passed his lips. I tipped my head back, a flash of surprise taking over. And then everything fell into place.

Why couldn't I have my cake and eat it too?

Why couldn't I keep him at arms lengths at work and close enough to touch outside of the office?

It happened in slow motion, tucking a rogue strand of hair behind his ear, he dipped his head, brushing his lips against mine in the softest, featherlight kiss. Unlike anything I imagined.

But it wasn't what I wanted so I let the alcohol take the reins.

My fingers danced across the taut muscle of his stomach before I slid my hands up his chest, fisted the fabric of his shirt before the collar, and tugged him in closer to deepen the kiss. We slipped into a world of our own, where the music and people all faded away and it was just us. Our moment, our kiss. Nothing else mattered and I wanted more.

Between us, space ceased to exist, but I needed to be closer. His hand splayed across my lower back, his mouth softer than I imagined as I fought for more, demanded more and took what he offered. My tongue licked into his mouth before nipping at his bottom lip. A deep grumbling reverberated in his chest that sent electric shocks throughout my body. Tiny little pinpricks of bliss.

Our breaths mingled in the centimeters between our lips when we broke free. "Do you live close to here?" I whispered, not at all taken back by my brazen request. You'll never get what you want if you don't ask.

"I don't."

My chest deflated, and I was seconds away from breaking my self imposed rule of bringing anyone back to my place when he pressed another kiss against my lips, lingering for a moment before breaking away completely, taking a step back. Decker's throat bobbed, swallowing nothing as he stalled his next words.

I wasn't at all surprised that I asked him to take me home, he wasn't the first guy and it was unlikely he'd be the last, but I was surprised at how his two simple words sucked all the fun from the night.

Warmth seeped into my side where his hands lingered on me, fingers ghosting along the dip in my waist. A look passed across his face before he spoke. "Even if I did live close, I'm here with them, for a make-shift bachelor party." My eyes followed the quick tilt of his head to where two men stood a few tables away, eyes locked on us with dumb smiles on their faces.

Surprisingly, a flood of disappointment washed through me as I pulled myself out of his grasp, and I refused to put any weight on the fact it felt like he didn't want to let me leave.

"Have a good night, Decker." My toneless voice clipped. I didn't wait for a response before I turned on one heel and slipped between people on the dance floor in search of Abby and Lennon and at least three more drinks.

Maybe I put too much stock into a fictional feeling, maybe the lack of sex was muddling my brain to think that he could have been there for me. Maybe I would blame the whole thing on being drunk and we could forget what happened by Monday morning.

He would never need to know seeing him sparked the feeling of being wanted inside of me, a feeling I was sure I buried deep enough to never bother me again. I never let people in because, mostly, they always found a way to let me down. It was an outlook on life I developed young, a side effect of growing up with parents that never saw you as a person and a relationship that demanded you change before it failed.

I didn't care about being wanted, I'd been getting through life fine without it, but it could have been fun, a few hours with him where he would look at me with his golden brown eyes and I could feel...something.

NINE

Carina

"Alright, I'm calling it. We're officially too old for bars," Lennon declared, finally breaking the silence at our table at Wake Up Cafe, and I was forced to agree with her.

Abby's shoulders shook at my side as she laughed. "If you say so."

My body ached as I tried to relax into the weathered vinyl booth. Dull pain beat against the base of my skull out of tandem with my pulse, muscle groups in my thighs that I hadn't used in years burned but I wasn't as hungover as I thought I'd be. The pain meds I took before we left for breakfast still hadn't hit but the next best thing would be caffeine, if only the waitress would magically appear.

Lennon slid into the seat across from Abby. Large, dark sunglasses sat firmly in place, hiding her tired eyes as her mahogany curls spilled around her shoulder and somehow were even bigger than the night before. Silence descended on us again as my prayers were answered. A waitress with a full pot of coffee appeared, filling our cups without even asking. She picked up on the no talking rule we had all implemented and left our table without so much as another word. The first sip barely even registered, expect for the bitterness that came with all burnt diner coffee. What I wouldn't give for a latte from Renaissance but this would have to do.

Our night passed in a blur after Decker left. All I remembered was a few more shots, more dancing, and Lennon leaving not too long after with Theo.

I slid my sunglasses off my face as the pain in my head started to dissipate. "How was the rest of your night, Lennon?" My words were playful but she gave us nothing, of course, ever the private one. All I wanted was to see her happy and while she was leaps and bounds better than she was when her husband passed away two years ago, I could tell she was still holding back. Even as blunt as I was asking if she and Theo slept together, she still was tight-lipped.

"Voglio solo che tu sia felice," I muttered to myself. These women are my family, my sisters. All I wanted was for them to be happy.

We parted ways after breakfast, as I climbed the stairs to the third floor of my apartment building with the late morning sun beating on me, I finally began feeling like myself. Sunlight streamed through my curtains as I walked through my empty apartment, illuminating my living room in a soft glow. Sinking into the plush couch, I flipped open my work laptop, left out from the day before, to let the sun work Vitamin D into my system while I searched for menial tasks to complete.

Within a few hours all traces of the hangover subsided and I figured I could manage an hour away from work... it was Sunday after all.

Work was my life, I loved every second of it but my first love was running. In high school the track team was the only thing that felt like it belonged to me, and I was good. Not good enough for a scholarship, as my parents, or really my mother, always reminded me, but it was a way to escape, and an excuse to not have to drop everything to help them.

Quickly pulling on a pair of biker shorts and a sports bra, I laced up my shoes before I lost all motivation and rushed outside only to be hit with blistering heat. This might be a terrible idea, it was likely to climb near the triple digits, but I needed to sweat out the last of the alcohol and frustration from last night.

Fairvale was old farm country turned suburb, most of the land plotted over a hundred years ago. Abby and Lennon both own their own homes it the older part of town but that wasn't quite my style. Which was why I lived in the newer buildings on the edge of Main Street. Not far from work, the shops always offered something I didn't know I needed when I had a free minute to roam around.

From my apartment building, it was a quick walk to the trail that led to the bike path along the river. It stretched for more miles than I was willing to run but it was the biggest perk of living in this small of a town. Within moments, my feet were hitting the pavement in rapid succession, my ear buds were blaring some random playlist that I was hoping would keep my pace up, and I was off.

I needed to make time for this more often, it seemed to be the only time my head was cleared of my thoughts. It was me, the river, and endless trees. Despite the heat, I was not the only one out, there were a few groups of people walking that I had to dodge or create a wide berth to get past parents with strollers stopped along the river to watch people on their paddle boards and cyclists that raced by. It was almost too much, but one of the best parts of this path were the side trails.

With a split second to make the choice, I veered to the left. I was ninety percent sure the trail looped back around to the main path so I didn't have to worry about turning around at a mile marker to get back home.

Sunlight filtered through the branches of the trees, dancing across the tall grass and leaves that covered the area like a canopy. With each deep breath, my senses were filled with clean, fresh air as I pushed harder up a small hill and the time whirled by me with each stride.

About fifteen minutes later, my memory was correct and the opening where the dirt trail met pavement appeared.

Maybe my toe hit a rock, or the brief second sunlight filtered through the trees blinded me, causing a misstep, but all I felt was the world tilting, my ankle turning a way it shouldn't, and the harsh bite of the pavement against my knee.

"Fuck," I shouted, as I threw my hands out to catch myself before my head smacked against the ground. My hip took the brunt of the fall as my heart sped up and a breath whooshed out of me. Pain hadn't set in so for a few seconds, I refused to move, or even open my eyes. Partly due to embarrassment, partly fear something might've broke during the fall and I would be stuck there forever.

After a few deep breaths, I peeled my eyes open, blinking out dirt before it began to sting, and gingerly shifted to sit up. The damage seemed minimal and thankfully no one seemed to be around to witness my mishap.

Blood pinpricks welled up in the scrape on my knee that I wiped away before giving it a bit of a wiggle. There didn't seem to be anymore damage than the scrape, so that was great. All in all, I was good; my pride may have taken a hit but at least nothing felt broken.

I remained on the ground for another second to calm my racing heartbeat that spiked once I fell. It wasn't until I was pulling the head phones from my ears that I heard my name being shouted. My head turned toward the sound and I immediately wished I never came outside. Or at the very least maybe fell while I was on the trail where people rarely went, because jogging up to me was Levi fucking Decker.

The urge to jump up and sprint back home, pretending I never saw him, lit up my insides but I couldn't peel myself up off the ground.

Instead the exact opposite happened. With each second it took him to reach me, I relaxed further into hard ground, fingers curling into the dirt beside me, ruining my once perfect manicure.

He was the picture of a knight in shining…well, not armor since whatever shirt he left the house in was tucked into the back of his black running shorts. Sunlight reflected off his sweat-covered chest, and I found the answer to every question I had about where his tattoos ended. When he finally reached me, in a span of time that felt like it lasted forever and was all too quick, I refused to look up at him.

"Holy shit, are you okay?" He crouched to my level and without asking, began swiping the rocks from my palms and dirt off my knees. And as if him witnessing my fall wasn't bad enough, goosebumps erupted over every inch of skin he touched.

Which one was I embarrassed of more? Who knew.

"Why are you suddenly everywhere?" I spit the words at him. He was in my files, at the bar, on my jogging trail when in all the prior years combined I never saw him out of work once. What game was the universe playing?

Pissed didn't even begin to cover it. Pissed off that I fell, pissed off that he was here, pissed off that he was touching me and not at all in the way I wanted. I scrambled from the ground, needing to be far, far away from him but two steps in I wished I hadn't moved at all. Pain shot through my ankle, sending me careening sideways.

Decker's hands darted out, latching around my waist to catch me. My body flushed. "I'm fine." I was not fine, I was burning from the inside out.

Pulling from his grasp and leaning into the feeling of my throbbing ankle seemed like a reasonable answer to quench the fire blazing through my body. I needed to escape, but if I was wrong and my ankle was broken, I couldn't do much about it.

He was still staring at me.

"Can you put your shirt back on or something?"

"Why? Is it distracting you?" His hands reached around to pull the piece of clothing from his waistband despite his tone telling me he was getting a kick out this whole situation.

"No."

Yes.

Finally he covered his sweat drenched skin and I could finally think. With as little pressure as possible, I placed my right foot back on the ground. Toes first, and then my heel. It felt like nothing so I stood up only to be met with Decker's careful eyes and hands that were slightly extended from his body, ready in case I fell again.

I ignored him.

One little step and pain bloomed through the joint again. My teeth pierced my tongue but I took another step, and then another, anything to put some distance between us.

"How does it feel?" he called out from behind me.

My molars clenched together. "Fine," I managed to grit out before he snorted, which only pissed me off more.

"I rolled it, that's all, it'll be fine. I just need to walk it off." I took a few more steps. I was about to start the longest walk of my life.

I didn't know what I was expecting but Decker falling into step beside me wasn't it. "What are doing?" I was a barrel of emotions that were currently imploding on each other and the question fired out of me.

Decker seemed not to notice. "Well I'm not going to leave you out here by yourself to get home on a bum ankle." He fixed me with a lingering look that softened with the milliseconds that swirled between us.

Each breath became more sludge-like, thick and difficult to expel from my chest as another wave of pain rolled through. "I said I'm fine."

"And I said I wasn't leaving," he shot right back, a no-nonsense look on his face.

"Decker."

"Carina."

We stood on the edge, where dirt met pavement in a staring contest I was determined to win. Seconds dragged on and the longer I looked at him, the more I began to notice. Like how his eyes weren't just brown, they were ringed in a golden honey color, a smattering of freckles but only along the bridge of his nose, where there also looked to be a healed over hole, like a piercing might have once sat there.

Another few seconds and he lifted a single brow and I did something I never liked to do.

I caved.

"Fine, let's go."

TEN

Decker

ONLY THE SOUND OF the river gently lapping against the rocks followed us as we slowly made our way down the bike path, before a myriad of questions got the better of her.

"What were you doing out here?"

"Same as you," I said with a smile. "Thought that was obvious."

Carina rolled her eyes. "I mean here, in Fairvale, running. Last night you said you didn't live close to the bar which is just up ahead."

The accusatory tone in her voice only made me smile wider. "I live in Cornelia but I come out here to run. I like the river." For a split second, she sympathized, tilting her head to the side and nodded as her nose wrinkled. Cornelia began where the highway ended. It was an okay place but had nothing on Fairvale, with its glittering river and scent of citrus that seemed to only exist within the town's borders.

We came to a stop at an indent in the tall grass that led up a hill, the apartment roofs were barely visible over the tops of the trees. "This is me. Thanks, Decker," she rushed to say and without waiting for me to reply, she started a slow trek up the hill through the brush. Like an invisible string kept me tethered to her, I followed her up the trail. Instantly, Carina noticed I didn't simply run off and leave her alone and she spun around, pinning me in place with a look that screamed she would rather die than accept my help.

"Humor me."

Her glare intensified but she eventually turned back around and continued walking.

We made it to the far side of the complex, to the building that looked out over the river, but only after stopping a few times for her to swallow tiny whimpers of pain. Over my dead body was I leaving her to climb these stairs alone, but as she pursed her lips and tried climbing the steps with her eyes, I knew getting her to let me help might be an issue.

Best I could do was wait it out and be there when she needed. Her fingers wrapped around the railing, quick breaths through her nose, but she still hadn't taken a step. I couldn't tell what she was saying but she was quietly murmuring to herself. I had never seen her do that before, talk herself up to get something done.

I didn't watch her, or I didn't watch her in a creepy way, but she was the type of person that made it hard not to notice her. She demanded attention any time she entered a room, an air of authority surrounded and I took notice. Like I took notice of the way her shoulder muscles flexed under the tight lycra of her bra. Last night's dress was incredible but this, simpler, tighter, lesser clothing made my cock throb and wearing thin running shorts that hit the middle of my thigh really wasn't the best at concealing, well...anything.

Statue Carina remained at the bottom of the steps. Cautiously, I stepped closer. "Do you need help?"

"No, I'm looking at it for fun," she bit out and repositioned her hand on the railing before finally taking a step. A soft growl filled her throat. My chest hurt with her pain and my cock throbbed again at the noise.

This wasn't the time to be thinking about what other situations might get her to make that sound, but I was in fact a man and I couldn't stop.

"Carina?"

She flung her hand back, swatting at me. "I got it."

"I know." She took another step and another growl erupted. My heart and dick really couldn't take it. "Can I help in any way?"

In a moment that seemed to drag on, a curt nod finally gave me the okay.

Without a word I scooped her up bridal style and started up the stairs. A surprised noise squeaked out of her as she slung one of her arms around my neck. Soft skin pressed against mine and I felt like I'd ascended to heaven. This was what I would be promised in the after life, I was sure of it. Her in my arms seemed like a fair trade for my life if any. Then, about half way up the first flight, delicate fingers wove through the stands of hair around the base of my neck.

It was almost as if I'd fallen into a dream. Or maybe I died and didn't remember?

The number of times I'd caught what Carina thought was a sly once-over was more than I could count on both hands and feet. And I always noticed when her eyes lingered on my hair. I fucking loved it, didn't know what it meant, but loved it.

Each flight of stairs was completed in silence but her fingers remained in my hair, curling the strands around her fingers, and by the third flight, her head relaxed and fell against my shoulder. It was more than anything I could ever dream up and if I could've I would've kept climbing. Give me ten flights of stairs, give me a stair master set for hours and watch me never tire of having her pressed against my chest.

Four doors faced us as I reached the top floor. I glanced down at her. "Which one?" She wasn't asleep but her eyes drifted closed at some point. One peeled open and she nodded to the one farthest on the right. "Keys?" I asked once I was in front of the door.

"It's open."

My breath froze. "Really?" I chastised. Didn't like that one bit.

Both eyes opened, looking up at me as she shrugged the best she could in my arms as I twisted to open the door. "I figured if someone came here to break in, they would hit downstairs first, easier to carry out the stolen goods." I barked out a laugh. "And I was only going to be gone for an hour," she argued, like it lessened my concern even a little bit.

We slipped through her door, and headed into her living room where I deposited her onto the couch as if she were a baby bird. What possessed me to then grab a pillow to prop up her injured leg was as much a mystery to me as it was to her. But I didn't let that stop me. I was here in her home and she wasn't immediately kicking me out, so I ran with it. "Let me get ice."

"No," she nearly shouted, lurching from the couch. "Thank you, but you don't have to do all," she waved her hand around her injured foot, "this." Her argument futile, I was already headed to the kitchen. Rummaging through her freezer, all I found was a bag of frost-covered peas, but it would work.

I walked back into the living room wrapping a towel pulled from the stove. I had no idea what I was doing, my knowledge of first aid was limited to three years of cub scouts, but I had this overwhelming urge to care for her. A dull pang in my chest drove my actions, because she was the one in pain and I *needed* to be the one to fix it.

Needed it like my next breath, my next meal. I needed her to see me and everything I was willing to do to have her. And if her eyes told me anything it was last night was an opening and might not have ruined it like I thought after running off. Carina watched me like a hawk as I knelt down by her propped up leg, unlaced her shoe and slowly slipped it off. Her sock immediately followed as I kept an eye out for any sign of discomfort. Something flared in her eyes, but it wasn't pain.

I stroked my thumb in slow circles on the inside of her ankle. "How does it feel?" I asked. When she didn't immediately give me an answer, my fingers glided higher on the back of her calf, testing the waters. She didn't kick me in the face, so that was a win. With skin like silk under my touch, I was finding it hard to keep my mind from wandering places it really shouldn't go. Peridot eyes roamed down my chest, cataloging every inch of me until her breath hitched when she noticed how terrible my shorts really were at concealing hardening body parts.

"Carina." My voice pulled her back to me.

"Hmm?" She blinked a few times as she answered, apparently not ashamed she was caught eye fucking me. I didn't want it to stop, I wanted so much more than her eyes.

"I asked how does your ankle feel?"

"Honestly, I wasn't even thinking about it."

Exactly what I wanted to hear. My touch danced higher on her leg before trailing back down. "What were you thinking about?" Peas laid forgotten, sweating water onto the floor that we'd care about later. If all I had was one time, I was going to make it count and I was going to make it last.

"A lot of things actually." A flash of pink darted out, wetting her lips.

"Tell me," I requested, my voice thick but eager for an answer as I continued caressing the skin along her lower leg.

ELEVEN

Carina

"Tell me," he said again. Voice deeper, more commanding.

I shouldn't, too many thoughts were spilling from the places I liked to keep them in the back of my head. Thoughts that would out me, thoughts that might have him running out the door.

Or maybe he was exactly what I had been looking for.

Decker's been under my skin for so long that maybe I needed to be under him to get it out of my system. Just once.

An immediate urge washed over me to pull him in and crash my mouth against his. Maybe then I could pour whatever these feelings were out of me and transfer them to him without saying anything at all.

But when I shifted, Decker's fingers latched onto my calf, far enough away from my ankle so there was no pain but hard enough my movements stilled. "Don't move, you need to keep that ankle elevated for a while."

I leaned helplessly back into the couch.

"Perfect," he praised, slipping his hand up my leg again, now past my knee. He had shuffled a few inches over at some point and had made himself at home between my propped up leg and the other one that I kept on the ground. "Now tell me all about the thoughts running through your brilliant mind." He ran his free hand through his hair, eyes focused on me.

Had I slipped into a dream? It had to be, it was the only logical reason for why I actually wanted to answer his question. If it were anything but a dream I would have told him to go fuck himself for thinking he had any right to my thoughts. But I was being held hostage by my libido.

It didn't feel awkward to have his hands on me, in fact I was being lulled into submission with every caress of his fingers against my skin. I felt wanted under his gaze and that was something I needed more of, so I would answer his question if it meant I got to keep him here longer.

He tracked the moment my tongue darted out to wet my bottom lip. "I don't like that you saw me fall," I admitted, getting the easiest one out of the way first.

My honesty was rewarded with fingers dancing up my thigh to toy with the edge of my shorts. "That's nothing, I once tripped and fell walking across the stage during graduation. College graduation," he added. "Not even high school so there were thousands of witnesses." He tucked his fingers underneath the fabric, but only enough that the tips of his two fingers disappeared. "What else?"

Languid strokes pulled another answer from me. "Work's been a lot lately, and I keep having to sub in at my parents' place. I can handle it, obviously, but I'm starting to see the line that separates me and burned-out-me."

He hummed, eyes roaming from my face, down my chest, lingering only a moment and I was reminded that I was sitting in front of him in barely more clothes than most people wore to bed. "Lucky for you, I happen to know someone at work who could help lighten the load if you ever need it." His fingers slid higher, any further and he would brush against the soft spot where my thigh ends and I would melt in his hands.

My heart began to slam against my chest but then he asked me something, or told me something, maybe. Everything was going hazy, I couldn't tell.

Right, help at work. "You're not assigned to me."

"That doesn't matter, all you have to do is ask. I live to please," he said matter of factly.

"Do you?" I arched a brow at him as he slipped up under my shorts even further. My next breath dripped from my mouth in a lazy exhale and my head drifted back into the cushion. He hit that melty spot of mine.

Decker noticed but only cracked a smile in response, and dragged a single fingertip along the edge of my underwear. "For you, absolutely. Whatever you need, I'm your guy," he said as if it was an obvious fact. "Anything else on your mind?"

"I was at a bar last night, met a guy, asked him to take me home but was turned down. Left me—" For whatever reason, I couldn't finish the sentence. Nerves maybe, or the fact I couldn't focus long enough to form a thought with the way his hands felt on me.

"Wanting," he finished for me.

I nodded and was rewarded with his finger slipping under the thin cotton, the only layer that separated us.

"Guy sounds like a dick."

"He is."

A genuine laugh burst past his lips, but when he pulled his hand from me, a soft whine fell from my mouth in protest. Decker studied me for a moment, warm amber eyes bore into me with a thousand questions and even more silent requests. For a moment I thought he was going to kiss me. He pushed up on his knees, bringing his chest close to mine, but instead of feeling his lips against my own, his fingers hooked around a stray hair tie I had around my wrist. He slid the purple tie off and onto his own wrist.

"What are you—" I started to say.

"It'll come in handy in a minute," he breathed into the small amount of space between us before sitting back onto his heels.

Was he about to do what I think he was?

"Wait," I rushed to say, propping myself up to look at him. "I was running."

He cocked an eyebrow

"You know, outside. I got sweaty and haven't showered, you don't have to—"

He cut me off. "Do you want to shower?"

"What?" I was so confused by this entire interaction and the sight of him on his knees was making it hard to think straight.

"We could shower," he offered with a sinful smile. "Or I could watch you shower, I'm not picky."

I scoffed. "Don't be ridiculous."

A beat passed without words but he still hadn't moved. I continued to stare at him in some unspoken game of chicken.

"Do I look like a man who's not about to have the time of his life eating this pretty pussy regardless of what you may have been doing half an hour ago?"

"No?"

"Exactly. I'm sorry I left you, will you let me make it up to you?"

I nodded my agreement and that was all he needed. His hands were back on me, sending electricity to every corner of my body, pushing higher, across the tops of my thighs, over my hip bones until he could tuck two fingers into the waistband of my shorts. He paused, leaving space for me to say no if I wanted to, but I didn't. I kept quiet and let him peel the fabric down my body, slipping my good foot from my shorts first, then with the most absolute care he dragged them down to the ankle that was propped up. Gently lifting it off the pillow to maneuver the clothing off and placing my foot back down so I felt nothing. He tossed the shorts to the side and turned his gaze back onto me.

A deep, masculine groan broke through his chest, his head lolling to the side slightly. The sound shot through me, my nipples hardening under the tight fabric of the sports bra but instinctively I moved to shut my knees the longer he went without making a single move. With only a tiny scrape of fabric that was a sad excuse for a thong, I was on display for him and nothing needed to be imagined.

"Don't, please," he whispered, large hand reaching for my knees to keep them from closing. "I've had this dream about a thousand times, I just need a second to admire you in real life."

"A thousand?"

He pulled the hair tie he stole only a few moments ago off his wrist and reached behind him, tying his hair into a quick knot at the base of his neck. "You have no. Fucking. Idea." Each word punctuated with a heated look as he leaned closer to the apex of my thighs, where I laid exposed and entirely at his mercy.

Each breath he took skated across the sensitive skin. "One day I'll take my time with you, learn what drives you to the edge only to keep you from falling off it for hours at a time." Another inch closer, he looked up and locked eyes with me. "But not today. Today I'm going to take care of you like I should have last night."

I used my good foot to stop his movement by pressing it into his shoulder. Turning back wasn't an option, this was going to happen and I wanted it. More than I wanted anything, but he needed to know what this was. "This is a one time thing, it changes nothing between us. Tomorrow we'll go back to work like none of this happened."

Something flashed in his eye, only for a brief millisecond before it was gone and replaced by burning desire once again leaving me with no time to discern what it might've been. "If you say so," he stated, a small laugh under the words and then his mouth was on me as his fingers pulled the wet fabric to the side.

My back bowed off the couch, my head sunk further into the cushion, all with one languid lick. I fell into a silent heaven where the only thing I had to focus on was the way he made my body feel. He was a starving man at a table laid with his last supper as his tongue dipped into my entrance. "Fuck, I knew you'd taste good but this is un-fucking-real."

One hand had my hip in a bruising grip as the other curled around the back of my knee, pulling it up onto his shoulder. "You keep this right here, elevation and all that." A quick kiss to the inside of my thigh and then continued with his original task, pushing me closer and closer to that edge he was talking about.

It was quick, and obviously a fluke, there was no way I was about to come this fast from Levi Decker's mouth alone because if that was true, I'd be in trouble.

I canted my hips up to meet his mouth, I didn't want a single second to pass without feeling him. His tongue swirled tight circles around my clit, pulling a sharp breath from me. He only laughed, a deep rumble that vibrated against my core.

The edge wasn't far; the tips of my toes had gone numb. The feeling travelled up my legs, then spine, wrapping around every limb until I felt nothing but bliss, but I needed more.

Without warning, he circled two fingers around my entrance, teasing me like he had all the time in the world to make me feel good. He pressed inside slowly, eyes glued to my core with rapt attention, brows drawn in, a glazed looked in his eyes, like the thought of missing even a second was unbearable.

The sound that climbed its way up my throat when his fingers slipped all the way in was obscene and like nothing I'd ever made before. Like dance behind my eyes immediately as he hit that perfect spot.

"Yes," I breathed, falling limp into the couch. He took that as his cue, grinding his palm against my clit, as he slipped in and out. I cried out again.

My eyes wouldn't open, and that was fine, I was lost in the moment. In the feeling and I was climbing higher and higher until...

"Oh god," I choked out, my thighs tightening around his head as every part of my body tried to draw him in closer, deeper, anything would do as waves of pleasure slammed into me from every corner. Decker didn't care about me possibly tearing his head as my orgasm ripped through me, and even if he did, I wouldn't be able to hear his protests.

Finally my muscles relaxed. Shit, that was good. Too fucking good. I was a blissed out mess, trapped under rolling waves taking longer than normal to subside.

Decker was still sitting in front of me, grinning like an idiot, lips and chin slightly shiny from me when I finally cracked one eye open. His smile turned lazy as he rested his cheek against my thigh, looking dazed and just as blissful.

It felt...good, and not because Decker ate me out within an inch of my life. Although, it didn't hurt either. It was a difficult to name emotion that I knew I shouldn't be feeling at all.

Normally this was the part where I left or snuck out of a guy's bed depending on the situation, but you couldn't run if it was your house. My high was wearing off, clouds were clearing from my head and the weight of what we did was starting to set in.

I just slept with Levi Decker. I just slept with a *co-worker*. This was wrong, so, so very wrong and yet so, so very right.

What the fuck was I doing?

He could sense the panic that was ensuing or maybe he saw it written on my face. Without a word he placed a quick kiss to the inside of my thigh, grabbed my discarded shorts he had set aside and slipped my legs back into them as gingerly as he took me out of them. Lifted me from the couch, careful to make sure I put no pressure on my bad ankle and shimmied them up until they were back in place.

"Ice it every hour and make sure you keep it elevated, you should be back to normal soon." The words were tight, as if it wanted to be another sentence entirely but this was the one that made it out first.

I nodded in acknowledgment and walked with him toward the front door.

Decker reached for the doorknob when I suddenly blurted out what I had been trying to convince myself was the right thing. "Remember, tomorrow, this never happened." He looked back at me, drifting over the features of my face with a wistful look in his eyes. And I did my best to drain all emotion from my face.

Except it didn't have the effect I wanted because all he did was smile. All he ever did was smile at me. "Okay, Carina." He reached up and hooked a finger into his tied up hair and let the black strands fall, then slipped my hair tie back on his wrist and strode out my front door.Cha pter Twelve

TWELVE

Carina

SOMETIMES I WONDERED HOW I fell into family law. If someone had asked me on graduation day where I would be in five years, a small-town family law practice wouldn't have even been on my list of answers. When I was starting out, I thought corporate law was what called to me. Skyscraper offices downtown, bringing businesses to their metaphorical knees in company takeovers and trials with complex arguments that would last for weeks.

One month into my first job out of law school and it lacked any of the luster I thought it would hold. I hated it, it sucked the life right out of me, and I was back on the market to find the type of law I was meant to practice.

Family law was a surprise but there was a sense of justice I felt when helping women who had been treated less than in their marriage or helping a parent retain custody after an unnecessarily long winded battle. It was hard work on my mind, but mostly on my heart.

Watching marriages fall apart week in and week out was not for the faint of heart. And sometimes, like today, I wondered why people ever got married at all.

"Ms. Leon, thank you for coming in," I said, plastering a small smile on my face.

The woman across from me was my age, maybe even younger but with heavy bags under her red-rimmed eyes, it was hard to tell. She was beautiful, her deep chocolate brown hair was pulled into a sleek bun at the nape of her neck, as she sat perched on the edge of her seat, delicate hands splayed across her pregnant stomach. "Please, call me Kelly," she said with warm brown eyes that shined behind a thin line of tears.

That happened a lot too, last names usually ended up being a sore subject. "Kelly. For the most part, today is signing a lot of papers, someone will be along with them shortly. Until then, can you tell me a little bit about what it is you're looking for?"

She was silent for a moment, staring blankly at the table between us. Her thumb rubbed small circles on the side of her belly, I wondered if she even knew she was doing it. Then her bottom lip began to quiver.

"First meetings are often hard." I slid a box of tissues across the small table toward her. "We can take as much time as we need, okay?" She pulled a tissue gently and pressed it to the corners of her eyes.

"My husband, or ex-husband, I guess," she shook her head, "he's very charming." That was not what I thought would be coming out of her mouth, so I waited for her to continue. "So charming that I worry no one will believe me and I will be left without a home, money, and family. Not only is he charming, but he's powerful and rich and I'm afraid that once this baby is born, he'll do whatever he can to take her just to hurt me." Her voice wavered as she spoke.

My mind began churning out a course of action. "I can tell you now, I cannot be charmed, so it doesn't matter. I am here for you and I will do my absolute best to ensure you are awarded what is yours and no one will be taking your baby from you," I said with venom.

There was an ever-growing list of things I hated in this world; men in flip-flops, being called sweetheart by older men, being told how to do my job by a man barely out of law school—honestly I might just hate men. But in the number one spot was men who twisted the love they received from women for their own personal gain, only to gaslight them into thinking they were the problem.

Kelly was married to the biggest property developer in Sacramento, Benjamin Leon. We're talking multi-millionaire, hand in dozens of business ventures, foot in seeder opportunities that made him even more money under the table. It made sense on why he would hire Ian Wheeler, their friendship probably went way back. I would even guess they belonged to the same dumb ass fraternity, Alpha Omega Asshole.

The door swung open and Decker slipped in with a stack of papers. "Hi, Kelly, Levi Decker, we spoke on the phone during your intake. Nice to meet you." He extended his hand which she took. It was quick but her eyes roamed over him before she released his hand. It wasn't the first time a soon to be single woman had checked him out in the office, and definitely wouldn't be the last.

Except this time I was participating.

This was the first I had seen him since I frantically kicked him out. I wasn't avoiding him on purpose; I simply made sure I wasn't where he might be because he was now two different people, and until I knew how to separate them, I needed to stay away.

At work he was still Decker, the all too annoying, leave everything to the last minute in order to mess with me layabout, whose neck I wanted to wring. But now, he was also Levi, the man who helped me even though I fought him every step of the way and ate me out like he was at a three star Michelin restaurant.

It was confusing.

Decker slipped into the last open seat and twisted the stack of papers toward her. "They are all standard agreements, along with fee agreement for you to sign." Kelly pulled the stack toward her and began flipping through.

"This is…"

"A lot, I know," Decker answered for her with a soft chuckle. "But that's what I'm here for. I'll be on your case, with Carina, to help with all the leg work to get you to the finish line. If you have any questions and you can't reach her, you can email or call me and I can track it down." He sat back, flipping the end of his tie up before crossing his hands in his lap.

Poker chips, his tie was covered in poker chips. I had to suppress an eye roll.

"Thank you. Honestly, I don't quite know what to expect," Kelly admitted, her shoulders relaxing slightly.

"Once these are signed, we'll have another meeting where you tell me about Benjamin. What he's like, what your marriage was like, how the decision for a divorce came around. It's not the easiest thing to do but it will help to see what we can do next. With all hope, I'll contact his lawyer and there won't be any issues and we can get this all settled."

A long shot plan, but maybe the divorce gods were looking down on her and it would be a quick process.

"He doesn't know I'm here exactly."

Or maybe they weren't ,and this would be a long one.

I glanced at Decker. His hand clenched in his lap.

"That's okay, have there been any discussion between you two about separation or…"

"No." The tears were back in her eyes, the word barely more than a whisper. "I'm scared but I need to leave him."

"Are you two still living together?" I asked.

She nodded. "But I'm moving in with my mother as soon as possible."

I gave her a small smile, it was really the only comfort I could offer. "Okay, good. Let me know as soon as you do and we'll make sure the divorce papers are served once you are out of the house."

Kelly didn't even bother returning my smile, the vacant look in her eyes told me everything I needed to know. She didn't want to be here, didn't want to be doing this. She was probably thinking about how she should have been picking out nursery colors with her husband, striking names off a list, or planning her baby shower. Instead, she was orchestrating her divorce.

I reached out and rested my hand on top of hers. "I know that this is probably the last thing you envisioned doing, especially while pregnant, but I am here for you, any time. Dec—" I stopped myself. "Levi and I are both here to make sure this goes as smoothly as possible." His eyes flicked over to me at the sound of his name.

He pushed the stack of papers toward her. "Why don't you take these, look them over, and then Carina will call you in a few days."

She reached for them but hesitated. "I don't think I can take these. What if he finds them and he—" Her words became panicked.

"It's okay, Levi can email you all the forms that way they go directly to you with no way for anyone else to come across them."

Her fingers rub the corner of the pages before she nodded. "Okay," she stated simply before getting up and walking out of the room with a polite goodbye, leaving Decker and I to a shared silence.

He spoke first, rubbing his hand across the faint stubble along his jaw. "That was something."

"Yeah, I know." I lounged back in my seat.

"But she'll be okay, right? I mean, she'll move out and get through this with nothing to worry about?" he asked, eyebrows drawing inward.

I wished I could tell him with ease she would be fine, give it three months this would all be over and she could move on, but I didn't want to lie.

We routinely dealt with hard cases. It came with the territory, but it was cases like this that made the hairs on the back on my neck stand up and enforced why I didn't bother with relationships in the first place.

"I will do whatever I can to make it as smooth as possible but with Wheeler on the case I know they'll be out for blood."

It was quiet for a moment before he spoke back up. "How's the ankle?" he asked.

Instinctively I rolled the sore joint. I attempted heels this morning, but I wasn't willing to push it and ended up in a pair of leather mules instead. "Another day and I'll be back in heels."

"Small miracles," he replied, hand over his heart. He turned in his chair, his knee knocking against my bare leg. The sudden intrusion was minor, barely even an event, and yet electricity zipped underneath my skin. Only for him to pull back the second we made contact "Sorry," he said, but his eyes told a different story. Darkness flashed in them as the tracked the hem of my skirt slowly upwards.

"Don't do that," I demanded.

"Do what?" He smiled.

"Don't do that either."

He laughed. "What?"

"Look at me like you've seen me naked," I harshly whispered through clenched teeth.

He leaned in, lips pulled back into a smoldering grin. "But I have seen you naked."

We sat, staring at each other and I felt like I was being pulled in two different directions. One half of my brain was screaming at me that I'd stayed single for a reason, people expected too much, they let you down, they held you back and in the end the only person you could count on was yourself. The other half was another story entirely. It was the softer half of my brain that only focused on the way his arms felt around me, the way my body melted into his and the way my brain was able to turn off completely for the first time in forever when I was with him.

"Knock it off, not at work, alright?"

He threw his hands up in surrender, smile only widening. "So does that mean I can say it outside of work?"

I opened my mouth but no words came out. I didn't know how to answer it. "Maybe," I ended up saying, surprising us both.

"That's all the hope I need."

I glanced up at the door and waited until I was sure no one was coming in. "I don't date."

"I remember."

I tore my eyes away from him, shaking my head and re-thinking every decision I made that led me to this moment. This was going against every rule I ever put in place for myself but maybe there was an alternative. Something that would be just for me and be able to scratch the incessant itch I had that he seemed to be the only cure for. "If that doesn't bother you, then you should come by my apartment tonight. I'm closing up my parents' restaurant but should be home by nine." For half a second I was horrified by what I said. I had just propositioned Levi Decker at *work*.

Somebody needed to study the effect of mind bending orgasms on my brain because it apparently made me stupid. Then his answer came in the quick nod of his head.

Did we need some ground rules? Absolutely, but we could go over those tonight.

THIRTEEN

Carina

THE RESTAURANT WAS DEAD as I walked in and waved to Noah who was wiping down a table in the back corner. Tossing my purse in the office, I sat down to go over the inventory order. It was all I was here to do. That, and lock the door behind Noah, and Anna, the only other employee my parents seem to have who can cook. An hour tops, and I would be back home.

I was flipping through the pages when Noah poked his head in. "Hey, is there anything that needs to be done? It's pretty dead out there." His baby face shined with the question.

"You want to learn how to do inventory?" I asked and watched his face light up. "And if no one shows up by the time we're done, we'll close up early."

He followed me around, clipboard in hand jotting down every instruction and small anecdote I mentioned. All with a smile on his face, and ordering was not a fun task. "Noah, why do you act like you're having the time of your life? This is boring," I teased.

"I don't know. I like working here and for your parents. I wanted to go to culinary school but turns out that's just as expensive as normal college, so I thought working in a restaurant would be a good start." He looked down at the paper in his hands, he had been folding it in half until the paper refused to bend.

"Can you cook?"

He shuffled back and forth, the toe of his shoe scraping over the linoleum flooring, avoiding my gaze. "I think so, and my mom always says what I cook is good."

I snorted in response. "Well I'm going to close up, but why don't you show me what you've got before we leave?" I plucked the paper from his hands and tossed it in the trash can nearby while he looked around the kitchen.

"You mean here?" His eyes widened with each passing second. "Now?"

"Obviously. What's your favorite dish on the menu?"

"Fettuccini," he answered quickly. That was everyone's favorite, and for good reason.

"Make me a plate of that and a plate of Penne alla Amatriciana. Both to-go. If they're any good, we'll see about giving you some shifts in the kitchen."

The kid was practically salivating over the thought of cooking and if it kept me from having to pick up extra shifts, it was a win-win, for everybody—but more importantly me.

Pans rattled against each as he grabbed one from the stack above the range. One slipped out of his hands, which he caught before it hit the ground. I guess having me stand near him during my experiment might not turn out the best results.

"I'll give you some space."

I didn't know what possessed me to ask for two plates. If I got home and Decker ended up standing me up, I was going to feel... Actually I wasn't sure what I would feel. Probably nothing but I did know I would go to work and pretend like nothing ever happened, that was guaranteed.

My sex life was great; you'd never hear me complain, but it lacked a certain quality. And I knew exactly what it was—connection. And not the touchy, mushy, tell me about your feelings type. I wanted someone to anticipate my needs, someone who knew me enough so I could throw caution to the wind, let go and not have to worry.

Maybe that was Decker, or maybe not, but something about him made me want to act without inhibitions, irrationally even. He made me want to unzip myself and step out of my hardened exterior. It was unlike anything I'd ever encountered.

Every chair was flipped up onto their respective tables throughout the dining room as I did my final pass through, ignoring the side work that needed to be done. I was here for inventory, nothing else, and even though I would be subjecting myself to a phone call from my mother in the morning, I had somewhere to be.

One last glance around and I was content with not finishing. I could always send her to voicemail.

Noah should be done and by the lack of smoke, I was assuming he did okay. I pushed the swing kitchen door open just as he slid the food into the containers for me. I walked closer to give everything a once over. "Well it smells like it's supposed to. Thanks, Noah. Clean up, then we can leave." He looked nervous as I took a bite of one of the dishes.

Flavors exploded over my tongue, as I flicked my eyes up to meet his waiting stare. "Well," I mused rolling my shoulders back and swiping my thumb across my bottom lip. "Not bad." That was all the praise he'd get out of me but I would talk to my parents about getting him in the kitchen. Supervised at least. Which would be a load off of my shoulders, one more person who could work more positions meant less time I had to spend covering shifts.

Noah raced through cleaning the station and we parted ways once I turned the lock over on the front door. The drive back to my apartment was quick, everything in Fairvale was a short car ride away. Carina's wasn't on Main Street like my parents originally wanted, but two blocks away was close enough that some foot traffic carried over, not that it needed it. Carina's was known across the county, my parents poured their life into this restaurant and it paid off.

A few minutes after leaving the restaurant, I was parking in my designated apartment spot and looping my fingers around the handle of the plastic bag in my front seat. Tasks pinged around my head. Shower, speed clean, stuff any clothes that were on my floor into the nearest closet, I was sure there was more that I was missing but I wasn't sure I'd have enough time for all of them.

Someone cleared their throat as my feet hit the hard stone of the last few stairs as I slipped my hand into my purse to feel around for the keys. My steps faltered. It wasn't often I was caught off guard, but seeing Decker casually leaning against the wall beside my door nearly caused the food to slip from my hand.

Dark jeans and simple white tee, so plain, so basic, but on him, my mouth physically began to water. No metaphor needed. And his hair, a curtain of black waves with one side tucked behind his ear.

What was it about that certain feature of his that seemed to rewire my brain?

"You're here," I blurted out the obvious.

My stomach fluttered and I immediately began plucking the wings of the butterflies forming. Butterflies had no place in my body.

His eyes flashed quickly as he turned his wrist to check the time. "You did say nine." He pulled off the wall as I came up to the door and slid the key in the lock.

"I did, I just didn't expect you to be so," I pushed the door open, "punctual."

Decker laughed and followed me inside.

"For you, Carina, I'm sure I will find myself doing all sorts of things I wouldn't usually do."

He only laughed harder when I turned to roll my eyes at him from over my shoulder.

I tossed the food on the kitchen counter, quickly untied the handles and pulled out both containers. "What's that supposed to mean?" I questioned only to see him shrug. Maybe inviting him over was a mistake.

The thought died when I finally I turned back to look at him and swallowed around the urge to rescind my invitation. If there was a flaw in Levi Decker I had yet to find it. I wasn't even sure one existed. Even in harsh apartment lighting he looked like a greek statute come to life. Warm whiskey eyes bored into me, heat flushed through my system.

Maybe I needed just one more time with him, actually fuck him, get it out of my system, screw my head on right and then we'd never talk about it again.

I had to force myself to look away. "I brought food if you're hungry," I remarked, pulling the plastic lid off one of the containers.

Soft footsteps had Decker at my back, peering over to see what I was offering.

"You brought me dinner?" he questioned while his breath skated over the back of my neck.

Telling him the truth was out of the question, but the lie came effortlessly. "No, it was just some extra we had that needed to be cooked or thrown out." I grabbed the food and walked over to my coffee table. Since it had always just been me and I spent more time at the office than anywhere else I never had use for a dining room table. Decker followed suit and made himself comfortable on the couch next to me. "Thank you, Carina," he said with so much sincerity it caused an agonizing wave of discomfort to flood my system.

I waved him and the feeling off and we both dug into the food. As soon as the first fork full passed my lips, I was reminded to tell my parents about Noah's skills. The guy could cook, he wasn't lying.

Silence ebbed its way between the cushion that separated us as we ate. And I only caught myself stealing looks of him a few times.

I thought it was the little things about him that I liked the best. The minuscule movements that no one else would even bother to pay attention to. Like the way his shirt strained over his arms with each bite he brought to his mouth or the one rogue piece of hair that kept falling over his eye that he had to keep pushing behind his ear.

Only watching him started to make my chest feel hot, so I had to stop.

"Wine?" I asked. A slight twinge in the word that was part question, part I needed a reason to pull myself out of his orbit.

This felt all wrong. This wasn't me, I didn't feed men I was trying to sleep with and yet that was exactly what I was doing and I did it almost without thought. Short flings, one night stands that was what I was used to. What I told myself was all I needed, a few weeks or months with someone that didn't mean much on an emotional level.

But with Decker, I didn't know what it was.

FOURTEEN

Decker

CARINA WALKED BACK INTO the living room with two stemless glasses full of red wine, both more than a standard pour. She handed mine over as she drank deeply from her glass before even sitting down. It was a funny thing to witness, she almost seemed nervous and Carina Pera was never nervous.

"You okay?" I asked.

"How do you feel about friends with benefits?" she blurted out.

Wine burned my nostrils as I inhaled the liquid out of shock. "What?" I sputtered out, while wiping the back of my hand across my mouth.

I heard her wrong, right? Those weren't the real words that came out of her mouth. I must've been confused. That wasn't an actual thing people did, a planned out situationship? It seemed like that would lead to impending disaster.

Sure, I've had a few one night stands but outside that, I was more of a relationship person. "Umm, I don't have any feelings about it," I answered honestly, "mainly because I've never done that before."

"Done what?"

"A no-strings-attached sort of deal."

She cackled, throwing her head back like I'd just told the world's funniest joke. It went on longer than she probably should have, as I edged closer to the line of embarrassment. "Oh, shit, you're serious," she finally came around to saying once she realized I didn't join in on her amusement.

"I mean it's not a big deal, but for the most part I only sleep with women who I'm in a relationship with." She only blinked at me. "I've had one night stands, just not regularly." I could count how many one night stands I had on one hand, and with only three fingers.

Carina leaned forward setting her cup down on the glass coffee table before she turned toward me, hugging one knee to her chest. "Would it bother you to know that I do the exact opposite?" She held my gaze as she asked. Not asked, actually, as she told me.

"What you do with your body is none of my business."

A smirk appeared on her face. "What if I wanted it to be your business?" Those words only had one meaning.

"I just meant—"

"I know what you meant," I managed to choke out. Why was my throat so dry and why were my hands sweating? My dreams and the real world were racing toward each other at high speed, with only a volatile collision on the horizon.

Could I have her this way and not let my own head get in the way?

Short answer, yes. Changing Carina's mind would be an impossible task but I would change everything about myself if it meant I got to be something to her.

"The only thing I would ask for is if this is going to be more than a one time thing that I be the only one." I knew it was a selfish ask but it had to be said.

Her eyes narrowed. Carina liked giving orders, and was passive at best when taking them. But that was fine, I wasn't lying when I said I would find myself doing all sorts of things for her I wouldn't usually do. Let that be tangling myself into a friends with benefits situation or simply obeying orders she commanded. I'd be happy to oblige either way.

I leaned in, letting my fingers curl around her bare ankle. "I don't think I could stand it," I said in a low voice.

"Stand what?" Carina murmured, eyes softening.

I wondered if she noticed how she inched closer to me, leaning further in so her face was inches away from mine. She was remarkable this up close and personal. There were so many details I never noticed before, like the pale freckles dusted across the bridge of her nose

"Sharing you," I finally answered.

Unable to stop, I pushed further into the space between us, closing the gap and claimed her lips with mine. It was gentler than I intended but I had waited long enough. A small surprised noise squeaked out of her before she relaxed. Every ounce of tension melted away from her body as I continued to kiss her, forcing her back into the couch as I climbed over her.

It had only been days since we were last together and yet it was like I was experiencing her for the first time. Her lips were petal soft as they moved against mine, hungry and exploring. A groan worked its way up my throat as her tongue swiped along the seam of my lips as a request.

Carina would be the death of me, but God, what a way to go.

I pulled back in time to watch her bite back a grin.

"I can do that," she answered. "But there'll have to be some rules." She wound her arms around my neck, her hands found their home in my hair as she looked me straight in the eye.

One thing I looked forward to about being a lawyer were the negotiations. A large scale give and take game, bringing one thing to the table so you could end up with exactly what you wanted. And what I wanted was Carina. Not for one time, not even for only the benefits she was about to lay out. I wanted Carina for good, for life even. I wanted her in the daylight as well as the night.

I wanted *her.*

But until then I would spend whatever time she was willing to give me and use it to convince her she wanted me the same way. Because I could see it, even if she would refuse to acknowledge it.

I didn't break eye contact. Negotiation 101, never be the first to lay out an offer. "What are you offering?"

A wide smile broke out across her face. I suspected she became a lawyer for a very similar reason, the thrill of the game. It didn't matter if it took us all night, I would spend whatever time I had and use it to convince her that I was worth it. And maybe by the end I could get her to call me by my name.

FIFTEEN

Decker

THE VENUE IS ABOUT an hour outside of Fairvale, and by the time I pull up to the place, Lola is pacing the length of the porch of an old white farmhouse. Instead of a smile, she met my eyes with a scowl. "Well this should be fun," I said to my empty car as I swung into a parking space.

Lola and I are the closest in age. Growing up we were often mistaken for twins with how much we look alike. In our house with as many of us as there were, it was like running a circus. We all pulled our parents in a thousand different directions but they did their best to keep up. Only sometimes their best meant some of us fell to the wayside and more often than not it was Lola. She was second to last in the line up and the fourth girl but she never let that dull her shine. She was always out for adventure and I stuck to her like glue growing up just to be a part of the ride.

She bounded down the steps barreling toward me. "What took you so long?" she whinged, looking like she was on the verge of tears.

"Why am I here again?" Crying women were not my specialty and I was very much contemplating getting back in my car and leaving.

"Because you love me and literally everyone else is busy today," she said as a matter of fact. I shrugged in agreement.

Within twenty minutes, I was really confused on why I needed to be there. All I had done was trail behind her and the wedding planner as I listened to details of things I didn't care about. I was struggling to keep my eyes open, and I learned there were more ways to fold a napkin than I ever knew possible when they finally wrapped up the meeting.

"Lola, seriously, why did I need to be here?" A threatening undertone padded my words but she only rolled her eyes.

"Thank you for coming, Brother. I didn't want to do this alone. Chase should be home soon and I just want to make sure everything is perfect." It was tough to be mad when I knew this had been hard on her to do this all alone. Anyone married or getting married to someone in the military had to be strong and Lola was the strongest person I knew.

"Do you at least have a date?"

"I don't understand why it's such a big deal to you?"

"I just want to see you happy, we all do." She gently punched my shoulder as she looked at me and it was moments like this where I was reminded that family was everything.

"That makes no sense, bringing a date didn't mean anything." I wanted to know what I did in a past life that I ended up with no brothers, but instead five older sisters who love to meddle. "I think you'd be happy with me bringing the mail person at this rate."

"You have to bring someone. If you don't, the head table will be all off and you'll be the lone man out."

What a lie.

"Alright, I'm leaving,"

Lola's laugh followed me back to the car. I had no idea what I was going to do but I needed away from her and any further excuse to keep myself distracted from the incessant thoughts of Carina.

It had only been a few days since I was at her apartment and we had the most straight forward conversation about sex since my parents gave me the birds and bees talk.

And our clothes stayed on the entire time.

We came out of negation with a no string, no feelings agreement where once to twice a week we get together to blow off steam as she put it. And I got...shit, I didn't get anything out of it.

Not a total lie, I did get to have the naked company of a woman who had been living rent free in my head for a long time, but I was beginning to realize I never asked for anything as part of the negotiation. I was too focused on giving her everything in order to get time with her.

Did that mean I was going to be a terrible lawyer?

Well fuck.

I pulled out my phone.

> you hustled me

The longest minute of my life passed by as I waited for her reply.

> **Whatever do you mean**

> **You are the best negotiator in the county. You hustled me**

> **That I am and I kinda did, didn't I?**

> **Our agreement is everything you wanted**

> **t is. And it only took you three days to notice. Impressive**

> **Well what do I get?**

> **Me. I thought that was obvious**

Well she got me there. Three dots popped up quickly after

> **What do you want?**

Through my rearview window I looked back at the venue.

> **I need a date to a wedding**

Bubbles appeared then vanished. Seconds ticked by before they popped up again.

> **Send me the date**

We had four rules. All simple, to the point.

No telling work, and nothing other than business at work. Easy enough.

No telling people in general. A bit overkill, but I went with it.

No lying. That one surprised me, I couldn't fathom a reason I would lie to her.

And the last rule, the most important one she laid out was absolutely, under no circumstances, were there supposed to be feelings involved.

So why did it feel like I was going to obliterate the last rule before we even started?

SIXTEEN

Carina

THE FIRST REAL MEDIATION meeting was always the hardest. For them, for me, for everyone involved.

A lot of cases that came across my desk tended to be women who, up until divorce papers were in their hands, didn't even know they were in a failing marriage. Across the board the story was the same, it didn't matter your social class or tax bracket, how much you thought you were in love or the vows you recited on your wedding day—men were some of the worst creatures on Earth. In my humble, professional opinion at least.

Luckily for Kelly's sake this meeting, wasn't in-person. Although from the slew of emails I'd received from Ian Wheeler's office, the pit in my stomach told me it was going to be a shit show, no matter where it took place.

"Carina?" Decker's voice preceded him as he pushed my office door open. And I didn't even have to look up to know it was him. I think at this point I could pick his voice out of a crowd in my sleep.

I pulled my eyes from my computer. "Yeah?"

"Kelly's here."

Shit, she was twenty minutes early. I roughly pushed back from my desk. I still needed to print her file, my eyes had been killing me all day and I wouldn't make it through the meeting during the last leg of the day if I had to keep staring at my screen. I knew I should have pushed harder for a meeting first thing in the morning.

I was steps away from the doorway he was leaning in when I noticed his day seemed to match mine. The knot of his tie was pulled loose, a dinosaur this time, the type with the long neck and as tacky as ever. His hair down and tucked behind his ears, which was rare to see on him in the office and usually was only a sight I got when the day seemed to throw more problems our way than solutions.

"Can you tell her I'll be with her as soon as possible? I need—" My words died as he pulled a thin stack of papers from behind his back and handed them to me. My eyes flicked downward. "What's this?" I asked, staring bewildered, as if he was offering me a birthday cake with trick candles and not a perfectly reasonable stack of documents.

"I printed out the account documents she sent over along with the list of demands you wanted her to narrow down." He pushed the papers closer. "I'll go tell her you'll be out soon."

He set them in my outstretched hand, fingers bushing against mine in the process, short circuiting my brain. I thumbed through the pages, it was everything I needed to put together. "This is exactly what I needed," I mused. "How did you...never mind. Thanks, Decker."

"Whatever you need," he said, lowering his voice so only I could hear and placed his hand over his heart. "I'm at your whim."

Oh, that was good. I almost forgot where we were for a moment, the urge to kick my door closed and splay myself across my desk was making its self a strong possibility. I was sure it was the fact that despite our wonderfully thorough conversation about being fuck buddies, there's been no fucking.

Paper crinkled in my hand as I gripped them to keep from reach out and brushing them across his chest. Or from pulling at his stupid tie and pressing my body into his.

I needed to pull it together. I was getting off track and needed to remind myself of rule number one. Nothing at work.

A tight lipped smile was all I had to offer him.

"I'll go get her," he stated and swiftly disappeared down the hall.

The few minutes I had to compose myself were hardly enough when he walked back through my door with Kelly trailing behind him. Sadness dripping from every pore across her skin. That was enough to sober me up.

"Kelly, come in and have a seat. Thanks, Levi," I greeted, without meeting his gaze.

He softly closed the door behind him as Kelly lowered herself into her seat. It hadn't been long since our last meeting, and I forgot how visibly showing she was and my heart ached for her.

This never got easier.

I took my seat behind my desk, it was best to rip the bandaid off. "We will call into their office in a few minutes. Do you have any questions?"

"Once we do this, will it be over?"

If only I could tell her yes, give her hope that by the time she gave birth she would be on the other side of this heaping mess but I couldn't.

"That is always the hope, but I want to be honest with you. Ben's demands are out of proportion to what you have asked for, I don't expect this will be the only meeting."

Her movements were minuscule, almost undetectable. A slight flex of her fingertips against her stomach, the quick uncross and cross of her ankles and the flutter of her lashes. Someone else might not have noticed but to me they were loud and clear. Kelly was at war with herself and was probably only now realizing she would be giving birth while still married and that was not what she had planned.

"What are his demands?" she finally asked and I debated not even telling her, but that would do no one any good.

I shifted through the stack of papers Decker had handed me and sure enough the email I had sent to him from Ian was there, highlighted and all. Even a few little sticky flags to make sure I saw the more ludicrous requests.

This wasn't the time for warm and fuzzy feelings, nor did I condone warm or fuzzy feelings in general but my heart seemed to beat out of rhythm at the sight.

I looked over the list, then back at Kelly, using every ounce of strength I had to give her the details with a straight face. "The usual, no alimony, or child support. He wants to keep the house and most assets that were acquired during the marriage."

Kelly scoffed, before leaning forward in her seat. "You've got to be kidding me."

That wasn't even the worst part.

"He's also demanding a paternity test at birth, and if he is the father, he would be pursing joint custody at an eighty, twenty split."

She nearly launched herself out of the seat. "He thinks the baby isn't his? Has he lost his mind? Of course the baby is his, I'm not the one who's been unfaithful. Eighty, twenty, how ridiculous. Of course he wouldn't want to spend any time with his child, it would infringe on his personal time." She seemed to be saying anything that came to her mind.

My tongue ran along my top teeth. "Actually, he's proposing he take custody of your child eighty percent of the time and you the twenty. It's the every other weekend schedule." I really wished I didn't have to tell her that part.

"Are you fucking kidding me?!" She shrieked and was on her feet. "That cannot happen."

Kelly began pacing the short length of my office in front of my desk, her hands cradling the bottom part of her stomach. I had no idea about her due date but God help me if she went into labor here.

I stepped around my desk to cut her off, placing my hand gently on her shoulder. "Kelly, I'm going to need you to sit." We locked eyes and it was like a punch in the gut. Her pretty brown irises burned with rage while simultaneously drowning in tears. I offered her a small smile. "I am an excellent attorney, which means I would make a terrible doctor and if you go into labor here, I'm afraid you won't be the only one freaking out."

Kelly blew out a watery laugh and shuffled slowly back to her seat. "Don't worry, I'm not due for another three months."

"Good to know."

Once it looked like she calmed down, or at least as calm as she could be, I gave her the run down of how I was going to steer the meeting. "His demands are ridiculous on purpose. They ask for the universe, so you'll settle for a few grains of sand. It's not real."

Men like Ben Leon don't back down easily, they force you to fight tooth and nail to get what you want and even if you win, they won't stop. That's what makes him terrifying. I would get Kelly what she deserved but it would come at a cost.

She nodded in acknowledgement.

"Let me do the talking, and if I need the answer to something, I will mute so we can talk. They should be doing the same thing. You won't be speaking to Ben directly. We'll get through this, okay?"

"Okay."

Finger poised over the keypad of my phone, I gave her one last look. "Are you ready?"

Kelly sucked in a depth breath. "No, but let's get this over with."

SEVENTEEN

Carina

"That's obscene, Ian, and we all know it," I said into the speaker of my office phone. It had been barely ten minutes since we started the call and I was grasping at invisible straws to keep a leg up. I flashed Kelly a sympathetic look, anything to calm her nerves that were fraying before my eyes.

A dark chuckle echoed from the other side of the call.

"We both know it's more than adequate. A paternity test will give my client assurance that the—"

Kelly exploded. "Oh, fuck off." Luckily, I punched the mute button before the first syllable left her mouth. Honestly I was a little proud. When they're mad, it meant they were on the verge of no longer feeling sorry for themselves. And Kelly got there quickly.

"Kelly," I chastised. Half warning, half I get it and I wished I could say the same thing.

"I'm sorry, I'm sorry, but a paternity test. We've been married for a decade, there's been no one else. Ever."

"I know, he's doing it to drag out the process."

She sat herself back into the seat and flung up her hands. "Of course he is."

I gave her a few more seconds before getting back to the call. "Ian, we can discuss the paternity test later, since he's the father it's a non-issue. Let's talk about the properties, the downtown bungalow was bought last year and still remains vacant. Kelly would like to keep the property to use as her main residence."

The place was adorable, I could tell why she would want to keep it. Great school district, walkable neighborhood, she even mentioned it was close to the penthouse Ben would be staying in, so whatever custody agreement was worked out, it would be beneficial to both of them.

Even when he was being horrid she still thought of him. I stood by my statement that men are trash and didn't deserve us.

"That property was bought and paid for by Ben."

"And last time I checked, it was bought and paid for during their marriage and this is still California. Communal property, Ian, or do you need to go back to school?"

The line went dead, I was sure someone was throwing a fit on the other end.

Kelly chewed at her thumb as I flipped a pen back and forth between my finger tips. We were going nowhere, that was a fact.

"We can discuss property once alimony is set. Ben won't be footing the bill for her not to work."

"No one's saying that, but Kelly has been a dutiful, *faithful* wife, and was urged not to work by your client for the decade they were married, alimony is going to be a part of the divorce settlement, no way around it."

"She's also the one that initiated the divorce, Pera," Ian barked.

I fought to not roll my eyes. If he thought a stern tone and putting a wedge of indifference between us by using my last name was going to get him anywhere, he was in for a rude awakening.

I wondered how Decker felt about me always using his last name? Did he even have an opinion about it or could he tell I used it for that exact reason. A way to keep him at arms length, and keep me from feeling anything toward him. Which had always been the goal.

"Doesn't matter who initiated the divorce." I shot back.

We did this for twenty more minutes and nothing was accomplished. By the end of the call, my nerves were shot and Kelly was fuming to the point I was surprised steam wasn't rolling out her ears. She left shortly after without much to say, disappointment didn't begin to cover it.

I reached up and pulled the pin from the French knot I had styled earlier. My head hit the back of my chair and my eyes drifted close. I only needed a moment to myself before diving back into work for the night.

That was how he found me as he slipped into the chair Kelly left vacant. "How did it go?"

"I've had nightmares more pleasant than Wheeler," I answered without bothering to open up my eyes.

"Hmm," he mused.

I cracked one eye open and glanced at him. "What?"

He did a quick lift and dropped one of his shoulders. "I've never heard you call another person by their last name. I was beginning to think you reserved that for me, is all." For a moment I figured he was joking, until I noticed he wasn't looking at me. No hint of his normal lazy smile that he liked to use around me. No suggestive waggle of his thick, dark eyebrows that he liked to tack on to comments that weren't work related. Instead he was running a fingernail along the grain pattern in the wooden handle of the chair, looking anywhere but my direction.

And I realized I didn't like it.

"Usually it is, but I don't like Wheeler, so it's not the same."

Watching his features morph was like seeing the first break of sunlight after weeks of rain. A sly smile unfurled across his face as he finally slid his gaze up at me. "So what I'm hearing is you like me?"

"Don't push it, Decker," I said as I sat forward, wiggling my mouse to bring my computer back to life.

The sight of that small smile put my mind on a track that led straight back to my bed with him in it. I wanted to ask him how late was too late for him to show up, but I was pulled from my thoughts when my phone rang.

Not saved by the bell, as the caller ID flashed Mamma.

"Not again," I groaned, reaching out to swipe right to answer.

"Everything okay?" he asked.

I didn't bother answering him as I took the call, switching to Italian.

"Hi, Mamma."

"Ciao, dolce mia. We need you again this weekend."

"Again?"

"Yes," she said with almost snapping tone. "Otherwise we will have to close the store for the night."

"What about Noah?"

"It will be you and Noah."

"Mamma, I don't understand what's been going on with you guys. Why do you need so many nights off, and why can't your regular staff help?"

I glanced up to see Decker watching me with a quizzical look etched on his face. I guess I would look like that too if I didn't understand the conversation.

"It's not important. You'll be there, Saturday at six then, yes?

Of course she would make it so I couldn't say no. "Noah and I, on a Saturday, by ourselves. Are you insane?"

"Carina."

One sharp word, a quick lash from my mother's mouth and I fell in line.

"Yeah, I'll see you on Saturday."

She ended the call quickly, not even a goodbye. I couldn't keep going like this. I needed to either put my foot down or figure out why they both kept slinking away from the restaurant.

Turning back around, I was surprised to see he was still sitting across from me. I tossed the phone onto the desk. If it broke, so be it, then I wouldn't have to answer their calls.

"Everything okay?"

"Yeah, just peachy," I said as I took out my aggression out on the keyboard and logged back in. "Just another Saturday ruined by that damn restaurant."

Why didn't he leave? Surely he realized that any agreement we had to meet outside of work this weekend was ruined. And if it was ruined, then there was no other reason for us to interact.

"Did you know, I used to wait tables?"

My hands paused. "What?"

"In college, I waited tables at some diner close to campus."

"Okay, and you're telling me this why?"

He pulled the chair closer, resting his elbow on the desk and his chin in his hand, with another smile playing at his lips. "You're smart, why do you think I'm telling you?" He raised an eyebrow, like I asked to be a part of whatever game he was playing.

"Decker," I replied as a warning

"Amore," he crooned.

My nose scrunched upward.

He sat up straighter, cocking his head to the side, a serious look washed over him. "Too much?" he asked.

"Yeah, don't do it again." The flushing feeling returned, blazing a path across my stomach and up my chest. I wanted to hear it again. I wanted my fingers in his hair and my thighs on either side of his hips and to hear it again.

"It's the only word I know so far," he answered with a small shrug. "Let me help you," he continued, a softness to his tone.

"I don't need help, Decker."

"Everyone needs help at some point."

Yeah, everyone else. Not me. I was the one who helped, not the one who asked. It was one of the first facts people ended up learning about me. That should have been the end of the conversation, but he lingered in his seat.

"Please?" he added lightly after a few moments.

"You want to come work at the restaurant?"

He nodded, his head still resting in his hand, amber eyes boring into me.

"Why?"

"I told you, to help you." He was acting like this was a run of the mill conversation for us. One where I reached out and he's there to lend a helping hand.

"I don't need your help, Decker," I reiterated, my tone much too harsh for someone trying to help.

He dropped his hand and reached across to drag his fingertips along the top of my hand. It was lightening fast, to the point that I could have imagined it. "I know, but let me anyway," he stated. "I live to please, remember?"

I should chastise him. Send him from my office with his tail between his legs. Rule one was nothing at work. We were barely into...whatever it was with us and he was already sweeping away lines we drew like we never marked them in the first place. I needed to pull the emergency break, I needed to shut this down before it spiraled out of my control.

"Fine, be there at six."

Well that wasn't what I was supposed to say.

EIGHTEEN

Decker

I was so fucked.

Didn't matter how many times I tried retracing my steps to figure out where I went wrong with our situationship, or right, depending on how I decided to approach our new reality. Didn't really matter how much I dissected the feelings, in the end it was clear—I was tightly wound around Carina's finger. So much so that one look from her and it wouldn't matter if I never actually got to touch her again, I was content in simply being near her.

Even if it meant stepping in as a server at her parents' restaurant on a weekend night.

Waiting tables was like riding a bike, no matter where you went, it was all about the same. Except it'd been so many years since I last did, it felt like the bike was on fire, the restaurant was on fire, and everything was turning into ash around me. And Carina couldn't stop laughing.

She walked me through the kitchen and introduced me to Noah who looked as skeptical as I did that I would survive one shift. The order system was easy enough and I trailed behind Carina while she pointed out the table numbers. Once I learned the order, everything else began falling into place.

As the sun slipped out of the sky and night fell over Fairvale, I was wavering in my ability. Most of the work was easy stuff; bring water, take orders, bring food, bus the table, repeat. But I forgot how hard the people made this type of job. It felt like every other table had some sort of problem, that was either directly my fault or had nothing to do with me but I was the one they looked to to correct it. It was slowly turning into my own personal level of hell.

The whole point of me being there was to prove to Carina I could be someone she could rely on, or be the person she could turn to when she needed help. Not that she would ever outright ask for help, even if she needed it, but at least if something did come up, she would think of me. But if I fucked this up for her, if she spent the night trying to clean up my mistakes it would only make more work for her and she would never see me as more than a... What was I too her?

Friend with benefits, were we friends? Co-workers, obviously. Person she set up a sort of sex pact with but we hadn't gotten around to the sex part. Bit of a mouth full but yeah, that sounded about right. Pushing through the doors, I stumbled into the kitchen, flushed and remembering why I hated waiting tables. "The lady at table five wants to know if she can get the cioppino without any seafood, she's allergic."

Noah stopped mid stir, turning to me with a look of horror slowly creeping over his face. "Cioppino is seafood in tomato broth, that's it."

"I know."

"So she just wants tomato broth?" he asked skeptically, trying to work out how he would even do that.

"I don't know. I tried to tell her, but she won't take no for an answer, she keeps insisting that you've done it for her before."

He looked back at the stove, then at Carina as she emerged from the office. She'd been out on the floor with me for most the night but once it slowed, she decided to make sure her parents were caught up on all their paperwork.

"Why do you two look like someone just kicked a dog?"

"A customer is asking for cioppino without seafood."

She rolled her eyes as she tossed the clipboard in her hand onto the table at her side. "That's Mrs. Andrews, she doesn't get cioppino, she gets ribollita and thinks it's cioppino."

Noah spoke up first, confused. "But that's not even remotely the same thing."

"I know."

I took her word for it and rang it up in the system. The printer near Noah came to life, spitting out the ticket that spurred him forward in his work.

Carina sauntered over as I took a moment to relax, stopping inches from my side and flicked her gaze up at me. "How's it going?" she chirped, an amused expression rolled through her eyes. Our height difference was on full display, as she tipped back her head, exposing her delicate throat in order to look up at me when she was without heels and

Images that shouldn't be occupying my mind filled my head. My lips against her pulse point, her back pressed against the wall, and me trying to pull all those little noises I know she makes from her. I think she can see them too. I stepped closer, needing to be in the air she breathed.

Normally Carina was hard to get a read on, emotions rarely gave away to what she was thinking so when her eyes broke our connection, flitting down to my lips then back up, I was finding it difficult to not do everything I just visualized.

I wanted her to want me as much as much as I craved her. I wanted her addicted to me, it would only be fair since I was already in so deep.

Maybe I moved first, dipping my head down, unable to stop making my fantasy from coming true but she pressed forward also.

It was like a count down, six inches, four, two; we were centimeters away and I was already slowly sinking into the haze she kept me in.

One more centimeter, one more breath.

CLANK.

Metal hitting the ground ripped us apart. Carina's head whipped to the side in time to watch Noah scramble to pick a pot off the ground, apologies spewing from his mouth. Fire and brimstone fury swelled in her stare.

"Sorry, sorry."

She stepped back from me, waving off his apology. And now I was annoyed "Noah, what have I told you about apologizing? Just finish the plate and take it to the table."

He worked quickly under the pressure of Carina's narrowing gaze but he did it without another mishap and she was back looking at me.

I decided to answer her earlier question, our brief moment fading with the ring of the pot hitting the ground. "These people are nuts," I answered truthfully. "Someone ordered diet soda, I brought them said diet soda, and they promptly told me that's not what they ordered. Another asked why there wasn't a soup, salad and breadstick option and proceeded to act like they didn't hear me when I told them this isn't Olive Garden, that's why."

Carina tucked her bottom lip between her teeth to keep from laughing. "What did they order, if not soup and salad?"

"Oh no, they still ordered soup, salad, and breadsticks. I brought them an antipasta and a few slices of whatever Noah had around. I forgot that I hated waiting tables," I said, as I pushed my fingers through my hair. "Also, I'm pretty sure some guy muttered that I needed to cut my hair."

A laugh she could no longer hold in spilled out of her, so loud Noah glanced over his shoulder to check on her.

It wasn't often that Carina laughed around me, maybe at me sometimes, a soft chuckle here and there but nothing like this. Uninhibited. Full of passion to the point her jade eyes crinkled shut, her nose wrinkled and dusty pink splotches bloomed across the top of her cheeks as she collapsed forward into the fit of giggles.

"I'm sorry," she said between gasping breaths before standing back up. She wasn't.

From my peripheral, I watched Noah take the dish he was working on out to the dining room. I knew the rules but I'd already blurred the lines at work, what's one more?

I stepped into her space, and seeing as we were already inches away from each other, my chest pressed into her body. Her laughing stuttered at the lack of space, but she didn't move. For a moment I watched as each breath caused her chest to graze mine.

She was so different here, loose and carefree. No polished suit or cool tone of indifference to keep things impersonal. This was who she really was underneath the mask she often wore. But if I was being honest, I liked both versions of her.

I watched as the corner of her lips turned up, like she was going to keep laughing at my misery. "I'm sorry," she sputtered, pressing her fingers against her lips to keep from laughing further.

"No you're not."

"You're right," she tilted her head back as unfiltered joy poured out, "I'm not." Color flushed her skin, painting her cheeks the color of roses. She laughed until her breath became scarce. It was beautiful. I wanted to jar the sound, carry it around with me for whenever I needed a pick me up.

It took her a minute but she finally reined it in, wiping tears from the corner of her eyes.

"Oh that was good. I swear I don't know what it is about food customer service that emboldens people but you wouldn't believe the amount of times I've had to read some guy the riot act while handing over a plate of pasta. The customer is not always right and I'm not afraid to let them know. But the hair comment, classic."

Teeth sunk into the soft flesh of her plump bottom lips as she shook her head, clearly amused.

I pulled down on her lip, freeing the soft flesh, as the urge to have my hands on her overwhelmed me. "Just wait until later. You can't laugh if your mouths full." Air vanished once the words tumbled out of my mouth.

I didn't know what possessed me to actually say what was on my mind but whatever it was, I wasn't about to stop. I needed her, desperately. Didn't matter that we were standing between an industrial sink and racks of folded napkins and tablecloths, I wanted to plunge my hands into her hair and haul her to my chest, forcing the atoms between us to figure out where I ended and she began. I wanted to stop fantasizing what she felt like, and remember.

Carina's next few breaths were quick pants, she didn't speak and the longer the silence dragged on, the faster the thought came that I fucked up.

"Tonight?" she asked, surprising me. My dick reacted first, straining uncomfortably against the fabric of my jeans; next was my heart rate which took off on an incline that threatened to topple me over. I'd never get used to how forward she was, in fact I hoped I never did.

I opened my mouth to answer but Noah came barging back in, returning oxygen to the room and forcing Carina to spring backwards, putting more space between us than before.

She disappeared back into the office and I took a minute to let the blood drain so I didn't make the customers uncomfortable and possibly get the restaurant shut down for indecency.

The next hour was a breeze, likely due to slow dwindle of people who showed up but still by the time the end of the shift was approaching I felt good about my goal. Which was to show her that I could be counted on for help, if she ever needed it.

Noah was walking me through what side work needed to be finished when Carina finally reappeared. She stopped in the middle of the kitchen and pulled her phone from her back pocket before asking, "How long has it been since the last guest?"

The small window in the kitchen door allowed me to see the dining room, to check if anyone new had walked in but it was still clear. "About fifteen minutes, last guests just left as well.

"Noah, finish cleaning your area then you can head home. We're going to close a bit early."

"But it's Saturday?"

Noah flinched as Carina leveled a glare in his direction. "And if my parents wanted to stay open for their full hours, they should be working. Just clean up and you're good to go." Noah started clearing dirty pans from the stove before the end of her sentence.

I was a hundred precent sure Noah wasn't purposefully going slow, but with Carina's gazed fixed on me, a small glint of lust lingering in her irises as I rolled silverware into linen napkins, I had half a mind to tell him to forget cleaning all together and just get out.

But I didn't, so ten of the longest minutes of my life passed by before he announced he was done. I leaned in the doorway between the kitchen and the dining area, as Carina followed him to the front with a smile and shut the door behind Noah, clipping his heels in the process.

For a moment, Carina stood at the door, arms at her side, her thumbs rubbing circles around her fingers. When she turned, a small crease formed between her eyebrows as her eyes pinged from me to the empty dining room then back to me but past my shoulder, like she was planning something. I knew this look, it was one of my favorites, where her mind ran through the obstacles standing in the way of her getting what she wanted.

Except, this time I wasn't an obstacle she wanted to get rid of.

Without a word, she stalked toward me, looped her fingers through the front of my apron and pulled me through the kitchen, down the short hallway and through the office door she had locked herself behind for most of the night. There wasn't enough time for me to get a word out before her mouth was on mine.

Hungry and demanding to be felt, full of teeth against my lips and fingers knotting in my hair. It was a punishment, and while I wouldn't consider myself a masochist, I wouldn't want to be anywhere else. "It's been I don't even know how long since we talked about being friends with benefits," she murmured against my lips. "But there's been no benefits."

Don't I know it.

"Are you going to do something about it or should I have picked someone else?" she challenged.

An unmistakable noise that vibrated in my chest, a deep grumbling that could only be taken as dissatisfaction. I moved on instinct, bending down, wrapping my hands around her thighs and lifted. Only one extra step had her back pressed against the wall and her legs wrapped around my waist, her core pressed against me white hot and the perfect height for me to bury myself in.

Layers of clothes were a minor setback in the moment but she was in my arms, and I needed to focus. This could be the only chance I got, honestly any moment she gave me I would treat like my last, and there was so much I wanted to do.

I shifted my hips forward, pressing her into the wall and grinding my achingly hard cock against her center. Carina's eyes fluttered shut as her grip around my shoulders tightened. My lips left her mouth, only to latch onto any other piece of exposed skin before pressing against her ear. "You and I both know I'm the only one you want taking care of this pussy," I whispered rocking into her once more. The whine that crawled up her throat as I kissed my way down her neck was high-inducing.

More. More. More.

The only thought in my head was more as she tore at the buttons of my shirt with swift precision. The office was cramped, barely enough room for two people. Definitely too small for two people to do what she wanted. A stack of papers fluttered to the ground as my hip knocked into the desk.

Was I really about to fuck her for the first time in an office at her parents' restaurant?

I was going to say no, until her hand fell from my neck and reached between us. With her eyes focused on me she pulled the apron ties and let the fabric fall to the ground, before reaching for my belt buckle. Metal clanking against each other filled the office in a deafening tone.

Carina flattened her back against the wall as her fingers held onto the button of my jeans. "Please tell me you brought a condom?"

But the answer was yes, I was about to fuck her in her parents' office. What else was I to do when she looked at me with lust heavy eyes, and lips reddened from my mouth? I knew there was no world in which I would say no to her.

Nineteen

Carina

THIS WAS THE BEST and worst idea I had ever had but fuck if it didn't feel good.

I was out of his arms but only long enough to rip my pants down my legs and step out of them and his to drop to his ankles. Tight black briefs pulled my focus from the crinkling of the condom wrapper opening.

Good God.

When you're a woman like me, who enjoyed sex and a lot of it, I'd seen my fair share of dicks. Some more impressive than others, but what Levi had was like a whole secret level that I never knew existed. "Holy shit." I glanced at him, then back down at his tented briefs, electric currents zipped down my spine. Whoever said you could know what a guy was packing just by looking at him was a liar, or maybe I had gone to great lengths to not think about Decker's cock because it was more than I ever imagined.

One corner of his lips pulled up in a small smile, almost shy. Which was a shock and honestly a wonder he doesn't walk around like he's the king of the world.

Plucking the condom from his hand, the wrapper landed on the ground next to my pants and with my eyes locked on his I slowly rolled it over his length. The way his eyelids slid closed and his head dropped backward sent a wave of arousal through my own core.

Suddenly his arms were around me again, pinning me up against the wall in the same position as before and the tip of his length notched against my entrance. Only a tiny piece of him and I was absent of thoughts, seeing it and feeling it were two completely different things and if this was the beginning, I didn't know if I could make it to the end.

"Decker," I panted, eyes screwed shut, wondering how it felt this good and barely anything had happened.

He didn't move, he didn't kiss me, he only stood still, forehead against mine with stuttering breaths longer than I could take. I rolled my hips as best as I could, allowing him to slide in ever so slightly.

"Decker, please," I whined.

"Please what, what do you want?" He slanted his hips, pushing in another inch.

"Levi, I don't think," I mumbled out after a moment as my brain slowly melted in my skull. "I don't think it will fit."

He chuckled, and I realized it was the first time I had called him by his first name in years. "Don't worry, Amore, it'll fit. I was made for you."

Oh, that was good. I was going to ignore it because no, he wasn't, but it was one hell of a line. He was made for this moment, but not me.

Decker slid himself in quickly, forcing a satisfying groan to crawl up my throat. The stretch balanced on that perfect line of pleasure and pain and I was so deliciously full.

"Oh, I fucking knew it." His breath stuttered as his head dropped into the crook of my shoulder.

Before I could even think of some snide remark one arm slipped from my waist and was at my jaw pulling me to meet him in a frantic sort of kiss. It was the type that not only stole your breath but melted your brain with how good it was, to the point that words no longer existed and all I could think about was him and this moment.

He snapped forward again, locking his lips onto mine, swallowing the sounds that I was unable to keep inside me. "Christ, you feel good."

My legs tightened around his waist, working on their own to drive him in deeper. Faster, anything really. He barely started and I could already feel my core tightening, I was on a short path to what I was sure was about to be a mind altering orgasm.

"No, not good, it's better than perfect."

Levi was a talker and I couldn't get enough of it. He pushed back from where he was pressed against my chest and I almost whined in protest, until his arms snaked under my legs, pressing me in to the wall. I was at his mercy, and it was my new favorite place to be.

Every thrust sent my head further into the wall and my fingers twisting in his hair. Every touch, every word that slipped out of his mouth piled on top of each other until I was teetering on the edge of bliss.

"Tell me, Carina," he panted. I cracked my eyes open to see him watching where we joined. His hair fell like a dark curtain across his face.

Goosebumps broke out across my skin as his thumbs pressed into the soft skin around my knees, opening me wider, my knees were practically touching my chest. I was exposed, there wasn't an inch of me I could hide and yet Levi's hips faltered on the next stroke. As if the sight of me caused him to malfunction.

"Tell you what?" I finally remembered to answer. He ripped his gaze from watching himself disappear inside of me to look at me. Amber colored eyes were blown wide in ecstasy, dripping in want, possession, and a hunger that surprised me.

Levi slowly pressed in his cock until every inch of him was sheathed inside of me, all without taking his eyes off me. "Does it always feel this good?" he asked, his face inches from mine. "Do you always feel this fucking perfect?"

The words sparked a new wave of pleasure as I clenched around him. A deep groan rumbled in his chest.

Did I have a praise kink? I must or at the very least I absolutely did now because all I wanted was to hear more about how perfect I was. I started to think it had nothing to do with the words and more to do with the man who was saying them.

I didn't answer, instead I closed the gap between us with a bruising kiss, slipping my tongue between his lips at the first break. I wanted to taste him, I wanted to feel the ghost of his kiss on me long after he left.

I needed it. I needed more.

Searching for any sort of friction, I rolled my hips to push in closer.

"Goddamnit, Carina, if you keep doing that, I'm going to come in five seconds and that's not the impression I want to leave."

He pulled out and snapped back into me. My head smacked into the wall at the blissful intrusion

"I knew you'd feel this good."

"Wet."

Thrust.

"Tight."

Thrust.

"Perfect."

A whine crawled up my throat

He smirked before his mouth landed back on mine. He was relentless, barely time for me to form a single thought.

"Levi, I need..." I couldn't form any other words. I was in a dense fog of bliss, my brain had turned off and I could only feel.

"What do you need? Tell me, I'll give you anything."

"Faster, fuck me faster." I managed to choke out.

He chuckled against my lips but gave me exactly what I was looking for. The room filled with the sound of our skin

That feeling was back, the tight coil of pleasure that snaked around my spine. Fuck did it feel good. I couldn't remember the last time sex with someone felt this good. Usually it was full of me trying to get them to place their hands or dick or whatever else exactly where I wanted or having to finish the job myself once I got back home, but not this. This was perfect.

"Fuck," he growled as I chanted his name in ecstasy.

The edge disappeared and I fell over into a wave of blissful euphoria with Levi following not too far behind, leaving us panting into each other's ears.

For a while, we didn't move. I stayed pressed against the wall until he slowly set my feet back on the ground, holding onto my waist as I swayed slightly.

"That was..." I didn't know how to finish the sentence.

"Yeah, I know what you mean."

Everything was about to change.

TWENTY

Carina

IT'S A FREAKING MESS that I couldn't seem to find my way out of. I didn't even know if I wanted to.

I tried and failed to keep him off my mind for the past few weeks but it'd proven to be impossible when he was everywhere I looked. Leaving for work, he was there just a head of me on the stairs. At work, there's been more times I've passed him in the printer room than all the years combined. My body refused to read the memo that the office was not the place to lust after him. But when he showed up in slacks that were a touch too snug in all the right spots, who could blame me?

Consistent, great sex turned me into an idiot.

Decker strode into my office this morning in a pair of coffee brown slacks with a dark sweater over a white button up looking like a librarian's wet dream come to life. Maybe his constant presence wasn't so bad after all.

He set a to-go cup on a file sitting in front of me. "Hey. Not on the paperwork, what are you thinking?" I chastised him as I shook my head and pulled the file out from under the cup. "Also, there's no need to bring me coffee every morning. A little over the top, don't you think?" I smirked up at him as he continued to hover around my desk.

"Maybe, but if I didn't, I wouldn't get to see that smile you keep attempting to hide." His voice was full of humor. I schooled my features and gave him a pointed look just to prove a point.

"If you say so." But he was right, every morning when he waltzed in with the simple coffee, it stirred up unknown emotions in my chest. In the stupidly small amount of time I'd spent with him, I seemed to have lost all sense of what I actually felt for him.

"Actually it's more of an 'I'm sorry' coffee. I know we had plans for tonight," he said with a grin. "But I need to cancel." He tucked his hands into his front pocket and replaced the smile with an empathic look. It took me a moment to realize his look was probably in response to the way my face fell at the thought of not being able to see him.

A second later, I lapsed into my normal air of indifference, waving him off. The last thing I wanted was to pull emotions into this. "No problem, I'll probably be here late anyway." That was news to me but he didn't need to know that.

"It's not that I don't want to," he stepped closer and I flicked a flat and hard look his way. He got the message and didn't move again, "but my sister needs someone to watch my nieces, and my parents aren't available." He rushed to say as if he couldn't bear the thought that I'd think he was ditching me for some other frivolous plan.

"You don't need to explain yourself to me, I'm not your girlfriend." The phrase slipped out before I could stop myself and my defenses slid into place. I had no right to an explanation, this arrangement was just that, an arrangement, that allowed me to feel something, anything.

Disappointment welled up in my throat for no reason at the first sign of a let down.

"Are you just going to stand around in my office all day? I'm already going to have to spend hours here after your day ends, I don't need you in here distracting further," I snapped out.

His head recoiled like I slapped him and regret pulsed in my chest, quickly replacing the pang of jealously that had flared to life.

I didn't know how to even explain my reaction but it needed one. I'd been so used to having nobody that his ongoing attempts to get to know me better had become my favorite part of the day and the interactions I looked forward to the most. And that maybe I'd become too reliant on him to brighten my days. I had spent so long trying to deny that I had any attraction to Decker that I didn't give any thought to how it would affect me if I gave in.

My head lifted to meet his gaze once again and his warm brown eyes gazed back at me The pull between us was undeniable. It flooded my system sending me reeling headfirst into an apology I was hoping he wouldn't make me regret. "I'm sorry, Levi."

His eyes widened before softening at my use of his given name.

I didn't apologize often, really ever. Not because I thought I was right all the time but I took the time to think before I spoke. I made a point to mean what I said because once you started apologizing for yourself it left the door open for people to think they could walk all over you.

My throat worked to swallow down my sudden insecurity before I continued. "What I said came out wrong. I didn't mean to be rude." Apprehension flickered in my voice as the foreign taste of an apology sat on my tongue.

"There's another mediation meeting next week for the Leon case, anything new come in that I might need?" I didn't make eye contact, I couldn't, so I switched the conversation as quickly as possible to avoid any further embarrassment.

Good switch it up, keep it professional, and don't let him see how absolutely rattled you feel.

Our eyes met briefly and I watched as he shifted. His initial playful attitude he came in with dissipated entirely. In its place a flash of confusion moved across his face before work-Levi made an appearance. He brought his fist up to his mouth and cleared his throat and pulled on the collar of his stark white shirt.

"Do you want to sit in on this one?" I offered.

The moment was back. One where the air felt heavy and more words that sat on the tips of our tongues, begging to be said but nothing spilled over. And I knew he could feel it too with the way he lingered for a moment in the door frame before disappearing back to his cubicle. It shouldn't have bothered me but it did and the worst part was being upset because I wanted to spend time with him but couldn't.

My ass was permanently altered, I was sure of it. It took on the shape of my office chair, and I wasn't sure if it would snap back. I kicked my door shut, flicked my heels down the entryway and shrugged my blazer off, letting it drop to the floor. I pulled my hair out of the lazy chignon I had attempted this morning and continued to the kitchen. The only consequence of staying late at the office was that the only open food options were drive throughs, but I was so tired, I couldn't even bother to stop for anything.

The tile of my kitchen floor was cool under my feet as I debated if the week old pasta was worth the inevitable food poisoning when a knock echoed through my apartment.

When you live alone, people showing up unexpected, in the middle of the night, was never a good sign. Pushing up onto my tip toes, I peeked through the peephole before almost stumbling backwards, because on the other side was Levi, loaded with what looked like grocery bags. The panic about a possible killer being on the other side of the door morphed into a new feeling.

He knocked again.

I panicked a little bit more.

Before I could think, my hand reached out and I pulled the door open. I wished I had something witty to say, I normally did, but as he stood in front of me with a lazy smile under the flickering porch light, everything I ever knew leaked from my brain.

"Hi." It came out way more breathy than it should have. He didn't answer. Instead, he crossed into my home and pressed his mouth against mine, in a surprisingly tender and domestic action.

"Good, you're here," he said after pulling away. Night air swept through the door sending shivers up my body. "I was afraid you'd still be at the office."

"What?"

"Knowing you, that could be any time into the night."

Was I that predictable? What was he doing out so late? What was in those bags and was it food because I was starving?

"Again, what?" I repeated.

"You mentioned you were staying late, when I cancelled, but I was out at dinner and all I could think about was coming home to you." His eyebrows pulled inward. "Well not home, home, we don't share a home, but here, to you," he rambled.

"Are you drunk, Decker?" I sputtered through a laugh, pushing the feeling from his use of the word *home* gave me to the back of my mind.

He held his finger and thumb up so they were practically touching. "Just a little bit." He kicked his foot out to close the door before crowding my space. A dopey smile etched into his features as he stared at me.

Levi had a dangerous effect on me. My heart was thawing and I didn't know how to make sense of it.

"How did you even get here?"

"Ride share, obviously. He didn't even mind taking me to store before but that might have been the tip I offered when I got in the car." He shrugged and brushed past me and disappeared into the kitchen.

I followed him out of sheer curiosity after hearing plastic crinkling. I peered around him as he continued to pull items out of the bag he showed up with. Slices of cakes, cookies, a candy bar and a whole freaking pie littered my counter.

"Decker, why did you bring me every dessert from the grocery store?"

"Why do you do that?"

"Do what?" I blinked up at him.

"Call me Decker," he replied but kept his eyes on his task of flicking open every container lid. "You always call me Decker, except for today. I think it was the first time I've ever heard my name from you when someone else isn't around to hear it." He turned toward me and his warm eyes marveled at me. "Or at least the only time you've said it was when your clothes were on." He kissed me again.

Even if I had a real answer for him, I didn't know if I'd give it to him. It started just after we began working at ALA. I used his last name because I was being childish and didn't want to be personable with him. But then he kept doing things that had my head spinning, so it stuck. "No real reason." Except for I liked the way he looked at me every time I used it, half annoyed, half amused.

The corner of his mouth ticked upward as he swept a fallen strand of hair off my forehead and tucked it behind my ear. "I like it when you say my name."

Without warning, I stretched up onto my toes and crushed my mouth back to his in a kiss that couldn't be labeled as anything but tender. He returned my enthusiasm, his mouth burning a path across my jaw and down the column of my throat. It was the type of kiss that left me panting, embarrassingly so, long after he stopped.

My hands had a white knuckle grip on the edge of my counter as he went back to his desserts and started rummaging around for silverware. Once I finally managed to get my breathing under control and I dove back in to my line of questioning. "Are you going to tell me why you're here with your bake sale?"

"I didn't know what kind of dessert you liked." He pulled open a few drawers until he found the one he needed and pulled out a couple of forks.

No one wanted to get to know someone—me, my brain whispered—that bad. I didn't know what to do with his outpour of affection.

For years, I worked long hours, filling my time with a career I was good at because maybe then I'd finally be worth all the trouble my parents went through to come to the States. Any free time I had I spent with the same two people because I didn't want to have to open myself up to anyone new and possibly face rejection. I did everything I could think of to be the person you don't think of because as much as I craved being seen in my career, I'm hopelessly terrified of being truly known in any other aspect of life.

But Levi stood in my kitchen, drunk on a Tuesday night with more desserts than I could count because he missed me. Because he wanted to be near me, see me, bring me dessert to find out which I liked best because he didn't already know the answer, and suddenly I felt more uncomfortable than I knew possible.

"Well?" He stepped back and waited.

What harm could come from him knowing a few, inconsequential facts about me? "Chocolate, anything chocolate, " I answered. "I'm a firm believer that fruit on dessert should be a punishable offense."

Levi laughs before sifting through a few plastic containers, pulling one from the bottom of the bag. "You're in luck," he proclaimed, turning to me with a a timid smile on his face and what looked to be a simple piece of chocolate cake. He flicked open the lid and stabbed the spongy dessert with a fork, but instead of handing the whole thing over, he simply lifted the bite of cake to my mouth.

Clearly he was waiting for me to acquiesce to his display of...affection? Was this what he thought would work? What he thought he needed to do in order to worm his way past my icy heart, ply me with grocery store cake and soft smiles?

And what did it say about me that it was kinda working?

"I'm waiting, Amore."

I found my tipping point, and it was that stupid fucking nickname.

Leaning forward, I closed my lips around the fork, leaving it clean when I pulled back and never took my eyes off him as I chewed the mediocre dessert.

We had what was supposed to be an easy, casual deal between two people. But I was slowly creeping toward a cliff I had never encountered before and I didn't know whether to jump or scramble back from the edge as fast as possible.

TWENTY-ONE

Levi

"Do I really have to do this?" My voice took on a whine I hadn't heard since I had to beg my sisters to tell me where they hid all my toys growing up. I gazed at my reflection in the oversized mirror at the barbershop. The plastic coat chaffed my neck as I caught Lola's wide smile in the mirror, eagerly nodding her head up and down. Reluctantly, I tugged the purple tie out of my hair and ran my hand through the strands one last time.

"It grows back, don't be a baby. I don't know why you kept it long in the first place."

My palms were slick against the armrest of the chair as Lola left to go wait in the front of the shop. I nodded at the barber to start because she was right, it was *just* hair.

Methodical snips of the scissors echoed in my ears as I watched the strands fall to the ground. Every snip brought me closer to a panic attack.

Forty-five minutes and more product than I cared to have in my hair later, Lola and I were back in the car. Sunday dinner was not a staple in our family like it was when we were growing up but every once in a while, our mother decided she missed us all at once and we would get summoned for dinner.

Lola prattled on about the last minute wedding details on our drive home, before turning her questions onto me. "Have you finished the speech?" she asked while staring at her phone.

"Uh," I stuttered out, and she glared at me.

All six of my sisters were bridesmaids in her wedding and our nieces were the flower girls. I would have happily stood by her side or by Chase's, but she surprised me by asking me to officiate. She told me nobody knew her better, not because I was her brother, but as her best friend. It was kind of hard to argue with that type of logic when it made your throat constrict.

"Levi."

"Lola," I mocked.

"I know you'll do great, just don't leave it to the last minute, okay? This isn't one of your English papers you can finish on a whim an hour before it's due." She laughed at her own joke from the passenger side of the car.

The gravel crunched under my tires as I pulled into our parents' driveway thirty minutes later. Lola hopped out immediately and bounded toward the front door, scooping up our youngest niece from the front yard on her way. Her tiny squeals of happiness rang out into the open air and I could hear Lola announce our arrival from the door.

Sunday dinners, when we did have them, never bothered me but for some reason as I dragged my feet toward the door, something felt like it was missing and every step closer I had to remind myself it was because of her.

But it couldn't be because of her.

That would be too real.

Carina had always been clear that a relationship was not part of her plan.

That didn't stop the want from building inside of me, and how every moment I spent near her, it seemed to expand, taking up all the room I had in my chest. It was kind of an awful feeling I was willing to deal with because even parts of her were better than none at all.

I sucked in a deep breath before I walked into the house. The second I stepped over the threshold the noise took over every single one of my senses. It seemed to be coming from every corner and crevice of the house, when there were sixteen people it was bound to get loud and stay loud.

A chorus of "Uncle Levi" was shouted and I turned just in time to catch both my nieces as they flew into my arms. My nephew followed on clumsy toddler legs, knocking into my knees before falling backwards. The girls screeched as I spun them in a fast circle in the entryway. "Again, again," they demanded in unison.

"Don't even think about it, Levi," Laura scolded. I turned to see her call out from the dining room with her hands on her hips, looking very much like a mother. "Remember how the last time you spun them one too many times, they threw up all over the carpet?"

"Sorry, girls, Mom's right." I pulled them in tight and they squealed again before I set them back down. I bent down further and hoisted up my nephew who threw his chubby little arms around my neck. "Hey, buddy," I said as I ruffled his hair before I set him back down.

Lena pulled me in for a hug as I passed her on my way to find my parents. "Be careful, Mom's really on one tonight," she whispered. And she was right. The second I stepped into the kitchen, her arms were around me pulling me down to her level so she could squeeze the life out of me.

I forgot how much hugging happened when we were all together.

"Oh, you're here, Levi. I've missed you so much," she croaked out.

"Why are you crying? Is someone dead?" I laughed in an attempt to lighten whatever mood she was in. She swatted my arm as my name rang out as the rest of my family acknowledged that I was there.

"Don't say things like that, no one's dead, Levi."

"Then why are you crying like someone died?"

"Who died?" My sister's husband called out while my sister Lydia also asked why no one told her someone died. I tried to stifle my laugh but the way my mom whipped around trying to shush and reassure everyone no one had died made it too much to handle.

"No one's dead. Jesus, Levi, look what you started. I wasn't crying, it's just been so long since everyone was home that I got overwhelmed with emotions." She threw her hands up in the air as my dad came around and hugged her from behind and planted a kiss on her cheek.

"Don't let these ungrateful kids spoil your night, lovebug." His affection was something I grew up watching and while we all gave them a hard time for it, there's something about seeing your parents together and knowing they're soulmates that made you feel all mushy inside.

A new chorus of "ew"s and "get a room" rang out, and it's times like these that I really missed being with my family. We all spilled into the dining room; the kids ran circles around the table while we piled food onto our plates. The only form of conversation was all of us talking at once, talking over each other in a slightly higher volume in order to be heard. But as the noise grew louder, it felt more and more like home.

My mom spoke up again with tears welling up in her eyes that had half my sisters shaking their head. "I am so happy you are all here. All we're missing is Chase," she said while looking glassy eyed at Lola.

"Okay, Mom." Her eye roll could be seen from my seat at the opposite end of the table. "He'll be here soon, and then I'm getting married!" she exclaimed and the table erupted around us in cheers.

With the amount of love and affection my parents had poured into us, their children, growing up was nothing short of a miracle. Even with six of us and just the two of them, never did it feel like they played favorites. They celebrated every one of our triumphs with such enthusiasm that for the longest time I thought all families were like ours. Loving, caring, and yes, nosey, but with the best intentions it was easy to overlook the intrusions done out of love.

Their chatter faded to background noise as I slid my phone from my pocket. Being around my family and their spouses was prodding something in my chest to reach out to Carina.

Hi

I was surprised to see how fast those three little dots appeared at the bottom of my screen. I stared at my phone, breath in my chest waiting for her reply, until my sister said my name.

"Levi, what are you doing?" Laura propped her head into her hands and stared me down from across the table.

"None of your business." These people really had no boundaries.

"Who are you texting?" she asked while leaning in to get a better look at my phone. My head dropped against the chair as that had peeked everyone's interest. Rounds of "who are you talking to", "who's 'her'", and "ooo"s ricocheted around the table. At least my dad had the decency to try and tell them to leave me alone.

"He's talking to *the* girl." Lola leaned further into my space to steal a glance at my phone. "She hasn't texted him back though."

I shoved the device in my front pocket. "Oh my god, there's such a thing as privacy, you know?"

Lola stuck her tongue out and went back to eating. It wasn't until I locked eyes with my mom that I knew I getting out of this conversation was unlikely. My phone buzzed in my pocket and I wasted no time fishing it back out, to which half the table snickered.

Hi

My thumbs hovered over the letters. I actually don't know why I texted her other than she was on my mind.

Are you busy tonight?

I could free up some time

Good, I'll be over soon

My mother's voice broke through the flow of thoughts showing me exactly how Carina and I were going to use the time she freed up for me. "Tell me about the woman you're bringing to the wedding." She lifted her fork back up to her mouth to take a bite casually, as if she had just asked me about the weather like there wasn't a table full of people who had been waiting to ask the same question.

It's not that I didn't want to talk about her, it's actually the one thing I was dying to do but I was afraid once I started, I might not ever stop. I could talk forever about her drive and ambition, about the way she talked with her hands when she was passionate. Which seemed to be a lot of the time. Or the way her blonde hair shined a bit like gold in the sun and the way I lose myself when I looked at her but in a way that made me feel like I'd finally found a missing piece of myself.

"She's...everything. I think you will all really like her." My honesty didn't surprise me but the silence that fell around me let me know everyone else was taken aback. I rubbed my hand along my jaw while I waited for someone to speak up. I would've taken anyone's response because the absence of noise was starting to freak me out.

"Well I can't wait," a soft voice announced and I looked up to see my sister Lena beaming. She offered me a small smile before steering the conversation away from me.

We all cleaned up the kitchen with little to no injuries and luckily no one pressed me further regarding Carina.

The drive back to Farivale was done in record time and I soon found myself knocking on her door. I bounced up onto my toes waiting for her to answer when the door swung open. I took a step forward, aching to touch her when a look of horror flashed across her face.

"What happened, what's wrong." Sheer panic swept through me as I crowded her personal space and pushed myself through her doorway but she just kept staring. I walked her backwards into her apartment waiting for her to answer me.

"What did you do to your hair?" she whined, sounding a lot like me when I was in the barber chair trying to get out of cutting it. Both of my hands instinctively went to my head and I carded my fingers through the shorter locks before they fell back down to my sides. She genuinely looked hurt and I forced out a laugh.

"Lola wanted it short for the wedding."

She took a step closer and all the air was sucked out of the room, her touch was feather light and my eyes dropped closed as her fingers raked through where my hands just were. "Do you not like it?" I asked and I was suddenly worried about what she thought of me.

"No, I do." I think she was trying to convince herself with the statement. "I just really like your long hair. Do you think you'll grow it back out after the wedding?" she asked, hopeful, and I dipped down to place a quick kiss on her lips before answering.

The way she melted into me in that brief moment dissolved any hope I had for keeping my feelings to myself.

"If you want me to, I will. I'll grow it long, cut it all off, wear it in braids. Whatever you want, whatever you need, tell me and I'll give it to you." I hauled her up into my arms as her legs wrapped themselves around my back and I walked further into her home.

"You keep saying things like that, Levi, and it makes it real hard for me to stay away from you."

"Then don't, stay close. Stay as close as you can get, *Amore*."

We didn't get very far before I pressed her into her couch. She laughed as I nuzzled into her neck and pressed my lips down the column of her throat. I was completely and utterly fucked, but I wouldn't have had it any other way.

TWENTY-TWO

Levi

CARINA WOULD BE AT the office any minute, but I was stuck in the world's longest line at Renaissance, praying someone didn't get to the last blueberry scone before me.

Paying attention to the little details that made up Carina had been my favorite pastime for so long that I barely questioned myself on why I was pushing through the glass doors into the coffee shop before work. I knew this mediation meeting would call for scones.

The little things were easy to figure out, anyone paying the slightest bit of attention would have noticed soon enough. But I wanted to know everything.

I wanted to know what thoughts formed in her brilliant mind when she woke up in the morning. If her dreams extended further than what she'd already accomplished. Did she want a husband and kids, or was she was like me and not quite sure how she wanted her life to end up?

Sure, maybe there was a chance I would never find out, but something in my bones told me that wasn't true.

"I don't care, I'm not handing over anything they asked for." A gruff voice growled from behind me.

Normally I wasn't a nosey person but without even knowing who he was talking to, I immediately was on their side. This guy sounded like an ass.

We all shuffled forward in the line when his voice grew a bit louder. "I told you if you don't do something about her, about both of them, then I will. Bring something to the table that I can sign today so it doesn't have to come to that. "

God, this guy was the worst. I was next in line but I felt like I had to turn and get a glimpse of him before I left.

"Morning, can I get the last blueberry scone, please?"

Before the barista lifted her hand toward the case the dick behind me let out a disgruntled groan. "Did you say the last scone?" His tone indignant and harsh. As he came into my view, I wasn't surprised at all by what I saw. Clocking his thousand dollar suit, greased back hair and golden watch gleaming in the sun filtering through the cafe, he was a textbook asshole. "Listen, man, I only come to this place for the scones, you wouldn't mind if I just got this one, would you?"

My face pulled into a grimace because, yes, I do fucking mind. Who was this guy?

"Sorry, man," I half apologized as the worker handed over the brown bag, which he watched like a hawk then muttered under his breath about how ridiculous I was being. Dude needed to find a mirror and take a good hard look at the douche staring back at him. Our interaction lasted seconds, a minute at max, and I already knew everything I needed to know. This guy thought the world owed him something, and he has probably used money to make sure he was always on top of it.

I paid and flew back to the office, arriving right before the meeting was set to take place. Carina was pacing the length of the window in her office when I found her, folder in hand and talking through points out loud. The plan was to sit the brown bag on her desk and walk out. I got half of that plan out before she stopped me.

"What is that?" she questioned immediately, stopping in her tracks.

She was a little scary when she was in the zone, I almost didn't want to answer. "Breakfast." Honesty seemed to work best with her.

The folder hit the table with a thwack, throwing me off a bit. "You're a life saver, I forgot to eat this morning," she said as she picked up the bag and pulled out the pastry.

Her body stilled as she registered what was in the bag, her eyes flicked toward me then back at her hands.

"Why did you bring me this?"

If I told her she would know just how much I watched her, knew her, obsessed over her. I opened my mouth to answer but it took a second. My tongue darted out to wet my lips and my heart started to hammer in my chest, begging to show itself to her.

"You eat blueberry scones before trials and big meetings."

"I do, but—"

This was my chance, and maybe it was terrible timing but something had to give.

"I wasn't done. You like blueberry scones before big meetings, your daily coffee order is a soy brown sugar latte, and when you're bored, you doodle on your notepads. Nothing particular, just lines and swirls, and when you're really concentrating, a little line forms right here." My thumb rubbed against the skin between her eyebrows, smoothing the crease that was deepening the longer I spoke.

Her lips parted, surprised I knew anything about her at all.

"I know you a lot about you, Carina, but it's all superficial, things any-one who paid enough attention would know. I want to know everything about you, even the things you're too afraid to say out loud, if you'd let me."

I'd always been slow to build romantic connections with people. Being outgoing and friendly with everyone didn't always translate into being close to someone, but it never felt like that with Carina. With her, everything was easy for me; the connection, the feelings, the want, desire, passion, simplicity.

Her fingers reached out and tangled into mine, I felt her pull but before I could sway her direction, Abby's voice preceded her into the office and Carina jumped like a live wire, pulling herself away from me. For a split second, Abby's eyes narrowed, glaring at the little space in-between us, and then it was gone. Carina and I were back to being a secret.

"Everyone's here, are you ready?" she tentatively asked.

Finally, she took a bite of the pastry and nodded.

———

"My client is willing to sign the papers today," Ian Wheeler announced seconds after telling Carina none of the records she requested would be produced.

A collective silence fell over the room. Carina kept her gaze trained on Ian, and I looked over at Kelly, whose fingers gripped the arms of her chair and was staring at her soon-to-be ex-husband, who in not a shocking turn of events was also the guy from the cafe earlier. Kelly described her husband as a quiet controlling type, the type of man who would go to any length to get what he wanted while keeping his hands clean.

To everyone's surprise, Kelly was the first to speak. "Why?" A simple question that could have a thousand different answers, all of which he would likely refuse to answer.

I wondered for a moment what they were like when they were in love. Did he bring her coffee in the morning and remember the exact way she liked it? When they would walk hand in hand through stores, did he ever keep his hand on the small of her back after she broke away because he couldn't bear not touching her? Did they whisper about the depths of their love for one another as they drifted to sleep?

"Do you want me to sign or not, Kelly?" he snapped, causing her to physically recoil.

If they did, I wondered how two people went from all of that to barely being able to speak to each other, and how do I make sure I never ended up that way?

"What are the terms?"

Ian flipped a page over from the stack in front of him. "Alimony and child support are outlined in the first section, along with the housing Ms. Leon requested." A page from his stack slid across the table. "Custody in the next, with a paternity test at birth, non-negotiable," he tacked on as Carina's mouth opened to argue.

She swiped the paper from the middle of the table and without glancing up asked for the room to confer with Kelly. I meant to leave with everyone but two pairs of feminine eyes stared at me until I sat back down. Kelly and I waited as Carina thumbed through the offer.

It was moments like this I wished she wasn't so good at her job. Nothing on her face gave away to what she was reading; was it good, bad, too much, too little?

"Its not the worst offer in the world but it's—"

"Yes, whatever it is, tell them yes. I want to sign today, I want *out* Carina." Desperation escaped with her words, a plea to be free was all too hard to ignore.

"Kelly, this is barely what you asked for, what you deserve. Alimony of two thousand a month for the next five years, child support five thousand, I mean these are no small numbers but Ben is worth hundreds of millions, this is a slap in the face to you and your daughter," Carina stated, trying to get her to see reason.

"It doesn't matter, the money, the house, none of it matters, I just want out."

"Kelly, please." Softness she normally didn't exhibit snuck into her words. Carina swiveled her chair to face Kelly and I felt like I was intruding on something private, something, that even though I'd been a part of, wasn't meant for me. "He's hiding something, I can feel it. It's the only reason they'd come and be so willing to settle. We were onto something with requesting his financials. As his wife, what's his is yours in this state, communal property is a thing for a reason. If you sign today, there is no coming back and arguing for more, this would be it and it's not enough."

"You don't understand, if I don't sign now, he'll..." The rest of her words stayed in her mouth. Kelly's dark hair swayed back and forth with a soft shake of her head. "He will never let me go, and I will die in that house if I stay with him."

I watched as she reached for Kelly's hand and her voice broke over the next set of words. "I would never let that happen. If he's said something to you or done something, we can help you." I had never heard Carina so soft spoken before. It was mesmerizing to watch and my heart ached over the whole situation and I had never felt so helpless.

"Please, let me help you," Carina pleaded again.

For a moment I thought she was going to agree, but she didn't and no amount of convincing from Carina would sway her.

The other party filtered back in.

Ben smirked as he signed the papers.

Tears gathered in Kelly's eyes when it was her turn.

And Carina and I only looked at each other once everyone left.

"Do you think it's always like that?" I asked, rolling my chair closer to her. Someone had shut the door behind them, leaving us to ourselves.

"Divorce? No not really, but when you're made of money, I didn't really expect anything less from him."

"No, not divorce." I nudged her foot with mine, no particular reason other than I needed to touch her. Even if it was only for a second, even if it needed to be a secret, even if she never realized that she was it for me. "Relationships in general. Do you think they all have an expiration date? That most people aren't meant to last unless you're, I don't know, soulmates sounds funny. I guess I don't really know what I'm trying to say, but I've seen more people break up than I've seen stay together so I was thinking maybe there's no point. Maybe you've had it right all along. No relationships, no dating, just going with what makes you feel good and not worrying about trying—"

"Decker, you're rambling," she interjected, rolling her chair closer to me. Her hand landed on my knee and that was all I needed. The helplessness I had felt dissipated. "I've been doing this a long time and to be honest love isn't everything. It's not a cure all, save all solution. You can love someone with every fiber of your being but that doesn't mean they can't grow into someone you hardly recognize one day." Her hand still hadn't moved, her fingers tightened around my knee. "And sometimes people you never expected to be part of your life end up being..." her eyes searched mine, trying to find the right words, "exactly what you need."

TWENTY-THREE

Carina

GOLDEN LEAVES CRUNCHED UNDER my shoes as I jogged through the early morning fog on my last mile of the trail before looping back around to town. Main Street was still sleepy this early on Sundays. I sped by the closed boutiques with their dark windows and impeccably dressed mannequins, and Vince's Pizza's neon signs still glowed through the mist as an elderly couple walked into Renaissance Cafe up ahead.

These were my favorite mornings. Ones where I answered to no one but myself, where I didn't stress over work or having to appease my parents' expectation of me. My head was free and clear from the constant buzzing that played on a loop like unwanted Christmas music too soon in the year.

Deep breaths, in through the nose and out through the mouth. It's methodical, required little effort and it's the only time I felt truly like myself.

A slick layer of sweat covered my body as I climbed the stairs toward my apartment with my hands resting on my head to regain my breathing. My mind was in another world as I slipped into my place but movement from my couch caught my attention. There was definitely a person on my couch that wasn't there when I left. My heartbeat rushed to my ears, and I had about half of a terrible plan to fight off a burglar when a head of dark red hair popped up from the couch.

"Not that I'm not happy to see you but what are you doing here so early?' I kicked off my shoes and curled up on the opposite end of the couch from Lennon. "And is Abby here too?" Where you found one sister, you were bound to find the other.

"She is." Abby yelled from what I assumed was the bathroom before she appeared and squished herself between us.

What I loved most about Lennon and Abby was the comfort we found in doing absolutely nothing together. The comfortable silence we fell into knowing just the presence of each other was enough. The sisters had an obvious bond that seemed to defy any logic that I possessed about what it meant to be a sibling. I assumed you felt some sort of bond when you shared blood with another person. I equated it to what I felt for my parents and vice versa; we loved each other yes but if I was honest, that's where I thought their feelings for me ended. It felt almost like an obligation.

But Lennon and Abby shared something that went beyond just the pull of familial ties and shared blood. The love they had for each other boiled down to the simple idea that come hell or high water, they would always be there for each other.

Being an only child wasn't something I thought of often, it was something that just was. My parents loved me, yes, they raised me well and provided for me the best they could. But in our home there was me, and then there was them. An invisible line that separated us.

When you are forced to leave your home, your country and everything that you loved all because you were pregnant, I didn't blame them for sticking to each other, but I didn't ask to be here and I certainly didn't ask to be the reason they had to move in the first place.

For years I often wondered what my life would have been like if they would've stayed in Crespano del Grappa and worked out whatever ridiculous issues their families had between them. Would I have ended up the same version of myself, as if we are predestined to be a certain way? Or could I have possibly ended up a warmer version of me, one where I didn't reject any semblance of a relationship or notion of love out of fear of having to give up something up in return?

My parents loved each other and it costed them their families.

My parents loved me and I costed them their home.

I once thought I loved a man who made me pay for our relationship by giving up the parts of myself that I loved the most.

All love did was break down the things we loved, little by little, and that price was too steep for me.

We all sat for a moment longer in the silence of the still early morning. I closed my eyes for a moment and basked in the warmth from the family I had found in them. Then Lennon shifted, breaking me from the moment. "So you two are here this early because...why?" I asked.

"I dropped Theo off at the airport this morning. It's his first overnight trip since the accident and I didn't want to just sit around the house all day."

"So you came to sit around my house?"

Lennon's foot shot out and kicked me in the side.

"Something like that," Abby chimed in.

I was surprised by how guilty I felt by not telling them anything about Levi. These two women shared everything with me, highs, lows and every mundane moment in-between. So why couldn't I bring myself to tell them I might have gone and fell for Levi Decker?

Oh fuck.

Did I love him? Did I repress feelings to the point I couldn't decipher when I fell?

No, that wasn't right, love didn't feel like this. It wasn't consuming me, or changing me. He wasn't on my mind all day every day, I didn't feel like I needed to be a certain, anything for him. Surely it wasn't love between us.

Although, I had nothing to compare it to, all I knew was I had never felt this way about anyone.

When the hell did that happen?

I thought I'd actually become sick.

The day was lazy, by noon we had watched more episodes of trash TV than we could have counted. Abby just left to pick us up mid day coffees, leaving Lennon and I to ourselves. Since reconnecting with Theo there's a new side to her. She was more radiant, kinder, and it had everything to do with being in love.

"What's it like being with Theo?" She turned her head to look back at me, her eyebrow arched.

"What do you mean?"

Asking for personal advice wasn't my strong suit. "After Camden, you were adamant that you would never fall in love again." I expected a look of pain to flash in her eyes but I was surprised to find nothing except a small smile.

"And you want to know what it's like falling in love when you thought it was something you swore you would never do?" She sat up straighter.

My face pinched. I should have kept my mouth shut, I wasn't falling in love with him, that would've been uncalled for but I could feel myself softening to him in a way that had taken me by surprise.

"It's only a question," I said pointedly.

She raised an eyebrow at me, and a sly little smile appeared at her lips. "If you say so."

"Loving Theo didn't come easy. It was almost tortuous, the back and forth of forcing myself not to fall, then teetering on the edge and wishing I had the courage to jump. I wish his accident wasn't the driving force that sent me flying, literally, into telling him that I loved him but once I did, I was sorry I didn't do it sooner."

"Is it worth it?"

"Yes," she answered immediately, no room for hesitation. "I know you don't do relationships or whatever is it that you say, but love is always worth it."

She turned back toward the TV and left me to my thoughts.

Falling in love must feel like jumping from an airplane. Adrenaline coursed through your veins tangling with fear and excitement. The free fall was a beautiful act of trust, where you knew that all you had to do was pull the string to let the parachute out and you'd glide back down to earth, safe and sound.

But what if it didn't open? What if you fell only to be met with a hard disastrous end?

Love didn't seem worth it when I took in the risk to reward ratio.

TWENTY-FOUR

Carina

"Do you want to go to dinner?" The words broke through the silence of my office, punching through to my nervous system. Looking up at the intrusion, I saw Levi standing in front of me.

Nothing was different about him but Lennon's words seemed to paint him in a new light, not quite golden but close.

The words 'I'm busy' were on the tip of my tongue, inching their way out until I swallowed them. "Sure." Surprise flashed across his face and the hope that was dwindling in them faded into excitement.

"Really?" he questioned.

"Don't make me change my mind, Decker. What time?"

He looked down at his watch and pursed his lips out. "Abby said you were finishing up some work on the Leon case, so how's seven?" His eyes glanced up to meet mine and I was stuck staring. Dark, thick eyelashes casted a shadow turning his normally golden eyes into beautiful burnt honey.

Weightless euphoria swept through me. Perfection is what I strived for but I liked to hide within my accolades and accomplishments, showing only what I wanted to people but somehow Levi saw beneath that. He saw the hard work and dedication I put forth in order to get the results I craved. He peeked behind the facade and instead of shutting the curtain, I wanted to pull it wide open and show him what was hidden to most.

"Seven's good," I cautiously replied. Fluttering erupted in the base of my heart and I feared if I said anything further, the pesky little butterflies might just show what I wasn't ready to admit.

He ducked back out, shutting the door and I was left to turn back to my work. I sucked in a deep breath dropping my head to rest my forehead in the palms of my hands. The Leon case was turning out to be more difficult than I wanted, or than it needed to be. I could handle hard cases, I thrived off the complexity of family law cases. But I knew what I saw, and I couldn't shake the feeling that he would not go quietly.

My fingers tapped out another email and I zoned out to the methodical clicks of my keyboard and I did this for the next few hours until Levi's head ducked back in. "You ready, or do you need more time?" My shoulders softened, the answer was yes to both, technically, but I stood to gather my things, pulled to the magnetic force he produced. My purse dangled from my hand, "I'm ready, Levi," I said with a smile.

Finding a decent restaurant late on a weekday was hard in Fairvale, which was why I wasn't surprised when he pulled into the parking lot of River House. The waitress walked us to the back of the restaurant placing the menus down at a two-top next to the large bay windows. Levi pulled out my seat causing me to pause. *Was this a date?* He said 'do you want to go to dinner,' he didn't ask me out on a date, but the chair pulling and waiting for me to sit before moving to his seat was telling me otherwise.

He looked so unbothered, as if we did this all the time. His eyes tracked over the words as he scanned the menu and I barely had the conscious thought to pick mine up. There were patio lights strung above the outside dining, and normally that's where I would have preferred to sit but the frigid November air wouldn't allow it. The cloudless night allowed the moon to sparkle and bounce off the top of the river below and I sat entranced until Levi cleared his throat.

I snapped back to the table while he lifted one solitary eyebrow up at me. "Is this a date?" Beating around the bush was never my style. His laugh came out as an almost bark while he clutched his chest, making my question seem foolish. My face remained stoic as I waited for a response.

"Oh, you're serious." He reeled in his amusement. "No... I mean you don't date, so no this isn't a date." A strand of hair fell in front of his eye, he lifted his hand to push it back into place while his eyebrows pulled inward. "Did you want this to be a date?"

"No," I replied quickly. "I just thought... Forget I asked."

He didn't press the matter further, and halfway through our meal it was like it never happened.

A sharp ring pierced the air from his pocket. He reached in without looking and silenced it, giving me his full attention. Until it rang again immediately after. "You can see who's calling, I don't mind."

His lips pursed when reading the name. "It's Laura." He looked up at me in question.

"Don't not answer on my account."

He paused, before answering, almost as if he hoped the phone would stop ringing on its own. The other end of the phone was loud and he was clearly annoyed by whatever was being said.

"I can't, I'm busy right now." More conversation from the other side I couldn't hear. "Doing things, Laura." The waitress stopped by to top off our drinks when he looked back at me. "Yeah, she's here." There was a questioning tone to his reply, and I had no idea what she said to him but his eyebrows shot to his hairline. "Okay, okay, just hang on and I'll try to be there soon."

Disappointment took up a spot in the pit of my stomach at his words. The call ended and he slid the phone back into his pocket. My fork stabbed into one of my last bites with a bit too much force. This wasn't a date, this was dinner and he was nothing but a co-worker who I sometimes slept with. I should not have had an issue with him needing to go somewhere after. "Do you have plans after this?"

"No, this was about it."

"My sisters are all about to take Lola out for her bachelorette party, Lena's husband was supposed to stay with the girls but got called into work." I saw where the story was going and the disappointment morphed into a soft feeling of vulnerability. His family came first. I could see that even from the little interaction I'd had with them, but I wanted him for tonight. "Do you want to come with me?"

Maybe I didn't know where it was going. I expected to be dropped off at home and forgotten like the groceries you buy and swear you'll eat, only for them to wilt and die a week later. Surprise overtook my face that I wasn't prepared for.

I wasn't sure I liked kids. I'd never been around them but still they looked sticky and that never meshed well with my outfits.

The desire for me to say yes leeched out of him and across the table. His thumb drummed against the table's wooden edge as he waited for a response.

"It's only fair, you helped me out at the restaurant."

Cornelia was only forty-five minutes away but the city moved at a faster pace there—it might as well have been a different realm. I pulled my car to the side of the street, where all the houses seemed to be built on top of each other, with no room for lawns or the chance to escape nosy neighbors.

There's a faint sound of music coming from the house in front of me after I got out of the car. The wariness of showing up to a house full of people I didn't really know shuffled through my veins. There's no one I was close to that I shared blood with, no aunts or uncles, no cousins, and my parents, well there was the divide between us.

With every step I took toward the porch, the more I began to shut down, and with every step I took, my defenses slipped into place. How could I possibly connect with a family that would bend over backwards for each other?

Right as my foot hit the porch, Levi's hand brushed against mine, tangling my fingers into his. He tugged, pulling my body flus with his side. "I appreciate you coming with me." He dipped his head low and pressed his lips to mine. It was sweet, coating my denial in a sickly sense of belonging. I didn't want him to pull away, but then the door opened wide and music poured out of the house along with the mingling of voices.

"Ewwww," two voices rang out as I jerked out of his embrace. "Uncle Levi, that's gross." I looked down to see two of the cutest little girls I had ever laid eyes on. They had dark hair, but not as deep as Levi and his sisters, it was more of a dark chocolate brown, that was pulled back into pigtail braids with matching bows in each. Everything about them matched, down to the bunny slippers on their feet.

The older one leapt forward off the porch into Levi's unsuspecting arms, forcing the air out of his chest in a loud 'oof'. I thought they were twins but once she was closer, I could tell she must have been a bit older than her sister, but not my much. "Are you his girlfriend?" she asked while staring at me with wide amber eyes that matched Levi's. The other sister snickered behind her hand.

I shook my head. "No, we're just friends."

"Why?"

"Why what?"

I wasn't around kids much, mainly due to the lack of people I knew with them but I could see the appeal. Not for me, but I could see it.

"Why are you not his girlfriend?"

For a tiny human, she was awfully persistent.

"Does he make you eat your vegetables? He made me eat them and I hate them. I wouldn't want him to be my boyfriend either."

"Okay, that's enough," Levi cut in before he swooped down and hoisted them up while their squeals pierced my ears. With a look back at me he cocked his head to the side for me to follow.

"Don't worry, they'll love you."

Them loving me wasn't what I was worried about.

TWENTY-FIVE

Levi

Not only did my body ache in places it shouldn't, but my brain hurt from trying to come up with ways to entertain my nieces for a few hours. The night wasn't awful, but I was pretty sure it cemented the idea that I never wanted children.

My body melted into the couch once I threw myself down, thankful for the quiet settling in around the house. "They're finally asleep." I yawned around the words and dropped my head onto Carina's shoulder.

Quietly, she chuckled before pressing her lips to the top of my head, and in that slight gesture my mood shifted entirely. It was such a small, simple act and yet colossal at the same time. And I wondered, at what point did I fall in love with her and not realize it?

My sisters fawned over her. All of them firing off questions which she fielded without batting an eye. By the end of it, they were all asking for her to join them and leave me behind, and she was close to taking them up on the offer. Seeing her fold into my family like she was always meant to be there, tugged at strings that held my heart together.

No one ever mentioned I was the only one without someone to share my life with, but it was always there. I'd be the one at Christmas in pajamas not matching anyone else or marking one in the guest column for events. It was just a fact that lingered around our dinners and holidays like an annoying family member you couldn't get rid of. But sitting here with her made me want all those stupid trivial things I'd been avoiding for the past however many years.

"Your nieces are adorable and you're great with them. I can tell why your sister calls you when she needs help." Her fingers carded through my hair as I shimmied down to lay my head in her lap. There really wasn't an angle where she didn't look good, I noted as I stared up into her eyes.

"They are. My sister's really lucky."

"Do you think you want kids?" The words slipped out causing me to wince in embarrassment. Her fingers stilled in my hair. I cracked one eye open to see her staring straight ahead.

"I don't think so," she admitted with a quiet voice and my chest swelled. Maybe we were more alike than we knew. Her fingers picked back up threading through my hair, lost in thought almost. "I'm an only child, my parents had to come here when my mom was pregnant with me. I didn't grow up with siblings or a large family and it was kind of lonely. I know I wouldn't want to do that to a kid of my own, you know?"

"You said they had to come here, did they not want to?" There was more that I wanted to ask... Like how she envisioned her future, but it didn't seem like the right time.

"Not everyone wants to move to America, Levi." She gave a little pull that sent shockwaves through me. She seemed to go somewhere else before answering and she went back to staring at the wall in front of her. "My parents are from Crespano del Grappa, it's a small town a little over an hour from Verona. And much like Romeo and Juliet, my mom's family and my dad's family did not get along. I don't even think my parents knew why, just that they were never meant to be friendly let alone fall in love and absolutely under no circumstances was my mom supposed to get pregnant out of wedlock." Her chest heaved as she said the words, as if she couldn't believe it. "They left everything they had to come here, their friends and family, their language and culture. All because they loved each other. I can't even begin to fathom being in a relationship let alone being so in love that I would leave everything behind for one person." Her fingers moved from my head, tracing down my arm to where her hair tie still sat on my wrist, the one I'd worn without fail since I took it from her.

Another spike in my heart reminded that we were not together.

"Could you?" she asked.

"Could I, what?"

"Leave your family for a woman because you loved her?"

It wasn't something I'd ever thought about but at that very moment it crossed my mind, if it was for her I'd leave everything behind.

"No. I guess not," I lied. "But they didn't leave just for them, they probably left for you too, right?"

She scoffed at my question.

"No they left to be together, I just happened to be a product of them being in love." She looked crestfallen at the admission, while she absentmindedly scratched at the fabric of the couch.

Carina was in control but as she sat there, I was given access to a part of her I never knew existed, a softer, more vulnerable version of her. A part of herself she didn't share with anyone and I wanted more than anything to be the first to explore that side. And I would, but at a different time.

She must be of the same mind, because she quickly steered the conversation away from herself. "You seem really close with your family."

"I am, they're a bit intense all together but they mean well."

"Your nieces are funny for small humans."

I snorted. "Small humans? You don't spend a lot of time around kids do you?"

"I'm an only child that has no extended family around, so you would be correct."

I liked this part of our *not* relationship. Getting to know her little by little, where the moments weren't so intense and we could relax into a rhythm that was our own. I reached up, catching a strand of her silk hair between my forefinger and thumb. "Brynn and Bailey are my favorite, they're little terrors to their parents, ridiculously funny and they get me all the best ties."

"Wait," Carina's face tipped down, golden tresses cascaded around us, blocking out everything but her. "Your nieces buy you all those ridiculous ties?" Her teeth clamped onto her bottom lip as a laugh shook her in her chest.

"Of course, you didn't think I bought frog prince ties myself did you?"

A smile erupted across her face. "Kinda." She chuckled, amusement playing in her gaze.

Before she could move out of my reach, I wrapped my hand around the back of her head and crushed her lips to mine. Excitement sang through my veins as we kissed. It started with a buzzing deep in my skin as the softness of her lips countered my demanding movements. Then the buzzing turned to bone deep desire.

Carina broke away, leaving my mouth burning for more. "I'm partial to the one with poker chips," she whispered against my lips before finally pulling back.

Moving from her side, I sat back on the couch and dragged her onto my lap, each of her knees landed on either side of me. My hands slipped past the hem of her shirt and up the expanse of her back only to drag her closer to me.

I wanted to get lost in her the way people found religion to be saved from the darkness. I would worship her body like someone would at an altar, begging for salvation and I would be redeemed even if it was only in her eyes. My fingers pushed into her skin, I needed her closer and judging by the way her hands were tugging at my shirt, so did she.

"Come closer, Amore." The endearment was effortless. I knew exactly one word in her mother tongue and never had an excuse to use it. Until her, almost as if I had always been waiting for Carina.

Her eyebrow quirked up but she leaned forward, pressing her chest against mine.

"Like this?" She challenged me, lips hovering an inch away from mine.

"Closer."

Her lips brushed against mine as she shifted on my lap, rocking into me. Her body reacted to my gentle command before she could catch herself and my head fell back in bliss.

"Is this what you want?" Her voice washed over me like a haze. Thick and sweet, desire was attached to every particle as she continued to grind on my lap.

Fuck.

"Yes," I breathed.

I wanted her.

I needed her.

It was more than this moment but she wasn't ready for that, at least not yet. I would hold out hope for as long as she needed and for now take what she was willing to give. My hand slid further up the back of her shirt as I finally claimed her mouth with mine. Within a second I had her shirt up and over her head and flipped our positions so her back was pressed into the couch.

The way her eyes widened with surprise before falling heavy with lust only spurred me one further. I pressed my lips to every inch of skin I could find. Neck, collarbone, chest, anything I could get my mouth on.

Her chest rose and fell in a rapid pace, her hands grasped at my clothes and I was more than happy to help her shed them. I was down to my boxers, her long legs wrapped around my waist as she panted into my mouth.

"Levi, please," she whined.

"Please what, Amore?" I said it once and I didn't think I'd ever stop now. I was painfully hard straining against the thin fabric of my boxers, when the door flew open.

Carina shrieked, hands planted on my chest when she shoved me with more force than I would have ever expected. I went tumbling to the floor, shoulders breaking my fall right before my head. My head whipped around to see Laura's husband step over the threshold and then freeze.

"Oh, shit," Kevin shouted with an amused tone tacked on to the end as he twisted from side to side frantically, looking anywhere that wasn't me practically naked on the ground and a woman he'd seen once at a distance scrambling to put her shirt back on. Carina shrunk behind my body in order to hide, pulling on her shirt as if a fire alarm rang out.

Embarrassment stabbed at me like a red hot poker had been stuffed down my throat. It was also the quickest way to go from hard to limp in under a second.

Kevin trained his eyes on the ceiling and swatted his hand around until it found the edge of the door and flicked it shut. "Having a good night, Levi?"

I snorted out a laugh. "I was about to." Carina shoved me from behind. "What, it's true." I flashed her a smile from over my shoulder that she only glared at.

"Do you want to, I don't know, maybe get your clothes on so I can stop looking at the ceiling?" Kevin asked, an amused smirk taking over his face.

Less than a minute later and I was fully clothed and Carina's cheeks were a pretty shade of rose, but she was still hiding behind me.

"Okay, you can look."

He dropped his head, a shit eating grin blasted on his face. "Not that I'm not always happy to see you, but what are you doing here?"

"Babysitter cancelled after you got called in."

"Ah." Kevin walked over to us. "Everything with the girls go alright?" he asked, as he looked at me before flicking his gaze toward Carina.

"Oh yeah, they were great, like always."

He raised his eyebrows again, tilting his head to the side. "Are you going to introduce me to your friend?"

Carina groaned before stepping out from behind me. "Hi, I'm Carina," she introduced herself, extending her hand to him. Business Carina was front and center.

They shook hands politely as my mind tried to work out how fast I could get her back to my place. Or it was.

The door flung open and all of my sisters flooded in. Loud overlapping voices and what sounded like someone on the verge of a breakdown engulfed the room. "This cannot be happening. What kind of caterer double books a wedding and only figures it out the week before?" Lola's shrill voice pierced through the noise. "How does that happen?"

The three of us watched as all of my sisters filed in, heading straight for the couch we were hovering by without a second glance. Kevin was the first to speak. "Why are you guys back so early?"

All of their heads turned to look at us.

"You're home," Laura commented, before pushing past me, throwing her arms around his neck and kissing him like they weren't in a room full of family.

"You weren't gone long, but seemed like enough time to do some damage at the bar." He laughed as he pulled back from her.

Carina stood silent at my side, taking in the theatrics around us. I wondered what it was like for her growing up an only child. I wasn't even fazed by what was going on, one sister crying while another other tried to fix the issue, another walked past all of us and staggered to the kitchen. Everyone talked over everyone and to me it was almost relaxing, but I wondered if it was too much for her.

It was almost too much for me.

"Where am I going to find a caterer this close to the wedding? It was nearly impossible to find the one I had in the first place!" Lola was in tears and speeding down a road to inconsolable as our middle sister Lainey rubbed circles on her back.

Nobody spoke up, because what can you do two weeks before a wedding? Carina approached the group of sisters from around my back. "I can help," she announced, and as if on queue, all eyes snapped to her. "Or well my parents can at least. They should be able to pull together a menu in time for the wedding," her eyes flicked to me, "if you're interested."

Lola stood abruptly from the couch, swaying for a moment, before stepping toward Carina. "Have they catered a wedding before?"

"A few, it's not something they advertise, but they can do it."

She stepped closer, teetering on her heels, a white and glittery bride to be sash hanging off her shoulder. The short veil that was pinned to her hair when they left was clinging on to a few strands of hair. "Do you think they could make that appetizer I had when Levi and I came for dinner, the rice ball thing?" She tapped the tips of her fingers together like a toddler asking for more.

When Carina smiled at my sister, something inside of me cracked wide open and flushed my system with a warm, calming sensation. It wasn't her polite business smile, the one she would use on clients she needed to wear a mask for. No, this was tender and genuine. This was Carina at her core, jumping in to help others when they needed it most. Not because she felt like she had to but because she cared.

I loved her willingness to help.

I loved seeing her amongst my sisters without finding them intimidating or feeling like she was an outsider.

I loved everything about Carina.

Did I love her?

I wanted to; that much was glaringly obvious, but there was something blocking me from falling completely. From the beginning, she was adamant we were nothing but a way to pass the time, a secret she meant to keep behind closed doors. And if we had stayed the way she intended, I was inclined to agree. But we didn't. Whatever it was we had morphed into something entirely new.

None of what we were doing felt like it was meant to stay behind closed doors. Instead, it felt like the door was cracked, waiting for us to make our way out.

Changing her mind was the only way past her well-placed defenses and when was the last time a man was able to change Carina Pera's mind about anything, let alone her heart?

Never, was the answer.

"Arancini, absolutely."

"Oh my God, thank you." Lola flung herself into Carina's unsuspecting arms. Muscles tensed in her shoulders at the intrusion, but only for a moment before lightly placing her arms around Lola in brief hug. "Levi, your girlfriend's a life saver."

I waited for Carina to correct her but it never came.

Maybe it wouldn't be so hard after all.

TWENTY-SIX

Carina

"No, no, no, you're doing it all wrong," my father's gruff voice called out from the other side of the kitchen. I looked back in time to see him shoo Noah away with a large knife in hand, and Noah's eyes nearly doubled in size.

"Papa, leave him alone, the onions are fine."

My father tsked, waving the knife at me dismissively. Noah's eyes flitted over to me, warning alarms for help flashing in them, but there was nothing I could do. If my father said it was wrong, there was nothing you could say that would change his mind, I learned the hard way.

"Carina, are you not done yet?"

The knife in my hand slammed into the table harder than I wanted at my mother's voice. Two seconds of peace, that was all I wanted but was that possible? Absolutely not, not when I had her breathing down my neck over a simple task and my father acting like no one could chop a fucking vegetable but him.

It didn't matter that I was there to help, they somehow always made me feel like I was more trouble to have around.

"Almost, Mamma," I answered between a clenched jaw.

"Once you're done here I need you to pack the truck with all of the serving trays, and we still need to count that we have enough loaves of bread for each table, oh and—"

"I know, I'll have it all done."

"Well it would have been a lot easier if I knew you would be here tomorrow."

I resumed chopping the toppings for the salads. The quicker I got this done, the quicker I could leave. "I told you, I'm a guest at the wedding. I won't be able to help, you will be fine."

My parents were thrilled to take on a wedding, it wasn't something they did often but any opportunity to get their business name out there, they took. They said yes as soon as I asked, barely even listening to the details, but the inevitable disappointment was etched into their features once I told them I could only help the night before.

It was a look I had grown up seeing. Didn't matter how many straight A report cards I brought home or how many stoles I wore at graduation, none of that mattered if I wasn't there to help them whenever they wanted.

My mother walked away without saying another word. It would be a miracle if Noah and I ever heard the words 'thank you'. I didn't need it but it would be nice, every once in a while you know, to at least hear the words.

They loved me, that much had always been clear but sometimes knowing you're loved wasn't the same as hearing it. So I kept showing up to help them, because maybe one of these days, I'd finally hear it.

Silence lasted maybe fifteen minutes before my father was griping about how behind we all were. Noah took refuge in the refrigerator claiming he was double checking labels on the food we had already prepped.

I took a page out of his book and stepped out the back door for a moment to removed myself from the heat of the kitchen and their overbearing gaze.

The phone rang twice before he picked up. "Carina?"

"Hi."

"Is everything okay?" Panic outlined his words.

What was I doing? I never called him. I didn't know I was calling him until I heard his voice. He probably answered thinking the office was on fire or something equally as devastating.

"No, I'm fine," I rushed to say. "I'm at the restaurant helping prep for the wedding, it was getting a bit tense and," I glanced around like someone would be waiting around to catch my vulnerability on camera, "I just wanted to hear your voice."

A brief pause filled the air. "Let me start again." The line went dead and not even a second later his name was filling my phone screen with a new call. I hit answer and brought it back to my ear. "Hi, Amore," he greeted.

He had been calling me that more and more, and each time he did, it unlocked a part of me.

"Hi, Levi," I chuckled.

"Do you want to talk about it?"

"No," I said quickly. Talking about my feelings, any of them, was not my style. Talking about my feelings about my parents was off the table completely. "This is enough."

I listened to him breathe a few times, the rhythmic sound doing wonders to lower the stress I was feeling while inside. "So are you all ready for tomorrow?" I asked.

"I think so, I'm still working on the speech but other than that, I think I'm good," he said.

I suppressed an eye roll, even without anyone around to see me. He would wait until the last minute for something like that. "Your sister is getting married in less than twenty-four hours and you're not ready, how am I not surprised?"

"It'll be fine, I do my best work on a tight deadline."

I laughed into the receiver.

"Do you want to run it by me? Make sure it's up to standards?"

"No way, it's a surprise."

The door pushed open behind me, I whipped around to see my mother's pointed face waving for me to come back inside. I held up my hand, letting her know I'd be in soon. "I have to go, but I'll see you tomorrow."

"I'll find you right after the ceremony and not a second after."

"Night, Decker."

"Goodnight, Amore."

When I walked back into the building I didn't notice she was waiting in the doorway by the office, I was too busy smiling at the small illuminated screen in my palm, like an idiot. "Who were you talking to?" she questioned, arms crossed over her chest like it was an interrogation.

I clutched my phone to my chest as if she could somehow see my call log and then know everything about him. "Nobody," I answered quickly, slipping the phone into my back pocket.

She leveled a look at me and I understood why some people were afraid of me. It's in the eyes, staring at and through someone simultaneously.

"Is he the reason why you have been too busy for the restaurant?"

Was she joking right now? "Too busy for the restaurant? I have been here more over the past few weeks than ever before. Every time you've called me I have been here to help you and Papa, but did you ever stop to say thank you? No, you just call me again and demand I show up like I don't have a life."

"You have no husband or children, the least you could do is help when we need it."

"I have a career," I shrieked, finally finding my tipping point. "And an important one, I help people during the most stressful time of their life, I help women find their footing after having the rug pulled out from under them so excuse me for not dropping everything to come running when you and Papa are off doing whatever it is you're doing." I pushed past her, rage leaking from every part of me.

Did they not see me? Did they not care about all I sacrificed to help them? Would I ever be good enough for them?

"You know nothing of what we have been going through," she shot back at me, switching to Italian. Noah and my father looked up from the stations. "You think that we are beneath you because we work here, and you can't be bothered to help."

"That's absurd, I bought you this place, why would I think less of either of you for working here?"

Noah set his knife down and wisely found something to do that took him out of the kitchen. My father only watched with careful eyes.

"Yes, you bought the restaurant but you do not care about what happens here or what happens to us."

Decades of feelings were becoming harder to bite back, but why hide them, it never did me any good. "The same way you never cared to learn anything about me." When my father's hand comes down gently on my shoulder, I slink away. "Neither of you ever cared enough to get to know anything about me and what I want. It was always Carina help with this, Carina you must be available for us, Carina you can't do that you have to help us. What about me, what about what I want?"

"I don't understand where this is coming from?" The softness of my father's voice only made it harder to keep my emotions inside.

"That's my point, my whole life, it's always been you two, and then me. You two came before everything," I shouted as I stepped back again. "And I wouldn't even care that much if either of you at least once thanked me for anything I did."

My chest twisted with an unfamiliar tightness that threatened to boil over and turn me into a puddle of tears. The duality between them was a familiar one, my father's softness and my mother's hardness when they looked at me and it was like I was being pulled in two different directions. I could scoop up everything I was feeling and stuff it back inside of me, or I'd bleed out my frustrations in front of them and force them to face the damage they had inflicted on me.

"We don't have time for this." She pushed past both of us, calling Noah back into the kitchen, and went back to acting like nothing was wrong. Nothing was ever wrong in her world, not if work needed to be done.

"Do you see?" I waved my hand toward her, turning to my father. "This is what I am talking about. I am here on a Friday night after working over ten hours to make sure everything goes smoothly for you guys tomorrow and I get nothing, only some dig about how I won't be there to help tomorrow." I followed my father into the office as he shut the door quietly behind us.

I dropped into the office chair and ran my hand across my face. This couldn't have come at a worse time, but it was bound to at some point even if I was content on living my life and never addressing this with them. All I wanted to do was leave, actually all I wanted to do was find Levi.

I didn't want to have to deal with any of it, but I knew if I pushed the matter any further, it could spill into the wedding day and I wouldn't do that to Lola, not when my parents stepped in to help.

"Carina," he said, and I reluctantly turned to him. My father was a giant of a man, over six feet, burly, full of laugh lines and humor but as I looked at him, I saw none of that and I didn't know when he changed.

He was thinner, face weathered by more than the lines time etched into him, his movements slower. "Your mother doesn't mean to be harsh, you know this, but lately we've been under a lot of stress and it's been too much for her to handle on her own."

"Please don't make excuses for her, you've been doing it forever and at some point she needs to own the fact that she hates me."

I had never said that out loud. My father and I had never even had a heart to heart before. "Hey," he barked, standing up a bit straighter, although the movement was guarded. "Your mother does not hate you, she is just so used to doing everything herself that she won't ask for help, even with all that we're going through."

"What do you mean, what have you been going through?"

"It's nothing," he stated, waving me off.

I sat up in my chair. "No, don't do that, don't shut me out. What's wrong, what aren't you telling me?" I knew there was a reason I'd had help more these past couple months. More than them having meetings out of town.

He took a deep breath. "It's not a big deal, just a little issue with my heart."

That got me out of my chair. "A little issue with your heart? Your heart is pretty important, you shouldn't have any problems with it, not even little ones." My eyes swept over him as if I would find the answer pinned to his clothes.

"It started with a little fluttering every once in a while, some dizzy spells and then I collapsed at home a few months ago. Your mother has been dragging me from doctor to doctor for appointments, for answers, and I had a procedure a few weeks ago. When she asked you to cover a Saturday night shift it was because I had to stay for observation. I'm okay now, doctors are monitoring it, I'm doing better and can work in the kitchen more but your mother's been stressed with all of it and the restaurant."

My own father was sick and I didn't even notice. I was so set on how they were treating me that I barely registered how I was treating them or the way I was distancing myself from them. "Papa, I am so sorry I didn't notice."

"We know we've been relying on you more, and we are so grateful for all the help, but you know us, not so good with our words sometimes." His shoulders jerked into a small shrug. "Your mother didn't want to tell you. She said we already ask too much of you and she didn't want to burden you with this as well."

"*You* should have told me." My arms crossed my chest as I stared him down, trying not to let any of the fear that welled up at his omission show.

"I know, I know, and I," he paused. "*We* will try to do better."

I wasn't sure if I believed it, but it would have to do.

"So tell me about the boy?" he asked after a few minutes of silence.

My faced pulled into a look I hoped conveyed innocence. "What boy?"

He only smiled at me before answering. "Did you know we installed cameras back here last year and a security system that tells us when the doors lock and unlock?"

My face paled and his widening smile told me all I needed to know.

"My procedure was very easy, and I was very bored that night so when the little app thingy told me the door was locked, then unlocked and locked again an hour later, I was curious."

Oh God.

"Exactly where do you have these cameras, Papa?"

"Don't worry, bambina, nothing in here. Actually, I haven't even been able to do any work in here since I saw you drag that man in by his apron."

My hands covered my face, mortified I shook my head back and forth. "Oh my God, please tell me you're lying." I peeked between two fingers.

"No."

"I'm so sorry."

"Ahh, don't be we've all been young and in love before."

"I'm not in love," I quickly answered.

"Does he make you happy?" he asked. I hesitated before I nodded my head, I was still too afraid to admit it to myself let alone out loud. "That's all I want for you, that's all both of us want for you." He pushed off the small bookcase he was leaning on and took my face between his hands. He squeezed my cheeks quickly three times, much like he would do when I was little. "Your happiness is the most important thing to us and I will be sure to tell you more often, il mio sogno." He placed a quick kiss on my forehead and left to finish prepping.

It had been years since the last time he called me that, my dream, and it took me right back to when I bought this place for them and they told everyone that came in that the restaurant was their second dream.

I was their first.

Parents were complicated, but underneath all the push and pull to be what they expected, it was simple. We were all just trying to be the best we could be.

TWENTY-SEVEN

Levi

It wasn't my wedding, I reminded myself for the millionth time, so there was no need to be so nervous. At first I thought it was the speech that had my stomach flipping in circles like a paid dolphin. Public speaking had never been an issue for me, but with this family, if I messed up, no one would let me forget. Which was fine I could handle that. My nerves had nothing to do with officiating the marriage between my sister and her soon-to-be husband. They had everything to do with realizing I was in love with Carina and not knowing what to do from there.

That was obviously it.

I was using every minute I had to go over my speech before the coordinator would be hunting for me. With the black leather portfolio in my left hand, I scanned through the pages, pacing in the living room of the house on the venue's property until the click of half a dozen heels pulled me from my speech. All my sisters and the two bridesmaids I wasn't related to walked down the stairs, donning dresses in all shades of purple, right as the wedding coordinator came around from the back room.

"Is everyone ready?" she called out and a chorus of yes' replied. She moved toward the front door to start lining us up when Lola finally made her way downstairs. I didn't think I would cry, she wasn't my first sister to get married or even the second, but there was something special about the bond I had with her, so seeing her beaming with happiness, clutching flowers in one hand and holding her dress up in another, it all hit me like a run away car.

She stopped in front on me, our dad was already a blubbering mess beside her. "What do you think?" she asked as she did a quick twirl. The fabric of her dress skimmed across the floor.

"I don't know, I think you could have used a few more layers, it's not quite big enough." Lola landed a smack to my chest with her bouquet, only loosing a few petals in the process. "Only kidding. You look beautiful, Lola."

She leaned in. "Are you going to cry?"

"I think I hear Joan calling me, you know I have to walk out first as the officiant."

She rolled her eyes as I walked away.

Joan was standing on the porch trying to get Brynn and Bailey to keep the flower petals in their baskets until they got to the aisle, but was slowly loosing the battle.

"Let's get everyone lined up and we can head out to the starting point. Levi, you're up first."

"Yes, ma'am."

Time was slowly ticking by as we waited for the music to start and as each moment passed, my eyes scanned the crowd for a glimpse of Carina. Would she mingle into the middle, hoping to blend in with the mass amount of family and friends or would she stick to the outskirts since everyone she did know was in the wedding party. All I knew was I couldn't wait for the ceremony to be over so I could be with her.

Finally the queue came and Joan ushered me forward; it wasn't until I was a few steps away from the start of the chairs that I found her. She was in the back, perched on the edge of an aisle seat with her hair sparkling in the sunlight as she turned with the rest of the crowd to watch the precession. My footsteps nearly faltered as our eyes locked. It was common knowledge that nobody could outshine the bride on her wedding day, and while Lola did look beautiful, Carina was glowing in a radiant halo, she made it hard to look away. Didn't matter that she wasn't in white, the dark blue floral dress dipped in all the right places, just enough for my eyes to linger but subtle enough that no one would think twice about it.

My heartbeat seemed to be the only thing to keep me on track when I reached the aisle as my hands itched to reach out and touch her but the last thing I would do today was ruin it for Lola and Chase. Instead my fingers flinched just as I passed her, as if they had a mind of their own and knew what I wanted.

I took my place at the head of the ceremony, clutching the leather folio that held my speech in front of me and I did the only thing that would keep me tethered to this moment—I watched her.

Her features morphed from an almost anxious look to one of comfort with each groomsman that walked down. I watched while she beamed at each of my sisters as they passed her and I nearly choked on a watery laugh when Lisa mouthed a quick 'hi' as she glided by Carina. I watched as she stood with the rest of the guests as Lola and our dad made their way from the house and down the aisle, her hand clutched softly at her chest when we all noticed Chase begin to cry at the sight of his bride.

I'd yet to decide if marriage was for me. Monogamy, yes that was something I knew, but marriage wasn't an act I ever really thought about. One day, once I was able to convince Carina we were something to each other, I would have to get her thoughts too. Or not. Honestly I was happy with what we had, whatever that might end up to be.

Lola handed off her flowers and came to face me with Chase's hands in hers. With one last look at Carina I gave her a quick wink, opened up my folder and began.

"Today, you embark on the next chapter of your lives. You have found in each other what most spend their lives searching for. You have found a partner, a best friend, a home. You have found the person who has seen you at your worst and at your best. The person you can show your scars, cracks and bruises to because you know that they will love you like you were never damaged in the first place. I've had the privilege of knowing you both as a couple and as individuals and while we all know relationships take work there is no doubt your unwavering devotion to each other will continue for a lifetime."

My voice wavered but the rest of the ceremony was a dream and by the end, my sister was married. Cheers rang out as I pronounced them husband and wife and I stepped to the side while Chase dipped Lola, kissing her with all the love in the world. All eyes were on them, but mine were on her.

Carina clapped along with our family, beaming as she spoke to someone I didn't recognize beside her. All I wanted was to get to her but it felt like an eternity as the bride and groom walked back down the aisle, followed by the entire bridal party, then their parents, until everyone followed after them and made their way to the reception area.

I slipped the folio under my arm and was the last to leave. Carina kept her eyes on me until I was only a step away from where she remained in her seat.

"Speech wasn't half bad for leaving it to the last minute." She turned to the side, crossing one leg over the other. Light green fabric fell open over her knee and fluttered in the slight breeze. For a moment I stared while she said nothing. Only looking back at me with a small smile on her face.

I'd seen many versions of Carina over the years, hardened work versions, relaxed work party versions, drunk and dancing versions of her but this one was new. A content in the moment version, where she was relaxed and happy even with no words being exchanged. A version where she looked at me and it didn't feel like a secret.

TWENTY-EIGHT

Carina

EVERYONE LOVED A GOOD wedding. The food, dancing, getting dressed up, free wine, and yeah sure the love part too.

Feelings that were hard to name surfaced during Levi's speech. I didn't know if it was the scenery or his words invoking them. Maybe it was the way his gaze flicked to where I sat near the back as he talked about finding that one person who knew you and loved you regardless. Maybe it was a culmination of all three that did it but I think I was right in my thinking the other day.

I might not be in love with him yet, but I was certainly falling into something.

And to my surprise, I didn't hate it.

Music wafted through the outdoor reception as the night turned the wedding to a party in full swing. Families with young children, older grandparents or guest with a long commute home had left, leaving what seemed to be most of Lola's and her husband's friends to the dance floor. Someone had brought out light up batons, the type you find at sporting events and I was pretty sure someone was walking around with enormous cut outs of the bride and groom's head.

I approached the bar behind two bridesmaids and watched the party unfold from my spot in line. My eyes snagged on Levi, who was twirling around both his nieces on the dance floor. All three laughed as they danced around to Whitney Houston's I Wanna Dance With Somebody as it blared through the speakers.

A soft chuckle from behind me caused me to turn. Laura was watching Levi with her children, just as entranced as I was. A few bridesmaids I didn't know moved from the bar with their drinks as Laura and I stepped forward. "Can we each get the bride's special?" Laura ordered for us without missing a beat.

We hovered near each other in an awkward silence as the bartender began mixing our drinks.

"The food was spectacular, please make sure you tell your parents that our entire family is so grateful they were able to step in at the last minute. It meant the world to Lola."

"It was our pleasure. They don't cater often but they love it, so this was perfect for them."

Two glasses, both full of a pale pink drink slid across the wooden bar toward us. Grapefruit and tequila, a superior combination and if marriage or a wedding was something I was into, this would have been on my drink menu as well.

We moved from the bar to the edge of the dance floor, where Levi held Brynn and Kevin had Bailey in his arms, both men swaying gently back and forth. It seemed that in the short time it took us to get our drinks the girls had run out of steam and were close to crashing.

"He's really great with them," Laura stated.

Without hesitating, I answered, "He is."

"And it's nice seeing my brother happy with someone finally," she casually volunteered.

I sputtered around my drink. "We're not...he's not my...no I'm sorry I think you're confused."

"Well are you seeing anyone else?" Laura seemed unfazed by my reaction.

"No."

"Are you sleeping with anyone else?"

Eyes wide, I stared at her. Laura was the oldest I think, maybe that was where the bluntness was coming from. She felt some sort of protectiveness over him, probably over all of them. "I don't think that's appropriate to answer." I was baffled by this line of questioning.

"I'll take that as a no." She took another sip. "Neither is Levi. Which sounds weird that I know that but he's my best friend as well as my brother. I love him and want to see him happy and what's making him happy right now is you, so I'm sorry but I think you're dating."

I took a moment to sit with her words. What *were* we doing if not dating? I could deny it all I wanted, call it all sorts of other words—friends with benefits, a way to pass the time, an arrangement but in the end he was who I called when I felt overwhelmed. He was who I leaned on when I needed help. He was all I thought about. "Shit... I think you're right."

"I'm glad you've realized it."

The men approached us, each with a girl fast asleep on their shoulder. "I think this is our queue to leave," Kevin said.

Levi swiftly and carefully transferred Brynn over to Laura. She immediately placed a kiss on one the girls forehead, and kept it there for a brief moment. "She feels a bit warm," she said to her husband, a look passed between them before they said goodbye and headed toward the parking lot.

"Dance with me?" Levi asked with dazzling determination. He extended his hand to me, palm up. I had somehow avoided dancing all evening but I could easily be persuaded. I discarded my glass on a nearby table, slipped my hand into his and was immediately spun onto the black and white tiled floor.

The music had shifted into a slow melody that allowed our bodies to press against each other as he moved us around the floor. My fingers toyed with the shortened hair at his neck as his hand drifted up and down my spine.

Everything faded away and it was as if it was just the two of us.

"I can't wait for it to grow back," I mused.

Levi laughed, somehow pulling me closer. His cheek pressed against my temple. "I'll grow it as long as you'd like. I live to serve, remember?"

My shoulders shook with quick laughter as I laid my head against his chest. "How could I forget?"

We danced the length of the song until it bled into another and then another. Never bothering to peel ourselves apart. I had no sense of time or when the wedding was actually over. All I knew is I didn't want the night to end. "This is nice."

"What's nice, Amore?"

"This, being here with you, feeling like I'm a part of the family. Just everything." I lifted my head enough to look at him. Soft overhead lights cast the night in a romantic glow and when Levi looked down at me it became abundantly clear. Fighting the feelings or not, they were here to stay.

His lips parted, but then closed as he worked over in his head what he was about to say, until finally it spilled out of him. "I know that this was supposed to be casual between us, but I don't know how much longer I can go on pretending like you are anything but the person who holds every piece of me."

I tightened my fingers on his shoulder, and rooted my feet to the dance floor, halting our movements. Music continued to fill the night air along with laughter in distance. When I finally looked around, we were the only ones still on the dance floor, a million miles away from everything.

"What?"

"I know I'm not what you wanted," he said in a hushed voice, "but you are all I want."

Oh.

Oh.

In my quest to hold onto my independence with an iron grip, I was blinded to the effects it had on those around me. It kept me from reaching out to Abby and Lennon in moments where my feelings seemed foreign. It kept me from connecting with my parents or even attempting to resolve our issues because I was too focused on silently proving to them that I didn't need them, they needed me.

It kept me from seeing the man in front of me and everything he was willing to offer me; a chance to belong without ever having to change and I had a choice to make. The first choice was the easiest, the safest one, the choice I had always made—stick to my self-imposed rules of no dating and either keep this casual or run from it altogether.

Or I could do the scariest thing I could think of and let him in.

Both options petrified me. While I was always determined to never lose myself, I realized I was also afraid of losing him.

I once told him never to ask me on a date again, in a throw away conversation that had little meaning, but for once, I was changing my mind. "Ask me." A faint tremor followed my words as my eyes burned into him, unaware of what my choice was going to be until it escaped my mouth.

His heartbeat changed, speeding up under the tips of my fingers as I trailed my hand from the back of his neck to his chest. It took only a moment before he realized what I was demanding. He brushed a curl from my forehead, his fingers trailing tenderly down the side of my face. "Are you free next weekend?"

"Yes." I breathed not even a moment after he finished his sentence.

His smile was enchanting, like a child on Christmas excited about the possibility of what the day would bring. "All I want is a chance, Amore. Me, you, and that restaurant downtown you have been talking about. Let me show you how good we can be together."

"It's a date."

Maybe we were doing this all backwards. Sleeping together, falling for each other all before our first date, but none of that mattered because when he finally stopped smiling, bending down to claim my lips with his, there was a new found intimacy in the act.

It was no longer a means to an end, a path that we knew would lead us to bed. Instead this simple act of his lips on mine was a statement, he was telling me that I was his, he was mine, and I was finally ready to listen.

I wasn't falling in love, that would be absurd, but I was absolutely stumbling into feelings I didn't know how to comprehend.

TWENTY-NINE

Carina

I NEVER EXPECTED TO be here, waiting on a man, a boyfriend, my mind reminded me and I still kind of wanted to belch at the word. Gentle wind swept through the street as I paced waiting for Levi to show. Chiffon and the night's air did not mix, I was having to stop every few steps to smooth down the fabric before any passerby got an eye full.

I should have just let him drive me like he wanted to, then I wouldn't have been here, by myself with a belly full of fluttering, jittery butterflies. I didn't intend to make tonight harder than it needed to be, but even as much as I wanted to be on this date, I was still going to hold to any scrape on independence I could.

> Are you almost here? They'll give away our reservation if we're late.

God, my hands were clammy. What's next, was I going break out in a full body sweat the longer he took to get there? He was probably lost in the mirror fixing his hair, or picking out an outfit. He seemed like the type to really put some thought into a night like tonight.

It was a normal date, our first date technically, even though we'd been seeing each other for months at this point. I told him this was ridiculous. I didn't need a fancy dinner to know what my gut had been yelling, but he insisted. Telling him no was always a challenge when he looked at me like I healed sick babies as a hobby.

I checked my phone for what felt like the hundredth time. The reservation time had lapsed by 10 minutes, and he still wasn't there. *He would be here, he had to show up.* Why spend months getting past all the walls I'd put up only to leave me stranded once I finally stopped pushing back?

There was no use standing in the cold to wait. With one more passing looking down the street, I reluctantly headed inside to get seated so our reservation wouldn't get passed over. Within a few minutes a waiter came by and I ordered a glass of merlot so I could, at least try to, calm the fuck down.

Maybe this was why I didn't like dating in the first place. Waiting was a nightmare.

A few more minutes and a basket of bread was placed on the table and I sent another text.

Levi I will leave

It was an empty threat, I knew that. He didn't.

I wanted to be there, and I knew he did too. So where was he?

Aggression was building in my chest, I did the only thing that crossed my mind and took it out on the bread and chewed vigorously.

A few more minutes passed and I ordered a new glass after draining the first a bit faster than I should have.

Where are you?

"Are you ready to order, love?" the waitress asked brightly as I stared at my phone willing for the three little dots to appear.

I mustered my stomach began to turn in on itself. No, just a few more moments, please."

She backed away from the table with regretful eyes, and suddenly I had the feeling I would never forget the way humiliation polluted my insides.

An hour. A full sixty minutes passed before I asked for the check and when it came back with only one glass of wine instead of three and the appetizer I ordered, I felt like I could've exploded.

He didn't call.

He didn't text.

He didn't show up.

Walking back out into the night, alone, was a type of low I thought I would never see and it had me teetering on an edge there was no coming back from.

With each passing moment the more everything began to hurt. Each breath that came was shorter than the last, catching in my throat and making it hard to fill my lungs. A weight sat in the pit of my stomach making each of my steps heavier and clumsier as I rushed to get to the safety of my car. I refused to break in public, if that's what was happening. And my chest vibrated with white hot embarrassment but it was my heart that hurt the worst. Pain sliced through the organ, cracking in half.

None of this made sense.

Logic was my superpower. I saw a problem, I fixed it with facts and level headed reasoning, doing what it took to find the answer but that part of me was lost in the wind. Instead I was a flurry of frigid anger, steadily working to replace each brick Levi tore down.

One chance, that was all he asked for. One chance and he threw it away? Threw me away? None of it made sense.

Cool glass from my phone pressed against my ear as I made one more call, that's all I was going to give him, an attempt to explain what was going on. I never bought into the whole 'put into the universe what you want out of it' like Abby did, but as the ringing continued I silently demanded, to whoever or whatever would listen, that he'd pick up.

Devastation washed over me once I reached his voicemail. For a second I thought maybe this was like Lennon and he was hurt, but unlike Lennon and Theo, nobody would know to call me if he was hurt. I was no one to him.

That had to be it, an accident on the way here, otherwise what was the alternative? He simply decided not to show up? Decided that these past few months were some sort of game?

My hands gripped the wheel of my car with such force, I was surprised it didn't crack under the pressure. Incoherent thoughts raced around my head, each one a string that wove itself around another until dozens of knots cluttered my head.

There had to be an accident; otherwise, it meant everything we had meant nothing.

THIRTY

Carina

LEVI DIDN'T SHOW UP—ANYWHERE. Not the restaurant, not my apartment. He never called. Didn't text. Not even a smoke signal.

Nothing.

By Sunday afternoon I was so worried, I broke down and began calling hospitals in the area but nobody matching his description or name was found. Which should have been a relief, but it wasn't. I scoured every news article I could find for any mention of a car pile up, or maybe some freak kidnapping—adultnapping—that I could talk myself into thinking he was a victim of. By the time night fell, I was furious.

When morning came, I hadn't slept, and for the first time in my career, I didn't want to go in to work and almost called in sick. Instead I was only an hour later than normal. No amount of concealer or caffeine could hide the bags under my eyes. I was a zombie walking into work on Monday and everyone could see it.

"Woah." Abby came to a halt in her doorway.

"Don't, I don't want to hear it," I snapped.

She lifted her hands up in surrender. "I only came to tell you a meeting was just called and we're all supposed to go to the conference room."

I just wanted to work and forget. Urgent meetings were never a good sign.

I pushed back from the desk and fell in step with her as we walked down the hall.

"What did you do all weekend? I never heard from you," she asked.

"I don't want to talk about it."

She must not have been picking up on the need for silence.

We walked through the door and took our unassigned, assigned seats. The chair in front of me was empty. Abby leaned over and whispered just as Diane walked in. "Where's Levi?" she asked.

"Good morning, everyone, I know, I know Monday meetings first thing in the morning are never a good sign and I am sorry to say that's what's happening. Unfortunately, I received notice late last night that Levi Decker will not be returning. While this is sudden, work does go on. About his caseload..." Her words were drowned out and I felt as if I had just stuck my head underwater.

My next breath went nowhere. The air I attempted to gulp down didn't even make it past my throat. Everything felt like it was drifting away — my co-workers, the table, even the room felt like it was about to crumble underneath me. Before I could lose myself entirely, I reacted and did the only thing that felt right. Shooting up from my chair, I bolted for the door in the middle of Diane's sentence. Once I made it out of the office doors, I was running toward the stairwell door, pulling it open and didn't stop until I was down the staircase, pushing past the side doors and stumbling into the courtyard.

Air finally hit my lungs but I barely registered the change. The area was empty but there was a strangled, pained noise from somewhere around me. My body swayed, seconds away from fainting but my hands hit my knees to keep me from falling as my world fell apart around me.

Abby appeared, shouting my name through the pained sound ringing out around us. She hauled my body against hers, wrapping her arms around my shoulders, when I finally realized the noise was coming from me. It tore out of my chest and into the space around, echoing until it was the only thing I could hear.

"He didn't show up," I finally choked out.

"Who didn't?"

I knew I was screaming but there was a chance I was about to cry too.

"Levi?" Abby questioned, finally coming to the right conclusion with no help from me.

I sucked in a deep breath, but it only felt like daggers into my chest. "We've been seeing each other." If Abby knew, she gave away nothing. "I've been pushing back, telling him I didn't want to get involved with him or anyone but he kept coming around, saying all the right things, doing everything he could to make sure I knew he was in this. That I was what he wanted." I sobbed the words, clutching my hands to my stomach.

Only then did Abby look alarmed, she had moved in front of me, reaching her hands out to wipe away the tears that had welled and spilled down my cheeks. I waved her off and stepped backwards.

"He's kind and funny and he didn't care that I worked through dinner or late into the night. Nothing stopped him from showing up but in a way that was endearing and not creepy." I laughed through the pain. "He was infuriating and then all the sudden the things that I would roll my eyes at where the things about him I liked the most." My voiced cracked and was thick with emotions. "I finally told him I wanted to give it a shot, us being together, a real couple who told our friends and family and went to the pumpkin patch."

Abby's brows pinched as a hint of a smile pulled at the corner of her lips. "You hate the pumpkin patch."

"I know, that's the point. With him I wanted to be the couple that picked out pumpkins together."

I didn't know what it was about that image but a fresh wave of tears stained my face thinking of us, all of us—Lennon and Theo, Levi and I, Abby and whoever she would eventually end up with—in a field under the warm October sun. I didn't know it was possible to yearn for a moment that never even happened, but my heart ached for a time I realized I would never get.

"We planned to meet Friday for our first date," I said quietly, as I turned to sit on the patio bench. "I waited over an hour at the restaurant. I called and texted and heard nothing. I spent yesterday calling hospitals."

"Oh, Carina," she breathed and came to sit beside me. It had pity written all over it. She shifted in her seat after a moment of silence. "I asked Diane why he left so suddenly. She either didn't have a lot information or maybe just couldn't tell me, only that he called her late yesterday and said he had to move out of the area," she said quietly, almost as if she regretted opening her mouth at all.

Nothing broke inside of me as the words registered. Instead I went to work, methodically picking up the bricks he pulled from around my heart and began rebuilding with masonry precision.

Moved. He moved.

How could he up and move within a day's notice? That didn't seem possible because home was here in Fairvale, with me. So where did he go?

"Did she," I wiped my hands under my eyes, "uh, did she say if it was an emergency or something or if he's coming back?"

She shook her head slowly and my carefully crafted world, where I was strong and independent, where I didn't need or want anybody to hold me up, seemed to crumble from underneath me. Tears fell as a sob shook my body in a move so foreign I had no choice but to let it take over. I was ill equipped and didn't know how to stop the pain from escaping where I liked to hide this overly human part of me.

Abby reached over and began rubbing slow circles on my upper back as I rested my elbows onto my knees and pressed the heel of hands into my eyes, staving off the flow of tears. I felt the small press of her chin on my shoulder. For a moment it was comforting, being in her arms, having someone to confide in, until she spoke again. "She only said that he sounded fine, and he should have told her sooner."

My body stilled, Abby's hand registering the change, stopped her ministrations. I popped up from the bench to look at her. "What?"

Abby's eyes were wild, unsure if she should have told me at all. "I don't know, Carina, I'm sorry," she sounded pained. " All Diane said was the call was quick, and that he should have told her sooner."

"Should have told her sooner," I repeated, then I scoffed at the ridiculous notion. "So he knew he was leaving and what, never said anything to me, to anyone, led me on anyway?" Anger morphed my voice, turning it scornful and accusatory, but in the direction of the wrong person.

Abby flinched at my outburst. "I don't—" she stuttered, unable to answer my question.

Sadness turned to rage like a waves hitting the shore, there one moment until the next piles on top of it. How stupid could I have been?

I had rules for my life for this very reason. Rules that kept my life on track and my head out of the clouds and yet that's exactly where I found myself. No wonder it felt like I couldn't breathe, I got lost in the sky for a moment and forgot the higher you float the less oxygen. But I was back, firmly planted on the ground now.

"Okay." I walked a few paces before turning back to her, locking every emotion I ever associated with him—joy, bliss, lust, *belonging*, down tight. It was a snap decision that would have benefitted from more time but when I didn't hear from him that night I had already put a plan in motion. I just figured we'd work it out once I saw him at work. "Okay," I said once more to myself for encouragement. "I need a favor."

"Anything," she said but there was air around it that told me she didn't know if she would keep the promise.

Swiping my hands under my eyes, I wiped away any remaining tears. That was all he would ever get out of me, and I was thankful he wasn't around to see them. I stood taller, and tugged the bottom of my suit jacket, squaring my shoulders. "I don't ever want to hear about Levi Decker again," I demanded with an air of authority, the type I brought to court. That was the last time I would say his name.

"But wh—"

I didn't even let her finish. "Nothing, Abby, I want nothing to do with him. He knew he was leaving and didn't even have the decency to send a simple text to tell me that whatever we had was a lie. I don't ever want to hear about him again." The words came out as a low snarl, an animalistic request that demanded to be heard.

"Okay." She finally agreed after a handful of seconds.

I felt foolish, entirely simple minded to think I could change what I already knew; I was the only person I could rely on, for anything it seemed. I let an altogether infuriating man strip away my defenses until I was left with only bones and nothing to hide behind.

He *forced* his way in, despite all I had told him.

Didn't I tell him I didn't date? Didn't I remind him that I wasn't interested in anything more than a physical relationship?

God, I hated myself for allowing him to barge his way into my heart with no failsafe in place. It was like I learned nothing from the last man

I was in a relationship with. When he asked me to change I left without hesitation, knowing I didn't want to give up any part of myself and then I went and freely changed for Le—I couldn't even think his name. At least I was young back then and could blame it on my frontal cortex not being fully developed, what excuse did I have now?

None, I would argue.

There was no excuse for what I allowed, for how he made me feel, for leaving me without so much as a goodbye to savor.

Abby and I stood in the empty courtyard for a few minutes longer. She carefully studied me, waiting for the break in my armor to appear again but that would be impossible. I said logic was my superpower, but so was my ability to cast people out without so much as a second thought. I was a steel fortress, impenetrable, rooted in the notion of self-reliance.

"I have to get back to work."

I may never forgive myself but I would move on. I would be fine.

I was always fine.

Two Years Later

THIRTY-ONE

Carina

ONE OF MY BEST friends was getting married and I was having a hell of a time finding even a scrap of happiness. In the grand scheme of things I was happy for Lennon, really I was, but the moment Lennon flashed me the ring, my heart dropped. Just a fraction, before I was able to pull myself together and wrap her up in a brief, affectionate hug.

Most people craved companionship, some might've even considered it a basic human need. I got it, I respected it, for the most part, but it had been so long since I last let anyone close to me that the reason people relied on others was beginning to fade from my memory.

But marriage.

Absolutely not.

Couldn't be me.

Wouldn't be me and it wasn't because I lacked prospects.

Abby would call that bitter, and maybe she was right but I no longer cared.

I did it once, or well, almost did it once. The relationship thing, not marriage, and it blew up in my face, leaving me scrambling to find a foot to stand on again.

Levi Decker was a name I scrubbed from my vocabulary, and in my mind it was as if he never existed. And yet, when Lennon told me she was engaged and flashed that sparkling rock my way, a vision of his face flashed in mind.

"Carina, do you think we could reserve the patio room at your parents' restaurant for after the ceremony for lunch?" Her words pulled my focus back to her and Abby. My head turned to see the hopeful look on her smiling face.

"Absolutely, I'll stop by on my way home and put it on their books."

I needed a drink. Or five.

Lennon's hand darted to grab something off the counter, the diamond caught the light, sending rainbows bouncing off the counter.

That diamond fucking ring.

Yeah, five should do the trick.

She checked off something in her notebook.

Lennon wanted a quick wedding, something fast and easy. A courthouse by the end of the month because they loved each other so much, fast and easy. Which worked for me, the faster we all got through this the better. For a second my mind attempted to replay the last wedding my parents restaurant catered but of course it was the wedding I went to with *him*.

Quickly, I slammed shut the vault that held those memories. I didn't want or need any of those memories coming up.

"All that's left are the dresses. I know I'm not doing traditional bridesmaids but would you guys like to wear something special?" I was half present for the rest of the conversation, I chimed in where I knew my input was needed but by the end of it I only wanted to get back home or even back to work. Didn't matter that it was Sunday, at least the office would be quiet, and quiet is what I wanted to stop the throbbing headache forming in my temples by the time I left.

My car pulled into my usual spot and I breezed through the front door right as my mother walked out of the kitchen to close up. "Vita mia," she exclaimed and shuffled over to me and wrapped me in hug.

"Hi, Mamma."

"Why are you here?" She knew I wasn't here to see her, she knew better than that.

"Lennon got engaged, Ma."

She clapped her hands in front of her chest, clearly overjoyed. "Oh, that makes me so happy, what do you need from me?"

"Can we have the back patio next month for a lunch after the ceremony?"

She walked over to flip through the reservation book that sat near the front door. "How about we shut down the whole restaurant, huh? Give them a real party to remember."

"That's too much. Lennon and Theo are having a small wedding the patio is more than enough."

She waved me off. "Nonsense, Papa and I will close down the restaurant. It might be cold, I don't want you all outside in case it rains."

There was no use in arguing, when my mother made up her mind, nothing could change it. One of the few traits we shared.

"Thanks, Ma. That's all I needed. I'll get out of your hair."

"A wedding, how wonderful. Maybe you'll be next?" I couldn't remember exactly when she started dropping, not so subtle, hints that she was waiting for my life to move forward, but it was getting more and more frequent. It wasn't enough I was successful, driven, independent. All she saw when she looked at me was an unwed, childless thirty-four year old woman.

Somebody else might have been offended but I was so use to not feeling like I was enough for them that I remained unfazed and chose not to answer.

"Are you alright, Amore?" Her hand came up and rested on my forehead.

I hated when she called me that. It seemed like I couldn't get away from his memory even if I tried. "Just tired, that's all," I lied.

It had been two years and I have been skating by on auto pilot. Letting work dictate everything about my life to the point I was buried under my career. It was the only way I knew how to get over what happened.

———

There was busy at work and then there was 'down two attorneys with more cases coming in than we could keep up with' busy at work.

The conference room was empty as I walked in, triggering the lights to flick on. My legal pad landed on the table with a loud whack before I sat in my usual chair. There were only a few moments before the rest of the office slowly started to trickle in.

Abby walked in next and sat down to my right. There's no assigned seating and yet that didn't stop us from always taking the same ones. My focus was on my pen dragging back and forth across my paper and not the perpetually empty chair across from us.

Diane started the meeting the moment she walked through the door. "Good morning, this will be Jody's last week." My eyes closed at the words, I knew what came next. "We wish you all the best in your next endeavor." She smiled at the middle aged woman across the room. I heard from Abby that Jody was moving out of the area last week, and normally that would be fine except now there were two open positions whose work would fall on me until they were filled.

"Luckily enough we have been able to conduct a few interviews and we should have at least one of the positions filled soon." She looked over at me with a bit of sympathy as she said the words. "Oh, and don't forget, the partners purchased a table for the upcoming gala so make sure you have that on your calendar." The rest of the meeting breezed by and soon enough I was back at my desk plucking away at emails.

There was an easy enough mediation meeting just after lunch which meant I was spending the next five hours glued to my seat. The work was soothing, and while I wanted to pull my hair out every once in a while, my desk was a welcome distraction.

This was what I wanted, right?

Thirty-Two

Carina

If I wasn't part of the planning, I wouldn't believe a wedding could come together as fast as theirs did. Dresses, flowers, cake, music, everything fell off Lennons's checklist faster than I could blink. The only thing she didn't need to worry about was the food. My parents worked at a frenzied pace the past week ensuring everything would be perfect. And it absolutely was.

Tables overflowed with plates of raviolis, pastas, and chicken piccata. Trays of black and white cookies overflowed the dessert table, which I personally ate a half dozen of and I heard no less than ten people rave about the dishes as I passed by.

Everything was perfect.

The room filled with the delicate sound of glasses tinkling together as the guests tapped their knives against their wine glasses. Lennon's head tipped backwards and laughed until Theo dragged her in for a kiss. The whole scene was something out of a movie. A romance that made you swoon and cry and feel as if the world is a better place because two people fell in love.

I hadn't been to many weddings, all of our family was still back in Italy and my friend circle barely extended past Lennon and Abby, so I didn't have much to go on, but this had to be the most beautiful wedding to ever exist. Even if it was small and at my parents' restaurant.

Lennon pinned her auburn curls so that only small tendrils fell around her face with tiny pearls tucked in between the strands. I watched as Theo moved one out of the way to place another quick kiss on her cheek before standing up from his seat. It was achingly sweet and if my heart wasn't frozen, it might have melted.

Bistro lights casted everything in a romantic pale yellow glow as he plucked the champagne glass from in front of him and called for everyone's attention. His dark suit was a stark contrast to the white satin dress Lennon was wearing. It was the first one she tried on and we instantly knew it was the one. A plunging back and straps that fell from her shoulders; she was ethereal, a vision.

"Thank you, everyone, for being here," he called out as his hand came to rest gently on Lennon's shoulder, her cheek pressed into him while she gazed upwards. The rest of the guests turned toward the front as my parents pushed through the kitchen doors to listen. "This day has been twenty years in the making, and it's almost hard to believe I get to call this beautiful woman," he paused to look at her, swallowing back his emotions, "who's had every part of me since I was sixteen, my wife."

A few murmured awes floated from the tables.

"I would also like to take just a moment to remember the man that came before me. You all know that Lennon was married before and since reconnecting with her, I've had the honor of getting to know him through her and let me tell you it will be an incredibly hard act to follow." A few people chuckled. "But I know that if I can love Lennon even a fraction of how Camden loved her, I'll be the luckiest man in the world."

The frozen organ in my chest did thaw, just for a second.

Theo pulled Lennon to her feet, she clung to his chest as tears slid down both of her cheeks.

I hated crying, but I was having a hard time remembering that. If anybody deserved a soft life and a happily ever after it was Lennon. The day of her first husband's death was a day that still floated through my nightmares and left me jolting in my sleep gasping for air.

"Lenny, my love, every day you amaze me with your wit and compassion and I am forever in awe of the way you love those closest to you. Being your husband will be the best thing I do with my life, and loving you the greatest honor I will ever hold." He raised his glass and the room followed. "To my bride, I would have waited lifetimes for you but I am grateful I get to love you in this one." He bent down, placing a delicate kiss against her lips and despite the tenderness woven into action it was the type of embrace that told us their commitment would rival every love story that came before theirs.

The room cheered and everyone took sips from their respective drinks as the bride and groom kissed. Abby was crying, loudly, from behind my shoulder, as we watched her sister and new husband walk out on the makeshift dance floor. My parents shared a quick kiss before disappearing back into the kitchen, married thirty-five years and I don't think they ever had a bad day together.

The Newlyweds swayed back and forth, lost in each other as the rest of us faded into the back. Abby sighed from beside me and when I turned to look at her it was evident not wearing waterproof mascara was a bad idea. "I can't wait to be married," she said with a dopey little smile on her lips.

I snorted. "That makes one of us."

Abby sighed like she'd heard me say that a million times. Which, to be fair, she definitely had.

"You've said that before. You sure you'll never get married? " My stomach soured at her question. "Wouldn't that be lonely?"

Why must I alway be subjected to a constant inquisition into why I chose to remain alone. Why was 'because I don't want to' never an acceptable answer? Marriage didn't need to be the blue print and love didn't guarantee a happy life, so why was everyone hell bent on finding it?

I had a career and friends, I was fulfilled. Asking me when I was getting married, or why I wasn't, frustrated me to no end. It was as if they were saying my life would be worth more if I was tied to someone. My life was what I made it, not who I spent it with.

"I'm sure. I have no desire to be someone's wife." I took a sip of my champagne. "Be anybody's anything, really." Abby rolled her eyes and left to get closer to the dance floor with her phone in hand and the camera open.

Marriage never interested me, even before, but after *him*, I couldn't even think of relationships without wanting to burn down the town. Despite the achingly sweet picture in front of me.

I knew I was the only person I could rely on.

THIRTY-THREE

Carina

You know that feeling in the pit of your stomach, the kind that screamed a message you couldn't quite understand and then sent your stomach flipping back and forth? It was a weird sixth sense that was almost impossible to figure out?

Well that was what was happening to me.

I woke up before my alarm, with my insides twisting. I didn't feel sick, no flushed feeling or sourness in my stomach, but I felt off. It was as if my world titled off its axis, but only by a degree. Subtle differences that wreaked chaos.

Everything that could go wrong did as I started my day. I was out of coffee, the blush I was using tumbled out of my hand and shattered as it hit the bathroom floor. While I was internally complaining about the first two issues I rammed my toe into the side of my bed getting dressed. Hopping around on one foot I contemplated crawling back in bed and not getting out until it was the next day.

My heart raced along side my thoughts, until I couldn't delineate one from another. They were weaving in and out of each other until I was left with a pile of knots that I couldn't undo. Something was telling me the day was going to be a disaster and the feeling followed me to work.

I set the white to-go cup I picked up from Renaissance on my desk and sat down. Abby walked in as I was staring at the touching hands logo stamped into the sleeve of the cup, trying to will the feeling out of my body.

"You okay?" she asked. Her wide-eyes questioning me as she walked further into my office.

"Yeah, just a rough morning."

She nodded in agreement. "You ready for the meeting? I just saw Diane, she was excited about an announcement she has and I want figure out what it is."

With the morning I had, I was planning on skipping but maybe it would be a turning point. "Maybe they finally hired someone to fill one of the spots," I mused out loud as I lifted back out of my seat and fell into step with Abby.

We filed into the conference room, quiet chatter between employees filled the space as we waited. With one leg crossed over the other, I swiveled gently in my chair staring down at the black stilettos I had opted for.

Diane started the meeting as normal and I only halfway listened to the usual announcements. Instead I used the little time I allowed myself to let my mind shut down and began doodling in the top corner of my legal pad. Words floated in one ear and out the other, I barely registered what was being said.

"Ah, right on time," Diane stated as the door was pulled open. "I am happy to announce we have filled one of the open attorney positions." Those words peeked my attention, finally I was going to get some relief around here. I wondered which option they went with, sometimes management would ask for input but I didn't remember anyone interviewing in the office recently.

"Some of you remember Levi Decker. I am pleased to announce that he is rejoining the firm but as an associate attorney."

The pen came to a halt on my third spiral on as her words sunk in. Suddenly I understood what my gut had been trying to tell me all morning. I didn't want to look but I had to. There was a visceral need to confirm the words she had just uttered were true and not in fact some cruel trick.

My head turned slowly toward the back of the room, and my eyes landed on him. No tricks, it was actually *him*. I sucked a deep breath through my nose at the sight of him.

For a moment I feared I fell asleep in the meeting and was plunged into a reoccurring nightmare.

It went on for months after he disappeared, I would wake in the middle of the night, slick with sweat and a pounding heart. Every night was always the same.

I'd be at my desk, working as usual until he appeared in my office doorway. His shoulder would hit the doorway as he flashed me the same smile that once warmed my insides and he would tell me he was sorry for being late. He would hand me a latte and my favorite blueberry scone, take the seat across from me and all would be forgiven.

That was it, four words simple words, and I would wake up shaking, devastated and hating myself.

My nightmares weren't of him disappearing. That would be too simple.

It was him returning, realizing how much I missed him and knowing how quickly I was willing to forgive him.

That's what my gut was trying to tell me.

It had been two years and in that time everything and nothing had changed. I still worked at ALA Law, I still saw Abby and Lennon every weekend. But I no longer ate scones from Renaissance, I changed to their danish pastries instead. I no longer worked at my parents' restaurant to help, or sipped brown sugar lattes.

I never re-downloaded the dating app, too afraid I might stumble upon him again. Instead, I went the old fashion way and let men pick me up at bars when I had the time or who I already knew and understood I had nothing to offer them other than a night or two.

All the days and hours that separated me from the last time I saw him standing in the door way looking exactly like my nightmares seemed to fade from memory. He was just as tall, and lean as I remembered him. Midnight hair that fell into a soft wave, pushed back and out of his face. It wasn't as long as it once was but it was still my favorite feature.

And of course he would be wearing a stupid fucking tie.

Some things never changed for him either.

It took me longer than I would ever admit to anyone to get past what happened. I didn't want to be the type of person that spent their life hung up on someone who paid them no mind. Eventually I stuffed my feelings deep into the abyss of my mind and willed myself to forget him the best I could. But all that work went right out the window.

The five stages of grief are denial, anger, bargaining, depression and acceptance. I experienced three out of five in the moments it took him to find his seat, that perpetually empty seat in front of me, before I could tear my eyes away from him. I focused on anything but the man sitting across from me, counting the seconds until the meeting was over.

"And that's all I had for today," her words finally rang out.

I was up and out of my seat before the last word left Diane's mouth. I needed out of the room, out of his orbit.

I needed to go back home, crawl into bed and get away from this nightmare that followed me.

The last thing I heard was his voice. It was like a knife in my back and the sweetest thing I'd heard in past two years all wrapped up in one devastating word. My name.

That's what my stomach was trying to tell me.

My nightmares were correct.

Fuck.

THIRTY-FOUR

Decker

THERE WERE DAYS YOU knew would change your life, for better or worse, and wouldn't even know you were balancing between the two. But that wasn't my case, I knew I was in one of those life changing days, and the arrow was leaning toward worse which had my body breaking out in a nervous sweat before I even woke up. I had to change my shirt twice before leaving because I sweat through the cotton of each one moments after putting it on.

I stood outside the doors at Alcala, Lane and Associates waiting for—I didn't really know what. A sign? Someone to appear and tell me coming back was the right decision? To find an encouraging note in my pocket to give me strength to pass through the doors I abruptly left two years ago?

Gripping the leather strap of my bag I pulled in a lung full of morning air, trapping it in my chest for moment. If in the next three seconds nothing happened, then I'd walk inside.

Three.

Two.

One.

My phone buzzed in my pocket a second after my allowed time as I exhaled.

> You're coming for dinner tonight, right?

Moving to Fairvale was one decision, the easier decision by telling myself I was staying close to family, and that was all. Coming back to ALA was another decision entirely, an agonizing decision made over countless sleepless nights and arguments in the mirror.

I knew she still worked there when I applied, when I interviewed over video with Diane and when I accepted the job. At each step I tried to convince myself not to move to the next one but I couldn't. Not when there was a chance to finally right all the wrong I caused.

Everything was still the same as I walked through the elevator doors and into the familiar space. Dull brown carpet muffled my steps heading to the Diane's office, taking the long way around to avoid Carina's office altogether. I may have came in early to get onboarding paperwork out of the way before most people arrived but I knew that wouldn't stop her from logging billing hours before the sun fully rose.

And I couldn't see her, not yet.

I knocked on the door frame. "Levi." Diane rounded her desk to greet me, her short brunette curls bounced as she shook my hand. "It's so good to see you again. Everyone is going to be so excited to see you." I bit down and swallowed the bile threatening to show itself. This was a terrible idea. I couldn't do this.

What was I thinking, coming back to the only place we shared? It was a fantasy, thinking I'd show up and all would be forgiven. How could I expect her to forgive me if I hadn't even forgave myself? It was selfish to come back, I thought I should have left. There were other jobs, other firms that would be willing to hire me, I was sure of it.

But there's no other her.

"It's great to be back," I forced out the words as I sat down.

I took a seat at the open table with a pile of papers stacked up. We went over the paperwork, all standard documents I had filled out once before. Diane spoke of a few changes in the office but was quick to excuse herself.

"I hate to run out but everyone should be in soon and we have a standing Monday morning meeting. Once you're done pop on over and we can introduce you as a little surprise."

My hand froze as I flipped through the pages. 'A little surprise' were not words I wanted attached to my introduction. I cleared my throat as acid began to climb back up it. "Does everyone one know you hired me?"

Diane smiled as if having spring this on the office was the only thing she had to look forward to. "Oh, no, not yet. We filled your position quickly and I haven't found time to announce it yet. Both Abby and Carina are still here, along with Oliver and Emma. I'm sure they'll all be thrilled to have you back. Carina especially, she has been drowning under the amount of work with the two positions open, she won't say it of course, but, well, you'll find out." She clasped me on my shoulder and walked out, shutting the door behind her and left me alone with my racing thoughts.

Carina had no idea. Out of every possible situation I had conjured up about how my return could go, this was the worst. Assuming there was some sort of announcement about me filling the position was too much to hope for apparently.

She had no warning, no time to prepare to see me like I did before coming here.

I was about to walk into a meeting that would feel like an ambush.

Chatter drifted out of the conference room toward the office I was finishing up paperwork as people began filtering in to start the week. Sweat forced my hand into an iron grip around my pen, which then began to cramp. I tossed it onto the table after my last signature. Maybe I should have brought an extra shirt to change in to. It was too early in the day, and also my first day, to shuck off my suit jacket and loosen my tie but it was entirely too warm inside.

I pulled at my collar for even a fraction of relief, repeating the process on the right cuff and then the left. As I did, a flash of purple caused me to pause. My fingers plucked at the fraying cord, wishing the small object worked like a crystal ball and would tell me I wasn't a fool for being there.

She was so close, and I could already picture the scene I would walk into. Carina would be sitting in the chair next to the head of the table, a small legal pad in front of her littered with tiny doodles in the top corner, and since it was Monday, she would be in a suit of some sort of color other than black or blue.

It never mattered that two years had come and gone, I still remembered everything.

I put off the meeting long enough, any further and they would come in search of me. I walked down the hall and paused at the door. Diane's no nonsense voice was my only focus point. I swallowed down the lump of nerves, pulled open the door and crossed into the room at the end of her sentence.

"Ah, right on time," Diane said to me. "I am happy to announce we have filled one of the open attorney position." There was murmuring around the room filled with faces I mostly didn't recognize. My eyes fell on Abby first, her mouth hanging open, unabashed. Carina had yet to look up from the doodling I knew she'd be doing. "Some of you remember Levi Decker and I am pleased to announce that he is rejoining the firm but as an associate attorney." A few polite claps reached my ears.

A few things happened the moment she said my name. First the pen in Carina's hand stilled mid loop she was drawing. Next my heartbeat sped up and felt like it was about to thrum out of my chest at the sight of her. Finally, her head lifted and she looked at me.

For a moment I thought sea glass eyes, the ones that littered my dreams for the past two years, would be staring back at me, but when she looked at me, really looked at me, I hardly recognized them. Shock made its way through her features, that was to be expected, until it mixed with agitation, disgust and what could only be described as resentment.

And it stayed in her eyes as she tracked my movements while I took the seat across from her. It wasn't on purpose, but it pulled me like a magnet.

It was too much. I wasn't ready for it, I would never be ready to face all the hurt I caused. I wasn't strong enough. I wasn't anything, coming back was a mistake and she was making sure I knew.

Carina spent the meeting boring holes into the side of my head, and even though I desperately wanted to look at her, I didn't.

Soon enough, Diane was concluding the meeting and a flurry of activity began as people filed out, heading back to their desk to start the day. Which is what I was supposed to be doing, but she hadn't moved, so neither did I. Instead I mustered up what little courage I had left and lifted my gaze to hers.

I had been gone two years, four months, and twelve days. If I looked at my watch, I would have been able to get it down to the exact hour as well. Each day a special sort of torture of knowing the truth behind leaving without giving her any answers.

Carina was knowledge and reason incarnate. A person who moved through life using her head, barely listening to what her heart had to say. Leaving her without an explanation would feel like a knife to her back after spending so much time breaking down the barriers she had built.

I opened my mouth, unsure of what to say but a fire burned in her stare as she swiped the paper and pen off the table and shoved herself back from the table. I wanted to stop her, tell her how sorry I was, that it was all a misunderstanding blown way out of proportion. I followed her lead, lumbering out of my chair as she slipped through my fingers, evaporating like smoke in the wind.

She was steps away from the door and I did the only thing I could think of. "Carina," I called out but she didn't turn back.

At one point I straddled the void that was love and lust with Carina. She was my favorite person, the person I wanted to turn to when I was happy or frustrated or just to have someone to talk to. She was my person, and I was nothing without her.

Which was worse, remembering everything about her or knowing she wished I knew nothing at all?

THIRTY-FIVE

Carina

AVOIDANCE WAS THE ONLY plan I had. Avoid. Avoid. Avoid. If I could avoid him, I could pretend he wasn't in the office and for me that was a solid enough plan. The only plan, really.

My office chair saw more of my ass than ever before. I kept the door shut as much as possible and the blinds closed. His office this time around sat directly across from mine, our windows perfectly aligned so that either one could see into the other at any time.

For the first week, any client who requested a meeting, I took it outside of the office. We'd meet for coffee at Renaissance, or at a park so their kids could play while we talked.

I did anything to keep myself busy but it barely worked.

There were glimpses of him from the corner of my eye as he walked down the hall in the morning. A few meetings where I had to wait a few beats before walking into the conference room so we didn't walk in together. Moments where he would glide past my office and for a second, only a second, I would think he was coming to drop off coffee like he used to. That maybe I would look up and see his shoulder hit the door frame and his strong arms cross over his chest with that sly smile on his lips. The one that told me I was his favorite secret.

And I hated it. I hated that I missed it. I hated that he was here.

But most of all I hated how he hadn't even tried to talk to me since his first day.

I was invisible to him.

My computer chimed with a meeting reminder that I needed to be down the street to meet a new client. I grabbed a fresh new legal pad, no doodles yet, a few pens, shut my laptop and slid it all into a bag before walking out of my office. I was too busy slinging the bag on my shoulder to notice he walked out of his new office at the same time. But once I did, I spun on my heel to head back toward my office but Diane appeared out of nowhere.

"Oh, I'm so glad I caught you both," she said. Levi's head popped up from the screen. He looked from Diane and then to me, his eyes lingering on my face before jumping back to her.

"I'm on my way to meet a new client," I said, hopeful it would get me out of whatever was coming next.

"Out of the office?" he questioned. The first thing he'd said to me in two years and he's questioning how I did my job. I could only muster raised eyebrows and a curt nod.

"This should be quick," she stated. "Do you two remember the Leon case you both worked on during your last stint here, Levi? I think it was the last case you were on."

He slipped the phone back into his pocket. "Yea, that was the one that had the husband who was putting her through the wringer just to sign the papers before Carina really started digging into him." Suddenly he snapped his fingers, startling me and before he turned toward me. "Wasn't he the one that tried to bribe you?"

I was surprised he even remembered, I had only mentioned it in passing. My gaze slid over to him. "Yeah. What about it?"

If Diane could sense anything was strained between us she never mentioned it, she carried on without missing a beat. "Right, well the wife, or ex-wife and now wife again is retaining us...again. Looks like after the spilt, they reconciled, there's a new pregnancy, and lo and behold, things still didn't work out."

Not the first time it'd happened. Sometimes it was easier to look past a few flaws, fall in love again and forget why you tried to get out in the first place.

"I think it would be best if you worked this one together. You both are familiar with the case from before. It would be a good way to dip your toes into this side of the pool and Carina is the best mentor you could find." She beamed at both of us like she solved an impossible riddle. "A win, win for everyone."

"Do you really think it would need both of us, I mean—"

"I can take the case myself, that's not a problem," Decker offered and I had to close my eyes to keep them from rolling.

"She specifically requested both of you again, actually. It's like fate almost, she called the day after you arrived, Levi. What are the odds?"

Fate's a fucking bitch.

"I know you two will knock it out quickly. We know all the tricks this guy has. Should be easy." She waved her hand above her head as she walked away, leaving us in an awkward bubble in the middle of the office hallway.

His mouth opened to speak, but I was faster. "Have Abby set up a meeting for Friday and we'll get started."

"Carina—"

"I can't, Decker. Talk to Abby."

As I pushed through the front doors and out onto Main Street, I wondered if I could even do this.

Even a simple conversation seemed like air was being tugged from my lungs. Words were hard to form, even my thoughts were muddled in my head. It was hard to separate past-Levi with the man that stood in front of me — I didn't even know who he was. That was the hardest part.

I was punishing myself by punishing him and he probably had no clue.

THIRTY-SIX

Carina

FRIDAY CAME TOO QUICK and yet not soon enough. I'd been walking on pins and needles knowing it meant I'd have to sit across from Decker and have a conversation with him. A conversation that had nothing to do with what happened between us. That part would hang over our heads like a dense rain cloud ready to drown us.

"Do you want to go out tonight?" Abby asked as she popped her head into my office. "Lennon and Theo are getting ready for their honeymoon and are busy, so it would just be us." My lips pursed out in thought. That didn't sound too bad and I was no psychic but there was no way I came out of my meeting later a happy person. "It would be like old times," she sang the words.

Fuck it.

I needed it, I deserved it. "Yeah, but let's go downtown to the bar near the courthouse. I want a man who wears power like cheap perfume to buy my drinks." She might not've understood exactly what I meant but was happy to oblige anyway.

Hours ticked by and my computer dinged with the meeting. I got to the conference room early. My laptop whirled beside me as I scribbled in the corner of the fresh legal pad. Endless loops and stars started to appear in the margin, and my nerves slowly began working themselves to where they belonged, deep in my chest where they couldn't bother me.

The door opened and I willed myself not to look up at him as he crossed the room to take his seat. Instead I listened to way the carpet muffled his steps and counted how many it took for him to get to his chair.

It was seventeen. Seventeen steps before he pulled out the chair we both knew he was heading for. Only once he was situated was I able to set down the pen and double click the mousepad on my computer to bring it back to life.

I could do this. I was made of strength, I spent years bowing down to no one and caging any remote feeling of softness to get to where I was. I would not let anyone sway me.

"Have you had any contact with Kelly in the past two years?" he asked and it felt like a punch to the gut.

I could do this, I only needed to treat this whole interaction like I would any other case. This was just a routine Friday meeting for a new case.

That was all.

"No, the last time I spoke to her was the meeting we were both at." I wanted to add it was also the last time we saw each other. Our date he never showed for was planned for the next day.

The keys of his computer clicked loudly in the otherwise quiet room. "From the email Diane sent over, it looks like they reconciled six months after we finalized their divorce and custody agreement, and she is currently six month pregnant." A tiny scoff followed his words. "I'll never get it."

"Get what?"

"Why go back? You remember that case, he was horrible to all of us, even his own attorney. I could only imagine how he was with her behind closed doors. We did all that work just for her to go back to him." He shook his head, the dark locks of hair moved with him.

"We don't know what happened, you don't get to judge someone for how they handle their life." The words sliced across the table like a double edged sword. "I have no idea where you got your degree, or why, or if you had been working elsewhere, but here, we listen to the clients and we don't judge because you're right, we don't know what it was like behind closed doors. Behind closed doors anything could happen, bad men can turn good and good men can turn into a walking, talking contradiction," I sneered, no longer talking about the case.

Oh, this was bad. This was so so bad.

I had no leash on my emotions that were lashing out and Decker knew it. He sat in front of me, eyebrows in his hairline, worry glinting in his eyes and I would bet something like regret was blaring in his head for ever coming back.

I pulled back a bit. "I'll have Abby reach out to set up a meeting with Kelly so we can get all the details. Who's your assistant?" I asked, words more calm than a few seconds prior.

"Oliver," he replied reluctantly.

Served him right, I hoped Oliver was as lazy as ever and Decker ended up doing most of the work himself. "Good, he's good. Have him send the request out to a forensic accountant, we knew last time he was hiding accounts that we couldn't find, and I'm sure this time is no different. I want his employment history, his leasing portfolio, I want to know everything he's done in the past two years."

Funny sentence seeing as it could apply to two different people.

When I finally looked back at him, he was smiling. It was only a small pull at the corner of his full lips and I had no idea what it meant.

I shut my computer a little harder than needed and began stuffing my bag full of my items, intent on leaving the room without another word to him.

He cleared his throat. "I don't know if you still live in the same place but you should know I'm renting an apartment in that complex."

Whatever my face contorted into, I had no control over. Him showing back up after two years was one thing, an annoying plot twist I could work on being okay with. But him in my apartment complex felt like I would be trapped, forced into seeing him more than I wanted. I would see him for hours on end at work and also possibly run into him while taking out the trash or picking up my mail.

It was a fucking nightmare.

"Why are you in Fairvale? Why not Cornelia or literally anywhere else in the world or hell, why not stay wherever you have been. Why here?"

"My sister and nieces moved here. Something about the schools being better than by my parents in Cornelia. And when I was told I got the job, it was the best fit. I looked elsewhere, I did," he added quickly before I could throw a snide remark, "but with such a short notice, your complex was the only one with something available."

I could only muster up a glare.

"Do you still live there?" he asked.

"Yes."

He only nodded. "My place is on the other side so I don't think we'll see each other much. I just thought you should know."

Hoping he would change his mind and suddenly tell me it was joke while standing around in the middle of the office hallway apparently wasn't going to happen, but I stood for another second just in case.

"Have Oliver send out the subpoena and I'll let you know when the meeting with Kelly is." Those were the words that came out, when really there were a million other questions on my mind.

THIRTY-SEVEN

Carina

ABBY WAS WANDERING THE dress section a few feet away. We'd been there for hours, Lennon attended for moral support, while Abby and I looked for dresses for the gala next week. Although, knowing I had to sit at a table with Decker, it all seemed less appealing the closer we got.

Lennon held up a deep green dress with a knee length slit up the right leg and a bow tied at one shoulder. It was pretty and I was tired of looking.

"Oh, thats pretty, are you going to get it?" Abby asked, approaching as Lennon handed over the dress, a golden colored gown in her hands.

"It's fine." I tossed it over my arm with little care.

Both sisters stilled at my clipped answer. "You okay?" Lennon, ever the older sister, asked. She never found out about what happened between me and Decker. Maybe Abby told her about my breakdown, and subsequent demanded that we never speak of him, but I never confided in either of them.

I wasn't hiding him, but it was nice back then having him all to myself. Not having to worry about what people thought about us or having to disclose it to work.

He was a secret, but he was my secret.

And then he was nothing.

I felt as if I was living life behind a bubble since he left, everyone could see me but no one could hear me. I'd been screaming for someone to notice how miserable I was. Under all the layers I had piled on myself, I just wanted someone to notice I was lonely so I didn't have to say it out loud.

Then he showed up and suddenly I had two sides wrestling. One side wanted to tell him how much I missed him. That side of me wanted him to tell me he never meant to leave that it was all some misunderstanding. What that could be, who knew, but if he had a case to make, I would listen.

Then there was the other side of me that was so hurt and embarrassed, I wished he would have stayed wherever he was and left me in peace. I would have found my way out of the bubble I put myself in eventually. I always did.

An alarm blared from my purse. I fished it out in time to see the meeting reminder.

"I have a meeting," I said to the sisters. "I'm just going to get this one. No use of spending all day stressing over a dress I'm only going to wear for an hour."

"Wait," Abby called out. Trailing after me as I walked toward the checkout stand. "We always stay the whole night. You know I love people-watching at the end to see who leaves with who." Abby's eyes doubled in size as she tried to use her softness to charm me.

"Normally, I love that too but I don't know about this time." I waved goodbye to both of them, paid far too much for a dress I'd barely wear, and headed out to meet Kelly.

———

Evening traffic downtown was the eighth gate of hell. I fought against it the entire way to a cafe near Kelly's house. Her daughter would be at a toddler gymnastic class next door and she only wanted to meet when it wouldn't take time away from her.

I pulled into the parking lot to see Kelly sitting at a table in front of the glass window but she wasn't alone. I wondered if there was going to be a time when I saw him and my blood didn't run cold.

Sitting at the table with Kelly, was Decker, smiling brightly at her as he shrugged out of suit jacket and pulled at the knot, loosening his tie. If I was a gambling woman, I would have put money on him being late. And yet there he was, before me, talking to a client, putting her at ease without anyone around to see.

The Decker I knew, was perpetually late, forgetful and all around lacked the ability to take anything seriously. It was part of this charm. Even if it drove me mad. I didn't know what to do with a confident, capable Decker, being a weakness I never knew existed.

I snatched my bag from the passenger seat. Whatever was happening inside, I should've been a part of. Not sitting in my car reminiscing.

A bell dinged above me as I pushed into the cafe only to be hit by a cloud of coffee aroma. I breathed in deep, salivating at the thought of getting a latte but it'd have to wait. He straightened in his seat as I approached their table. Kelly turned to meet me as I called out a greeting.

"Carina," Kelly said as she stood and pulled me in for a hug. I forgot how touchy she was.

"Kelly, thank you for meeting me," I looked over at Decker. "Or us I should say."

Her laugh was as soft as a wind chime in a summer breeze. Everything about her was soft. Her voice, her demeanor, she was the blueprint of a 1950s housewife. Everything I never wanted to be.

The chair screeched over the floor as Decker reached out one of his long arms and pulled it out for me. I slipped into it without a thought. Their polite chatter continued as I pulled out a notepad when, from the corner of my eye, Decker slid a to-go cup in front of me. It was nonchalant, like it was part of a normal routine, as if we had a routine.

I listened as he continued asking about her daughter without a pause in his words as I stared at the cup.

I should ignore it, right? Who did he think he was? Showing up at my work after two years then, two weeks later, slipping me a coffee.

I hated the coffee, I hated him but I was running on fumes. Drinking a hate coffee didn't mean I forgave him or at least that was what I was telling myself.

"So, Ms. Leon," I started, my eyes flicking to the cup.

"Kelly, please."

"Kelly. You've been through this process before, so it's going to be pretty similar. If at any point during our conversation today you want to take a break or need a minute just let me— us—know, okay?"

She nodded.

Finally I gave in and reached for it, the paper cup was warm in my grasp as I quickly brought it to my lips and took a sip. Light, sweet flavors filled my mouth as I drank the first brown sugar latte I had had in two years. I pushed forward with the conversation, trying to not let that little fact deter me even though it felt like I was careening off a cliff. "Let's start with how you two got back together. The last time we saw each other you were determined to get away. What changed?"

She barely flinched at my words. Which was good. The words weren't meant to inflict pain but the story mattered

It wasn't unheard of, people end up back with someone they swore they would never be with for all sorts of reasons. But Kelly was different, she was scared of him, almost, even if she never came out and said it.

She took a steady breath and launched into her story. A few months after their divorce finalized, she fell ill and was in the hospital for over a month. Ben was apparently overly attentive, taking over all the care for Amelia who was only two months old. When she was discharged, he convinced her to move back in, under the guise it would be easier on her with his help and with her still being weak, she agreed. She wove us a tale that over weeks of close interaction, she realized that the man she originally fell in love with was still there, so she never left. A year later, they re-married and six months ago she found out she was pregnant again.

Thats when the cycle began to repeat itself.

Decker's fingers flew across his computer just inside my peripheral view. The notes were meticulous, no detail missed. At some point, I sat down my pen to focus on Kelly and let him take the lead. Which I had never done before and felt almost sacrilegious.

My mind raced while she told her story. And the questions I was asking myself had nothing to do with the client in front on me. By the end of her story, I was convinced she was conned into a new relationship with the same cold and calculated man as before and I felt an array of emotions for her.

When it hit six o' clock, she suddenly stood. "Sorry, but Amelia's class is over and I need to get her."

"Of course. Thank you, we'll be in touch soon."

She breezed out the front door, leaving us to each other and the sounds of coffee being made. Buzzing of a grinder, the hiss of steam clearing the wand, mindless chatter from the few other people occupying tables close by. It was common for people to gravitate there for a quiet place to relax, except I was anything but finding peace.

Every noise amplified the distress in my body. *If only I could leave.*

I started tossing my useless notepad into my bag, but that was as far as I got. "Can you send me the notes?"

"Already done," he said on the heels on my question.

Get up, I screamed at myself. *Leave the coffee, get up, and leave.*

Until I was able to put the pieces of what happened between us together, I couldn't be alone with him. It was too much. Too much wondering, too much hurt trying to make its way out of the cage I placed it in, too much of him and me and memories I didn't want to think about.

But my legs didn't move. I grabbed the cup and took another sip to occupy my hands from taking matters away from my head and acting on their own. Would they strangle him or pull him in, who knew? Certainly not me, my brain had turned itself off in order to stay in the moment.

We sat inches apart, with stupidly good coffee between us as his golden eyes roamed over my face. And I let him as everything faded into indistinct background noise. I just didn't think it would be painful as he slowly categorized what stayed the same and what may have changed.

I needed to know. I needed at least one scrap of information of where he'd been for the last two years. "Where did you get your law degree from?"

He must of sensed I was fishing for information and for a second he seemed like he wasn't going to tell me. "SW Law," his monotoned voice replied.

Finally I turned to look at him, his eyes a replica of the pain pumping through my veins.

What the hell was he doing in Los Angeles?

THIRTY-EIGHT

Decker

THE QUESTION WASN'T WHETHER or not I should have told her where I went to school. It was more of I should have made her stay so I could tell her the whole story. Carina left in a hurried rage after telling her where I went to school. Los Angeles held no meaning for her. It held no meaning to me, until I moved.

I could have cleared this entire issue up with only a few more words. So why couldn't I bring myself to say them?

Was I punishing her without realizing it? Was I still hurting and taking it out on her by withholding the information? Making her hate me more with each day that passed, letting her think I left her without reason.

And which was worse?

My phone sat propped on a shelf in my kitchen while I prepped a sad dinner for one. The video ringer was going as I waited for Laura to pick up. It took longer than usual but finally her face filled the screen. "Hi, little brother," she exclaimed.

"Hey." I moved the phone near the stove with one hand and flipped the burger I had on the pan with the other.

"Wow, don't sound too excited to talk to me. What's up, what's wrong?"

"Nothing's wrong."

"Sure, and I'm not your favorite sister." She rolled her eyes at me. I slapped a piece of cheese on and waited for it to melt then pulled it off the heat and placed it on a bun. "Don't get in to too much detail, I might not be able to keep up," she mocked after the prolonged silence on my part.

"How's Brynn?"

She side-eyed me from the screen, her finger coming up to tap and the view changed. "She's good, tired still, but good." The relief in her voice palpable. It soothed a piece of my heart that has been on fire for years.

My niece appeared smaller than she was, curled up in her bed, surrounded by more stuffed animals than one kid really needed. Soft curls, as black as mine, and were finally long enough to tuck behind her ears. They didn't live far from my apartment but I ached to be close to them. Spending two years as my sister's roommate, or live in nanny as I liked to joke, would do that to you.

The camera flipped back to her face. "Now tell me why you really called."

My phone balanced on the plate as I walked to the couch as I still didn't have any dining room furniture to sit in.

"I didn't think working with her again would be so..." Laura waited in silence as I paused, "hard," I ended up on. "I don't know. She's angry, keeping me at arms length, won't talk to me directly, or at least not really. We're stuck on a case together so we have to talk but it's cold. I don't know how to explain it to her in a way that doesn't seem like one giant excuse."

"Hold please." The screen went fuzzy as I tore a bite of the sandwich off. I was mid chew when another face appeared.

Lola appeared. "Sup, bitches?"

"Why is she here, Laura? I called you," I whined. My back hit the couch as I began to pout.

"Yeah, and you're bitching about the girl. Of course I'm going to call her."

Lola's wearing a shit eating grin. "Ohh, is he talking about her again?"

Laura nodded and I contemplated hanging up.

"Why don't you just tell her?" Lola practically yelled the words. "She'll understand once you tell her."

This was a revolving door type of conversation. Her and Lola liked to gang up on me about it, every chance they got. But they were the only ones who knew everything about Carina. *Really* knew.

"You make it seem so easy," I said.

"It is and I don't know why you didn't go back right after Brynn's surgery, but that's just me," my ever-so-wise oldest sister chimed in.

She was right, not that I would tell her that, it would only go to her head. What did I expect to happen when I left without a word? Blocking me was the easiest thing to do, I should have expected it, but instead I let the anger from the situation with my sister and niece get the best of me and used it as an excuse to never go back. It was the stupidest realization I'd had to date but it was the truth. Even if it was dumb and I was left to pick up the pieces I shattered.

If I didn't go back, I wouldn't have to see the hurt I caused. It was the easier choice and with everything that happened, choosing my family was something I wouldn't regret.

"You like her still, we all know it. The two years you spent here I never so much as saw you as flirt with another woman. Tell her that it was a misunderstanding and show her you are in this Levi. You owe it to yourself to tell her at the very least," Laura rationalized.

I hated when they were right.

My phone was close to a cracking point as I gripped it.

Laura spoke up again. "I will be grateful for everything you did for Brynn and me, our whole family. But you deserve to have your life back, you gave up everything for us. If she is still what you want, then you need to tell her."

My thumb rubbed across my eyebrow, a tactic to keep tears or a headache from forming. I couldn't tell which I was trying to stave off though. All I could mange was a nod. They both said their goodbyes and I was left with a blank screen, a half-eaten sandwich, and a blackhole where my stomach should've been.

There was a chance she would see it as an excuse and I wouldn't be someone worth forgiving. Maybe what we had was built up in my head and we weren't on our way to being a great love story. But I couldn't move on until she knew.

Thirty-Nine

Carina

The gala should have had me on a high. Usually I relished slipping on a pretty dress and drinking until my limbs were warm. Staying until the tables were cleared and lights flicked on with Abby, but this year was different.

Levi was sure to be at our table, even if he was a last minute addition. Sitting around and watching women fall over themselves to talk to him wasn't what I wanted to be doing. It was inevitable, no matter where he went there was always someone trying to get his attention. The dancing, and fake smiles, everyone at their best while I was dying inside was like being trapped in a nightmare.

I procrastinated as long as I could before I had to go home to get ready. My makeup was rushed, my hair barely gave off the old Hollywood glamour I was going for which pissed me off ,and I was seconds away from faking sick and staying home.

But I sucked it up and pulled the dress up my body. It fit my form like a glove and the sheer green organza fell around my feet like I had been sketched for a fairytale story. Except I didn't feel like a princess, I felt like the carriage after it turned back to a pumpkin. There was no white knight waiting for me, no one to slip a glass slipper on my foot, no one for me at all, but that was what I had always wanted? Wasn't it?

Even if I didn't feel like royalty, at least the gala would.

Tall cocktail tables draped in black table cloths, with lush red rose arrangements were spread out in the large ballroom as I walked through the door and headed straight to the bar. Large circle dinner tables covered the area on the far right of the room and I was glad to see the absence of a dance floor.

Once the bartender handed over my drink, I plastered a smile to my face and started my initial round around the room saying hello and introducing myself to guests I didn't know. Networking I was good at, great even. Zeroing in on what made people feel good about themselves and by proxy good about their work was one of my top skills.

A booming laugh escaped the man in front of me as I told him some fabricated story about my childhood. He was the head of the forensic firm we used and I wanted that report Levi had requested sooner than later. Behind him, I finally spotted Abby leaning against the bar. I politely excused myself and escaped over to her.

The gold dress she chose shimmered in the bar light. It was as if she was covered in thousands of twinkling fairy lights and the copper in her hair shone through more than ever.

"Hey," I breathed out as a relief. She smiled wide as she handed me a glass of champagne she got from the bartender.

I plucked the delicate glass from her hand. "Ugh, you know me so well." I took a small sip and let the effervescent bubbles dance along my tongue, my eyes closing for a moment to savor it.

"Damn," Abby breathed.

My eyes popped open to see what she was talking about.

He was the first thing I saw. And damn was right. No, damn was an understatement.

Sometimes a tux wears the person, and then other times the person wears the tux. In Decker's case, it was the latter. He was wearing the ever loving fuck out of the tuxedo he had on for lack of a better term.

It was a stark black that almost looked almost like velvet with stain lapels and gold buttons to top it all off. His hair was in an in-between growth phase that slicking it back was the only option to appear put-to-gether and it worked. His whole demeanor was a man who was confident in himself and everyone in the room was buying it.

"Your mouth is hanging open," Abby whispered behind her glass.

I closed my mouth. "Shut up." Abby only laughed.

"Anything you wanna talk about, Carina?" she asked with a tilt of her head. Ignoring her was my only recourse. I took another sip and looked back to where he was.

Decker looked past the man he was talking to and locked eyes with me. A slow smile crept across his lips until they moved to form the words excuse me and made a bee line toward Abby and me.

She spoke up first. "Well, well, well, Levi Decker, you clean up real good when there's not a dorky tie around your neck." His hearty laughed filled the area around us.

"Thanks, you look great as well, gold looks good on you." Abby flipped her hair behind her shoulder and basked in his praise, causing my stomach to burn.

Well that was new.

She took another glass from the bar behind her and handed it over to him. His left arm extended out, the fabric around his wrist scrunching upwards.

"That's a funny thing to wear," Abby commented, nodding toward his wrist.

He grabbed the glass, his eyes flicking toward me lightning fast before he tugged down the sleeve of his dress shirt over the purple tie around his wrist.

That day seemed so far away. It was barely a blip on my radar as something significant, and surely not something that needed to be kept. The sight of it fogged my senses. Or maybe it was the champagne I slammed at the sight of my hair tie on his wrist. Or maybe it was because he smelled divine, clean and sensual. I didn't know but I was on high alert in this small moment of time.

"Carina."

"Decker."

People began to move in rushed flurry to take their seats. He gestured to the bartender and a second later he was handing me another glass.

"Should we find our seats?" he asked.

I'm not generally easily charmed, but there was something or everything about him that was making it hard for me to remember why I was ever mad in the first place. A tight lipped smile was all I could muster before the three of us found the table with our names. Of course it would have been too much to hope for to have Abby between us, but the world was against me as I took my seat to his right and Abby to his left.

He pulled my seat out and I sat down silently, I could hear a faint chuckle from him at my obvious attempt to ignore him.

I turned my attention to my table mate on my other side.

Ian Wheeler.

He was older than me by about ten years, but still incredibly good looking. Unfortunately he knew it and loved to use it to his advantage if he could. Light hair cropped short, large build, like he spent most of college on the field but when he didn't make it pro being a lawyer was the next best thing. He was a bit on the sleazy side, where all his words were sweeter than sugar and nothing was genuine, but nice enough.

A perfect distraction from the man I was pretending to be over. Or not talking to. Or whatever it was I was not doing with him.

"Ian." I leaned in for a hug but his lips pressed a kiss into to my cheek. *Gross.* I ignored it and kept to my plan. "It's so great to see you again." I could feel Deckers's back stiffen behind me. I hadn't seen Ian since the final meeting during Kelly's first case, but he didn't know that.

"Hey, sweetheart," he crooned.

Again, gross.

I ignored that too.

We spent the dinner talking, before it led to whispering back and forth, and my hand touched his arm as I faked a laugh—Decker was hating every second of it.

He remained tight lipped and stabbed angrily at his food every once in a while. It was thrilling almost, knowing my lack of attention was getting to him. I wondered what else about me would get to him.

FORTY

Carina

It was going a little too far, but the champagne had dulled my senses enough to not care.

The dinner dragged, but I was so preoccupied about the visceral reaction I was pulling out of the man to my left that I was having the time of my life. A laugh escaped my mouth that was so fake I wondered how Ian couldn't see it.

Dessert was placed in front of us in unison. I turned my attention to the slice of cheesecake that had strawberries dripping down the sides and quietly let out my disappointment. It was probably delicious but it wasn't the chocolate cake placed in front of Decker I was trying not to stare at.

I hated fruit in my dessert.

An internal debate was taking place in my head about whether or not I should eat it when Decker's hand entered my space. He gripped the edge of the plate and pulled it toward him but before I could even think to ask what the hell he was doing, he placed his dessert in front of me.

Not a single word.

Nothing.

But he remembered, and he needed to stop.

He needed to forget everything he knew or at the very least stop letting me know he remembered because it was slowly killing me.

I abandoned my cheap flirting and picked up my fork, dessert always deserved my full focus. Before sliding in what was about to be the greatest thing I have ever tasted between my lips.

I audibly moaned the second flavors exploded on my tongue and it wasn't on purpose.

Levi tracked my movements like a religious experience. Ian, well, I didn't really want to pay attention to him any more.

"Good?" Decker asked.

I nodded, not even caring that I was actively not engaging in casual conversation with him as I scooped up another bite.

He placed his own fork between his lips. "It's not the tiramisu served at your parents' place, but it's not bad." My hand stalled. This was the first either of us mentioned what I've coined as the 'before' time. Before he left, before I was more of an ice queen, before everything.

He was right though, nothing beat my mother's tiramisu.

After the plates were cleared, I looked to Abby to let her know I would be leaving, but she was gone. I would love to linger around until the end like we used to but I flew a little to close to the sun with Ian and I was pretty sure he was two seconds away from asking me to get a room with him. And that was not something I was interested in.

I left the table in search of her, not realizing she had disappeared at some point. My heels clicked down the hallway against the tiled floor, echoing in the empty space. When I turned to the hallway that led to the restrooms, I ran smack into the man I was avoiding.

When the fuck did he get up from the table too? Was I that drunk that I didn't even notice people getting up and leaving?

"Ian, sorry about that," I said sweetly as I tried to back away but I was locked in his unsuspecting grasp.

He smiled down at me. "I thought you left without saying goodbye," he remarked in a way that made it feel like a threat. "The night doesn't really have to end, you know?" His hands trailed down from where he had caught my upper arms. The smell of whiskey polluted the air. I took another step to pull myself away but his fingers dug into me. My only hope was that Abby was in the bathroom and would walk out and rescue me. Heavy flirting was a mistake. A bad, bad mistake that I was having to do cartwheels to get out of.

"It does, Ian, I have an early morning and was just leaving. I only needed to say goodbye to a friend." I teetered on my heels. My head swirled looking for a refuge, anyone would do but the only person I saw was Decker.

Because of course he would be the only one around.

Even at this distance, the scowl on his face was noticeable. To anyone else, this might have looked like a wanted embrace but it wasn't and I was doing everything I could think of to make sure that was evident. The closer Levi got, the faster the look morphed. A bit more angry, a bit uneasy. I rolled my shoulder, breaking the hold Ian had on me in time for him to reach us.

"There you are," Levi announced, eyes blazing and looking only at me. With what emotion was impossible to tell. A tick in his jaw told me annoyance. The slow inhale as he slipped his arm around my waist told me something else entirely. Every nerve ending lit up like the firework finale on the Fourth of July. I melted into his side out of instinct, as if my body rejoiced in being back home after a long vacation and for a few heartbeats it was almost as if he never left.

A bubble appeared around us, where time was simply a construct, one where two years were nothing but a blink of an eye. One simple touch and the sound of ice cracking filled my head as the parts of my heart that froze over the moment I realized he left without so much as a word, melted.

"Abby's been looking for you. I told her I would come and find you before she left." His hand didn't leave me as he tugged me in closer. He turned, finally acknowledging the other person with a quick tilt of his head. "Ian." Then his attention was back on me.

Ian blinked at the interaction.

"It was great to see you," I lied to him, before allowing Decker to lead us out the side door.

The cold night air a welcome respite to my flushed skin. We walked in silence, until we reached the rooftop pool, only then did I pull myself out of his grasp. Darkness blanketed the area, lounge chairs like headstones in a forgotten cemetery.

Goosebumps erupted over my skin. "You didn't need to do that but I appreciate it," I said, staring at small ripples in the pool instead of him. "I flew a little too close to the sun with that one." A nervous laugh, probably the first bit of a nervousness I felt in a long while, made an appearance. Another gust of wind pushed through the patio we were on, sending shivers down my spine. This dress was beautiful but was no match for the late September air.

"You were laying it on pretty thick," he said, his voice as chilly as the night.

"Yeah, well, it was that or..."

"Or what, Carina?" The statement more of a pained demand than a question. "Talk to me?"

Yes, exactly. I would rather lick the sidewalk on Main Street for all to see. I would rather see the gynecologist every day of the rest of my life. I would rather flirt with a grease ball like Ian Wheeler, of all people, than make small talk with him at dinner. How did he not get that?

I walked the length of the pool to get away before I accidentally said all that out loud.

"Are we just never going to talk about it?" he yelled after me.

"Not if I can help it," I shouted back over my shoulder, anger bubbling like thick lava in my chest at the notion he could just ask and I would, what, turn around and say 'yes please, I'd love to'? Please tell me all about how you left me rotting in that restaurant and how I never heard from you again never.

"Carina." My name echoed from his mouth as a plea.

I could feel him at my back, a breath away and I didn't know whether to lean in or flee. How did he have a hold on me after all these years? I was strong but I was floating between anger and torment. Each fighting for the upper hand.

Deft fingers ghosted across my skin and all my resolve crumbled.

"Please—" I choked out but I didn't know what I was begging for?

"Please, what?" His voice was low and gravelly.

Please touch me again? Please leave me to my misery?

This was a trap, an enticing, desire inducing trap. His cologne diluted my senses, leaving me pliable to his advances. His head dipped, lips at the shell of my ear. "Amore, please talk to me," he pleaded again.

I whipped around. "NO," I roared, my hands hit his chest, shoving him back. The word spewing out of me like a vengeful volcano, and I was ready to rain fire. "You don't get to do that. You don't get to show up after two years and say that."

I couldn't take it.

I didn't want this, my gut said to flee so I listened. I turned on my heel, my dress spinning around me dramatically.

Only, he followed as I stalked away.

FORTY-ONE

Decker

Her dress flowed behind her as she swiftly sauntered away from me. Moonlight bounced off the green of her dress, and illumined her porcelain skin. She was like a fallen angel. An angry fallen angel, but an angel nonetheless.

"Carina," I shouted. "Please talk to me."

"Why, Decker?" she yelled at the wind without turning around, and kept walking until her hands clutched at the wall that over looked the city, shoulders rising and falling with each breath. I reached my hand out slowly, but she sensed me coming and shrugged me off like an unwanted bug. I didn't need to touch her to feel her body vibrating with the anger she was holding in.

"I cannot keep going on like this. You have to hear me out please." Her grip on the wall tightened, any more and it would crumble beneath her altogether. "I'll do anything, *please*. Yell at me if you have to but please just talk to me," I begged.

I think I would beg for a lifetime for the chance to explain myself. My sisters were right, I still wanted her. I wanted my life back, her back.

"You're too late." Her voice three octaves higher than normal, her dress spun with her as she whipped around. "You never reached out, I moved on. We should both move on, Decker."

Move on?

I couldn't move on. I was stuck in the past with her because it was the only place I got to have her. I had to tell her. Once she knew why, it would all make sense and she could forgive me. But my anger got the best of me. "You're the one who blocked me. I called and texted, hell I even emailed you, but everything bounced back. How was I supposed to reach you? I don't understand why you are so mad." My fingers ran through my product riddled hair, turning my hands sticky.

The time Carina and I had before all this wasn't long, a few months of being together but not *together*. I didn't know every corner of her soul but I knew what she looked like when she angry and this wasn't anger. Or wasn't only anger. Pain shimmered in her eyes, turning them a vibrant shade of green, as she forced her tears to stay beneath the waterline.

"Why am I so mad?" she nearly screamed, her voice cracking over the last word. "Why am I so mad? I cannot believe you would say something that stupid." Her heels clicked as she paced along the concrete. This wasn't going as planned. I didn't have a plan but I knew it wasn't wherever this was going. "I never wanted this!" she shouted at me. Pink tinging the tops of her cheeks, wind blowing her curls loose. "I never wanted to be the woman who put man in the forefront of their life. That wasn't me. I worked too fucking hard to get where I am and I was fine with how my life was, Decker. I didn't want anything like what Lennon has or what Abby is always searching for." She took two steps toward me, arms flinging out with the words.

It felt like a win, she was talking to me, until I saw tears slipping down her face.

"Until you." Her voice broke, nearly toppling me over with the flood of emotions that came with it. "You ripped apart the wall I spent decades building and I wasn't even mad about it. I thought... I thought, finally—" She choked on the words and my fingers itched to touch her, to do anything but I was rendered useless. "I thought, *finally*, someone could see past the mask I wore and thought that this cold, detached woman I made myself into was enough." She confessed with her hands pressed into her stomach.

"I—"

She held up her hand, cutting me off.

"You took up space in my chest, in my fucking heart, that I wasn't going to give to anyone. Parts of me that never even crossed my mind to give away and then you were gone. Leaving a hole in the shape of your stupid body that I can't get rid of. So mad doesn't even begin to cover the vast array of emotions I have been filled with since you left."

"I tried, Carina, but what was I supposed to do?"

She took a menacing step toward me, her heels putting us eye level and in them I saw years of anger burning. "You could have tried *harder*. For fucks sake, Decker you fed me all these sweet words for months, and then you just left. I'm fucking livid." Her anger boiled over and it was white hot. "Two years." She shook the fingers in my face. "You have been gone doing god knows what for two years. I thought I mattered, you made me feel like I mattered." Her chest heaved up and down.

"You do ma—"

"I don't want to hear it," she screamed back at me, fingers trembling as she threw up her hands before spinning away and clutching the sides of her head as if she was in pain. "You and I never happened, okay? That's how I've been living the past two years and that's how I will keep going. You being here now changes nothing, nothing you can say will change that."

I begged her to talk to me and I didn't have any words for her. I didn't know what to do in the face of all the destruction and pain I caused. I wanted to tell her how I wanted to come back the moment I got to that hospital. That as soon as everything calmed down and I caught my breath, she was the first thing to come to my mind but at that point it had been a few days and I panicked.

She deserved the truth and I couldn't stand there and watch her walk away from me. The pain of my niece being diagnosed was unbearable but this was an agonizing type of torture. It was like I was losing her all over again. The satin of her deep green dress hugged her curves, dipping so low on her back that made it nearly impossible to speak but I had to tell her.

"My niece was sick," I managed to get past the lump in my throat. It was a bit too loud, a bit too direct, but not in anger at her, but with the world and how everything played out.

Carina spun around, confusion morphed her angelic like face to one I hardly recognized. "What did you just say?"

It was hard to pull one over on Carina, she's known in our industry for having all the details before you even knew you needed them. She was always one step ahead of everyone, and if I was being honest it was how I kept going all these years. I talked myself into believing that she somehow found out and still chose to block all forms of communication. It was easier for me that way.

Clearly I was wrong.

"I didn't want to leave, but I got a call she was being admitted to the hospital after collapsing at soccer practice. I was in my car and driving to be with my sister and my nieces because they needed their family."

She needed to understand that I didn't want to leave her, I left because I had to.

Every moment of that night still played on a loop in my head. I remember holding two shirts and going back and forth in front of a mirror, trying to decide when my phone rang. A part of me figured it was Carina calling to cancel, she was going to tell me she thought about it more and decided she was going to call off the whole thing. Instead I picked up my phone to see my sister's name. When I answered silence hung in the balance for so long I figured it was a pocket dial, but then came the crying.

"When I got there, my sister told me she was being life-flighted to another hospital, for treatment. They couldn't figure out what was wrong with her here. My sister flew with Brynn, but I drove Kevin and Bailey straight to San Fransisco so they didn't have to be separated."

Carina hadn't moved, she was listening, but I couldn't tell what she was thinking.

"I left so fast I forgot my phone." I swear she looked as if she was going to roll her eyes. "I know, I know how it sounds, but it's the truth. All I thought about was my sister and my nieces when I left, and I'm not going to apologize for that."

I didn't want to leave but I felt like I was fighting a losing battle. I couldn't make her forgive me. Nobody could make Carina Pera do anything she didn't want to do, I always knew that. I just didn't realize how much it sucked being on the other side of a tug a war with her.

My fingers ran through my hair, the strands reached past the top of my ears. I spent the last two years mad at everyone and everything, without thinking, and out of spite, I kept my hair cropped short. I did anything to make sure I didn't have to think about her.

When I looked back she was shaking her head but not looking at me, contemplating something. I could see the wheels turning in her head as she tried working out whatever problem was there. "Then why would

Diane say when you called to tell her you weren't coming back that you should have told her sooner." Her words were demanding.

"What?"

"That's what I was told."

"What are you talking about? How would I have known she was going to get sick? That's ridiculous."

"Abby asked her what happened when you called her and she only said you mentioned that you should have told her sooner."

I wracked my brain to pull forward the conversation but I was at a loss, that whole night and day were a blur.

Until it clicked.

I breathed out my frustration. "She mentioned that if I ever wanted to come back I could and I told her that I was in law school, and I said maybe I would come back as an associate." I began to pace. I hadn't thought about this conversation since I had it. Diane was shocked to hear I had to write but was speechless to learn I was in school. "She asked why I didn't tell the firm I started school."

"And why didn't you?" she demanded. "You never so much as mentioned to me about starting school or that you applied. Was that your plan all along. Get into school, leave the firm, leave me without ever mentioning it?"

"No, Carina, no. It had nothing to do with not telling anyone and everything to do with my fear of failing. Law school and leaving had nothing to do with each other and nothing to do with you." My throat ached with relief of finally having the truth come out. "I never wanted to leave you."

"I sat in that restaurant for over an hour waiting." She mirrored my position, arms limp at her side, defeat washing over her features. "On Saturday, I was inconsolable, by Sunday I was blind with anger and blocked every form of communication with you that I could think of. By

Monday I was terrified and spent the day calling hospitals and morgues because I still hadn't heard from you. When they told us on Tuesday that you had left the company, I was numb. What was I supposed to think, Levi?" Her eyes closed and she slowly shook her head.

"I left with nothing," I said again, like it would help. "I don't know how to tell you how sorry I am. I didn't leave the hospital the entire weekend. I ended up being the donor for her surgery and put in my notice for leave that weekend."

Everything about this situation was fucked and I didn't even know how to fix it, all I knew was that I wanted to, but the story had so many layers and they were all piling on top of one another.

My fingers inched closer until our fingertips brushed against each other. When she didn't immediately move I breathed a sigh of relief. "I don't know what to say other than I'm sorry. I'm so fucking sorry." Someone's eyes could tell you everything you needed to know and for a split second, I saw the hurt in her eye break. I think she knew it was no one's fault but that didn't erase two years of thinking I left her without so much as a word.

"Tell me how to fix us, Carina."

Her fingertips traced the purple band on my wrist, the one I hadn't taken off since the day I put it on. "There is no us, Decker," she whispered. "Not anymore."

Without a second look she left me standing out in the cold while remorse burned deep in my stomach.

FORTY-TWO

Carina

COULD NOTHING GO MY way? Just once, that was all I wanted, something, anything to happen that was good. But no, life was on an agonizingly slow, downhill spiral for me. "You've got to be kidding me." I shifted more boxes around in the supply closet, but it appeared the new office manager decided to no longer stock my favorite pens.

I wished it didn't matter, or that I was less rigid about...well, everything.

The metal door of the supply locker rattled after closing it a bit harder than anticipated. I turned on my heel to go sulk about having to purchase my favorite pens when the air heaved out of my chest as I collided with a person walking into the small room.

An apology hit my tongue but before I got it out, I looked up. "Oh, it's you." I backtracked into the room as Decker took a step in my direction, crowding me. My heart stuttered at the closeness. This whole town felt five times too small since he came back, being trapped in a room that was no bigger than a closet was no better. We hadn't even spoke since

263

the gala, at least nothing more than a few professional emails answering a quick question he had about filing court documents.

"What did the door ever do to you?" He flashed me a small smile and chuckled under his breath.

It was really hard to focus on his words when he looked like *that*. Tailored suit, golden eyes, and just a hit of an arrogant smile. An almost deadly combination.

I was distracted, oh so very distracted. His tie vanished at some point, and the top two buttons of his shirt were left open, exposing the hollow point at the base of his neck. Damnit, he also smelt good, like the citrus trees along the river.

I shook the fog out. "Nothing, I just went through my last pen and apparently we're not stocking them anymore. There's only the cheap ones with our logo on it." I held up the pathetic writing utensil.

"I have some in my office, if you want one," he offered casually, but it wasn't lost on me that he knew exactly what type of pens I would be looking for.

"Oh." I had been avoiding him for a reason—realizing everything you thought you knew was a lie will do that to you. But I really wanted my pens. He patiently waited for me to figure out if I was going to keep ignoring him or not.

Damn it.

"Yeah, that would be great."

We walked the length of the office in silence, and as the last two people, it was eerily quiet. We had the same four walls for our offices and yet his was not what I expected. It was homey, with a faux tree in the corner and art on the wall. But not the typical office art that looked like it was printed in the nineties and adorned at least ten offices in every county. It was a castle, a very familiar castle.

I walked over for a closer look as he rounded his desk and pulled open a drawer. "Huh." I leaned in closer to the glass and sure enough Theo's name was scribbled in the bottom corner.

"What?" he asked. I turned to him watching me, two pens at the ready in his hands.

"Did you know this photo was taken by Abby's brother in law?"

His gaze flitted over to the print. Immediately, the landscape of his face told me he didn't. "I had no idea. I bought it from the gallery across the street, wanted something local to liven the place up, you know?"

Not really, my office was much like my home—stark and lacked warmth. Another reminder about how different were are.

"Here." He held out the pens, my hair tie on full display. If he had something to say about the way I snatched them from his outstretched palm, attempting to touch him as little as possible, he didn't say it out loud. Instead he regarded me with eyes that were too warm, too penetrating, too familiar. Too much of so many things I forced myself to forget.

Stick to the plan.

Did I even have a plan?

I stared at the purple, worn threads which looked as if one small movement would cause it to snap and fall from his wrist. "Why do you still wear that?" Well if I had a plan, I was pretty sure that question wouldn't have been part of it.

His features morphed all at once, eyebrows squeezed together, lips pressed as if my question turned his stomach queasy. And then, as if without thought, his hand drifted toward his wrist and began toying with it. It was silent for a moment too long, him lost in caressing the weathered band, me warring with myself for asking about it in the first place.

I took a step back, making my way toward the door. He didn't have to tell me, and honestly I wasn't sure if I wanted to know. Too many emotions attached themselves to his answer and neither one of us were ready, really ready, to talk about them if our last conversation was any indication.

This seemed like a good time for an Irish goodbye, he'll see me leave of course but we didn't need to acknowledge it. I was only there for pens after all. Another two steps and I was at his door, turning to make my exit when he answered.

"It's the only thing that reminds me we were real."

I wished he said nothing because now I knew all my nightmares were right.

——

Do you think if I Googled 'how to act when your not ex-boyfriend shows up after two years apart' it would give me an answer? If you answered yes, you'd be wrong. It gave me nothing. Nothing but fluffy articles about knowing your worth, or how to get him back by looking your hottest. Which was not what I wanted, because first of all, I wasn't trying to get him back, and second of all, I always looked good, so no article was needed on that front.

What I wanted was for something to tell me all these buried feelings trying to claw their way out were normal, and not a weakness. Because that was what I felt like, weaker than a baby deer on their first day of life. It was easier when he was gone, I fed myself a reason for his disappearance and ate it up until I was too full to look for the real answer. And I was fine with that, I could've lived with it, but that wasn't what was happening because I knew the truth.

There were still a thousand questions in my head and so many missing details but knowing I wasn't carelessly abandoned threw me into un-charted water.

"You coming?" Abby's head popped into my office on queue to grab me for the weekly meeting.

I clicked out of the useless article and fell into step with her toward the office. "So, how's it going?"

"How's what going?"

Abby's been treating me with kid gloves since Decker returned, 'checking in on me without checking in on me' type of deal. In turn I'd been ignoring her but not ignoring her. It was a shitty move, especially knowing I didn't have to act with her at all. Abby was my confidant but I didn't want to confide in her, in anyone. I wanted to not have to deal with him, my feelings and having to talk about it with her.

"Oh, so we're doing *that*. Got it." Abby didn't mean the words to be harsh, I genuinely believed she meant for them to be reassuring, for me to know she understood why I was deflecting but all it did was make me feel like a shitty friend.

Another thing to add to the list, I guessed.

We took our normal seats as everyone's good mornings rang out in unison.

"Not too much on the docket today but first I would like to congratulate Levi on his first closing," Diane announced, and polite clapping ensued.

Giraffes with sunglasses. That's what I noticed about him first, his tie. Next was his tight lipped smile at our co-workers. Last was how he noticed me staring at him. I tore my eyes away, and distracted myself with endless loops around the border of my notepad. Except every time I thought the coast was clear and looked up, he would glance my direction. The entire meeting was a constant cat and mouse game of who's looking at who.

For whatever godforsaken reason, I couldn't stop.

"I wanted to try out a new way to end our meetings, a way to get to know each other better," Diane said the words and I closed my eyes briefly in disdain. We may see each other more than we see our partners or friends but that did not mean I wanted to know personal details about any of them. "So, for today, what is something that we are all learning or would want to learn?" She was way too cheery for someone taking up my time.

You could hear the metaphorical pin drop with how silent it went as everyone stopped breathing at once and did their best to avoid eye contact. All of which was felt by Diane. "Okay, I'll go first, I would love to learn how to roller-skate. I did it when I was a kid and loved it but it's been, I don't know, forty years since I last strapped on some skates." She looked genuinely happy about the possibility of reliving a part of her childhood and you know what good for her but I was not about to share a damn thing.

Another collective breath holding competition started back up but then just before it seemed like she would give up altogether and leave us be, Decker spoke. "I'm learning how to cook."

Diane's eyes lit up. "Oooh, really? What kind of food?"

His eyes ping ponged between everyone as he adjusted in his seat, everyone but me. "Umm, Italian, actually."

"That sounds fantastic, what kind of dishes are you making?

"I'm making a ribollita this weekend."

"You're making ribollita?" I slid into the conversation with about as much finesse as a pushy salesman, making myself known when nobody asked and every pair of eyes snapped to me. Abby smacked my thigh with the back of her hand, a warning more than anything, about my tone, which probably was coming off more accusatory than anything.

"Yes?" he reluctantly answered.

I didn't know what to do with this information, so I acquiesced and let Diane wrap up the meeting. But as we filed out, I stalked Decker back to his office, slipping in behind him closing the door.

He acted oblivious, as he casually slipped back into his chair and dove into work as I stood fuming across from him. I didn't get it, it felt like every time I turned around, he was leaving a bread crumb trail of facts to remind me that we weren't strangers and it was a glaring reminder that at one point, we were something bigger.

"Since you're here, I got the records for the subpoena, would you agree with setting the first mediation meeting in person instead of a conference call like we would normally do given the history of their last case?"

I didn't want to talk about work. I wanted to talk about us—what was I saying? Not *us*, but the fact he was deliberately making it so I was forced to think about the past.

"I would. Best to get in front of everything, they hated having to meet in person last time, so I would make every meeting face-to-face now if you can. Ben is too self-absorbed to just let Ian handle it and will insist on coming, so stick to a hard schedule and don't let him change dates or anything to fit his needs. Really mess with him."

If I didn't like him reminding me of the past, I sure as hell didn't like the way he peered intently back at me. On the surface it was professional, a look you might give a stranger on the street, but it was layered. Underneath was unbridled desire, and a flash of heat burned across my skin. Finally, under it all was longing and that was the layer wrestled with the most.

"You're good at this."

"I know."

He smiled and I felt feverish.

"Ribollita," I finally say.

"Yeah, I got tired of canned sauce and pasta."

My nose curled at the thought. "Blasphemy. I promise it's way easier to make your own sauce and tastes a million times better than anything out of a can."

After a beat, he spoke up. "Will you show me?"

FORTY-THREE

Carina

I LIED. OR PARTLY lied but it was to myself, so it didn't count.

I really did try to find enough work to keep me at my desk past an hour. I figured I'd send him some 'I'm sorry, something came up' text and leave it at that. Or better yet I could have not shown up at all and given him a small dose of what I got two years ago.

I really did try not to go. I even three way called Lennon and Abby to force my way into their plans but with each of them now happily in a relationship, it would be very pathetic.

I really did try, I told myself as I stood in front of his door exactly an hour later.

He answered not even a second after I knocked.

As I walked inside and quickly noticed how homey it felt, not that I wasn't expecting much, but men living alone didn't generally have a good track record of turning a house into a home.

A small entry table sat by the door, with a bowl for his keys and wallet, a few hooks in the wall next to it held some of his work blazers. His TV was on but only music was softly playing from it instead of a show, making the moment less awkward. What surprised me the most was the wall you saw once you closed the front door. The entire space was covered in framed pictures, all different sizes and shapes but nothing looked out of place. Every picture looked as if it belonged, a miss matched puzzle of memories. They mostly looked like his family, all jet black hair of various body forms, but I didn't get a close enough look at all of them when an acidic burning smell assaulted me.

My face contorted and I had to restrain my hand from coming up to cover my nose. Although I'm sure my face said it all.

"I tried to start without you but you lied. It's way harder than opening a can of sauce."

Yeah, seemed like there was a lot I was lying about lately.

Our apartments were the same, I didn't wait for him to lead me where I knew the kitchen would be, where the strong burning smell was originating from.

Every counter was littered with bags from what looked to be three different grocery stores, vegetables, and herbs were in various different forms of prep, and a large new pot sat on the stove with the fire still going and smoke escaping from the top.

I couldn't help but laugh. "Okay, first rule. If it's smoking, turn off the heat." I turned the dial down and pushed the pot to the back burner, then flicked on the hood fan for good measure.

"Noted."

"What were you trying to make?" The black sludge really wasn't telling me much.

He ran his hand through his hair, the strand barely long enough to tuck behind his ears before reaching for his phone. "The recipe said 'easiest red sauce you'll ever make.'" He turned his phone to me and some blog with too many ads displayed on his screen.

"Second rule, cooking is a lot easier and smoother if you can prep as much as you can first." Slowly walking the counter length, I went over all the items he had and sure enough, it was everything I needed. Within minutes, I had the sauce simmering and the rest of dinner well on its way to being edible.

I picked up the wine glass Decker had refilled and sank back in his couch. "I forgot how much I love to cook."

"What about the restaurant?" A sudden look of terror crossed his face after he asked. "It's still open, right?"

"Yes, it's still open, I just don't work there anymore. On rare occasions I'll help test cook some new entrees but I haven't worked a shift since..." I didn't finish the sentence. "It was getting to be too much and turned out my dad was sick and I never even noticed. I much prefer having them as only my parents and not also as my employers." A thoughtful look passed over his face as I took a sip from his glass. "So tell me, what's new?" I asked, quickly moving the spotlight off of me.

He told me about law school and we went over some points I thought would be helpful for Kelly's case. He asked my opinion on another case he was assigned at work that seemed to be a straight forward divide in half and sign the papers type of divorce.

I told him about the divorce I just finalized for a woman who was talking up a storm about celebrating this weekend by seeing a local rock band in Cornelia. We both laughed until we were out of breath when I told him about two of the law clerks getting wasted at last years Christmas party and were caught in the bathroom together by our receptionist, Jan, who's about ninety years old and as up-tight as they make them.

We didn't talk about what was between us before. We didn't talk about where that left us now. But it was nice. Sitting there with him, eating pasta and laughing.

By the time I made it home, it well past midnight, and despite living alone, I crept in like I had snuck out to break some rules. Which I had, kind of.

When he left, I told myself I would never forgive myself for what I allowed to happen, what I allowed myself to feel for him. I made a silent vow that something like that would never happen again but a few hours alone with him and those vows were a tiny, tiny voice that was getting harder to hear.

How did I go from being constantly irritated by him, to falling in like or love or whatever it was, to hating his existence to friends?

Were we friends?

I didn't want to be friends with him.

I wanted something entirely different, something I didn't even want to say out loud.

Something I thought died a long time ago.

I knew it would be a terrible idea.

Forty-Four

Carina

My weekend was useless, so it was me and the Leon file on a Sunday. My pen tapped on the glass coffee tabletop in one hand as my finger toggled the mouse in another. The emails never ended but I couldn't find the one he was supposed to send over.

My phone sat beside me as I tried to convince myself not to reach out to him, but it was futile. I could text him real quick to see if he heard back from the financial investigator, figuring he was normal and not monitoring his email on a Sunday.

A text would be fine.

One text wouldn't hurt anybody.

I grabbed my phone and my thumb hovered over the Messages app, and before I could overthink it, I typed in his name, but nothing came up. Because I blocked him in a fit of rage and never looked back.

I scrolled through my settings until I found my blocked contacts and a part of me wished something would happen once I unchecked his name. Maybe messages or voicemails would flood my screen, proving he was telling the truth. It would have been simpler if that had happened then, rationalizing how I wanted to forgive him would be easier.

But phones didn't work that way, and unblocking Decker was as simple as a single tap.

The first sentence I typed out, I deleted immediately. The second sounded way too formal and like a robot had taken over my phone, so I deleted that one too. "Pull it together," I muttered to myself out loud, as I jumped up from the couch and started pacing.

What do I say, do I introduce myself incase he doesn't have my number still? Pretending like he'd know I'd be the one texting seemed too weird. What if he had my number blocked and it didn't even go through?

> Hey.

> It's Carina.

> Sorry to bother you but did the finical investigator email you the report on Friday like he was supposed to? I know it's the weekend but I was hoping to look over it today.

That was too many texts in a row. He was going to think I was incapable of conversations.

Where was confident, to the point Carina? The Carina who wasn't rattled by anything, let alone men? I wanted her back, wherever she went.

Minutes passed and I was beginning to assume I was blocked as well.

> Working on a Saturday. How very Carina of you.

> Looks like he emailed it just after I left the office. You should have it in your inbox now.

That was that, simple and to the point.

I pulled open my email for the document. Following the money was all I had to go off.

When I first worked the case, Kelly and I were certain there were hidden accounts. It didn't make for a prominent man that boasted often about his business ventures and real-estate dealings to have only one account. Even if that account had more money than I would see in one lifetime. We looked during our first round of mediation, Kelly had little information about their finances, Henry handled everything she told us. She had a credit card with no limit and was always told she didn't need to worry about anything, let alone bills or accounts.

By the fifteenth page of what seemed like nothing, the letters started to blur despite the readers I started wearing last year. A knock at my door pulled my focus, and after a few quick steps, I was pulling it open.

Standing on the other side was Levi.

A gentle breeze wafted through the entry as we stood, locked in a stalemate. Each waiting for the other to talk. Except I had no idea what to say.

"I just wanted to bring you this." He handed over a thick stack of papers. "I know your eyes bug you when you have to look at more than five pages on a computer and I figured you didn't want to wait until Monday," he stated, like it was completely normal for him to know—or I guess remember—that about me.

My face flushed for a moment at the fact he remembered passing details about me as I hesitated but eventually reached out to grab it.

Having someone pay enough attention to my habits was one thing, having them remember and go out of their way to make my life a bit easier was another. Creeping in was an alien feeling, making it hard to form words. "I...um. Thank you. You would still be correct, my eyes started going blurry before you knocked." I half laughed.

"I'll leave you to it." He smiled warmly, turning the breeze into stifling air. His dark hair gleamed in the sunlight, matching the dark joggers that hugged his thighs.

The thought of him turning around and leaving, even if I wasn't expecting to see him made my stomach flip. "Have you read through the report yet?" I blurted out before he could turn away from me. He shook his head, a slow back and forth, his eyes never leaving mine.

"Did you want to come in? I was about to make lunch." I wasn't but that felt like an easier excuse to get him to stay.

It didn't take two people to read a report no matter how long it was. He knew that. I knew that. But that didn't stop him from walking into my home, sitting on my couch, and reading through a few pages with me, never commenting on how lunch never came.

In the three months that he'd been back, I'd wrestled with the reminisce of my feelings for him. Hate was exhausting. Every time I saw him, it ate away at my insides and I was tired. I was tired of fighting it, tired of not feeling.

Ice filled my veins when he left, and I was tired of being cold.

I wasn't innocent in the exchange, something I come to learn the moment he told me his niece was sick. Decker was a family man through and through, he would choose them over me, a woman he was barely in a relationship with, and I couldn't fault him.

I'd been riddled with guilt over my part in how we ended up here but I was determined to change it. I just didn't know how so I'd treat it like a case. It was the only thing I knew how to do well.

Get all the facts, and go from there.

"Is Brynn okay now?" I asked after we came to a break in the report and the silence between us craved to be filed.

He hesitated and for a moment, I thought the worse. "She's good. It was touch and go for a while after her transplant but she's been in remission for almost a year and is as bubbly and talkative as ever."

In my anger after the gala, I didn't even bother asking how she was.

"And what about you? You said you were her donor?"

His hand went to his hip, I don't even know if he did it as he responded. "I'm fine," he remarked softly. "It was a stem cell transplant. By the time we got to San Fransisco, they had already told Laura that it was Leukemia. They were still formulating a treatment plan, and didn't know if she would need a transplant but decided to do match tests that day just in case." The work in front of us fell to the wayside as he recounted what seemed to be a harrowing weekend. He slipped from the couch cushion onto the floor next to me, one long leg propped up. "Laura and Kevin weren't a match, but Bailey was, and that just didn't seem right. My five year old niece having to be the one to hopefully save her older sister wasn't natural and it wasn't something I could wrap my head around so I asked them to test me. It was a long shot, but crazier things have happened." He took a deep breath and began running his nail against the fabric of his pants over his knee.

Perhaps I should have told him I didn't need all the details, he looked almost queasy telling me the story, but shamefully, I wanted to know.

"The test was quick, side effects were a bitch, and then they were in her room telling us we were a match. It was so quick, faster than I could have imagined, I figured it'd take a week to get the results. Kevin asked me no less than a dozen times if I was sure I wanted to go through with it, and my sister, she just looked at me with these big eyes silently begging me to say yes. It was the easiest decision I've ever made."

"At first I thought I'd come home, tell you, explain what happened and grovel for forgiveness, let work know, file for FMLA leave and commute back and forth between here and San Francisco while Brynn was in treatment." He glanced over at me, where I sat rapt in attention. "Except the hospital ended up not being in their insurance network for the type of surgery and radiation she needed. Did you know stem cells transplants can cost up to seventy thousand dollars out of pocket?"

Why was I not surprised, this country loved to kick people when they're down.

"Kevin has family in Los Angeles, close to a pretty prestigious children's hospital, that luckily accepted their insurance." He laughed under his breath. "Because I was the donor, I had to go with them, and commuting that far wasn't really an option." He lifted his shoulder in a small shrug, like it answered everything. And honestly it did, because I knew the next part of the story already. He probably tried to call, or text but nothing went through or connected because by then I had already blocked him in a child-like tantrum.

If there was ever an excuse to forgive and forget a heartbreak, this would be it. He literally saved his niece's life. "They are very lucky to have you as an uncle."

"Trust me, I'm the lucky one. I'd do it again in a heartbeat."

His hand was pressed into the carpet between us, centimeters from my fingertips. I itched to crawl my fingers forward to brush against his.

"Before you left, why didn't you tell me you started law school?" He was on a roll, might as well rip the bandaid off every wound at once.

"I wasn't lying when I said I was afraid of failing. I'm still afraid of failing, just because I passed the bar, doesn't meant mean I'll be a good lawyer."

FORTY-FIVE

Decker

When I was younger, my mom would call me her little lawyer. She would yell at Lola and I to get off our Nintendo and I'd have five different reasons why we needed ten more minutes on the fly. As much as I liked to argue, I liked being right more, but when you have six kids, there's nothing left by the time you get to the end of the line when it came to a college fund.

During undergrad, I worked myself into the ground waiting tables but it paid off when I graduated without debt. I thought it would be easy enough to do the same thing with law school except I was couldn't get away with riding out the free rent and clean laundry at my parents anymore. Lola had moved out and my parents wanted to travel. After raising all of us they deserved it. Moving out was easy, paying bills myself wasn't.

Getting a paralegal certificate seemed like the best way to keep my foot in the law world while I saved to go to school. And then life happened.

The work kept me on my toes and my head on track that being a lawyer was exactly what I wanted to do when I grew up. It just took me a while to grow up. I moved around a few different offices testing out which specialty of law was the best for me before finding myself at ALA. Years passed and I found myself compliant in my position but when Jody left, the drive I was lacking returned and I applied to a local school to start night classes.

"I didn't tell anyone, not at work at least. Not when I applied, or when I got in. Then classes started and I was afraid of failing. So I figured it was easier to not say anything at all in case I couldn't hack it."

She flipped a page and continued to stare at the stack of paper. She invited me to stay but hadn't given me anything more than a sideways glance, but it was something. The glacier she placed me in when I came back was thawing. She wasn't going to forgive me and invite me all the way back in one day, I knew it would take time, and I would wait in the blizzard for as long as she needed.

"I took night classes here for the first two years, a couple of summer courses, and when I left, I was able to pull some strings and got in to SW Law in LA and completed my degree." She was silent as she processed the information. I shouldn't have piled everything on her at once, but I was desperate for her to know the whole story, so I continued. "It felt like I was being forced to choose between you or them, and I chose them."

Pity crossed her delicate features, a slight downturn at the corner of her eyes.

"I don't regret my choice though, my family is important to me, but I do regret the way I did it. I handled the whole situation carelessly, and I will have to live with that for the rest of my life."

"Levi." She said my name with such sweetness that it would dissolve at the first hint of rain. A mere whisper of my name fell from her lips and those two syllables bloomed a sense of hope that maybe not all was lost.

I was always Decker, when she was mad, when she's indifferent toward me, even on her good days, I was always Decker. Every so often though, I would make it out of the box she put me in and would become Levi.

We inched closer together on the couch. I thought it was just me at first, being pulled into her by sheer gravity, but the subtle way her knee moved toward me told me we were finally finding common ground.

She was coming around to not hating me or at least not *only* hating me. There were other feelings there too.

"Do you want me to beg?" My voice dropped to a low whisper.

She laughed.

"I'm not too proud to get on my knees for you. You are worth any amount of groveling you demand and I am more than willing to give you whatever you need in order to forgive me."

Her voice dropped to match mine. "But what about me?" she asked as I searched her face which was a vast pool of questions that shimmered with vulnerability. "How can you forgive me? For the way I cut you off without any remorse?" For a moment I thought she was joking, until the regret was seen simmering in her eyes.

If I didn't take a chance at that moment, I never would.

"There is nothing to forgive, I was the one who left." Gravity pulled at the impulse to reach out and touch her and was far too strong to ignore. My hand brushed the strands that had fallen out of the loose bun and tucked them behind her ear. "And I have lived the past two years figuring out how I could get back to you," I confessed.

Touching Carina always felt like a divine rite of passage, and as my fingertips lingered on her skin, I wistfully remembered how much I truly missed her. And when she didn't pull from me, I took that as a sign I was on the right path home.

Carina was a labyrinth. Take one turn and you couldn't tell where you began and or where you needed to end; another turn and you'd face the same corner you'd already seen about five times. But every once in a while, when you're feeling stuck, you'd take a corner assuming you'd come face to face with a wall, only to find a straight path to the middle.

Seconds passed by and she was back in work mode, peeling herself away from me and focusing back to her computer while I picked up the report and began reading it through.

I'd follow her lead, wherever it took us.

I turned back to the papers in front of us. "I'll be honest, I'm not a hundred precent sure what I'm look at or for in this thing." I flipped another page.

"You and me both," she said as she reached out for the report and then pulled it from my hands. "Normally these aren't needed. In a general divorce case, there's maybe a round or two of mediation depending on the assets or if there are kids involved. This isn't a straight forward case. You remember what he was like last time. I was so sure he was hiding accounts from Kelly before and he liked to use money as a weapon to keep Kelly."

"Keep her, how?"

"In line, with him, however he can. He uses money to scare her, to buy her affection. The guy is a monster dipped in gold and it's up to us to crack him open and expose him for who he is."

She splayed four different pages on the glass coffee table before us.

"Look here," she points to the first page that had an account, "this appears to be a regular account."

I scoffed. "Yeah a regular account with eight million dollars."

"Regular to him. See how over the last eight months payments are going out and nothing else is coming in?"

Millions of dollars were disappearing until a few columns down and there's only one million left. What a life.

"The money isn't appearing in any other account and there's been no new businesses with his name or within his LLC. No new residential purchases, nothing."

"So where's the money going?"

"Exactly. My guess is an off-shore account so it doesn't get brought up in the divorce. He probably started funneling out money the moment he felt Kelly slipping out of his grasp."

I raked my fingers through my hair, I was only about halfway following what Carina laid out in front of us. "And now we have to find it. That seems like trying to find a missing piece from a thrift store puzzle."

She smiled at me. "We just need to prove it's there. This account didn't exist until they were married again. California is a community property state, that money belongs to Kelly just as much as it belongs to Ben. He wasn't dumb enough to forgo a prenup this time but unfortunately for him we are very good at our jobs."

A sinister feel attached itself to the smile sliding across her face. "It's time for another mediation, Decker." Carina was scary when she was on a mission and Ben Leon was now firmly in her crosshairs, God help him.

FORTY-SIX

Carina

IT WAS LIKE SLIPPING on a suit of amour. There's no chainmail or metal plates but the heather gray polyester suit still did the same thing. It was a facade of strength that took me years to actually believe in and as I slid the blazer over the high neck black top I felt more like myself than before. And I needed to feel like me.

It had been weeks since the charity event and his words played in my head like a broken record. Stuck on the same part, driving me to the brink of madness. I finally had my answer, and it was worse than anything I could have imagined.

Him leaving for any other reason would have been easier. I could have stayed floating in my anger, giving him none of my time. But no, he left for family. His niece, tiny little Brynn, was sick and not only was he there for them but he put his own body on the line to help her get healthy again.

How can you stay mad at that?

You couldn't.

I almost wished I didn't know because it made me feel like a monster.

A lying monster.

I leaned toward my bathroom mirror, dragging the soft mauve colored lipstick across my lips as a finishing touch. My gaze caught the time and I realized even if I left that second, I wouldn't have time to stop for coffee or a pastry, leaving a sense of foreboding in the pit of my stomach. I never started a big meeting without something from Renaissance. For a while I stopped but then I realized I could only punish myself so much until I switched to the danish pastries. I fucking missed those deliciously dense blueberry scones that always put me in the mood to win but the last thing I needed was to be late the day of the Leon case's second, first mediation meeting.

Last time, Ben gave in right at the end and opted to give Kelly everything she asked for in order to not go through with the trial. I doubted we would have the same outcome this time.

The short drive in did nothing to squash the feeling. My heels clicked against the floor as I made my way down the hall. Initial meetings were like pulling up to a fire with no information and being ready for anything. It could be small, both parties split their assets easily, custody was either a breeze or nonexistent, and the fire was put out with little effort and I was on to the next. Then there were times you arrived to a wildfire with only a garden hose and you're left to battle an inferno by yourself.

My gut told me to expect a wildfire. Or a tornado. Anything could happen with this guy.

Popping my head into Abby's cubicle, I asked her to prep the conference room for the meeting beginning in an hour.

"Levi already beat me to it. Rooms ready to go," she said without even looking away from the computer screen as her fingers flitted across her keyboard.

"Oh." My voice carried a tone of surprise. "Thanks for letting me know."

The switch from laid back Levi who'd never so much as lifted a finger out of his job description to this over achieving counter part of a co-worker made my head spin. I always thought I couldn't rely on anyone. I would tell myself my standards were too high and it wasn't that I worked with incompetent people, it was that I went for the overkill and didn't want to burden anyone else with my insane need to have everything perfect.

Levi had the all the documents sent out to Kelly for signatures almost immediately after our initial meeting. He did all the follow up calls and drafted the initial settlement documents once she narrowed down the details of what she was hoping for.

Those were sent off with no answer. Which was why this meeting was set.

Every time I checked in to see how it was coming along, he was there with completed tasks.

And yeah, sure, it was technically his case and I was shadowing since it was his first with ALA but I expected to be more hands on. I didn't quite know what to do since figuring out he was surpassing every mental benchmark I gave him.

It shouldn't be attractive and if anyone was stupid enough to ask, I would deny it.

I liked the before Levi, he was like all the best parts of a vacation wrapped up in a man. When I was with him, I could forget about my responsibilities. I could relax and have fun. He eased my headaches and melted away any tension but when he disappeared, I was left hungover in a post paradise fog that seemed like it would never lift. That Levi was still there, I thought, but there's a new side to him and with that came a new, or maybe even an old, fluttering of feelings rising from the grave I haphazardly buried them in.

I rounded the corner into my office. The morning sun cascading through the glass caused me to squint as I walked in. In that short stint of blindness, I almost missed what was waiting for me on my desk. My hand stalled on my bag strap once I was able to focus.

Sitting front and center was a coffee and a pastry. Not any pastry though, on my desk was what I was sure was my go to coffee order and my lucky blueberry scone.

Before putting too much thought into it, I tore open the bag and took my first bite in two years. My teeth broke through the crisp outside with a slight crunch as I bit into the soft inside. It was always the right amount of sweetness from the glaze paired with the tartness of the blueberries. I swore, if Renaissance ever stopped making these, I would actually riot. Like a march in the street with malatov cocktails kind of riot.

My tongue licked across my top lip gathering any crumbs left behind when he walked through my door. Dark blue suit, hair perfectly tousled, but I couldn't tell what his tie was right away.

"Oh, good, you got your pre-meeting baked good." Amusement could be heard in his voice and seen in the half smirk on his face.

I still had half a mouth full when I answered in confusion. "What?"

"The little blueberry thing you eat before big meetings, you get from Renaissance," he answered, sauntering into my office and into the chair I was standing next to. "So I stopped by this morning to get two. One for you, and one for me," he said as he pulled another small brown bag from I didn't even know where.

He drew out another scone and promptly took a large bite off one of the ends. He looked up from his seat with almost child-like wonder as he chewed, bits of glaze stuck to his bottom lip. We were like two opposite halves as we finished chewing.

I swallowed what I had in my mouth and brushed the back of my hand across my lips. "How did you all remember that?" I asked, mildly confused and intrigued. "*Why* do you remember, is a better question maybe?"

"Knowing you is my favorite hobby." He slipped the last part of the scone into his mouth in one large bite and got up from the chair. "Meeting starts in thirty. Kelly should be here in fifteen. I'll let you finish and come get you when we're ready." Then he was gone.

Is his favorite hobby, not was. Not past tense, not something he once did but something he was still doing.

It was happening again.

He would drop some achingly beautiful sentiment without much context and would leave me yearning for more.

FORTY-SEVEN

Decker

My first real mediation meeting started and all I could think of was her.

Which was fine, I was fine, everything was *fine*.

I had a plan. Actually, it was more of a loose list of things to try which would hopefully allow me to slip back into her good graces. It was a semblance of a plan.

First, put everything I knew about her to into action. I knew where she got her coffee, I would have her order ready every chance I got. That little pastry trick was something I had been sitting on for a while, and it worked like a charm. If it came down to it I'd show up at her parent's restaurant four nights a week with the hope she would be there, all to spend more time around her.

If that didn't work, I knew the next best thing to do in order to get on her good side. Carina prided herself in her work. It's where she drew her strength from. It was who she was and she liked to surround herself with people that did the same. I would be the best damn associate attorney she'd ever mentored. She thought I was lazy before, and to a point she was right. I was. But it was because I wasn't being challenged, I could do half that work in my sleep. She would never come out and say it to my face but I knew it.

I also wanted to be the best for myself. Carina just so happened to be great motivation.

Kelly sat next to me, hands on her round stomach as we waited. I know you're not really supposed to ask women how far along they were, but it seemed safe enough.

"How much longer?"

"Hmm?"

I nodded toward her stomach.

"Oh, about two more months," she said while smiling down at herself.

That's all I really had. I might love being an uncle but pregnancy kind of freaked me out. Having kids in general freaked me out. I was the fun uncle, and that was it.

Carina saved me from making a fool out of myself by asking any more questions and breezed into the room a moment later. She shook Kelly's hand before setting her space up right next to mine.

"Okay. We can hope that he will realize that we know his tricks and decide it's not worth the evasiveness and we'll all be done but we're prepared for the worst," she said, her face giving away nothing. Only an air of authority to her. "It's part of the reason I suggested doing the first meeting in person, to try to bypass all the nonsense."

"And what's the worst?" Kelly asked trepidatiously.

I stepped in at this point. Trying my best to channel Carina's confidence. "Worst case, he drags his feet, again, refuses to sign for months. His attorney will argue for less child support, less alimony. They'll fight every request you've made. We'll go through depositions, more mediation meetings, comb through every aspect of his life until a trial is the only option. Much like the last time."

She looked queasy at the thought.

"But that's the worst case scenario. You're not asking for the moon, even though you should. We will get this over as fast as we can," Carina chimed in, resting her hand on top of Kelly's. They smiled at each other. "You did it before, you can do it again."

"You must think the worse of me. Not only getting back together with him, but marrying him again, getting pregnant again." She wiped her hands under her eyes, catching the tears before they fell.

"Absolutely not," I chimed in. Both women looked toward me. "We don't think less of you or differently, people can change and then change again. We are here for you no matter the situation." Carina was right, we didn't know what happened behind closed doors and who was I to judge?

The doors swung open and in walked Benjamin Leon with not one, or two attorneys, but three. Talk about overkill but I guess when you're worth a quarter of a billion dollars, you could afford the dog and pony show.

"Ahh, great to see you both again." Ian Wheeler swooped in to shake Carina's hand first as she got up. His thumb swiped gingerly over the back of her hand, that she had to snatch back from his grasp. A pang of jealousy hit me square in the chest over the movement, even more so when he fixed his gaze on me and smirked.

The guy was a dick and obviously still pissy over the charity event where he didn't get to take Carina home.

"Ian, good to see you." They shook hands and he moved to the other side of the long table and dropped his briefcase. Ian jutted out his hand toward me after moving past Carina who took the opportunity to sneak in an eye rook when only I was looking. Once his large, clammy hand let go of mine he stepped to the side and I finally noticed the one other person who wasn't a lawyer in the room.

"And Mr. Leon. It's good to meet you." She extended her hand which he took eagerly.

"Ms. Pera or is it Missus?" he mused as a slimy smile crept across his face and he still held her hand. He did that politician thing with his handshake to where her hand was now held hostage between his. He leered over his words and I saw the start of her frustration bloom in her eyes even from over in my corner. I cleared my throat louder than needed. "Carina is just fine," she snapped out with a smile on her face and pulled her hand out of his grasp. She gestured for him to sit and flicked her eyes over to me and offered a small smile. I returned the gesture with a quick wink and I could tell she was working hard not to roll her eyes one more time.

Benjamin Leon looked exactly like the pictures on his website, or the press releases or the news stories that came out every time he donated a large sum to one charity or another. Polished, self-important, and so incredibly fake. Only the pictures missed the layer of slime that seemed to cover him as we walked around to the head of the table and took his seat like he owned the room.

He fixed a stare across the table and onto his ex-wife. "Kelly." His voice was calculating. The single syllable held a menacing tone. It was enough to put me on the defense as Kelly's shoulders slumped and her hands wrapped around her stomach protectively.

If you never took part in a deposition, consider yourself lucky. They were fairly boring if you're an outside spectator like I normally was. You listened to people answer mundane questions about who they were, what they had done, and half the time, none of it even mattered. Sometimes you got lucky and they'd out themselves and admit to a piece of information they probably shouldn't have. On very rare occasions there was enough information that came out of these things and we'd end up signing all the paperwork on the spot.

"Let's get started, shall we?"

FORTY-EIGHT

Decker

My suit was constricting my body in all the wrong spots as I reached up to pull on the knot of my tie for what felt like the millionth time since we began the meeting. No amount of adjusting was working so I gave up on trying to be comfortable.

This was my first real mediation meeting and I was tanking. Which I probably could have been fine with, if it was anyone's but Kelly's case. When you have three of Sacramento's top lawyers sitting across from you, it was hard to feel like you were even remotely competent. The middle lawyer scribbled something in his notepad and slid it across to Ian, who only smiled.

"Right, um, Mr. Leon can you please confirm the properties listed on the fourth page were bought during the last year?" I couldn't get a handle on my voice, the words shook in my throat as I said them. I swallowed around the dryness and tried clearing my throat but nothing helped.

He barely glanced at the list before flicking the page and answering, "Yeah, that's all."

"Kelly would, again, like to use the bungalow as her primary residence.

"That property is currently on the market with three pending offers."

My eyes darted between Ian and Ben before looking toward Carina. Kelly spoke up first.

"You knew I wanted to go back there, why would you sell it and not tell me?" she demanded.

"That property is still only in my name, it's been vacant since you moved out, why would I not sell it?"

"You're selling it on purpose and you know it."

"Give it a rest, Kelly," Ben spat. She shrunk back immediately. This entire meeting was spinning out of control and I didn't know how to rein it in.

I flicked through a few pages as my knee bounced a thousand miles a second under the table, nerves begging to escape my body. The meeting was two seconds away from being my thirteenth reason when suddenly a pressure appeared on my knee, pushing down slightly to get the movement to stop. Which it did but it also short circuited my brain.

She was touching me. I mean, she was probably annoyed by the bouncing but still, she was touching me and I all at once forgot where I was, what I was doing, everything. But with that, the nerves I was battling seemed to dissipate. All from one single touch, like they never existed in the first place. But then her hand slipped from my leg and I almost whined in protest.

"Ian, remind your client that I won't tolerate Mrs. Leon being talked down to," Carina stated, almost lazily as she looked down at the file in front of her. Ben scoffed at her side and I'd hate to be on the receiving end of the look she flashed his way.

"Did you have something you wanted to add, Mr. Leon?" She left him no room to answer. "No, good, let's move on." She pulled a sheet of paper from the file and slid it in front of him, and waited for his eyes to scan over the information.

About a week after Carina and I went over the financial reports, she burst through my office doors and smacked that same piece of paper on my desk with a smile wider the a Cheshire cat. I wasn't even remotely surprised she figured it out. To me it was a jumbled mess of numbers that was impossible to decipher.

"That's not the first property you sold, was it?"

Ben's eye's flicked to Ian, but didn't answer, so she pressed on.

"I'll answer for you, it's not. In fact you've sold over half a dozen smaller properties starting about a week after you were remarried. I'll hand it to you—"

"Carina," Ian warned.

"I'm not done," she shot back and I relaxed back into my chair to watch the takedown unfold. Learning, and all that.

Carina was ruthless with her questioning, it was amazing to watch. Ben's face was getting progressively red with every second that ticked by. Ian shifted in his chair as he went over his copy of the listings as well. They knew this wasn't going to end how they thought it would and she was just about to let them in on it.

"At first the two bedroom house out in the Pocket, it was pretty run down so you only got about three hundred thousand. Then it was one of your businesses in Carmichael, hundred fifty thousand, tough times."

God, she was so fun when she was on a roll.

"Where are you going with this? He has every right to buy or sell his own property."

Carina whipped toward Ian, the other attorneys were decoration more than anything. "But not if he's going to hide the money because he knows it's only a matter of time before his wife leaves him," she slowly looked back at Ben, "again."

His eyes narrowed as she stared back and he visibly stiffened in his seat. His attorney looked over at him then flipped through the papers in front of him, a bit frantically if you asked me. It felt like an eternity before he spoke.

He spoke through a clenched jaw as he shifted in his seat, next to him his attorney was still completely lost but interjected. "You can't prove any of that." It was fantastic to watch, there was nothing like a smug man getting beat down. Ian flipped the pages back and forth.

"I don't have to, your financials speak for themselves." She smiled while she talked. I felt like there should've been a slow clap afterward, but that would be unprofessional, so instead I ducked my head to cover my laugh.

Ben shot from his chair, startling all of us. "You fucking bitch. You just couldn't stand that Kelly didn't get everything she asked for the first time." He shouted as his attorney attempted to get him back in his seat and to calm down. He shrugged him off and planted his hand on the table, leaning across it to get closer to Carina. "You won't get off that easy this time. If you keep pushing at me, I'm going to push back and I would hate for something to happen to you."

My body lifted from my chair at his words and I was half a second away from flying over the table and removing him from the building myself when Carina held her hand out and stopped me before I could move, as if she was reading my thoughts. She rose from her chair, a steady, swift movement and without any of the rage I was holding inside of my chest.

She mimicked Ben's movement, placing both hands on the table and leaned in. "Next time you threaten someone, Mr. Leon, make sure it's not on record." She looked toward Ian. "I think we're done here." She grabbed a few of the folders she brought in, turned on her heel and exited the conference room without a second look back at any of us.

Leon continued his sputtering while the rest of us looked on. The court reporters fingers flew across the keys while looking shaken and Ian seemed as if he'd lost all capacity to wrangle in his client. A second later, security dashed in the room to escort him out, Carina must have called, or the receptionist who's just on the other side of the wall and likely heard everything.

Carina.

My mind snapped me back to the moment, I needed to find her.

I stalked out of the conference room and went straight to her office, doubtful she would be anywhere else.

The blinds were drawn as I approached her door, everything about it told me to stay out. She wouldn't want me in there, she made it perfectly clear she didn't want any involvement with me but I couldn't not check on her. And if it made her mad...well, when was I not pushing her buttons?

I knocked softly before turning the handle and stepping inside.

She's pacing the length of the window behind her desk as the door shut with a click behind me causing her to stop and her eyes bore into mine.

I couldn't tell what emotion was brewing behind her eyes but it didn't matter because in that moment, I knew there quite possibly wasn't anything I wouldn't do for her. And right then, I wanted to let her know that I would never let anyone or anything hurt her.

FORTY-NINE

Carina

My heels were beginning to etch a permanent track in my office. It was only five steps from my desk to the window but that didn't stop my feet from carrying back and forth, back and forth. His words were blaring in my head, an endless loop of screaming and I had yet to convince myself that I wasn't in danger. Every part of my body was fuming with rage. I could feel the pinpricks of electricity roll through my veins from the top of my neck into my fingertips and into my toes. Even behind my eyes there's the telltale sting of tears beginning.

I couldn't believe what just happened.

Crying and I didn't mix; there's nothing wrong with crying, I guess, but it wasn't for me. Growing up I was constantly told "tutto passa", everything passes. I didn't think my parents meant for it to be ingrained in the fabric I was made up of but it was. It was imprinted into me that nothing last, and sure they might have meant just my fears and worries but also it leeched its way into my happiness and joy. It shaped the way I felt about everything and everyone around me, nothing lasts and everything passes. So from a young age, I learned to push down any emotion that threatened its way out of me, crying about an issue would get me nowhere so what was the point, tutto passa?

Some would say it made me hard or cold but it's also what had gotten me exactly where I wanted to be and it was always a price I'd been willing to pay.

Another minute passed and nothing let up. Almost as if someone walked into my office and lassoed me, and then began pulling the rope tighter and tighter. Each breath came quicker than the last and my body erupted into flames. Maybe the heater turned on or maybe I had fallen into the middle of the sun, something had happened because all I could feel was the white hot burn licking at the inside of my chest.

I pressed my hand to my heart, feeling each rapid beat as it tried to rip through my chest.

Maybe I was dying.

That had to be it. I was dying, there was no other explanation for the feeling that was trying to claw its way out of my chest.

Everything was closing in on me. My clothes sat like thousand-pound weights on my body, my office transfigured into the size of a matchbox, and every coherent thought in my head drifted out to sea like an untethered sailboat.

After what seemed like my hundredth pass across my office floor, my door opened and quietly snicked shut. Turning toward the noise, I locked with the last pair of eyes I wanted to see.

"Carina, are you—" He stopped mid sentence as he continued to stare at me.

His eyebrows pinched inward slightly as I held his gaze and tried to convey a warning. It didn't work, he took another step into the room. If I were a kinder woman, a woman who believed in romance or even just a warmer person I would be able to see that he was coming to check in on me because that was the type of person he was or as a sign that his feelings for me hadn't all disappeared, but I was none of those things.

"I can't with you right now." My voice teetered on the edge of panic.

Is that what this is, am I panicking?

It didn't faze him. Two more steps closer and I could feel my resolve to be tough and unbothered snap like a brittle twig, but I couldn't break in front of him. I wouldn't do it.

He studied me for a moment. I had no idea what he was seeing but it couldn't have been good because he finally stopped stalling and walked further into my office, past my desk and was suddenly so close it launched me further into my spiral. A war broke out in his head, like he was stopping himself from doing something as his hands flexed at his sides.

"I think I'm having a heart attack or maybe just out right dying. I'm not sure," I blurted out, each word a heavy breath. If I was dying someone needed to know, that way they could call 911 or something.

"Okay." His voice tender and cautious as he took another step and placed himself at my side. With that one small move, the tightening lessened but not enough.

He was right next to me but I couldn't quite see him.

Was I going blind too?

My hands trembled and my heart was a second away from taking off and ripping right through my chest. Darkness crept in from seemingly nowhere, threatening to collapse my world in on me as my head reeled. It was as if someone was using Earth as a spinning top. "Something is really, really wrong."

"You're having a panic attack."

Well, that didn't make much sense, I never panicked. And even if I did it *never* felt like this.

"I want you to look at me." His voice sounded like he was talking underwater.

When we locked eyes, his face gave away no emotion, and I wondered if he did that on purpose because of me. Did I make it so he couldn't, or maybe refused, to feel around me? Did I do too good of a job at the gala?

"Good, now take a deep breath in." He pulled a long breath in through his nose that I mimicked and held it in, but it didn't relax me. Being around him did the exact opposite for me. Maybe this wasn't a panic attack; maybe this was me locking down each emotion he stirred up because if I let them run rampant, they would take over every aspect of my life.

"And now blow out." A long exhale escaped through his mouth. I followed his lead.

Across my back, he spun, slow, light circles with the palm of his hand. I counted in my head each time a new one began and I wanted, more than anything, for them to continue on forever. Maybe it was the breathing, or the warmth seeping into my skin from where we were connected but finally a light broke through the darkness as I waited for more instructions.

Another small smile from him. That helped too, but I didn't want to think about that. "Again, in and out," he commanded gently.

It took three more rounds before the darkness faded completely and his words became clearer. My heart rate fell into a normal pulse, but the jittering feeling continued to cascade up my chest and down in my arms. A thousand tiny bugs that couldn't be flung off no matter how hard I tried shaking the feeling out of me.

Nothing changed, not until his hands wrapped around my upper arms. I had no time to freak out, thinking he was about to hug me, when he squeezed once, then twice, and a third time followed in quick succession. My eyes slid shut and he moved an inch lower on my arm, above my elbow and another three squeezes came.

Maybe it wouldn't be so bad if he did wrap his arms around me.

"One more breath in, Amore."

My chest cracked open at the word.

On the exhale, his hands were around my wrist with the same methodical squeezing and yet just hearing him call me that again threatened to send me back into the dark. Everything remained at a standstill as he repeated the soothing motion once more but on the last squeeze, he let his fingers thread through mine.

It had been so long since his hand had been in mine, but nothing about the feel of his skin had changed. If anything, it was bringing everything I forced under my cold exterior to the surface. I had been so full of resentment for the past two years, I hardly noticed there was anything else I was feeling. That I could feel anything else but regret lingered in my veins alongside the bitterness he left behind.

I missed him.

"What was that?" I asked with my eyes still closed, afraid of what I would find when I opened them.

"That was a panic attack," he confidently answered.

A panic attack. I'd never panicked a day in my life so where the fuck did that come from?

"And what did you do?"

"Brynn had a lot of anxiety when she was hospitalized, I learned a few tricks to help where I could."

I hummed in response. Delaying the inevitable could only go on for so long. I forced myself to open my eyes and was hit with a sight I knew would be devastating.

Breathtaking whiskey eyes stared back at me, full of hope, and pain, and endless longing. He really was beautiful. All dark brows, sharp jawline and angled cheek bones. Sometimes it was hard to even look at him without beginning to feel the ice around my heart begin to melt.

"Thank you," I whispered the words.

"Any time."

Did he move or did I lean in?

All I knew was he was closer than he had been since he left, breathing in the air I was exhaling.

"Kiss me." The words fell out of the depths of my heart. "I need you to kiss me until I forget about what just happened. Until I can't think of anything else." A soft roar started in my ears, and the only other thing I heard was my own heavy breathing as I tried and failed to regulate myself. "Kiss me until I can only think of you."

Longing pushed forward in his gaze with desire not far behind.

"I—" He was going to come up with an excuse not to, I could feel it, but I knew I wouldn't survive another second without his touch.

Another centimeter gone between us as I leaned in a bit more. "*Please.*" My voice cracked over the word. Jagged pieces of the plea lodged themselves in my throat. I was not the type of woman to ask for help, I didn't beg, it wasn't who I was, but here, right now I needed help. I needed him.

Gravity tripled as he closed the gap, never taking his eyes off of me. Perfect lips hovered near mine, so close that I could practically taste the fruit from his drink.

"Carina," he whispered.

There it was again, my name. So simple but coming from him an infinite amount of feelings were attached to it. He said my name in a way that made me think there was still so much more to us and I wondered when or how that even happened.

"Levi," I replied. His name a breath of long awaited air to my starved lungs.

Fingers squeezed mine at the sound of his name.

A knock pierced through the veil of the moment jolting us back from one another as Abby flew through the door with one of the firms partners in hot on her heels.

"Carina, are you okay? We just heard what happened," she rushed to say. Her voice was an octave higher than normal as worry seeped through her words. A look flashed in her eyes when she glanced between the vacant space between where Levi stood facing the window and where I was gripping the side of my desk, as if she could visibly see tension in the room.

Scott seemed, a small mercy. "Carina, security has already escorted both Mr. Leon and his attorneys from the building. Are you okay?"

"I'm fine, Mr. Alcala. Nothing I can't handle." A bold face lie but I wasn't even thinking of the threat.

His lips pressed into a hard line. "Maybe you should call it a day, take some time for yourself and start the weekend early."

Between the Ben Leon, the supposed panic attack, and the almost kiss, that didn't sound too bad. "You know what, I think I'll take you up on that offer," I acquiesced as I reached for where my purse sat on the desk.

Abby remained silent, eyes drifting back and forth between Levi and me that flared with worry but almost a hint of suspicion.

Levin turned around and spoke up. "I'll walk you out."

We approached the elevator and stood, waiting in silence. The doors finally dinged open and I stepped inside as Levi hovered on the other side. My smile was fake and weak but it was hard to muster anything else as he was studied me, concern flickering through his features. "I'm okay, don't worry about me," I said, shaking the haze that had a hold on me since he entered my office.

"I will always worry about you." A small smile played on his lips. "Whatever you need, Carina, all you have to do is ask."

That spiral feeling came back as the doors slid close.

FIFTY

Carina

A DAY OFF, OR half a day, was such a foreign concept to me I genuinely had no idea what people did during the day. My apartment was clean, I went grocery shopping for the first time in months, I even ran a few miles along the river. Beating a personal best, might I add. And yet once the day faded away I could hear were the threatening words as a soft echo in my head as inlaid in bed.

I flung back the covers and told myself it wasn't a good idea. As I pulled on the nearest sweatshirt that hung loose and covered my sleep shorts, I told myself this was the worst idea anyone's ever concocted, ever. And as I walked out my front door, down three flights of stairs ,and across the apartment complex to his door, I suddenly didn't care at all.

It's what I wanted.

If he'd have me.

I winced as the knock pierced through the still night air. Wind swept in through the entryway, crisp enough that my skin pebbled. I thumbed the fabric at the hem of my sweater. Another five seconds and I would walk back to my apartment in shame and never speak of this to anyone.

Only nobody tells you how long five seconds actually feels like. By the third, my stomach twisted in knots and I was ready to bail until the door creaked open.

Levi blinked the sleep out of his eyes, before pressing the heel of one of his palms into them. "Carina?"

I was rendered temporarily mute at the sight of him. Black sleep pants slung dangerously low on his hips, like he haphazardly stepped into them seconds before answering the door. Every inch of skin on his torso was on display. Rippling muscles went straight to my head and it was better than I remembered.

"I couldn't sleep."

He stepped back to let me through without another word.

Turning, I faced the wall of pictures, a wall that held what was most important to him. Inside the wooden frames held all the people that meant something to him, people I barely knew, but I was envious over what they had.

Because I wanted to be someone worthy of being in a frame on Levi's wall.

A million thoughts raced through my head, all of the fighting to be the one that was said. Instead, I asked, "What was it like growing up around so many people who loved you?"

"Fun. Messy. Annoying, sometimes. I was never alone which at the time wasn't the easiest thing, but looking back, I don't think I'd change a single thing. They are by my side no matter what. Doesn't matter if I needed a place to stay after a bad break up or I'm stuck at home with the flu, if I call, one of them will come."

"That sounds nice."

"It is." A heavy pause filled the space. "Why are you here, Carina?"

My eyes continued to scan each photo starting from the top. I never looked at all of them last time I was here, but I wasn't sure how to answer his question when I didn't even know why. I feel as if I owed him an explanation, for everything, and that would only help if I started at the beginning.

"I fell in love with a guy just as I was starting law school, he was a few years older and was finishing up his degree when we met. It wasn't love at first sight or anything like that but we were together long enough that I thought maybe marriage wasn't the worst thing I could do."

Levi didn't rush me, didn't look at me like it was the middle of the night and I was rambling in his living room with no point in sight. He simply waited for me to keep going as I continued not looking him. "At some point I lapsed into my usual habit and was so focused on school and working to put myself through school and helping my parents that he kind of fell to the wayside without me realizing it. I thought he knew going into the relationship that graduating and passing the bar was what I was working toward and I wasn't going to let anything get in the way. Even him, it didn't matter if I thought I loved him or not. So when he told me I wasn't paying enough attention to him, that I was too focused on school, all I could hear was 'your goals, your passions in life, are not important to me.' So I ended it."

I was coming up on some of the last photos when a smaller one caught my eye. Stepping closer, I swore his breath caught in his chest as I reached out to touch the frame.

"He expected me to take the time and energy I was putting into school and give it to him. Even though we had the same goal, and we were in the same relationship, *I* was the one who was expected to make the sacrifice in order to make us work."

My sentence ended and my rapid blinking did nothing to change the fact that I was staring at a photo of myself. I trailed the tips of my fingers along the thin frame holding a picture I didn't even know existed. A preserved moment in time hung on his wall, a moment from Lola's wedding I thought only existed in my memories was right in front of me. The string lighting, my dress and his tux, the way we looked at each other, it was all real and he'd held onto a version of us this entire time. It felt like an eternity since he held me in his arms as we danced, where it felt like he was mine.

I wanted that feeling again, that all consuming warmth of knowing there was someone in this world that might have be made with me in mind. But wanting something only another person could give me felt like I had to give some part of me away in order to have it.

That was the part that no one understood, I didn't bend easily and I was willing to lose anyone over it. No one was safe from my inability to change.

I stepped away from the photos and took a breath. "And I wasn't going to do that. I am who I am and I refuse to change for anybody. For years I told myself relationships and I don't work, that I am too selfish for a happily ever after. I would rather live a life on my own than live one where I might have to chip away parts of me so I can fit into someone's version of who I should be. I'm not willing to change. "

Finally I turned around And I waited. If he tells me I wasn't worth it, I'd understand, but it would only solidify my of rest of my life would be spent alone.

"I've always known there was someone reason behind not wanting to be anything more with me than a physical relationship back then. You're the most logical person I know, it made sense. It was never my place to force it out of you, so if you said that was all you wanted then who was I to say otherwise? I'll be whatever you need, but Carina, you're perfect exactly how you are."

My eyes squeezed shut as I pulled in a deep breath. This wasn't the rejection I was convincing myself would follow my confession. This was acceptance and I was overwhelmed by the way my heart seemed to swell in my chest.

I cracked my eyes open after minute. "You have a picture of me on your wall."

"I do," he responded with a soft smile. "I have pictures of everyone I care about."

One of us moved closer but again I didn't know who, only that suddenly my hands were pressed against his chest and I was tilting my head back to look up at him as I asked, "If I said, for one night I'd like to pretend that I'm not cold or heartless, and I asked to stay?"

"I'd give you anything you'd ask for."

"Can I stay, Levi?" Warmth flushed my cheeks over the simple question. He'd say yes, wouldn't he? He had to see that this was me trying. This was me...not bending but softening.

There were no words as he threaded his fingers into mine and pulled me along as he walked back to his room. Every inch of his apartment was drenched in the spicy scent that always followed him, simply breathing it in repaired my frayed nerves while I waited for him to speak.

Anything would do. I didn't want to be the one with all the answers. I didn't want to be the one to fix what was broken, even if I was the cause of all the misery between us. One time, that was all I needed. At least once, I wanted to know what it was like to hand over the reins, to have someone take over and melt the frigid parts of my soul.

Still no words, only the deafening sound of the zipper of my jacket being slowly undone. It was almost effortless, slipping into a softer role for him.

His fingertips delicately swept across my jaw, then down my neck stopping only for a moment for his thumb to brush across the spot where my pulse throbbed.

Maybe we didn't need words at all.

Maybe he could hold me through the night and that would be enough.

Longing bounced off of every inch of him as he peeled the jacket from my body, before finally allowing his eyes to drift across the rest of my appearance. I left in a hurry, barely registering I would show up in fabric so thin it was practically see through.

"Carina," he whispered, an agonizing sound that awakened something in me.

I was wrong, I didn't only want to be held.

I wanted more, so much more and I wanted it from him.

"Kiss me?" I asked and there was nothing to stop him.

His lips met mine in a frenzy, like he thought if he took too long I'd change my mind and he didn't want to risk it.

It was exactly how I remembered. Soft lips that moved against mine, strong arms that wrapped low around my waist, digging into me as he pulled me close. With my body flush with his, there wasn't an inch of space between us, but I wanted closer. I snaked my arms around his neck, letting my finger run through his hair, gripping the strands slightly. Levi groaned and I took the moment to trace his bottom lip with my tongue.

Nothing else mattered besides the moment we were in, besides us.

But I needed more.

I broke the moment, leaving Levi gasping and a wave of satisfaction through me, knowing I still had the power to drive him to the edge. With my hands still around his neck, I pushed him down until he hit the bed and I took a step back.

His hand reached for me. "Please don't leave."

"I'm not, but we need to talk first."

Apologizing wasn't my strong suit but if anyone deserved the words, it was him.

FIFTY-ONE

Carina

SLIVERS OF MOONLIGHT BEAMED through the window, but even in total darkness I wouldn't forget the sight. It was always satisfying to watch a man fall apart under my hands, it was another thing entirely to watch Levi fight his last bit of restraint. His white knuckle grip on the edge of the bed, the deep line settling between his brows, and the long, slow inhales of air he kept in his chest before finally breathing out.

Perhaps I could live in the moment, freeze time and live there with him. Instead I took a step forward and slotted myself in-between his strong thighs. His head fell back, eyes dark and dripping with hunger as his arms slipped around my waist like a vice.

"Some days it feels like I'm still stuck in that restaurant," I quietly admitted. Not only to him, but to myself. My usual voice of authority gone, replaced by the soft femininity of a woman who's lived with a broken heart for far too long. "You ruined me. You brought a color I never noticed or cared about before into my world, and then you left, and everything went back to being black and white."

His arms tightened around me. "I'm sorry. I'm so fucking sorry. I should have came back for you, I should have—"

Both of my hands ran through his hair, stopping when they rested on either side of his face and cut off his words. "*I'm sorry.* I should have tried harder to figure out what happened. I should have fought harder for you. I shouldn't have jumped to the conclusion that you were out to hurt me and made villain in our story be default. This is not on you, this is my fault."

He looked at me with such tenderness, I was surprised the dam I built around all the tears I wanted to cry over him didn't crack and spill out between us.

"Maybe it was no one's fault. Maybe it was a fluke in the timeline of us, maybe somewhere out there, something knew we weren't ready," he finally said. I pushed in closer, his chin fitting into the dip between my breasts as he continued to stare up at me.

"But I'm here and I'm ready." Levi's breath skated up my chest, and the stillness of the room gave us nothing but time to sit with our forgiveness "Give me another chance, let me get it right this time. Let me be the person you lean on."

"I don't need anyone's help." Weak words, from a strong woman.

"I know but I want to be there for you anyway." The words rolled across my chest, skin pebbling under the sentiment.

"Okay."

"Okay," he replied before sealing the promise with a searing kiss. One hand tangled in my hair the other wrapped around my waist holding onto me like I would slip from his grasp and he couldn't bear to let me go.

My clothes weren't the only thing being stripped away. With each scrap of clothing he pulled away from my body, he exposed the parts of myself where he'd lingered for the past two years. Nothing was rushed, fabric fluttered to the ground and in its place his lips found my skin.

Lips littered my collarbone with soft brushes of his mouth, before dipping between my breasts letting his breath skirt across my skin before he sealed his lips around one nipple. My fingers shot out and gripped the soft strand of his hair.

My head lolled to the side as his tongue swirled small circles around the tightened peak. His other hand explored the expanse of my stomach with feather light touches. He pulled from my breast and placed a kiss to the middle of my chest.

"I missed you," he mumbled against my skin, almost as if he didn't want me to hear them. But the sincerity of his words were unmistakable.

Coarse stubble pricked at my finger as I tilted his head up to meet my gaze. In the two years since he left I dreamt of this moment almost weekly, where I would hear those exact words and my broken parts would be stitched back together. But this, this was more than being put back together.

This was like being born again.

I was a completely different person at the sound of his words, I was whole and new.

Levi deserved to know the truth even if I'd been denying it. "Not as much as I missed you," I admitted, to him, to me, to the universe. The skin of my palm rested against his cheek, my thumb stroking the high planes of his face as every muscle in his body relaxed.

Our thighs brushed as I lifted my knee pressed into the soft blankets of his bed near his hip. That one small movement and hunger darkened his eyes, blowing his pupils wide and swallowing all color. My other knee followed suit until I straddled him, hovering inches from where his cock strained against his sleep pants.

With my eyes locked on his I reached down, fingertips teasing the band of his pants. Levi's chest heaved with each breath.

"There's been no one since you." His voice thick and unsteady. I paused, my hand moving away from where I knew we both wanted. "There's been no one since you," he repeated.

My voice shook. "I can't say the same."

"That doesn't matter, Amore."

That was all I needed, my hand made quick work of his pants, pulling enough to free him from the confines of his pants. I would take my time later, on my knees or any other way I could get him, but I was burning and vibrating with the need to be as close to him as possible.

I closed the gap between us, my hand on his, swiping him along my entrance gathering my arousal and working it down his length. Simultaneous groans of satisfaction escaped from us.

"Tell me again."

His brows pinch, but he answered. "I missed you."

I lowered an inch, taking only the tip of him inside me. For a moment, I stopped breathing as his fingers dug into the soft skin of my hips. When I managed to open my eyes again, Levi's gaze was glued to the spot where we'd finally rejoined.

"Again."

"I missed you," he said painfully, erratic breaths escaping his mouth. Another inch.

He took a sharp breath. "Carina, please." His eyes pleaded with his words.

I gave in, letting gravity take over, dropping myself and taking all of him in one swift movement.

Colors flared behind my eyelids as my head dropped backwards. If it weren't for his arms around my waist I would have floated away altogether. The stretch was better than I remembered, that inescapable feeling of fullness that made you wonder how anybody could get anything done in the world when you could feel like this all the time.

A sharp tug at the base of my skull brought me back to the moment as he hauled my mouth back to his lips, his other arm lifted me slightly in order to snap back into me. And then again, and again. He pressed his forehead against my shoulder as I met each of his strokes.

Seconds in, my thighs began to shake and my vision grew disoriented.

"Fuck, I forgot how good this pussy was, how could I forget?"

He didn't lighten up, he didn't pull back. He remembered everything that I liked and that only drove me faster toward the edge.

"I thought I was going to have to live the rest of my life with only the memory of how you feel wrapped around my cock," he panted and thrusted up into me. "I'm so fucking happy that's no longer true because this is a million times better than my faded recollection of you."

It happened, quick. A sharp spiral down a technicolor hole as my climax barreled through me. My hand tightened around his neck and with one last unforgiving stroke he sheathed his entire length inside of me and followed over the cliff, panting with the side of his face pressed against my chest.

The night was spent in various versions of this position until the early hours of the morning, making up for lost time I didn't even know I wasn't missing out on.

It's wasn't until Levi's soft snores filled the room that I slipped out and walked back home in the cold because old habits die hard, no matter how much I wished I could bury them.

FIFTY-TWO

Carina

I SOMETIMES WONDERED WHY I even bothered with my mailbox when the only things I got were coupon packs and more credit card promotions than I could count. I slipped the small brass key into the lock and pulled the door open. Sure enough, that was all that was there. I stood over the garbage, thumbing through the envelopes, tossing them in one by one when the mailroom door creaked open.

Absent-mindedly, I glanced over my shoulder and I immediately wished I hadn't. My hands stilled. It took me all of two seconds to recognize her and remember who she was, if the striking black hair wasn't enough.

Stuck in the doorway, looking back at me was Levi's sister. I knew it was the oldest, the one whose daughter was sick. I started racing through L names to remember.

Laura—the oldest one was Laura.

She must have clocked who I was as well, her eyes never left me as she entered the small area and went straight to a mailbox. Best guess she was

319

there to see Levi, last he said they moved here but to a house on the other side of town.

I'd been in my fair share of awkward situations over the years or but I had never been intimidated be someone. Normally I wouldn't be bothered in the slightest, but her look twisted my insides.

Did I say something? Did I acknowledge that we've meet?

Did she even remember anything about Levi and me? My guess would be no, with everything surrounding her daughter I would think everything else would have faded into a forgotten memory.

"Carina," she acknowledged.

Shit.

"Hi, Laura, it's nice to see you." I donned the voice I usually reserved for clients, sweet, to the point, and fake.

She opened the mailbox door, pulling a small package from the slot then flicked the door close. "Funny, Lee didn't mention you lived in these apartments," she mused with a playful smile. I dumped the remaining mail into the garbage.

"Oh, well I'm sure I'm the last thing on his mind, so..." What a terrible answer.

Laura's laugh bounced off the glass walls. "If you say so," she replied.

My brows furrowed. What did that mean?

The world's longest awkward silence passed between us and I'm pretty sure it was less than a second. "Levi told me about Brynn, I'm glad she's okay."

Her face softened, as her eyes instantly turned glassy. "Thank you, so are we. I don't know what we would have done without Lee stepping in to help."

I nodded in agreement but I needed to get out of there. I stepped past her, kicking myself for ever coming down here in the first place.

"He told me about what happened as well, between you two." I forgot how close they all were. "How he didn't reach out to you until it was too late."

My hand wrapped around the door handle, white blooming over my knuckles. I didn't want to think about it, I stashed away the memory of that weekend hoping I never had to encounter it again. "I won't apologize for asking him to come with us to LA, it saved my daughter's life, and I wouldn't trade that for anything but I'm sorry for how it happened, for what it might have cost you."

It was as if she ripped open my jaw and forced a rock down my throat. My pain was not up for interpretation, it was mine to deal with and I was fine pretending like the soul-crushing abandonment didn't exist.

"It's okay." My voice thickened with the lie.

Strands of her dark hair waved as she shook her head back and forth. "It's not and he would kill me for telling you this but for those two years, he was not himself. I'm not even sure he could see it, but my brother was a watered-down version, putting on a brave face for the rest of us." She took a step closer to me. "He chose us, but he missed you, and it was hurting him."

What was I supposed to do with this information?

Did she mean for the words to make me feel better, because it didn't. If anything, I felt worse. Not having any insight of how he felt during those years was a preference. Imaging he was as miserable as I was and suddenly being told he was out there for two years, just as lovelorn, was wall shattering.

I could put on a good front, another superpower of mine, but my heart was broken and no one even knew. I was so convincing that I almost believed him leaving had no effect on me.

The moment he told me about Brynn. I forgave him, none of the anger compared to the position he was put in and if the roles were reserved I would have chosen my parents over him as well. "For whatever it's worth, I hope you two can work your way back to what you had before."

"It wasn't anything, it's not like we were in love."

"Maybe *you* weren't."

I didn't have it in me to say anything else, instead I fled like a coward back to my apartment.

FIFTY-THREE

Carina

COULD I HAVE FILED what I needed online? Yes, was the obvious answer, and in this day and age, everything could be done online, even filing for divorce. Or in this case, filing a motion to compel the other worthless party to present his full financial portfolio. But I needed to be out of the office, or more like I *wanted* out.

I needed space from him, but also didn't? For the first time I didn't know what I wanted. Nothing was standing out, nothing telling me 'this is what you need to do to get where you want to be'. I had spent more time convincing myself he wasn't what I wanted and normally I could argue anyone to my side, with facts and clear reasoning on why I was right but apparently I was immune to my own tactics.

I still ended up in his bed every other night, because why deny myself life's little, or rather above average, pleasures. Never staying long enough to see morning, and by the time we came to work I went back to avoiding him, kind of. He just didn't know it, or maybe didn't care because he continued to act like whatever we were doing was perfectly normal.

Space was not a word in his vocabulary when it came to me. So when he heard I was going downtown, he also had some motions to file on a separate case. How convenient.

Sacramento's Courthouse was a boring building, the less time I spent inside of it the better. Filing the discovery request was quick but Levi disappeared to another floor for his request and was taking far too long.

The elevator doors were closing but I managed to slip in at the last moment to the next floor to find him. Blank corridors that all looked the same had me working on memory, but I was certain the office to modify divorce decrees was right around the upcoming corner.

"Did you see who's opposite counsel on the Leon case?"

I stopped in my tracks before turning the corner. I didn't recognize the deep voice, but the dickish tone made my chest burn.

"Don't tell me," another voice chimed in, "is it her?"

What the hell was happening? I was about ninety-nine percent sure they were about to mention my name unless there was another case on the docket today with the same last name. Which not out of the realm of possibility, but the way my skin pricked, I doubted it.

One of them chuckled. "Of course it's her, what people see in her is beyond me."

"Last case I had with her was a nightmare. My client ended up having to pay double the alimony that was originally agreed on and ended up selling the house to split the profits instead of being bought out. She's a fucking nightmare."

Oh, they were definitely talking about me. Not the first time, sure as hell wasn't going to be the last time.

"Any time she's in court, she walks around with her nose in the air, like she does no wrong, frigid bitch. I'd hate to be the man attempting to warm her bed."

One of them barked out a laugh. "I doubt that's possible, someone should really take her down a peg or two."

Then the first voice lowered, I took another step closer, right to the edge of the corner. Their sentiments were nothing new, I'd heard them before and would hear them again. Men hated a woman in power, and men especially hated a woman in power who was good at her job.

"Last I heard, Ben Leon had a few things up his sleeve for Carina Pera." The thinly veiled threat made the hairs on the back of my neck stand up at the mention of my name.

"Excuse me." That voice I did recognize, but in a tone I had never heard fall from his mouth. "If you assholes are done bitching, you're next in line." I peaked around the corner. Levi stood with his back to me, facing two men I had never seen a day in my life. Both looking at him with faces ranging from sheepish from being caught to disgust for being called out.

"I take it you know her?" the shorter of the two bit back.

"Whether I know her or not, I don't like the way you're speaking about someone who's not even here to defend themselves."

The taller guy nudged the other. "Oh, he knows her alright."

Levi straightened and took a step toward them, putting enough inches on them that they both had to look up, and neither of them liked that fact. "Carina has more brain in her fingertips than you two combined. I'm sure you're both just bitter because, what, she was able to interpret the law to her favor? It's her fucking job, she can't help it if she's better than you. Although I doubt that's very hard, I passed the bar six months ago and probably better at my job than you."

Both men seemed to be grasping for words to hurl back but he left them no room to speak. He took another step toward them.

"Carina will always be two steps ahead of you. She will always be a better lawyer than you, and more importantly, a better person than you could ever hope to be. Now as I said, you're next."

They both turned and disappeared into the next room.

Levi shook his head. "Assholes," he muttered to himself. I waited a few moments before joining him in line. "There you are," he said brightly, like his whole prior conversation never even happened.

"Come to my place tonight," I blurted out.

There were so many versions of Levi, it was hard to choose which I liked best but this one always topped the list. Where his smile was slow to take over but once it did, it made everything better and it was all for me. "I'll make it worth your while."

His fingers tangled into mine and squeezed. "I don't need an incentive to want to be with you."

Fifty-Four

Levi

"So, you don't work at the restaurant anymore, but does that mean we can never go back, or..." I called out, already thinking of ways I could spend more time with her.

She popped her head around the corner of the closet she was standing in. "Really?"

"Yeah, really, I would never lie about loving the food there. I came to see you but it was the food that really brought me back," I said, smiling, and ducked as she lobbed a shirt at me.

If Carina only meant for me to come over and not stay the night, she never said a word, because we were both startled awake by alarms going off within five minutes of each other. She of course immediately rolled out of bed and began getting ready, while I was lying back in her bed with the morning light barely even past the horizon.

Carina was it for me. No one else compared, I only had eyes for her. But it would help if I knew what was going on in her head, if she felt the same. It could be anything, the smallest scrap of information that this could be something, that we could be something. There's been nothing yet, but that hadn't stopped me from hanging on.

Actually it's almost unfathomable I'd been welcomed so long. Carina liked her space and I loved to give her what she wanted but I couldn't help but like the new version of her I got more.

She walked back out, pulling a dark pair of work pants up her legs. I needed to get up to go get dressed, if I spent any longer in her bed, we'd be late. She buttoned the pants, grabbed a silk shirt from the chair she had in the corner, and slipped her arms in before walking toward me.

"Okay, we'll go tonight after work."

I snagged her by the waist and pulled her down onto me, not wanting to move outside the little bubble we created. My hands snaked up her chest, pulling the shirt back off and kissing my way across her chest, feeling her heartbeat kick up with each press of my lips against her skin.

"Great answer."

More clothes fell away; from me, from her. "We're going to be late, you know," she said on a sigh but made no move to leave.

"We can be late for once."

Fairvale was beginning to feel like home. It was easy here, slower, meaningful. Maybe it was Carina, maybe it was everything feeling like it was falling into place but all the trepidation that went into my decision on coming back slowly melted away, leaving me confident I had made the right decision. Work had never been better, we were getting closer to the trial date for the Leon case. I had taken on a few more cases of my own, with no shadow. This was the life I dreamed about getting back to.

We walked into the restaurant about an hour before closing. Carina made some comment about it being easier on the kitchen. She hated ordering off the menu and it was better for them if there wasn't a dining room full of tickets for them when she put in her complicated order.

A hostess I had never seen took us directly to the booth tucked in the back. Carina didn't even bother opening the menu, she was too busy scanning the room.

"What are you looking for?" I asked.

The answer came in the form of an older woman shuffling up to the table. Her apron dirty, greying hair that was obviously once the same shade as Carina's.

"Vita mita, non vieni mai a mangiare." She reached in and placed a quick kiss on her cheek. Then looked at me. "E questo di chi è?"

My chest filled with buzzing nerves, filling my chest rapidly until I thought they would burst out and onto the table. I had one chance to do this, and while I knew I would stumble all over and probably make a fool of myself I had to.

"Levi Decker, signora." I held out my hand. Both women looked at me wide-eyed.

"Conosce l'italiano?" She points the question at Carina but pierced me with the same look Carina liked to dole out when someone gave an answer she didn't expect.

Carina immediately answered 'no' the same time I said, "Non parlo bene...ma ci provo." It had been awhile since I actually used the language out loud. I bumbled over the pronunciation and I never could get my r's to roll.

Carina gaped at me like I had grown a second head, then a third.

I leaned across the table. "Did you know you talk to yourself when you concentrate? And that when you do, it's in Italian? I started learning before I left."

"But why?" she questioned.

"I told you knowing you is my favorite hobby. I figured I should start with your language."

I turned to her mother who was watching our interaction in rapt attention.

"Tua figlia è una donna incredibile e voglio solo continuare a conoscerla. Per tutto il tempo che me lo permetterà." And I meant it, she was incredible and if she hasn't figured it out by now that I was willing to be in this, whatever it was, then I needed to start telling her.

Her mom's arms darted out, grabbing my face with both hands before pulling me in for my own hug. Carina asked her to make whatever she wanted and watched as she disappeared back to the kitchen.

"So you just know Italian and didn't tell me?" Her voice a bit higher than usual, still staring out across the dining room.

I couldn't tell if that was a bad thing or not, but I answered her anyway. "Yes, and I meant what I said. Besides, I've told you before, knowing you is my favorite hobby. One of these days you'll believe it."

"And you want to stick around?" She chewed on the inside of her cheek as she asked the question, studying me as if waiting for me to change my mind. But I wasn't going to, I knew what I wanted. I'd always known.

"For as long as you'll let me."

Waters were dropped off as we lapsed into a silence that seemed like it would last forever. Before I might have started contemplating if I was giving her too much insight onto how I felt but not this time. This felt natural, a peak in the rollercoaster of our story.

"What if I said I didn't want to not do this?" She waved her hand between us.

And this was the thrilling downhill slide. The moment you stood in line looking forward to, when anticipation turned your stomach into a fluttering mess as you sat at the track peaks. "I would say I'm pretty sure I know what you're saying but just to be clear, spell it out for me."

Her lips rolled, hesitation rippling off of her as she tucked her hands behind her elbows. "Maybe we could try being something?" she asked softly.

"Carina Pera, are you asking me to go steady?"

An exacerbated laugh burst past her lips. "You're being ridiculous and I detest labels," she argued playfully, leaning on the table further, resting her chin in her hand. The insecurity from a second ago gone and all I thought was *there she is.* The woman I fell for, always headstrong and sure of herself. The woman who looked at me like she wanted to throttle me and kiss me simultaneously. "But maybe we could try being something. No labels or titles, or work disclosures. We'll just see how it goes because I don't like being without you." The words spilled out of her full of caution.

"I want nothing more than to be something, anything, everything with you."

"Good." She nodded, and took a sip of her water. That was it, as if we just concluded a business deal.

"But, maybe we should tell work? There is a disclosure clause in the handbook we all signed."

"No, no. Work is work, they don't need to know and they don't get to dictate what we are. But outside of work, we're together. We can tell our friends but not work."

This moment was burning itself into my mind as a distinct, core memory, the type I would look back on and pinpoint as the moment everything changed. It was something I would never forget. I wasn't lying when I said I would be whatever she wanted, whatever she needed. As long as I had her, that was enough.

FIFTY-FIVE

Carina

OUR CONVERSATION WAS BARELY a week ago at the restaurant and his sisters already knew, he wasted zero time telling people. Made sense, his sisters were his favorite people, so I understood why he would want to tell them so soon, but a week? I hadn't even been able to wrap my own head around the fact that I had a boyfriend, let alone tell Lennon or Abby. And we'd only been on one date since dinner at my parents' restaurant.

Maybe I should tell them, get it all out into the open and over with so it didn't feel like lead strapped to my feet. The sooner they knew, then sooner we could pretend like it wasn't breaking news.

"So, are you guys a couple?" Lennon asked Abby as she brought her glass of wine to her lips. She smirked behind the cup before taking a sip.

"No, or maybe," Abby stated. "I think so?"

"You think so," she laughed gently, "how familiar."

This would be the perfect opening, slip into the conversation about Abby finally getting with her neighbor that I was with Levi. Maybe they would gloss over my statement and we could stay focused on Abby.

"This isn't like you and Theo, this is different. I don't want to rush things or make a bigger deal out of what we are and ruin it. Like I always do," Abby explained.

> **What are you doing? Can I see you?**

> **Very clingy, I know, I know but can you blame me**

I turned the corner with my phone in hand, and walked back to join Lennon and Abby on the couch. It was clingy, and a few months ago I would have cut him off at the head and refused to text him back but I wasn't so sure anymore. It was almost nice, knowing I was wanted.

Slipping onto the open couch cushion at the end of Abby's couch, I shot him a quick text that I was in fact busy for the night but would see him as soon as I could.

"Oh, you know, Kaiser took me to that new restaurant out in Palm Grove you've been talking about." Abby's voice barely registered as Levi began texting all the things he was planning on doing once he did see me.

My eyes didn't move from the screen when I answered. "Oh, really, did you like it?"

"It was fantastic, not as good as your mom's place, but still, fantastic."

I hummed out my agreement. *Maybe I could have him come pick me up*, I was three too many glasses of wine into girls night to drive anywhere and apparently Levi's ability to make my brain go quiet wasn't limited to the bedroom.

"Have you been there yet?"

My head snapped up, and I set my phone to the side. "What do you know?" There was only one reason she would be asking me.

"What is happening?" Lennon asked, but neither of us answered.

"I might know something, or saw something." Abby shrugged.

"And...?"

Lennon leaned in and stage whispered. "What is happening?"

"Carina's been keeping secrets," Abby whispered back. I rolled my eyes and made an annoyed tsking sound. "But that's okay. We don't need to be all in each other's love lives all the time."

Lennon faked a gasp. "Does Carina Pera finally," she threw her hands up, "finally have a man?"

"You two are the worst and there is not nearly enough wine here tonight to get into details," I muttered into my empty glass.

"I'll be ten minutes." Abby flew off the couch, scooped up her keys and was out the door before Lennon and I could even think to argue.

I should've just told her about Levi, Abby obviously knew, and if anyone would understand me, it would be Lennon. I needed to tell someone in order to make this real between us I needed to let them know.

So why was it so hard?

"Will it be different this time?" Lennon was the best of us. Even though the three of us had a habit of trying to deal with our personal issues on our own, it was always Lennon to be the first to notice when we needed a push. However, not enough wine was an understatement, if I was going to talk about my feelings, I preferred to have something to blame it on.

"Will what be different?"

"Between you and the guy, will it be different than last time."

"How—I, I'm sorry, what?" I stuttered.

She gave me a knowing laugh with a tilt of her head. "You may think you are oh so very secretive but I see you, Carina."

I didn't know how to answer her. The answer was yes, it had to be different this time, but stepping out of the comfort of who I was, wasn't easy and it didn't happen overnight. It would take work and there would be times where I fell back into a space where I craved privacy over everything but I was committed to making us work.

"It will be worth it," Lennon said once she realized I had no intention of answering her. "I love you Carina. You wear the weight of the world on your shoulders and you do it beautifully, better than any of us that's for sure, but you also deserve someone that is willing to lift it off of you, someone who doesn't wait for you to ask for help. Abby and I would do it, if you let us but you're too stubborn for your own good." She laughed. "I think maybe this guy can be that person for you. Don't let it slip through your fingers because love is always worth the fight even if the fight is with yourself." Lennon's eyes shined like the deepest part of the ocean as she spoke, and I feared mine mirrored hers.

My mouth opened but no words formed. I shook my head a little, and really, really wanted Abby back with more wine because maybe then I could get around to believing what she said.

I titled my head back, begging gravity to put the tears back where they came from. "What if, umm..." I cleared my throat. "What if I can't let Levi," she smiled when I finally mentioned his name, "in the way he deserves? What if I'm too...me, and I lose him all over again?" The words were filled with watery pain. "I'm scared, Lennon," I finally whispered.

They weren't the words I meant to say. Those words were meant to stay inside my head, where I could unpack them myself once I was ready.

She slid across the cushion that separated us and grabbed my hand. "I'd be more worried if you weren't scared. Second chances don't happen for everyone but they happen for reason. If you don't go after what you want, what you *deserve,* you will regret it for the rest of your life."

It almost sounded like a warning but if anyone knew about almost squandering second chances, it would be Lennon.

Before I could be trapped into any more heart-to-hearts, the front door opened and Abby was back. She came around the corner with a bottle of red clutched in her hand and a distant look in her eyes.

Lennon noticed immediately. "You okay?"

A look flashed across her face, before she pulled her usual smile back on. "Of course, now where were we?" she asked, swiping the bottle opener from the table in front of us and made quick work of the cork. Lennon moved the conversation away from me and Levi by launching into where her and Theo were going on their next trip.

I'd been so scared of what Levi and I were to each other that I almost forgot that even if it didn't work out. I would be okay in the end. Abby and Lennon were my family, my soulmates, having a man or not having a man in my life would never change that.

FIFTY-SIX

Carina

THERE'S A BRIEF BRUSH of his lips against my head, extracting a deep sigh from my chest even as I balanced between sleep and awake. We'd spent more nights together than apart at this point and I was surprised about how much I didn't hate sharing a bed.

I peeled one eye open. "Are you leaving?" Sleep coated my words, making them low and raspy.

"Yeah." Levi pressed his hand into the mattress and kissed me once more. "Brynn has a scan today. I'm gonna go wait with them."

Clutching the sheet to my body, I sat up as he pulled back. "Is she alright, she's not sick again, is she?"

"No, she's fine. They're doing a routine scan to confirm she's still in remission." He leaned over, pressing a gentle kiss to my forehead before dressing quickly, stepping into last night's jeans.

"Oh, wait," I called out and reached over into my nightstand, pulling open the drawer. "I have something for her." My hand sifted through the years of discarded junk until I found the small black box. Wrapping the sheet around my body like a makeshift toga, I padded over to him and held out the box.

He looked at me, then the box. "What's this?" he asked cautiously.

"It won't hurt you, just—" I shook my hand. "Take it and look."

He plucked it from my grasp and carefully took off the lid. He stared at it for a moment then looked back at me confused.

I moved closer to him, looking down at the small coin that sat by itself in the box.

"I can't take this." Levi tried pushing the coin necklace back into my hand.

I pushed his hand back toward him with the box. "You can and you will. I'm not a child anymore and it would do more good for Brynn than me."

"Come with me," he asked abruptly.

"That, I can't do. This is your family they are what's important. I shouldn't be there."

"You're important to me, you know that, right?"

I'd never been this far in a relationship. Not only was I going to meet his parents but I was going to be in a setting with most of his family where there was a minuscule possibility they were going to get life altering, devastating news. It had my stomach in knots.

Levi was devoted to his family, what if they used the rash takedown I exhibited to convince him I wasn't worth the second chance we were pursuing. How would I stand up to that?

"I was only going to hang out in the waiting area. Please come?"

This second chance was about moving out of the bubble I put myself in and allowing him to step into my space. This was a chance for me to show him I was different.

"Okay."

——

When he said he was going to wait, I didn't realize how long the appointment was. My head had just dropped onto his shoulder and I was about two minutes away from snoring in the middle of the hospital waiting room when Brynn and her parents bursted through the doors.

"She's still in remission!" Brynn's dad yelled out, scooping the little girl up to twirl her around. Her soft giggles were contagious as Laura laughed through the tears.

Everyone seemed to jump up at once, latching onto each other, while laughing through the instant tears.

Brynn's eyes snagged on Levi. "Uncle Lee, did you hear? I'm not sick." She wiggled herself free from her dad's arm and launched herself toward Levi. With zero hesitation he swooped her up and hauled her in for a bone crushing hug. For a moment it was just the two of them as we all watched a moment pas.

I couldn't imagine the feelings that were probably floating to the surface, here was a man who gave parts of himself to save her, but that was just the type of person he was. I think Levi would give parts of himself, or all of himself to help anyone in need because he was simply a good person.

Levi whispered something in her ear that caused Brynn to smile and nod before taking a step closer to me.

"Brynn, this is Carina."

He might only be her uncle but it was almost like looking at a carbon copy of Levi in Brynn.

"I remember you," she whispered.

"I remember you too, and I'm so happy to meet you again."

"Are you his girlfriend now?"

Levi bit back a smile and placed a quick kiss to the side of her head.

Everyone was looking at us, but I didn't feel caged in. "Yeah, I think so."

Brynn snickered behind her hand.

"Carina brought you something." Levi dug into his pocket and handed over the box I gave him earlier. She tore off the lid and lifted the small coin from the box, turning it over in her hands. Both Laura and Kevin stepped forward to see what it was.

Brynn spoke up first. "Who is she?"

"St. Philomena, the patron saint of children." Confusion morphed her tiny features, making me laugh. "When I was about ten, I caught a nasty flu that turned into pneumonia. I was really sick and had to stay in the hospital for three weeks and every day my mother would kneel at the edge of my bed to pray, and each day that I had to stay, she would find a new saint to pray to, anyone that could help me."

It was so long ago, the memory was blurred around the edges, the only part that remained clear was my mother's prayers. It was the first time I felt as if they truly cared about me, the first time I felt as if I was a child they wanted and not just a child they had. If she was praying that hard to save me, then she must've loved me and for years afterward it was what I clung onto as a reminder that maybe I wasn't the burden I believed I was.

The silver was cold under my fingertips as I brushed a finger over the woman in the metal. "My mother said she was the last saint she prayed to when the doctors told her I was cleared to go home so she bought me this." I looked up at Brynn's soft brown eyes and, while I would always firmly plant myself on the hill that I never wanted children, I understood the pull as I looked at her. "I think I just liked her flower crown and the fact she was a princess, and since you're not sick anymore, I thought that you might want to hold on to her for me," I said softly.

My eyes flicked toward Laura, who mouthed 'thank you' but before I could say another word, Brynn tangled her tiny arms around my neck and pulled me into her and Levi. My body froze, but only for a moment before I thawed and wrapped my arms around both of them, laying my head onto Levi's shoulders.

On purpose, I'd always kept myself on the outside of relationships, and not just with men, but friends and family by telling myself it was better to skate along the edges to make a quick escape if needed, but this moment firmly planted me in the middle. Not in the middle of a relationship with Levi, but it placed me in the midst of his family and I would be lying if I didn't say I was terrified.

Levi once told me that he would find himself doing all sorts of things out of the ordinary for me, and it was about time I started to do the same for him.

Not all at once of course. None of this meant we would be walking into work holding hands, but it was a start.

FIFTY-SEVEN

Carina

SOME LAWYERS MIGHT LOVE going to court, but if I could avoid a trial, I would. At all costs. It was time consuming, and all together draining. Not just on me but everyone involved, the clerks who put together all the paperwork, the paralegals who kept my long hours researching anything that might possibly be useful, everyone was on overdrive if one of our cases went to trial so we worked hard to settle before we even got close.

But trial was inevitable.

Ben and Ian made sure to fight everything I brought to the table in order to get to this point. I'd been beating myself up for even letting it get this far but at least by the end of the day it would all be over. They might have gotten their trial but that was all they were getting.

It didn't matter how many times I did this or how well I thought I knew the judges and the way they swung; it was nerve inducing, every single time.

Levi and I sat at the courtroom table with Kelly between us. One wrong decision from the judge might actually send her into labor but Levi gave everything he had to the case, and I was filled with more pride than I knew what to do with. More than pride, I was filled with an overwhelming sense of love, filling parts of my heart that had never been used.

Kelly was going to win this, again. She had to, or I had no faith in the system any longer.

After an agonizingly long wait the judge appeared. "Good Morning, everyone," Judge Riviera greeted as he took his seat at the head of the courtroom. He shuffled through a few folders before looking out at all of us. "We are here today for the final divorce decree of Benjamin Leon and Kelly Leon, is that correct?"

"Yes, Your Honor," both Levi and Ian answered. I cut over to glance at Ian in time to see a smug smile cross his face. How or why he thought his client would get anything he wanted was beyond me. This case was air tight and Levi was going to prove it in a few short minutes.

"Does either party wish to provide oral key points or are the filings up to date?"

Ian stood from his chair. "We have a few additional items to present, Your Honor."

Kelly shifted in her seat, head turning to Levi who was already anticipating her reaction. "We prepared for this, remember? They're going to try to throw a few more things at the wall to see what sticks."

"But what if—"

"We're at the end, Kelly, and everyone at the other table knows it. This is it, you're going to walk out of here with everything you wanted."

She let out a breath and nodded.

Trying to see what stuck was an understatement but in the end Judge Riviera saw right through it.

"I have reviewed the evidence submitted and nothing further will be submitted." He looked over the rim of his glasses at Ian. Judges should be impartial, but the look that crossed his face was anything but indifference.

Ben's reaction is instant, turning into a steam engine before all our eyes as he harshly whispered something to his counsel.

"In the case of Kelly and Benjamin Leon, I hereby grant the order for divorce. Mrs. Leon will retain ownership of the residence in Land Park, as well as her current residence in the Penbrook building downtown."

Ben's discomfort could be heard from our table as he angrily whispered to Ian.

"The accounts will be split in half, awarding Kelly Leon five point seven million dollars."

Ben's voice broke through the whispering. "You can't be serious."

"I'm not done, Mr. Leon. Alimony is also awarded to Mrs. Leon of fifteen thousand a month for the next five years, or until Mrs. Leon remarries, whichever comes first."

The amount of pleasure I was getting from Ben's downfall needed to be memorialized.

"In the matter of the unborn child, upon the birth, Mr. Leon will be granted visitation of three hours every other day for the first six months, we can reconvene at that time should the parties not be able to come to their own agreement for custody for a reevaluation."

Tears streaked down Kelly's face as she looked at us in shock. The other side of the room was in an uproar but all it told me was that you could have all the money in the world but in the end, if you're a dick, life could still fuck you.

Ben shouted and raged to the point Judge Riviera ordered him to be removed and the three of us watched as he was walked backwards out the side door of the courtroom before we all exited through the front of the building.

"It's over again?" Kelly finally asked, looking between Levi and me.

He spoke up first. "It's over and you are now a very wealthy woman."

"I never wanted the money, I never really wanted any of this."

"We know," Levi answered.

"I just wanted him to love me enough to change, or at the very least love our daughters enough to but he couldn't. At least they will grow knowing that I did everything I could to protect them. Thank you for helping me again."

"It's been a pleasure, and I mean this with all the love, but I really hope we don't have to see you again," I joked and luckily she was on the same page.

Kelly smiled and bit back a laugh. "Me too." She was eager to get away from us, or the court, I really didn't know which, but either would be justified.

I'd handled hundreds of cases, all of which left some sort of impression, mainly the impression that love wasn't forever but this one was different.

After seeing so many fairytales with the headstrong, over-worked woman giving up parts of herself in order to fall in love, I convinced myself I would be better off alone. I convinced myself that love wasn't worth it, but even I could admit when I was wrong. Never in my wildest dreams did I imagine I would be able to find someone who not only saw me for who I was, but lifted me up higher to continue to achieve what I'd set out to do. Which was to give everything I could to the people who walked through the office doors. Levi gave me room to be selfish, something I didn't even know was possible.

"I'm so proud of you, Amore," he whispered, leaning in so the words felt like velvet caressing my skin. It was sincere, so full of love, and it didn't send my mind reeling wondering if I was even good enough for the praise. Levi said he was proud and for the first time, I actually believed those words. This was his case, his hard work, and yet he was telling me he was proud of me. He was perfect, and I wasn't sure that I deserved him.

It didn't even register we were in public, that people might see. Before he could get too far, I turned and pressed a quick kiss against his lips. Shock appeared first but quickly melted into an adorable, dopey smile.

"What was that for?"

I shrugged. "I'm proud of you too."

I liked that he didn't use it as a gateway to kiss me again, or to slip his hand into mine. He still understood that I struggled with having my personal life in the open, or out in public, around work. He was happy taking what I offered and not expecting anything more.

There'd come a time where I felt the need to bend. I wish I was ready then but when the time did come, I'd give this relationship everything I had. Until then, this was perfect.

Fifty-Eight

Carina

I'D ALWAYS BEEN HAPPY with my life. Despite the amount of hours of work I put in, issues with my parents, or anything else that life thought to throw at me, there wasn't a time where I wasn't truly happy. I knew how lucky that made me. So it was hard to find some way to distinguish this version of my life, because happiness didn't even come close to the almost euphoric feeling I'd been drowning in.

Kelly's case wrapped up and Levi and I fell into a comfortable routine of working together during the day, and nights split between his apartment or mine—barely any nights were spent alone. My friends finally knowing about us was a weight lifted off my chest and it felt like, well I didn't know exactly what it felt like except that it was good.

A squealing noise erupted from the large printer I was standing in front of, followed by the sound of ripping paper. I groaned along with the machine before opening the front hatch to look for the paper jam.

"Ms. Pera, it's good to see you." The voice came from behind me causing me to jump before whirling around and met with the older face that belonged to one of the office partners, the A in ALA Law...Alcala.

"Mr. Alcala, likewise." He hovered in his spot with a stack of papers in his hands. "Sorry, the printer is jammed again, just give me a minute," I rushed to say.

"No worries, take your time."

I started pulling open the machine, acutely aware of the awkward wavelengths my boss was putting out behind me.

"Great job with the Leon case by the way, it's not often a judge sides completely with one side, especially when the other side has a person like Ian Wheeler at his disposal."

I could see the edge of the paper in the far back. "Oh, thank you, but it was Levi's case really, he did a great job," I answered over my shoulder.

"How do you think he's working out?"

It wasn't that uncommon of a question, anytime a new employee started, one of the partners followed up with a few people to check in on how they were fitting in, or if there was room for improvement somewhere. Normally I had zero issue giving my feedback, but normally, I wasn't the girlfriend of the new employee.

"Oh, pretty well I think. I mainly only worked the Leon case with him, you might want to check in with his paralegal, they usually have the best insight." I pulled at the paper only to have it rip in half. Why, just why?

"You know I don't mean to pry," he spoke again while watching me fight with the piece still in the machine. That was never a good sentence to start with and my stomach felt like it was about to give away with whatever his next words were going to be. "My wife and I were out to dinner the other night and I saw you out, with Mr. Decker."

What should have been an innocent statement made me feel like I was being interrogated. My hand slipped, bashing my knuckles against the metal of the printer. A hiss of pain seeped through my clenched teeth as I yanked my hand out of the machine. There were a few layers of skin peeled from my hand as I bit back the curse on the tip of my tongue. Instead I rolled it around and tried to play along. "Oh?"

Fuck. Fuck. Fuck.

My hand hurt, my mind was reeling and who knew what the next thing out of his mouth would be. I paused for a second until the pain subsided, schooled my face into the picture of calm and turned to my boss.

Should I lie and act like Levi and I weren't out together? Say we were only together to discuss a case. Or maybe we just so happened to have ran into each other while we were out? For once in my life I didn't know what to say. Words wouldn't form, only a swelling in my throat that was making it hard to breathe and a fluttering heart beat that was making me dizzy.

"I didn't realize you two were together." No inflection ended his sentence. It was a statement, not a question. Lying went out the window.

Fuck.

Having Abby see us without knowing was one thing, but my boss, a partner whose name was on the building, who could easily remind me that all relationships needed to be disclosed and if not my position here would be in jeopardy was exactly what I was afraid of.

FIFTY-NINE

Levi

BY SOME UNKNOWN GRACE, I ended up wrapping up at work while the sun was still out. A small miracle. Since the trial, it had been a little slower but both of our caseloads were still filled to the brim and we often ate our dinner in the break room before getting back to work in the office.

I popped my head through her office door. "Do you want to get dinner?"

She hummed out a response without taking her eyes off the screen.

"You, me, maybe take out from that Chinese place you like from the town over? I can call it in now so it's ready by the time we get there?" I offered but honestly I just wanted a night with her. To think of nothing but her and leave work behind for once.

"I don't know. I'm pretty tired and thought I would just call it a day."

I stepped into the room. "You okay?" Something was off.

Carina clicked a few more keys before finally meeting my eyes. "I need to tell you something."

That was never a good sign. I waited for her to continue.

Her chest filled with her next breath slowly. "Alcala was asking about you and how I thought you were fitting in now that the case was over."

"O-kay?"

"He then mentioned he saw us out to dinner and that he wasn't aware we had a signed disclosure statement on file."

"And what did you say?"

"I froze but I told him we didn't. He wants us to sign it as soon as possible."

I could see the wheels turning in her head. "Carina, it's just a piece of paper, we both know that, we can sign it and forget about it."

"It's not, though. It's not just a piece of paper. You know how I feel and this," she took a deep breath, "this feels like it's forcing us to be something that maybe I'm not ready for."

"I wasn't lying when I said whatever you needed, we would do. We can call us whatever you want, partners, boyfriend/girlfriend, people who exist beside each other, whatever, as long as we're in it together it never made a difference to me. But work doesn't get that, they want assurances that we won't blow up on each other and take it out on the office." I took her face in between my hands. "It's just a piece of paper. We sign it and go right back to what we are now. "

It never bothered me that Carina didn't want to put a label on us, I never thought twice about it. We were together, we both knew it and if she struggled to call it what it was then I would be there to remind her that labels didn't matter.

Her fear of commitment was rooted in the notion that she would be forced into giving up parts of herself in order to mold herself into what the other person wanted. It would be a lie if I said I understood exactly what she was feeling but it wasn't my place to tell her how to process it. It was my place to keep showing up for her though, to keep letting her know that I wasn't going anywhere and that I would take whatever parts of her she was willing to share with me and love her for who she was.

It was evident that I loved her for a while but I knew telling her had the potential to send her running away from me again.

Waiting was fine. I would wait months, years, decades for her to be ready. I was just happy to be in her presence.

"Levi, I don't want it to change what we have."

"Nothing could change us. Don't you see that all I care about is you? You don't believe in true love, fine, but what's stopping you from believing that I love you. Why can't I be one of the soulmates you say everyone has?"

"Because I'll hurt you!" she shouted, and without thinking I took a step back as her words hit me. "It's inevitable that I will hurt you because it's all I know. I will break your heart and I'll never be able to forgive myself." She pulled back from me and it felt as if she was a million miles away. "I told you before women like me don't get happily ever afters," she proclaimed but it was like she was trying to convince herself.

"Let me love you, anyway," I nearly yelled back at her. "Just let me..." Me voice teetered on the edge of desperation, and I wasn't above begging. I couldn't lose her, not now, not when I just got to have her. "I would endure a lifetime of heartache if it meant I got to love you for even a second, Carina. You are worth the heartbreak."

"What if I said I didn't want to sign it?"

A pained looked crossed her face, sending a chill down my spine. Maybe she was trying to tell me she didn't want to sign it because she wasn't as into us as I was. Maybe I came on too strong and this was her tipping point.

Maybe she was all I wanted, but I wasn't what she wanted.

It would be an impossible reality to swallow, but I would if I had to because it didn't matter what timeline we were in; I was in love with

Carina Pera in every single one. And if I had to wait for her to be ready to take a step or wait for her to decide if a relationship was even what she wanted, then I would wait. I would wait for her even if it meant making a home in the sidelines of her life without me.

God, I loved her and if begging would have helped my cause, I'd let my knees hit the pavement and never come up. But I knew her; she wouldn't want me to grovel or list the reasons we were perfect for each other, she would want her decision respected and I would give her whatever she wanted.

Whatever her next words were, I'd live with them and I would love her regardless.

"Carina, if you don't want—"

"Carina Pera." A voice boomed from behind her. She turned as I looked up to see a man I didn't recognize standing a few paces away.

Something changed in the air, the wind turned and with it brought a sense of wrong. It didn't matter that I was mid afternoon on a sunny day, a chill suddenly fell over the area at the presence of this man.

I took a step to the side, then forward, while keeping one hand on her waist. "Can we help you?" I asked as something prodded at the back of my brain to look at this stranger, really look and to remember.

Blue shirt.

Jeans.

Shorter than me, 5'10, maybe.

Beer belly.

Brown hair, cropped short.

Older, mid fifties.

I played the list over and over in my head.

"I have a message for you." He took two quick steps toward us.

It happened in a blur, and yet I moved out of instinct pulling Carina from where my hand was still stuck to her waist, pushing her behind me.

Then came a searing pain through my right side as the sound of lightening cracked around us, louder than anything I could have ever imagined. My mouth opened to call for her, to see if she was okay but nothing came. Words bubbled up in my throat but died before I could get them out.

Darkness started creeping in around the edge of my vision, it was like I was looking through a kaleidoscope of black and then my knees hit the hard sidewalk beneath me.

I still didn't understand what happened.

My body hit the pavement.

Someone screamed.

Then total blackness.

Sixty

Carina

For a moment, I thought I was back at my desk. Ringing filled my ears, like someone was calling my office phone over and over, but I had no way of answering it.

Why couldn't I answer the phone?

My eyes were squeezed shut as I pressed my hands against my ears to muffle the sound but it only grew louder.

Someone needed to answer the phone.

Nothing helped. If anything, the passing seconds only made it worse.

Where was Levi?

Find Levi. He'd be able to help me.

Finally, I forced my eyes open, only to realize there was no phone, and that was when I started screaming. The sound tore from my chest once I registered Levi's body on the cold ground. A sound so loud, so ragged, that if I wasn't the one who made it, I wouldn't think it was human.

Crimson slowly seeped from his side, soaking his shirt like a sponge dying of thirst. My ankles buckled in my heels as I stumbled toward him before falling at his side. A burning sensation radiated through my knees when the concrete tore at my skin, but I pushed everything from my head. He was my only focus.

Out of instinct, I pressed my trembling hands to his blood soaked body causing his dark lashes to flutter before squeezing shut. A pained groan escaped him.

"I'm sorry, I'm sorry." I pressed harder trying to snuff the flow as blood continued to seep through my fingers, growing heavier and heavier. Thousands of thoughts ran through my head as I pressed my hands onto his wound, and vaguely I sensed people gathering around us.

"Somebody call 911, now!" I screamed.

A man's voice yelled back that the ambulance was on the way causing my shoulders to relax a fraction of an inch.

Blood coated my hands, turning them slick.

There was so much blood.

Why was there so much blood?

My eyes squeezed shut and then realized I was chanting 'it's okay' over and over. I didn't know if it was for me or him.

"Carina," he croaked out and I finally willed myself to look at him. He was so pale already, but there was a hint of a smirk pulling at the corner of his mouth. "I'm going to be okay, Amore," he slurred the syllables.

"Why would you do that? Why did you push me out of the way?" Slowly, his hand drifted upward, like he was using every bit of strength he had left to cup the side of my face and wipe away tears I hadn't noticed were falling.

I wanted to take his face in my hands. I wanted to shake him until he answered me.

"What a stupid question," he whispered.

An ambulance wailed in the distance as Levi's face scrunched up, his head lolled to the side and his breath hitched in his chest. "They're almost here, Levi. You're going to be fine, you're going to be fine," I said between clenched teeth.

A distressed chuckle escaped him as he forced his head back to look at me, but his words were barely more than a whisper. "I like it when you say my name."

"No, no, no, no, you don't get to do that." My hands pressed harder into the wound and he barely moved. I leaned in closer, our noses almost brushing. "I'm going to fix this, I can fix this." Blood smeared across his forehead as I pushed back the hair that had fallen across his face. "Do you hear me, I will fix this and you will be fine."

Blood stopped pooling beneath him and I didn't know if that was a good sign or not.

"I know you can, but just in case—" His breath labored.

I knew what was coming, and I didn't want it. Not like this. "Please don't, not yet."

A weak smile appeared on his face, like this was all a part of one of his games to get on my nerves. His fingers brushed over where my hands were covering the bullet hole, they curled around my wrist with barely any strength. And that stupid, wonderful, god awful purple hairband was still on his.

"I love you," he breathed as he lost consciousness and went limp in my hands.

All sense of up or down, right or wrong faded around me as I screamed his name, over and over until my throat went numb.

His name morphed into a cry that shattered all sense of reality and rivaled the scream that tore through Lennon when they buried her husband. Back then, I thought I understood what she was going through, I sympathized with her, thinking I could imagine what she was dealing with.

I knew nothing of pain then and I wished I never had to find out.

Fear ripped through me like a freight train, bulldozing its way through my senses as I continued to scream in fury. Anger on heels of the fear swirling inside of me.

Anger at the man who shot him, at Levi for pushing me out of the way but mostly at myself. Seconds before I was complaining about signing a stupid fucking piece of paper that would have put a label on what we were.

Was the universe really this vindictive? Would I really lose him because I was scared to call him what he was to me?

Would I lose him right as I was ready to fall?

I couldn't.

I wouldn't accept it.

I refused to accept it.

Paramedics rushed from behind me to take over. It wasn't until one of them mentioned his pulse was weak, and they loaded him up on a gurney and pushed him through the ambulance doors, which then shut with me on the outside did I finally breathe. He was still alive and that was all the hope I needed.

As I watched the ambulance lights fade from view, I finally admitted to myself that I am wholly, without a doubt, in love with Levi Decker.

And if he died, no one would be safe from the hellfire I would rain down on whoever caused this.

SIXTY-ONE

Levi

THE FATES WERE PLAYING with my string, stretching and pulling it to its snapping point, scraping the scissors against the thread, taunting me. One quick snip and this would all be over, the pain would be gone and I could finally relax. Which sounded almost nice and for a second the call of the afterlife was the loudest voice in my head.

Poets write about heaven and tell us all the ways we'd live in splendor. In the afterlife we would never want, our every whim would be catered to in the land beyond life. Eternal glory with no pain as we blissfully existed in a state of euphoria until all time and space ceased to exist.

But none of that compared to a life with her.

I would live through a hundred heartbreaks, I would rather be destitute and on the brink of starvation if it meant I got to live my life with her. I would live with searing pain tearing through my skin and bones until the end of time if it meant I could even look at her one last time.

All I wanted was her.

Just this one life and to be able to live it with *her*.

Just let me have the girl and let her want me back, I thought.

That thought alone pulled me from the fog as my eyes fluttered open. The lights of the hospital blinded me as I tried to focus on my surroundings; I could hear about five different voices and my bet was every single one of my sisters was surrounding me.

"Can you all stop talking, please?" The words cut like glass in my throat as I croaked them out.

My request was not taken into consideration as every voice began calling out my name and asking me a million questions and all together started fretting over me. A gentle hand came down on my arm, my blanket was pulled up and I was pretty sure someone fluffed my pillow.

In my thirty-two years, I didn't think I had ever had all my sisters fuss over me. Or really any of them fuss over me like this. Usually I was being bossed around, asked to help with a project that I wasn't allowed to object to, and generally picked on by all of them.

The bright overhead light washed out my vision for a few minutes before I could bring anything into focus. It was obvious that I was in a hospital and the longer it took to get my bearings, the more things came into focus. My sisters' faces were the first thing I saw, Lola's tear streaked face smiling at me as Laura seemed to sigh in relief. Then came the steady beep of the IV machine with the slight pinching pain in my hand. I thought I would feel the gunshot first but whatever meds they had me on were doing their job.

My eyes scanned the room before a flash of blonde moved from the corner of the room. For a second our eyes met, pale green and full of every emotion, met mine. Pain, worry, relief—all of it flashed across her face.

I wanted to reach for her but before I could do anything, she gave me a gentle smile before she pulled the door open and left the room. Watching her leave filled me with a new type of pain and it was worse than any bullet wound could inflict.

Laura tracked the entire interaction before turning back to me. "She's okay, Lee," she said as panic washed over my stare. "I promise, she's okay. She just needs a moment."

"She's okay?" I tried sitting up but it was took much, the pain in my side flared to life and forced me back into the bed. "Are you sure, Laura?"

"Hey, hey, hey." It was my mother's voice and gentle hands urging me backward into the bed. "It's okay, Son." She ran her fingers through my hair. She hadn't done that since I was little and would crawl into her bed anytime I was sick. When I looked up at her she was easily a decade older looking than I remember.

My smile was weak, everything was weak. "Hi, Ma." Tears were instant in her eyes at the words.

"You scared us."

The machine beeped and a few moments later my body felt like it was being dragged back under. "I'm sorry. Don't be mad at me, I didn't think I just acted, I just—" My face pinched at the amount of strength it took to speak before I relaxed back into the hospital bed.

"I know and I'm not mad," she said. My eyelids became heavier with each pass of her hand over my head. "I talked to her while you were sleeping. It was easy to see why you did it."

A medicated induced smile crossed my face. "She's perfect, and maddening, and so smart. She makes most grown men cower in their shoes with just a look, she's one hell of a lawyer, and I love her."

There's a collection of awes from the room but my eyes were too heavy and I couldn't fight it any longer. Sleep took over and there was nothing I could do to stop it.

———

When I finally came back to, it had been hours, night had fallen and darkness overtook the room. Only the pale light coming from the machines and the steady beat of my heart filled the room. For a moment

I thought I was alone until I looked to my right and saw Laura fast asleep in a chair in the corner.

Or I thought she was asleep. Her eyes shot open the moment I tried to prop myself up in bed. Without a word, she was out of the chair and using the remote to lift the head of the bed so I was sitting.

"Thanks," I croaked out and she handed me a cup of water. It had always been like that, Laura anticipating our wants and needs, like a second mother growing up.

"How soon do you think I can get out of here?"

"Depends, is it because you're better or because you're going to go see her?" she asked with a knowing smile. I didn't even have to answer before she continued. "Doctors said you're doing pretty good despite being shot, it missed all your major organs so maybe in a couple of days."

Days, I couldn't go days without seeing her. "I need to get out of here, I need to get to her, *I* have to make sure she's okay." I realized it was the middle of the night but I was beyond any type of rationalization, all I knew was I needed her and if it meant breaking out of the hospital, then that was what I needed to do.

Laura flicked my blanket back over me and pushed back at my feeble attempts to get out of bed. "Okay, knock it off, you're acting worse than Brynn when she was in the hospital." Her stern mom voice was on display. "If I can get you out tomorrow, will you stay in bed?"

Tomorrow, it seemed so far and I didn't even know what time it really was. "By noon tomorrow?" I challenged.

"Yeah, yeah, I'll see what I can do."

When she sat back down, all she did was stare at me. A quizzical sort of look she normally saved for her girls when she knew one of them was lying.

"What?"

"I just... Nothing." She waved me off.

"Spit it out, you've never had a problem speaking your mind before, don't let me almost dying stop you now." Hopefully my smile would let her in on my sad attempt at a joke.

She rolled her eyes and I knew it worked. "I want to make sure that you think she's the right choice, is all. You physically put yourself in front of a bullet for her, Lee, that is not something you do for just anyone and I want to make sure she's in this just as much as you are."

For a moment I sat with her words, really thought about what it was that Carina and I were but I didn't take long for me to have my answer.

"Carina was never a choice, not really. Loving her is as much of a decision as drawing my next breath, it's done unconsciously, but doesn't mean it's not vital to me living. We may not have done everything the right way or the normal way but it's the way it was supposed to happen. She needed time and I never hesitated to give her what she needed because I knew in my heart or in my soul, or whatever cliche thing you can think of, that I'm meant for her. It was always going to be her."

Heart to heart conversations didn't really happen growing up, maybe a few attempts here and there after we both grew up and I really needed some direction in life, but if Laura needed to exert some sort big sister wisdom on me to make sure I was making the best decision then I would give that to her.

Laura lay back in her makeshift bed, drawing the thin blanket back over her body. "Noon tomorrow then." She gave me one last pointed look before closing her eyes while a small smile played at her lips.

SIXTY-TWO

Carina

Levi was set to be in the hospital another day from what Lola's last text said and I had been fighting the boiling urge to go back to him. In the end, the logical part of my brain won and I didn't go. Or maybe it was the illogical part? I really didn't know.

Sleep was elusive since I left him, my dreams were all plagued with images of him lying on the sidewalk as thick, scarlet blood seeped through my fingers and pooled on the ground. And that scream, it was a broken record that woke me up and was hard to shake.

Diane and the name partners told me to take the week off to decompress from the whole ordeal and deal with the cops. I gave my statement no less than a half dozen times to various officers and district attorneys about the events, and it never got easier. In fact, once I was told who was behind it, it only made it worse.

Benjamin Leon was always going to be a problem, men like him always were. When you had his type of money, you had the ability to get other people to do your dirty work. Ben hired Ian to handle his divorce, and then hired a random man to 'teach me a lesson' or at least that's what I heard. In the end, my life was worth ten thousand dollars, a bargain if you asked me.

Ben didn't like that Kelly ended up with everything she wanted in the divorce, and apparently it was my fault. Not his, or the way he treated Kelly, it was mine. He took zero accountability because he thought when you have wealth and influence, you could say whatever you wanted, treat people however you wanted and there would never be any consequences.

Only he was so cocky, he got sloppy.

The guy he hired was caught within hours of the shooting and sang like a bird the minute he was cuffed. Ben barely covered up his involvement and the transaction was easily traced back to him after a small amount of digging. A first year law student could have tried this case and came out with a home run.

All because he was a fragile man who didn't like to be told no.

Staying away from Levi was no longer working for me. I left the hospital two days ago and that was enough time apart. I had to tell him how sorry I was, that I loved him. Otherwise my fraying nerves would fall apart at the seams. We were forced apart once, and I would never go through that again.

I swiped my keys off the table and quickly walked to the door, pulled it open and saw the sweetest relief. Levi stood in the doorway, one shoulder pressed against the wall. Loose sweatpants hung low on his hips, a plain black tee, and for a moment it was like he simply ran out to get coffee and forgot his key coming back. But if I looked closer, I could tell his skin was two shades paler than normal and heavy bags lined his eyes.

It took me a second to snap back to the present. "Oh my god, what are you doing here? Get inside and sit down," I commanded. He took one wobbly step before I slipped under his arm and helped him to the couch. He sunk back into the cushion with a groan as his hand pressed against his side where thick bandages padded the area.

"What are you doing here? You weren't supposed to be out until tomorrow?"

"Good behavior?" He cracked a smile, before wincing.

"Thats not fun—"

"I love you," he cut me off with. "I love you an indescribable, insurmountable, incomprehensible amount and it doesn't scare me because out of everyone in this crazy entire world I know, in my soul, that I was made for you, Carina Pera. I was made for you and I think you were made for me."

My chest filled with an overwhelming buzzing sensation that cascaded out and onto my skin. My whole body reacted to his words, goosebumps pebbled over my arms, across my chest and up my neck, and tears stung the backs of my eyes as I hung my head in shame.

"I was going to tell you that it wasn't working out," I whispered, "because I'm a coward. I don't deserve you."

His hand wiped the tears dripping from my eyes before hooking a finger under my chin, forcing me to look at him. "You're not a coward."

"I am, because when I'm with you, I turn into this person who wants to do domestic things like go to the grocery store together or the pumpkin patch on the weekend and it terrifies me."

"I can't image you at the pumpkin patch."

I laughed. "Exactly." I blew out a shaky breath. "I think I could love you the rest of my life and it wouldn't be enough. I've never felt anything like this and for once, I'm scared and overwhelmed, but none of that compares to what I felt watching the life fade in your eyes as you bled out in front of me. So if I have to choose, I choose to feel scared of loving you over losing you."

"Then why did you leave the hospital?" he asked.

"Because even though I love you, I'm still no good at this. But for you I will try, for however long you'll have me."

Levi's fingers grazed my cheek. "Whatever you need, Carina. It's always been whatever you need to make this work."

"You're what I need."

Epilogue

CARINA

A FEW YEARS LATER

Two weeks in Italy wasn't enough, a lifetime there wouldn't be enough time, but it was all we could manage to take off from work. But at least it was a blissful two weeks. We made stops in all of the big cities, Rome, Milan, Naples, but by the end of our trip, I wanted to go home.

Crespano del Grappa was a blip on the map to most, but for me, it was where it all started. It was where my parents met, where my life began and theirs changed forever when they decided to make a life in America rather than stay and feel like they didn't belong. Sometimes I wished it didn't end up like that for them, maybe if they had stayed, we would have been closer but if it was any different, then I wouldn't have been there with a man who made it his mission to ensure I never I had to experience changing myself to make people happy.

"Lennon and Theo were right, this place is beautiful," Levi stated as we looked out across the emerald hills as we stood atop of Monte Grappa. I hummed my response, too overwhelmed at the sight to even speak.

We would need to leave soon, the sun would be setting soon and the road was not one I wanted to be on in the dark, too many turns and not enough maintenance already made it a white knuckle drive.

This trip was everything I could have wanted and sharing it with Levi was everything despite the amount of times we'd been asked if we were on our honeymoon when checking in to hotels. We weren't married but we might as well be. Didn't matter if we had a piece of paper defining our relationship or not, after this many years together, there was nothing that could tear me from him.

He'd hinted over the years, but nothing serious of course, and yet every time he did, a new crack appeared in my resolve. I guess it wouldn't be the worst thing in the world

"This would be a great place to get married," Levi suddenly mused, as if he'd heard my inner thoughts.

"You're not going to ask me to marry you again, are you?" I flashed him a smile, because at this point the jokes imbedded into our dynamic.

He laughed, treading his fingers with mine. "No, but give me the word and I will marry you tomorrow or right now or five years from now."

My heart squeezed and I wondered why I was so opposed to marriage in the first place. In fact, was it possible I was never opposed to marriage? Maybe I was opposed to men who I assumed would want to lead and demand me to change and all I needed was someone to walk beside me.

Someone who knew being flexible wasn't in my DNA but was willing to bend for the both of us if needed. Someone who saw how I thrived when there was work to be done and encouraged me to continue. Someone who was patient enough to wait for me to overcome my stubbornness on my own.

Someone like Levi.

"What *about* right now?" I asked.

He cocked his head to the side. "What are you talking about?"

"I don't want a piece of paper that tells me what I already know, what I feel, and we don't need a wedding to make vows. I am yours so why not right now, right here."

"Okay." A quick word from his smiling lips.

"Okay?"

"You're right, why not right now?"

Springtime in the Italian countryside would make even the most sound people act irrationally, this was anything but rash. This was what I wanted.

Levi reached out, taking my hands into his. Standing tall before me, with his hair down and the gentle breeze sweeping the long black strands across his face. My finger instinctively went searching for the hairband on his wrist, stroking the threads. It wasn't the same one from all those years ago, but he made a point to steal another one of mine once the purple threads finally gave away.

"Carina Pera, loving you has been the greatest adventure of my life and one I want to keep living until my last breath. Your drive, your passion, the way you pour everything you have into those around you to lift them to their fullest potential is your purpose and what makes you, you. It's why I love you, it's why everyone around you loves you." His grasp tightened. "And for the rest of my life I will live each day making sure you get everything you want out of this life because you are *my* purpose."

Who knew when I started crying, but tears fell like waterfalls. He brushed them free before placing a kiss on each cheek. And then it was my turn.

"Levi Decker, you were a surprise." He threw his head back with a laugh. "I told myself that I would never find someone. I was too driven and headstrong for love or happily ever afters, so I convinced myself it wasn't what I wanted. But then you came around with your relaxed look on life, and your dorky ties and *that hair,* and showed me I can be all the things I thought made me cold and unlovable and still be enough for someone. You showed me I didn't have to change in order to be loved. You love me for exactly who I am and I will live the rest of my life a better person because of you. You are entirely too good for me, thank you for taking a chance on me, thank you for opening up my world, thank you for loving me."

His hand cupped the back of my head as his dipped down and brought his lips to mine, sealing our vows with a kiss that was sure to top the list of history's most romantic moments. I was completely lost in his embrace and found all at once.

When he pulled back, one arm slipped behind his back and into his pocket. Confusion took over as he pulled out his wallet. I took a quick stock of where we were. "I don't think we can get away with doing that here," I chastised him.

A deep chuckle reverberated in his chest as he flicked open his wallet.

"I like where your head is at, but no. The first time I fuck you as my wife will be in a bed so I can have you spread out and comfortable."

I didn't know what made me melt more, the filthiness of his words or him calling me his wife. "I was getting," he made quick work of his wallet, drawing out something small, "this."

I looked down, then back up at him, then down again, where pinched between his thumb and pointer finger was a wedding band. It was a thin white gold band with diamonds along the entire perimeter.

"How long have you had this? Why do you have it?"

The metal was cool against my skin as he slid the ring on my left hand, a heavy weight that would take some time to get used to. "When I got shot, you were the only thought I was able to conjure. Not the pain, not the possibility I was dying, just you." He thumbed the band, pushing it from side to side, allowing the sinking sun to catch the stones which bloomed tiny rainbows from the facets. "My only thought was how I hoped that wasn't the last time I saw you because all I wanted was to spend this life at your side. I bought a ring not long after getting out of the hospital."

My mouth fell open. Years ago, he bought me a wedding ring and apparently had been keeping it in his wallet ever since.

"I didn't know if you were the type to get married, and there was no way I was going to ask you that early, but I knew I had to be ready for whenever you might be."

My arms snaked around his neck, forcing his head close to me. "Very presumptuous of you," I whispered against his lips.

"It was fate, nothing else."

I didn't like that. It was possible he was right, I wasn't so sure fate didn't play a role in our lives, but we also worked for what we had. We spent years learning and growing from each other, pushing, pulling and fighting our way to a future we believed in. Fate could have a footnote, but we deserved the credit.

"No, not fate, it was us, Levi. It was all us."

Loving Levi was a battle I would have rather ignored than join, convinced I was meant to spend my life alone. Nothing could have prepared me for the revelation that I was not better off alone, and nobody other than Levi could have done it. It had been years and I still found new ways to be surprised by him, and he had spent every moment showering me in so much affection I had no choice but to believe it.

In life, there were times when you put yourself first, sometimes out of necessity, others out of sheer determination, and you got to accomplish everything you set your mind to. You aim for the stars and if you worked hard enough, you reached them, but that didn't mean you had to stop there. I worked my ass off to get where I wanted to be. I paid for my position in life with determination, loyalty, sacrifice, hard work and the gut feeling I was meant for something great, something bigger. I made it to the stars, only to find Levi had the universe waiting for me.

Epilogue

LEVI

NOT TOO FAR IN THE FUTURE

I was a simple man, with simple wants and needs. Most of which were satisfied by my wife, or as she always reminded me, my *partner*. It had been a while since that day in the Italian countryside, and I wasn't lying when I said I didn't care about a piece of paper, but sometimes it was fun to watch the way her eyes narrow when I used the 'W' word.

"Are you almost ready?" Carina shouted from our bedroom in the back of the house.

"Yeah, I just need to change, there's no way I'm wearing any good clothes, not when I know one of Abby's tiny humans will inevitably get something on me." Her laugh grew louder the closer I got as I walked down the hall. "I'm serious, Carina, last time they were here, I ended up with jelly in my hair. *Jelly.* No one was even eating sandwiches."

We knew kids were never a part of the future between us, but we loved being the aunt and uncle to swoop in, spoil the kids, and then leave once the sugar kicked in. Between my sisters and Abby, we were no short supply. And this was going to be one of those days.

It was a quick drive to our destination—one of the perks of living in a semi-small country town, farms were almost a dime a dozen and within twenty minutes.

Theo, Kaiser, and I stood along the side of a field while the love's of our lives pursued row after row looking for the perfect pumpkin. Abby and Kaiser's children, Juliette and Fredrick, ran ahead in search of one while Abby, Lennon, and Carina trailed behind them. The three women as close as ever.

"You know she's going to find the biggest one and ask you to carry it back," I commented as Abby bent down next to a pumpkin with Juliette at her side. It was huge, came up to at least her knees, and was almost taller than Juliette. Kaiser pulled off his baseball cap, running his hand through his hair before putting it back on.

"Yeah, I know, but it's really hard to say no to her."

Theo laughed on his other side. "Who? Abby or Juliette?"

He paused to think. "Both," he finally replied.

Like clockwork, Abby stood and waved him over. "I think I want this one." Her voice carried across the field and before she even finished talking, Kaiser was moving toward her to haul their picks back to the truck. Their son stood proudly a few rows over next to an equally large pumpkin.

I went from barely knowing any of these people to realizing I could never live without any of them, and over the years, the lessons I learned on all the different ways you could love someone were invaluable.

Lennon and Theo showed all of us light could be found even when you were surrounded by darkness, and that grief wasn't the end but a passage you had to walk through for a new beginning.

Quiet love, like Abby and Kaiser's, was sometimes the loudest in the room and when you peeled back the curtain to show the parts of yourself you deemed too damaged for anyone to see, it could be the one thing that set you free.

And Carina modeled that being selfish didn't mean you were unworthy. It meant sometimes all you needed was to find the person who saw your ambition as a strength and not something that needed to be changed.

Growing up in a large family, I always assumed I would have had one of my own. And I did but not the way I had imagined it.

Family wasn't always blood. Sometimes, if you're lucky, family ended up being the people you found along the way and became who you leaned on in tough times, the ones who surrounded you to celebrate the highs and lows of life...or random Sunday afternoons at a pumpkin patch. The six of us made up a family that surpassed everything I ever thought I wanted, no dream or fantasy could even compare to what I had with them.

It would never matter if we didn't share a last name or genetics because whatever we were to each other, it was everything, and I would do anything for this family.

Thank You

Thank you for reading Whatever You Need!
I would love it if you could take the time to leave a review or rating via Goodreads or your preferred platform. Your feedback is not only important to me but can also help new readers find my work.

<h1 style="text-align:center">Acknowledgements</h1>

It's such a bittersweet feeling completing this story that I almost have no words. I wrote three books, three books with my heart and soul scattered across the pages for the world to see, and while writing is an art and art is subject to opinion and critique, I can't help but feel overwhelmed with pride no matter what others might say.

I never dreamed I would be here, at the end of my first series and with so many more stories on the horizon, and it would be criminal to close this book without thanking you, the reader. I've done this before, and I'll do it again because I could not do this if it weren't for people like you. Readers who choose my book when there are endless possibilities to choose from. Thank you for taking a chance and opening a book written by someone you've never heard of but had a story to tell, again.

Ellie, the editor of my dreams, the woman who knows I don't know how to use a comma but stuck with me anyway. None of this would be coherent without you.

My extraordinary beta readers, Britt and Kaila. Your feedback helped me refine the shape of Carina and Levi's story, and your words of encouragement pushed me into finishing when I felt like I wanted to scrap the project altogether.

But most of all, this series, with its found family, would be nowhere without a few certain people in my life. When I set out to write, I had one thing on my mind - how can I immortalize the people I hold closest to my heart? Which turned out to be easy because, as the saying goes, write what you know, so I did just that.

I wrote stories steeped in soul defining love - between sisters, between friends, between lovers because I am lucky enough to experience each of those relationships, and my life is better off because of them.

For Richard, Courtney, Eric, Lily and Elijah, for my soulmates, this was all for you.

Also by Brittney Lauren

Anything For You
Everything You Are

About the author

Brittney is a Northern California native who spends her nights crafting love stories. When she's not writing you can find her amongst friends deciding what game to play next, performing Taylor Swift songs to her unsuspecting husband, and binge watching period romance movies.

Follow Brittney on Instagram & TikTok:
@brittneylaurenwrites

To stay up to date with upcoming releases, join her newsletter:
https://substack.com/@brittneylauren